ELEMENTARÍ RISING

RISING

NANCY
HIGHTOWER

ELEMENTARÍ RISING

NANCY HIGHTOWER

Book One of the Elementarí

○△∪□

PINK NARCISSUS
PRESS

This book is a work of fiction. All the characters and events portrayed in this book are fictitious, and any resemblance to real people or events is purely coincidental.

ELEMENTARÍ RISING
© 2013 Nancy Hightower

Cover illustration by Siolo Thompson. Design by Duncan Eagleson.

Published by Pink Narcissus Press
P.O. Box 303
Auburn, MA 01501
pinknarc.com

Library of Congress Control Number: 2013910553
ISBN: 978-1-939056-03-0
First trade paperback edition: September 2013

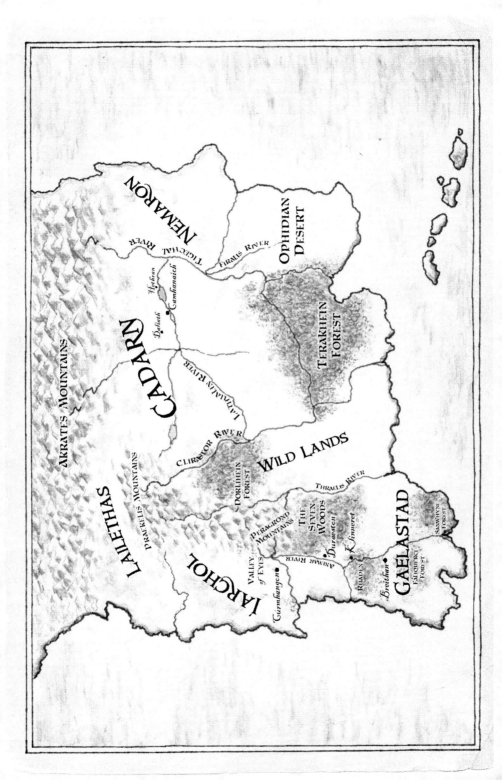

FOR MALINDA

PROLOGUE

The Three Sisters Inn was full tonight, possibly too crammed with traders, guild officials, and sojourners from Íarchol for him to escape the notice of prying eyes. The barber slipped the black hood over his head and drew the cloak tighter around his belly. It would not do if anyone caught sight of the three blue emblems emblazoned on his vest. Luckily, it was the hour when men had drunk enough of Molly's ale to dull certain senses and heighten others, but the girls were scarce tonight. Off in the corner two men danced cheek to cheek, keeping time to the melancholy song being piped by one of the Íarchins. He kept his head down as he wandered unsteadily between the long tables towards the staircase that led to the rooms. It wouldn't do to act sober or purposeful.

"Damn these stairs," he muttered as he began the slow climb up the narrow flight. He paused to catch his breath at the top before waddling down the dimly-lit hall to the fourth room on the right. Three knocks. Pause. Two more.

The door opened a crack, and an eye peered out. "Who's there?"

"I think my bulk alone would answer that question, Tarl," the man wheezed. "How many three-hundred pound barbers do you know?"

Already, the air felt stuffy, the room too small as he stepped across the threshold. The lamp cast scarcely enough light for the place. The barber had half a mind to keep the door open, but that's what fools did—trust in light to save them, just as the cruel believed darkness covered all sin.

Well, he was in between the damned and the saved, so one lamp would do just fine. He closed the door behind him and stood there, dripping with sweat and wheezing like an old man. Tarl looked scarcely better. The tanner was swaying side to side, his brown tunic and breeches still covered in soot.

"How drunk are you?" the barber asked.

Tarl looked down at his work-worn hands. "Drunk enough."

The barber glanced at the little girl lying on the small hay bed in the corner of the room. "How long has she been out like that?"

"Just a little while," Tarl said. "She'll stay that way for the rest of the night."

The barber nodded once. "Good enough. He'll be here soon. Then we can conduct business and be on our way."

"Is that what you're callin' it now? Business?"

"In light of the unfortunate circumstances that are about to plague us, yes." The barber unloosed the tie to his long cloak and flung it on the larger bed against the right wall. "I've made it my business to secure peace when war looms on the horizon. What else would you call it?"

Tarl pointed to the three blue emblems on the barber's vest. "I can think of a few other words—"

A sharp knock at the door.

"Who's there?" Tarl barked.

"Someone who'll slit your throat if you don't let him in," a quiet voice replied.

The barber heaved his body onto the center bed and motioned for Tarl to open the door. "It's him."

Tarl opened the door wide enough for a tall gentleman to step inside. He wore the maroon cloak and gold badge of the drapers guild, with knee-high leather boots. *A rather good disguise,* the barber thought. *Too blond, though.* He liked his men a bit more dark and brooding. His women too. Still, a handsome face, with a strong jaw framed by short hair and a neatly trimmed goatee. The barber had to admire the cut and shape of both.

The draper looked over to the corner bed. "Is she—"

"Asleep," Tarl said.

The draper nodded as he withdrew a small bag from his cloak. He opened it to reveal the gold coins that filled it to the brim. He picked one coin out and tossed it to Tarl. "Test it."

Tarl threw it back at the draper's feet. "Ain't doin' this for money, damn you."

"What my friend here is trying to say is that there are more important things at stake," the barber quickly added, picking up the gold piece. He bit into it. Soft, just as it should be. He dropped it back into the draper's money bag.

The draper drew the strings close. "You secure those stakes with this exchange, providing what you say about the girl is true." Four long steps brought him to the small form asleep in the corner. She could not have seen more than seven or eight years. He knelt down beside her and brushed a lock of dark hair from her eyes. "Are your certain this is the one?" he asked softly, his face unreadable.

"Oh yes," the barber answered. "Our sentries have watched her wandering the Seven Woods alone for the last six months now. It took some time to catch her, for she seemed to know the forest better than the woodland guards."

"I've heard legends about your woods," the draper said, still gazing at the little face. "Ours die so quickly."

"Any forest will die if you lay an ax or fire to it," the barber retorted. "Which is why we are all here. Now, let us get on with it."

The draper stood up. "Why are you so nervous, sir barber?" he asked softly. "Do you know, perhaps, of others?"

"I didn't know about this one until your visit a year ago," he said. "I found her. I know of no others, nor have I heard any tales of them. May Neáhvalar forgive us." He signed a triangle in the air then folded his hands. Tarl did the same, before quickly casting his eyes to the floor.

"If your god had wanted them safe," the draper said in a voice as smooth as the silk he wore, "he would have saved them in the first place, don't you think?"

"Such matters are beyond me," the barber sighed. "I am no priest, nor do I belong to the Order of the Seven Wood. I only wish to keep the passages between Gaelastad, Íarchol, and Lailethas clear of Nemaron soldiers."

"Don't worry, you'll have your peace." The draper hurled the bag of money straight at the fat man's chest. "And your pay."

The barber flinched slightly as he caught the bag. Let the brute think he was only doing it for the money and the security of the guilds.

The draper went to kneel by the little girl. He placed his hand gently on her forehead. "Where will you take her?"

"To the center of the Seven Woods," Tarl slurred, "where we found her."

The draper's ice blue eyes shone—with understanding or desire, the barber couldn't tell. "An excellent choice," he said, gently kissing her brow before reaching for a second time into the depths of his cloak.

Whatever their choices tonight, the barber thought, they were damned, all of them. *No, this is to keep damnation from coming,* another voice inside his head argued. The moonstone blade flickered purple in the candlelight, its jeweled hilt half hidden by the draper's hand. The barber turned his head away. *The Winter will invade before the Nemarons.* This little human girl could do nothing to stop the violent winds and snow that would come with the Elementarí's waking.

But the real Terakhein girl was out there, hiding. Somewhere. He prayed this sacrifice would buy them time. *Neáhvalar, let someone find her—before he does.*

CHAPTER 1
A WORLD OF THORNS

The little imp was up again. Jonathan waited a few moments, hearing the front door creak open and close. He crawled out of bed, pulled on his boots and cloak, and grabbed his dagger. Knowing his sister, he guessed it was well-nigh midnight. Jonathan threw back the blanket then crept to the door and listened. No one else in the house was stirring. He quickly felt his way across the pitch-black room, opened the door, and followed the small dirt path he was sure Jenna had taken.

The night was cooler than it should have been for mid-summer, but after the waves of heat they had experienced in spring, the cold air felt good on Jonathan's face. The run up the long grassy slope warmed him enough, but the eastern wind cut through his clothes as he traversed the semi-rocky descent on the other side. He slowed his steps as he came upon a vast meadow, shadowed black and gray by the light of the quarter moon. He squinted, looking for any movement in the darkness. If she wore her cloak tonight, she'd be hard to see. Not by his eyes, anyway. The Fáliquerci Forest bounded the southern and western side of the meadow. To the east lay a small lake. The grasslands were a primary feeding ground for white-tailed deer this time of year. And where deer grazed, wolves followed.

A sudden glint of silver flashed by the far end of the meadow, close to the dark line of trees. Jenna had her blade out. Jonathan sped across the meadow, holding his breath as he whipped out his own knife.

"Who's there!" she shouted, swinging her blade around.

Jonathan peered into the line of trees and saw nothing. The little scamp had just been play acting. "It's polite to wait for the answer before trying to kill a stranger," he said, sheathing his dagger.

"I am the Queen of Cadarn!" Jenna pounced towards him, knife held like a sword. "You will answer before taking another step, sir."

Jonathan laughed as he dodged a second swipe of her blade, picked her up and threw her over his shoulder. "What? Not the Lady of the Poisoned Bow?"

"Evanna died to protect the holy flame," she said breathlessly as she dangled upside down.

"So? Cierdwyn died to win the war."

"Stop! Stop!" she pleaded, amidst giggles of delight, but he just spun her around even faster. It had been so long since he had heard her laugh.

A howl pierced the night air.

Jonathan set Jenna down. She ran to pick up her knife.

"Quiet now, girl." Jonathan held out his hand as he scanned the perimeter of the wood. Jenna's fingers tightened over his as she pointed to the far side of the Fáliquerci. There, between two Elder trees, each as thick as two men wide, a pair of yellow eyes glowed in the moonlight.

"Walk, don't run," Jonathan said, as he pushed her towards the meadow. His skin prickled with fear as a wolf—almost twice as large as any full-grown male wolf he had ever seen—crept out from the trees, its coat gleaming silver white. He had heard of such creatures living in the most northern wilderness of Lailethas. So what was such a monstrous beast doing in the southern part of Gaelastad? "Keep your blade out, girl, and be my eyes," he commanded Jenna.

And Neáhvalar keep you from looking back and seeing this ghostly creature stalking us.

His sister led him through the meadow while Jonathan kept his eyes on the wolf, careful not to gaze directly at it. This wasn't a challenge, but neither could it be a rout—the moment you ran you became its prey. He had thrown back his shoulders so that his slim six-foot height might seem more massive, but that hadn't deterred it from coming even closer.

"Is it still following us?" she whispered.

"Of course. Probably saw me as a right tasty meal." Jonathan hoped Jenna couldn't hear the shaking in his voice; she always trusted him to rescue her. "This should teach you to stay in your bed in the middle of the night."

"The wind called me," she said quietly, her little palm sweaty in his.

"Next time tell the wind you're tired." *And to leave you alone, strange girl.* Six times lost in the Fáliquerci, twice as many stuck up in a tree, countless whippings, and their father bellowing curses weren't enough to stop her wandering.

She wouldn't have gone out tonight if Jeremy were still here.

"Jonathan." Jenna tugged on his sleeve. They were beginning the long stony path up the sloping hill, and Jonathan realized there was no way to keep his balance and still face the beast. He let go of his sister's hand.

"Now go for it." His sister was quick and silent as she lithely climbed the rocky slope, almost as stealthy as a Terakhein child would have done. Jonathan scrambled after her, listening for the sounds of the wolf's pursuit over his own rasping breath. Such a massive creature would surely make more noise if it wanted to attack them on the hill? *The lies we tell ourselves to get through,* Jonathan thought, breaking skin as he grasped a thorn bush to pull himself up.

Jenna cleared the top first. "Run home, Jenna, as fast as

you can!" he commanded. *I can at least stay this creature's hunt long enough for you to get Father.*

He reached the plateau and spun around, dagger out, half expecting to see that giant white form bounding after him. But no, the sloping landscape loomed as one continuous shadow; nothing stirred on the side of the hill. He took off at a sprint towards the house, looking back every once in a while to see if there was a hint of silver white in pursuit. Relief flooded him when he saw that Jenna had just reached the front door. He put a finger to his lips. No use waking Father now.

"What happened?" she asked, looking behind him.

"It returned to its pack," Jonathan said, although he wasn't so sure. "Must have thought you a scant dinner for such a pursuit, I warrant," he added, noting just how thin she had gotten. He would see that she ate better in the mornings, no matter what the night brought. "If either Mother or Father wakes, it'll be both our hides..." he warned as they snuck inside and felt along the wall until they reached their small rooms, one beside the other. Jonathan followed his sister into her room, and made sure she was tucked quite well into her bed. "Now, stay here for the rest of the night," he whispered, and kissed her forehead.

She caught hold of his hand. "Don't go, Jon."

"The wolf went away—"

"I'm not scared of any wolf!" she whispered furiously.

"You're not scared of the dark either." He sighed as he sat down on her bed. At only eight, his sister could wander into the fields at midnight without so much as a second thought, but she could not face the world of her dreams. The nightmares had started when she was three, and no tonics or teas could help her sleep through the night. *A fanciful child, your sister is,* the widow Samsone had told him when he and his mother first brought Jenna to her. Bawdy and brash hag that she was, she was still the best healer in the village. *Bosh and balls, talk to the child when she wakes up crying!* the widow had admonished them both. *Tell her to name her fear, name it and make it go back into the darkness where it belongs.* Jeremy had always been the one to lull her to sleep, and again Jonathan found himself intensely wishing his older brother were here. A year it had been, and Jenna's nightmares had only grown worse.

"What do you fear?" he repeated.

"Dreams," she said in a small voice.

"Dreams?" he challenged. "What are dreams?"

"Flowers that spring from sleep."

"So what is it that you fear?"

"Nightmares," her voice trembled.

"And what are nightmares?" Jonathan asked.

"Thorns and weeds that creep into the sleeping world of flowers."

"So what will you do?"

"Take a dagger and cut my way out."

"That's right," he said, standing up.

"Please stay. Just wait till I'm asleep. Please, Jon?" Her hand once more grasped his.

"Fine then." He threw himself on the floor beside her straw bed, irritated that once again he would lose a good night's sleep. "But you'll not grow up until you learn to defend yourself against the thorns, starling." He tried to get into a comfortable position so he might get at least some rest before dawn. Jenna was quiet. So quiet that he thought perhaps she had already drifted off. But his sister must have sensed his restlessness, for she crawled down beside him, drawing her blanket over them as she sought the safety of Jonathan's shoulder. She was shaking furiously, like he had never seen her, and so he held her tight. "What is it?" he whispered.

"I don't..."

"You don't want to tell me?" Jonathan suggested.

"I don't...understand."

"Is it the world of thorns? Are the serpent demons coming after you? You know what to do. Cut your way out with a—"

"It's not thorns or snakes, Jon. "

"Then what?"

"Winter. It's a world of winter," she cried.

⟿⟾⟿

Morning was brutal, despite the smell of frying eggs and onions that filled the house. Bleary-eyed, Jonathan turned over to see that Jenna had already gone. He sat up, and his shoulder spasmed in pain. He rubbed it hard while rotating his arm a few times, and felt it loosen as the spasm reduced to a dull throbbing once again.

"Jonathan," his mother said, poking her head around the tapestry. Sharp amber eyes peered down at him. "Dawn's almost come and gone, what are you doing still abed?"

"I don't call it a bed unless I've got feathers underneath me." He continued to massage his shoulder, regretting the fact that he had stayed instead of sneaking back to his own room. "One thin layer of straw on an earthen floor scarcely counts."

"Get out here before your father comes home—he and Lian are due back anytime now." She checked to make sure Jenna wasn't behind her. "Another nightmare?"

Jonathan hesitated, wondering how much to tell her. She had kept such a close eye on them both since losing Jeremy that if she knew about the wolf, his mother might never let Jenna out of her sight. Besides, he was certain it was a lone wolf, far from home—there had been no answering howls to its own last night—and wolves sundered from their pack did not survive long. "Yes, that's all."

Her thin brows crinkled slightly. "Your father thinks we should take her to the widow; perhaps bleed her a little and see if that helps."

"I've never known anyone to bleed out their bad dreams, and besides this one was my fault."

"What did you do?" she asked, exasperated. "You know better than to excite her imagination—"

"She was pretending to be Evanna, so I played along. That wasn't her nightmare anyway, and she's getting better, I swear. This was only the third time this summer." If they didn't hear her during the other times, why worry them? They had enough to think about with the bad crop from last fall. He ran a quick hand through his black mop of tangled hair and rubbed his temple. "Not half as bad as in the spring."

"I suppose you're right." Her forehead relaxed, immediately making her look ten years younger. "I'm still going to ask the widow about it—it makes me nervous."

"Aye, Mother, she'll turn out all right." It was more a hope than a statement. It was no longer the time for prophets—that happened long ago. Seeing visions or hearing voices were signs of madness, now, nothing more. He had to warn Jenna not to talk about the wind calling her.

"You'll take her into Breithan when you go to Cadman's?" His mother's voice broke into his thoughts. "It'll cheer her up to go play with Susanna."

"She'll slow me down by an hour at least." Jonathan followed his mother out into the main room, where a plate of eggs and bread were waiting for him on the table.

"No I won't!" Jenna bounded into the house and planted a kiss on Jonathan's cheek. Their father came stomping in after her, followed by Lian Tidwell. Both men looked worn and old, older than Jonathan even thought possible—especially his father, who at fifty could take on a man half his age. *'Tis a storm we bring to save the land*, he had said last week when he set off with Lian to convince the council to obey ancient Terakhein laws rather than fall to the will of the guilds. *Terakhein*—Cadarian for earth keeper. Such a strange word, Jonathan thought.

"Morning, Merthenna. Jonathan." Lian Tidwell nodded his greeting as he dusted off his heavy boots and stepped inside.

Merthenna set down a bowl of porridge on the table and wiped her hands on her apron, sighing. "Greetings be damned, Lian. Out with it. What news have you brought?"

"Nothing good." Lian shook his woolly head. "The Southern Council voted to break Dormín, so everyone can continue planting come next spring."

"Break Terakhein law and you break the land—"

"That myth matters little to the guilds, and you know it, Merthenna," Jonathan's father said between mouthfuls, egg yolk dripping yellow into his black beard. "They want more trade between Breithan, Klinneret, and Duraeston and will do whatever it takes to get it. Dormín was the first to be challenged, and just you watch that Centuras will be next."

"They wouldn't dare," Jonathan countered.

"You've got a lot to learn, boy, about the way politics work," Lian said coolly.

Jonathan felt a slow flush creep up his face. He was not so naïve as that, listening to his parents and others talk in the village about changes the guilds were asking for. Crops had been bad the last two years; of course, the Council wanted to break Dormín and plant instead of letting the land rest. The forests, though, were another matter. No other country had wood of such stature that didn't rot or grow weak as the years passed. Damn idiots didn't realize that the moment they killed Centuras, they demolished the Order of the Seven Wood, their only standing army. And then who would stop the soldiers of Cadarn, or even Nema-ron, from marching across their borders for more lumber? Granted cutting the trees once but every hundred years was hard to understand when a new barn was needed, and such laws now straddled the line between legend and practical politics.

"Centuras might stand for a little longer, I warrant," Jonathan's father said. "Especially with news about that girl in the Seven Woods."

"What girl?" His mother had that dark look again. "Jenna, go to your room."

"But I want to hear about—"

"I said go."

Jenna stomped off, but Lian waited until she shut the door before he continued. "Seems there's a little one living in the woods—maybe Jenna's age or younger. Sentries have been trying to catch her, but with no luck. And now people are worried about where she came from and who has lost her. No one in Duraeston has been asking to help find their daughter, so the priests have ordered double the guard for the forest. Still, you know the breadth of that wood takes weeks to traverse; it'll be a long time before the sentries can find her, I warrant."

"I could find her," Jonathan found himself saying, a thousand thoughts running through his head. He was a damn good tracker at only eighteen. Folk from Klinneret had even hired him out when an animal had been lost, or a criminal was on the loose. There wasn't a footprint Jonathan couldn't find. But more than that—

"You'll not be leavin' to rescue other's children," his mother glowered.

Jonathan felt the pang of guilt even though he knew his mother's words were not an accusation. Jeremy's death had not been his fault. But that did not stop the unspoken, desperate desire he had to save a life for the one he lost that day in the Fáliquerci.

"This news is somewhat good, as you say, Lian—stop your glarin', Merthenna, they'll find the girl. And soon, too. This weather ain't no good for being outside at night. But in the meantime, the Order of the Seven Wood will double its vigilance," Silas said. "As of late, I had begun to wonder whether or not the guilds have been paying for access into the wood for a little milling."

Lian took a swig of his ale. "That's not been proven."

"But you've had your suspicions, as have I."

Lian nodded. "Aye, and if they turn out to be true, Neáhvalar help the guilds who have purchased the land's blood, and the priests who let them. Silas and I will give 'em a thrashing such as they've never had, especially if they've convinced the Northern Council to fall in line with the decision to do away with Dormín too."

The hair on Jonathan's arms stood on end at those words. Lian Tidwell was a gentle man, for the most part. Father of six boys, his curly mop of hair was already gray, same as the giant beard that covered half his face. Jonathan's father barked before he bit, so you had fair warning. Lian was cool and calm as a summer's night until you crossed him, and then the storm descended. "I pity their backsides as much as I do their politics," he said.

"Time's done for mercy," his father growled. "Even Cadman's Iron Clads have begun to split into factions. Some say Terakhein law still stands; others say it's nonsense, especially since there's not been any emissary sent from their forest for twenty some years now, maybe more. At least, not here, and I'll not count that dribble that came of out Cadarn after the war."

"It was more than dribble." Merthenna shook her head in disbelief. "It was blasphemous, what they said. Such stories to scare children." She tossed a furtive glance back at Jenna's room.

"Dribble or not, that war cost us everything," Lian snorted, "even if we had no part in it. At least we had an understanding with Cadreyth and Evanna; they guarded their flame, and we our trees. *Live and let live alone.*"

"Do you think the fire really did heal?" Jonathan interjected, thinking now only of Jenna. Legend had it that the royal house of Cadarn swore fealty to it. Hundreds of Cadarians would line up once a year to bow in front of Ashyranna to be rid of smaller maladies. Its power was always suspect amongst Gaelastad folk—for certainly the fire was unable to grow new limbs or bring people back from the dead. It had never been a matter of concern for Jonathan, until he thought of Jenna and her nightmares...

The rumors concerning Ashryanna's disappearance brought no suspicion at first, with a verified report of the Nemarons taking the king's hall and killing Queen Evanna, who had been defending the flame herself. But that story became intermingled with stranger myths: Cadreyth being killed in single combat by an *embodied* Elementarí, who then murdered Cierdwyn, the king's sister. The folk in Gaelastad, Íarchol, Lailethas scoffed at the tale—what mattered was that Cadreyth had reinstated all the Terakhein laws that his father had been lax in enforcing. Such laws limited trade with the western countries, and the guilds stayed out. But all that was rapidly changing. There were darker whispers about the loss of the flame that healed—tales of madness and death.

"King Adolan's power keeps growing." The growl in Silas' voice brought Jonathan out of his reverie. "First mistake he made was to begin his idiot reign by sending all of Cadreyth's counselors into exile after they could not reclaim Ashryanna. He's twice the size of his cousin and half the ruler, yet every year he sends more guildsmen here, asking the purchase price of our wood. Our council probably hasn't thought of that. They just think of trade, as is their wont. And the disappearance of the Terakhein too, I don't like it. Not one bit—what happened to them all and why didn't we hear anythin' about it? Bad tidings are afoot, I'm tellin' ya. Now Lian, what word do we have from the tanners?"

"Cadman says Tarl's feeling pressure to swing the vote their way. He's been acting strange lately—let's have Riok talk to him," Lian suggested. "Sometimes family can persuade where mere friends cannot."

Jenna bounded into the main room. "Can I come out now?"

Their father turned and gave her a half-cocked grin—the

only smile Jonathan had seen on his face in the last few weeks. "I guess so, seeing as you're already here. We've had enough talk about other matters, for now."

Lian tipped his hat to Merthenna, then said to Jonathan, "You'll probably see Alec when you get into town. Tell him I'll be back by sundown."

"Yes, sir." He tickled Jenna's ear. "Provided this one doesn't dawdle about so." She had better not slow him down—he had much to talk about with Cadman.

"Then what are you doing wasting time now? Dawn is done," Silas said, "we've a farm to tend."

—⁘◉⁘◉⁘—

He and Jenna donned their cloaks and set out at a good pace down the little dirt path that led past their fields, a sea of golden wheat and barley waving in the breeze. They *might* just have enough grain to make do this year, provided a decent rain hit their farm every week for the next month. Given the unusually cool weather they had been experiencing, that was indeed a possibility. They'd never needed a coat in the summer months before, and yet the breeze nipped at the skin despite the sun overhead. Jonathan gazed at the gray sky and inhaled deeply. Southern winds always smelled musky and usually brought the storm clouds of the coast with them. "Jenna, come back here!" She was already running down a grassy slope to the meadow on their left. "Now!"

She sprinted back up the small hill, breathless. "I was just playing."

"We don't have time for that. Cadman's expecting me by midmorning. If you want to run, head straight." His godfather had been very strict about being on time as of late. Quite the nerve, too, after passing him over for first apprentice. *Bastard,* he muttered to himself then tried to shake it off. There was no more to be thought or said about *that*—it was done. What mattered now was the girl lost in the wood, the girl the Order was desperate to find to save their reputation.

His old dream of becoming a sentry of the Seven Woods suddenly took fire again. He had hoped that being apprenticed to Cadman would allow him to become a journeyman and gain him admittance to his Iron Clad guild in Duraeston. From there, he might be recommended to the Order. Jonathan had learned the art of wielding a sword as soon as he could hold one. Cadman had often practiced with him as a lad, and then when he went to work for him in the evenings, the training got more serious. *Test the weight in your hand, see what happens when the pommel is off in size or heaviness.* Sparring with the smith taught him much about what went into making a good a blade.

Wanting to be in the Order of the Seven Woods, well, that had been decided long ago, when he and Jeremy saw a few sentries ride through Breithan, dressed in cloaks of rich green with only a simple silver brooch clasp. Jonathan knew then and there that he wanted to be of the guard that protected the largest of Gaelastad's undying forest. It had only been strengthened when, at fifteen, he, Alec, and Jeremy ran off for a week and slipped into the Seven Woods, escaping the Order's pursuit. They had wandered forests thick with trees thousands of years old, and grown so tall that even the day was as night, so much did the foliage block out the sunlight. But oh, that forest was so alive it seemed to *breathe,* and Jonathan had felt for the first time that the Elementarí were more than just myth. He knew there had to be elemental spirits feeding that life, sustaining it, and maybe even *leading* him there. He couldn't tell anyone that. Not even Jeremy. *Yet it was I who led you out, brother,* despite Alec's loud complaints of being thoroughly lost amid that endless labyrinth of undergrowth, vines, and bramble that seemed to block every path.

They came back to Breithan and, despite a sound thrashing from their fathers, never confessed where they had been. It would take but a few days to find the girl who was close to Jenna's age. What would his sister do, lost in a such a wood? He saw that Jenna had reached the massive wall of trees that began the Fáliquerci Forest and was waiting for him. It wasn't so bad at the forest's edge, where the normal ash, oak, and elder trees allowed dappled sunlight in. But the true Fáliquerci began where the Atreal trees grew thick, with leaves of such dark green and blue hue. The Midnight Forest many called it, and once trapped in the middle of it, far from the road, it was rumored the trees conspired to keep a man lost forever.

Jonathan was probably one of the few who knew the truth of that legend, unless the widow had heard something that day she'd found him, cradling his brother as his last breath escaped his lips. The Fáliquerci had no sentries guarding it because the wood took care of itself; you were fine as long as you stayed on the road. He and Jeremy had wandered into the middle because Jonathan wanted to feel the trees growing, just like he did when they braved the Seven Woods. He still felt guilty that he hadn't seen the snake that had sunk its fangs into Jeremy's ankle—only heard it whip through the trees and saw his brother point to his leg before falling to the ground. No one else blamed him for Jeremy's death—at least, not to his face. But he often wondered about his father, who he would catch looking at him every once in a while with a worried, almost fearful expression. And Cadman had chosen another boy as first apprentice instead of him, citing Jeremy's death as the reason; he could not leave Silas a hand short on the farm.

"Jonathan, stop it." A small hand slipped into his. He looked down, surprised to see Jenna there. But she always seemed to know when he was thinking about his brother.

He gently squeezed the little fingers. "Aye, girl. No use thinking of what's past." *Nor what's to come.* They had entered the forest proper and were now completely sur-rounded by the dark Atreal trees, with trunks so thick three men could stand behind one and not be seen. Sinuous branches canopied the narrow road. Perpetual twilight. Today, though, the wood seemed darker than usual, the gray cast of the sky against which tall trees loomed over them like black-robed figures. The road was big enough for a small cart to wheel through, but he felt like it was shrinking with every step. *Warmth for winter, fire for darkness.* He silently repeated the old Terakhein chant, hoping to calm the faint buzzing that had begun to creep into his head. He passed the ancient oak on his right, bracing himself as he moved deeper into the wood. The buzz was as loud as a hornet's swarm. He tried not to break into a run, instead he merely increased his gait, but now Jenna was having a hard time keeping up with him.

"Jonathan, *slow down*," she whined.

But he wasn't really listening. Not to her, at any rate. *Just do it already, damn it.* A few steps more, and the horrific sound finally changed to soft whispers. Jonathan did not look to his right or his left as he strode forward, fists clenched, for there was no one hiding in the shadows of the wood, just as there was no swarm of bees. He found that out when it all started, the day Jeremy died in his arms. The low-hanging trees and thick twisted branches closed in all around him while the whispers increased in volume. Over to his right, two yellow eyes crouched low, and a coat of silver white. He should have known…

"Jon!" Jenna yelled again.

Jonathan turned around. Something flashed in the corner of his eye as he did so. Fire? He blinked hard, whipping out his dagger and placing himself between Jenna and the wolf now creeping out from the undergrowth. He was still a good five paces away from his sister.

"Jenna, stand still!" She froze. Behind her, a light flared. Not fire. More like a ghost of a flame trying to catch hold on wood. There was a hint of shape about it as it shimmered. And it was large. Was that a hand? A claw? It was moving, too, slowly towards Jenna. He could not reach her before the flame did, and thankfully, she hadn't seen it. But her eyes grew wide at sight of the massive wolf that kept inching towards them. Instinctively, she drew her out her small dagger. *Neáhvalar, help us.* "That's right, girl. Now walk slowly towards me, very slowly." He looked for any low hanging branch she could climb to safety—but nothing. As prey they were caught between beast and disembodied flame.

Suddenly they heard the wind barrel along the tops of the branches, a thundering gust that caused the Atreals to sway dangerously. The flame was snuffed out while the wolf let out a long, hungry howl. Jonathan grabbed his sister, but they couldn't run within the maelstrom of branch, rock, dust that now encircled them. Jonathan could barely see the oak off the road, so they dove behind it for cover, not sure of where the wolf was now, for its howling had been silenced.

Litchwáll, athera heran, Ventosus

The words came from all sides, and they were no longer whispers, but raging voices of fear. Louder than the words was laughter, a high cackling laughter that rode upon the fierce gales tearing the forest apart.

Ventosus! Athera heran, Ventosus

Jonathan was still crouched protectively around Jenna when suddenly he was knocked onto his back, not by wind, but by a force so powerful he felt like his skin would come right off his muscles. Was it the wolf? No. A burst of flame rushed past as he heard the giant branch above him crack. Jonathan rolled a few feet, the dagger dropped as he shielded his head. The branch hit the ground with such force that it splintered into pieces. At that very moment, the wind died and the laughter with it. Even the voices of the trees were silenced.

"Jenna!" His sister was still huddled at the base of the tree, eyes tightly closed. He immediately swept her up into his arms. "Are you alright?" he asked, eyes scanning the forest floor for any appearance of silver or golden flame. But nothing moved. At least, not yet.

She was shaking all over. "Jonathan"—her lip quivered —"the wolf—"

"Aye," he said, trying to keep his voice steady as he checked to make sure she was unharmed. "What? Not a scratch on you, magic girl. Now let's go before it returns."

"You're bleeding," Jenna said in a small voice.

"It's just a nick," Jonathan assured her. "Come." He held out a hand for her while with the other he reached up and gingerly touched the place where a flying rock had cut his brow. A thin line of blood trickled down the side of his face. *And now there's this scent to follow.* He hurried her along the small road that was littered with thick, gnarled branches. *Just like snakes,* he thought, as the forest once more grew dark around them.

—⟶⟨⟩⟨⟩⟶—

It hadn't meant to be seen, not by the boy and girl, at any rate. The boy's dreams were not ready to be culled from his mind. But it wanted the large silver-white serpent that closely trailed the young man and his sister. Oh yes, the flame wanted it. Badly. But then the wolf had to join in, too. It hadn't counted on that.

The snake had detected the flame's unseen shimmer and quickly coiled itself into the strike position. The fire, in return, had brandished one leg in warning. A foolish move, for the boy saw it, and they could not risk further discovery by engaging in battle. The fire hesitated, and in that space of indecision, the serpent hissed and extended its fangs.

Then they heard the wind.

It ripped apart leaf and limb as it circled among the tree-tops, howling and laughing in madness as it descended into the middle of the forest and surrounded fire, serpent, and wolf. *No no no,* the protest escaped the serpent's forked tongue just before they were caught up in the maelstrom of branches, dirt, and rock. The flame almost succumbed to the windstorm's force before it burst into a brilliant fireball, knocking the young man back as it sped towards the snake. White hot limbs seemed to erupt from the fiery orb as it snatched the serpent and dragged it far away from brother and sister. It wanted its prey alone, without distraction. The white wolf had run off—to its master, hopefully. The wind roared, but no raging tempest would shake fire and snake from each other's tethered grasp, and so they remained tightly intertwined, like lovers, until the wind died away, defeated in its attempt at sport.

The boy and girl escaped while the serpent still writhed within the golden-red flames. It was neither consumed by the fire's heat nor in pain, hissing only in fear of what was to come. In one fluid motion, it suddenly changed from a snake into a beautiful man with long silver hair and brilliant green eyes.

"Let me go, Bryn," the man said in a silky voice as he tried to stand upright. "You'll not want to do anything to me here, out in the open like thisss."

"You're not a good judge of what I am inclined to do, Trapher," the fire roared, trying to control its anger. Already a small tear in the earth formed where they stood, large enough for a small child to fall through. It would be noticed later by the townspeople. They would naturally ask what caused it. "Quick! Tell me why you were following them. Neither is your normal choice for sustenance, from what I recall."

"I'm not here for feeding."

"Then why?"

"Many reasons. Perhaps the almighty Bryn knows some...but not all," Trapher hissed as he slipped back into his serpent form and wrapped himself around two of the fire's many limbs. "The day we took the Terakhein's foressst eight yearsss ago...some of the little onesss ran to the river, oh tasty they were, and I was enjoying the hunt, but that wench of a water spirit sent two away to safety using the

Avexi Celarise. I'm glad I caught her before she left too. The children must have survived, now, don't you think? Or why elssse would you be here?"

Bryn blazed as the silvery snake continued to coil around him. The split in the ground grew wider. "What do you want with them?"

"Keep your fire down, love." Trapher reared his triangular head back. "What do I want? Probably the same thing you do. I hear when she cries out at night. Sssomething about serpents and wolves, don't you know. But it doesn't matter now, does it? Enough has been set in motion that one girl, Terakhein though she may be, couldn't sssstop it. But the boy interestsss me too... I'd like to find out more of what the boy knows...yesss...I think I'll do just that."

Trapher angled slightly to the left as Bryn tried to bring one leg around to stomp him. But the flame wasn't quick enough, and in one vulnerable instant Trapher struck Bryn's eyes. There was a burst of white fire as Bryn cried out and rolled onto his back, allowing the serpent to whip around Bryn's fiery legs. Then Trapher rose up, hissing delightedly, as he reared his head to strike again.

⁓⊰⊚⊱⁓

The road was not getting any clearer.

They tried to quickly scramble over the crisscrossed limbs of Atreal, oak, and ash that covered the dirt path, but branches scratched their hands and faces. A cold, steady breeze swept the gray clouds lower; the forest grew dark like night. "It's the winter," Jenna warned, breathless. Things were stirring amid the leaves and twigs, and Jonathan prayed that it was but forest creatures that, like them, had been trapped in the windstorm.

"It is *not* winter," he countered, not wanting her to fall into hysterics, here in the middle of the wood, with the wolf ever behind him. "You said yourself the wind asks you to come out and play." *And the trees talk to me, starling—* although now they had fallen silent—*while a flame walks the wood, so we're even.* When he was little, he had experienced bursts of light, brought on by intense head pain that the widow eventually cured him of. The flame he saw just now was different—it had shape and intention.

"But, Jonathan, with the winter comes the *wolves.*"

He gripped Jenna's hand. They still could not stop, much as he wanted to check her eyes and make sure they were not gleaming with fever. "What? Why did you not tell me this last night?"

"Because the wolf in my dreams is a black, and even larger than the one we encountered. I don't see the others that follow it—I only hear their howls."

A different kind of cold was creeping into Jonathan's flesh. Why was a black haunting his sister's dreams, and a silver-white one hunting their steps? "I'll take you to the widow straightway after work. She'll know what to do about all this." He didn't relish the idea of a visit—the old woman was as lusty as she was wise, and didn't mind a good pinch of his arse during most visits. But she knew things, strange things that others in the village didn't. Folks couldn't say where she had come from, but she had been there long enough—from before the Great War, at least—to be accepted.

Jenna nodded in assent to his plan.

Snap.

The sound of a large branch breaking behind them caused Jonathan to spin around even as he silently motioned for Jenna to keep walking ahead. They were almost to the edge of Fáliquerci, where thin beams of sunlight broke through the bands of Atreals. She at least, could make it out. He focused on the curving branches that seemed so still. What if something was *slithering* their way? He remembered Jeremy's purple-blue lips, mouth contorted in pain as he begged Jonathan to save him.

Another loud *snap.*

"Run!" he shouted at his sister. She scurried over the last

of the branch-littered path with Jonathan behind her, turning this way and that, looking for the unseen thing near
them, his blade out and gleaming. Another rustle as something darted to his left, but the path suddenly cleared and
light broke in from the mid-morning day. Jenna had sprinted
ahead, over the last hill and out of sight. Jonathan was right
behind her, listening for pursuit while simultaneously noticing that the road beyond the forest was clear. *As if the
storm was within only the wood itself.*

Within moments the tanner's place on the outskirts of
town came into view on the opposite plateau. Jonathan had
never been so glad to see the small line of houses and shops
that cut across the horizon. Two-storied and built from the
impenetrable wood of the Fáliquerci, the buildings of the
village looked like a fortress. Small wagons rolled past on
the road that cut across the Terakhein path that led from
their farm to town. He needed to get word to Lian about
clearing the path—true, few folk went out their way, but
still, no wagon was going to get through, and even horses
would have a hard time navigating around branch and
bramble. Jenna sprinted right, to the north and down the
wide dirt street, past the apothecary, the butcher's place, and
Lian's carpentry shop.

"Where do you think you're going, my little sprite?" Alec
shouted from the doorway.

"We escaped—"

"Monsters and all sort of fey beasts." Jonathan interrupted. Now was not the time to talk of such things.

Luckily, Alec provided the perfect distraction by tossing
Jenna into the air. Built as tight as a barrel just like his father,
Lian, he tossed her into the air as if she were light as a kit-
ten.

"If you make my sister wet herself, you're taking her
home," Jonathan threatened. "Methinks your stench would
cover hers no matter what." Alec's wide smile showed a row
of perfectly white teeth.

"This squire needs to be taught a lesson, don't you think, my lady?"

Jonathan had no time for this, but he could see that this horseplay was taking Jenna's mind off the terror they'd just experienced. He crouched down, but it was too late; Alec had already dived under his arm. The next moment he was lifted into the air and thrown onto the ground, to the sound of Jenna's cheers. Alec threw himself on top, just to be sure Jonathan stayed down. "Do you yield?"

"Yes, damn you, now get off me before someone thinks we're betrothed."

"No one would ever believe it; I'm too good looking." Alec stood up and reached out a hand to Jonathan, which he took.

"Remind me to get you a new looking glass," Jonathan said as he wiped the dirt from his breeches.

"Bitterness will ruin that fair face of yours," Alec smirked. "It's not my fault you have a brow as flat as a throck's."

"No, but those blond curls of yours are looking limp as a —"

"Jon-a-than!" Jenna reprimanded.

"Aye, where are my manners," Jonathan teased. "Now go on to Balfour's. I'll be by mid-afternoon and then we can stop by the widow's place." She nodded, knowing to say no more. With a quick wave of her hand at Alec, she skipped down the road.

"We are dismissed, Sir Throck," Alec said, with a slap on Jonathan's back. "Come, I'll walk with you to Cadman's. That man owes me some nails."

Together they walked down the dirt street lined with various peddlers—the aromas of sizzling meat, dried fruit, perfume and manure all blending into the scent of a village that was quickly transforming into a town. Today the square was bustling with more activity than usual—perhaps it was the odd nip in the air despite the faint sun that had momentarily peeked out of the gray clouds in the distance. Still, nothing compared to the scope of Duraeston, thankfully, with its Elementarí altars at every corner, offering up musky incense to gods that people didn't believe in anymore.

"So what is the word?" Alec elbowed him in the ribs. "Father hasn't come home yet."

"He stopped by our place first and said he still has affairs to attend to." Jonathan kept his voice low as they passed a group of men on their right. "The Southern Council voted to dismiss Dormín, and they are worried that the Northern Council will be of like mind. And Centuras is not far from falling as well, if Dormín is broken."

Alec narrowed his eyes at that. "Father said that Duraeston will be the deciding vote there, and the priests won't be able to stop the power of the guilds this time. The land will not rest this year, and the Wood will be cut before its time. It's been comin' for a long while, Jon. Since the war."

"You weren't even alive then," Jonathan shot back. It irritated him how much Alec was like Lian in mind—practical to a fault in the affairs of state. But his friend was right. The war between Cadarn and Nemaron brought to Duraeston a host of Cadarian exiles who, through the years, had not only adapted to local life but had also established a bustling trade of goods and services. Everything from spices to exotic fruit flowed up and down the villages of Gaelastad and into the lower regions of Íarchol. "But see here, we've still got Tarl on our side—Riok is going to speak with them. There's hope yet," he added as they came upon the smithy.

Cadman was outside and shirtless, his scarred arms laid bare to the sun, salt and pepper hair tied back to better see the ax he was filing. "You're late," he said, without glancing up.

"We had a few diversions in the Fáliquercí. Jenna's monsters and all that," he added quickly when Alec raised an eyebrow. "Will the widow's ax be done soon? She came by three times yesterday to ask about it, and didn't mind a nice pinch at my arse while doing the asking." If he had reason to go by Sienna's place, it would be all the better.

"She must have quite the grip after all these years. I'm almost done with the ax now, but I'll spare you being the one to take it to her, lest your arse become too black and blue. How are you, Alec?"

"Not as much in demand by wise-women as my throcky friend here. Are the nails ready?"

"They're inside on the bench. Help yourself."

"My thanks." Alec disappeared into the smithy.

Cadman had momentarily stopped his work and was staring at Jonathan in a strange way.

"What?"

"You do have a rather throcky brow, and those black eyes don't necessarily help. Think you can finish the pommel on that sword for the Duraeston buyer? The hilt is all ready, and I want to send it up with my journeyman tomorrow to show my Iron Clad brother before delivering it to the owner."

Jonathan held back a retort to the words *my journeyman*. "I'll see to it," he said, too brusquely he knew, but that could not be helped. "But wait…"

Alec bounded back out, a bag of nails in hand. "I'd like to stay and find out more about this Council nonsense, but if I don't run these over to my ma'am, she'll kill me." He shook the smith's hand in thanks and gave a hearty slap to Jonathan's back. "You'd better be thinking about who to take to the Harvest dance. I've heard Ida has her eye on you."

"You should say yes, lest the widow find you without a dance partner," Cadman quipped as Alec walked away. The widow. Now that they were alone, Jonathan could speak more freely. Alec was his friend, but whatever you said to Alec made its way back to Lian. "Let me bring her the ax, Cadman. Jenna had one of her nightmares last night."

"Is it getting worse? Sienna said the spring was bad."

"She dreams of a black wolf following her, which wouldn't normally concern me overmuch except that we found a white wolf last night, and it found us again in the Fáliquerci."

"What's this?" The smith now stopped his work and looked up, a scowl etching weathered lines on his face. "A wolf from the north?"

"Aye. Twice the size of a normal southern gray. I've heard they might be that big, but never believed it."

"It had been tracking you since the night? By Neáhvalar, how did you escape it?"

"That is the strangest of all tales. We were saved by the wind." He related how the windstorm had blown through the forest, tearing at the trees. "When it was over, the wolf was gone. I wouldn't think it a portent of things to come, but Jenna's nightmares now revolve around winter."

Cadman's frown slowly relaxed into an unreadable mask. Jonathan wasn't sure if the smith suddenly thought him crazy, or worse, overprotective, like his mother. But his tone was deadly serious. "What did she tell you?"

"Naught else but that the wolves come with the winter. She was shaken last night from our encounter with the White, and it was all I could do to keep her from weeping and waking up our mother. I thought the widow might be able to help her, and maybe see..." he had no words for what he was thinking next. His sister dreamt of a world of thorns, and he saw invisible flame and imagined whispers echoing from the Atreals. Jonathan didn't know if he wanted to tell anyone about such occurrences, except the widow. She was eccentric enough that you could say such things and not worry about it being repeated in the village gossip. Cadman was watching him now with that measuring look, listening and weighing every word.

"You're not worried that our summer fields will suddenly be covered in ice and snow?" Cadman asked, and Jonathan couldn't say whether he was in complete jest or not.

"We'll be fine," he said dismissively. "Just let me bring the ax to Sienna, and she can take a look at Jenna. Besides," he added, knowing that the smith had just come from Duraeston two days ago, "I want to know more about the girl lost in the Seven Woods. Lian and my father gave us just the barest of details, but I bet you have more."

"The priests are trying to keep it quiet for now—speaks of scandal, that a child could be living in the Wood for Neáhvalar knows how long without any notice." Cadman scratched the gray stubble on his chin. "There were only two reports that I know of that says she was spotted near the south end. But they lost sight of her, for she moved quick of foot, almost as if she was running from something. There's even been some talk that she's a Terakhein child running from whatever demons invaded her forest. That is the craziest of tales, though, and it certainly doesn't speak well of the Order's ability to protect the forest from others slipping in, either. There's been talk of the guilds poaching some of the Atreals." He looked shrewdly at Jonathan. "Don't think of rescuing her, Jon. Saving her won't bring Jeremy back, and there's Jenna to look after."

"I can take care of my sister," he replied, wishing he had not mentioned anything about Jenna's dreams. No matter, the smith had given him enough information to go on—the south end. "Now, where's that sword you want finished by today? I'd best start working on it."

—⚬⚭⚬—

From mid-morning to mid-afternoon Jonathan worked diligently on the sword's pommel to fit the tang, testing its weight and then reshaping it. He was still hunched over when Cadman walked in. "You had better leave off the work for now. I don't like what the sky is showing."

Jonathan walked outside to see green-cast clouds looming overhead, which promised hail, but they were never threatened with hail when the winds blew west as they were doing now. Hard rain was more like it, and the road through the Fáliquerci was already going to be difficult to traverse. Jenna loved thunder and lightning, but unless the water was still and deep with a nice bank around it, she hated getting wet and howled if she had to be drug through even the lightest sprinkle.

"Maybe you'd best both stay at the widow's place tonight," Cadman said as Jonathan walked back into the smithy. "I don't know that I want you two traveling on foot with that wolf loose and this storm."

"My mother will be worried sick if Jenna doesn't come home—no, I must at least let them know. Jenna can stay at Balfour's though."

"At least take Hammer; you can outrun wolf and rain on that steed."

Jonathan whistled at the offer since Cadman rarely offered his best palfrey for any errand. "The road still needs to be cleared, and it would take us just as long to find a way around all that wreckage. Thanks anyway, but I'll be fine if I leave now. The sword will have to wait—possibly for a few days since father needs me to help with the farm." He hoped Cadman would buy the lie.

"I still don't like it," Cadman said as he put away the sword Jonathan was working on. "And you could finish it if you stayed in town, instead of me giving the task to Jophil…"

"Wouldn't do any good anyway, would it?" Jonathan couldn't help the slight. While Cadman was trying to offer him better opportunities to do intricate sword work, the door to becoming a journeyman was essentially shut now. "I must be off," and he walked out before the smith could offer any other argument.

He hurried through a few streets over to Balfour's shop on the square. The chandler was in the back, patiently showing his son (who, at eleven, already promised to be as big and bushy as his red-haired father) how to dip a wool string in a pot of melted tallow.

"Keep your eye on the string, son, otherwise it won't be even all the way around." Balfour wiped his hands on his apron before extending one to Jonathan. "You here for Jenna already?"

"Actually, there's a bad storm coming and I was wondering if Jenna could spend the night here." He wanted to add that the candle maker could use the rest as well, for Balfour's eyes were bloodshot, as if he hadn't slept a wink.

"But of course, Jonathan," Balfour said as he lumbered over to the base of the stairs. "Jenna! Come down, your brother's here."

His sister jumped down the steps two at a time until she reached midway and saw Jonathan. "Why are you here so soon?" She frowned. "It's but mid-noon, if that."

"Look outside, Starling. The sky is green. Hail might be on the way, so you get to stay with Susanna tonight."

"We have a little cot in the cellar for you too, Jonathan." Balfour said. "It's not much, but it'll do."

Through the small window in Balfour's shop the clouds seemed to have grown in darkness. "That's kind of you to offer, Balfour, but I must at least let my parents know that Jenna and I are safe. My father will come for Jenna in the morning." He shook hands with the chandler, while Jenna flew down the rest of the stairs to give Jonathan a hug.

She squeezed him tight. "I'll try not to have a nightmare tonight," she whispered in his ear.

"A world of flowers," he said, and let her hold on tight still. "You sure you'll be alright?" He didn't want to leave her.

"Oh yes," she said, finally letting go.

"Then be good for Nellie and Balfour, and mind your manners, miss saucypants." He winked, and she giggled. One last kiss on her forehead, and then he was off.

Jonathan set his shoulders forward against the wind that had suddenly kicked up, and walked down the street, past the bakery to the hill. A raindrop hit his arm, prompting him to sprint down the green slope and up the next to the other plateau. Soon he was running through a light rain, with the green sky promising more. The edge of the Fáli-querci was in sight, just a half mile more until the road disappeared in between the dark line of trees. Once in the wood, he tried waiting it out under the cover of the Atreals, but even there he continued to become soaked to the bone. It wouldn't do to stay this wet and cold, and so for the next hour he trudged on in the deluge, glad he had left Jenna with friends in the comfort of a warm house. He didn't even worry about meeting beast or monster out in this mess of weather. It was almost dusk before he reached his house, waterlogged and in the worst of moods.

"Take off those sopping clothes before you step one foot into this house," his mother warned as she brought him a blanket. It took her a moment to realize that Jenna wasn't with him. "Where's your sister? Has something happened?" She gripped his arm with such force that Jonathan was sure he'd have a purple mark there tomorrow.

It was a reasonable question, but walking through storm and wind had put him in a sour mood. "Calm down," he snapped, wrenching his arm free to snatch the blanket and wrap it around his shivering body. "I let her stay at Balfour's for the night. The storm looked for the worse when I started out."

"Don't talk to your mother that way," his father bellowed. "But you did right keeping her there; she might have caught a cold from getting so wet. We'll pray you don't."

"Yes, well, I'd rather have her here, but come now and have some supper," his mother said. There was bread and cheese on the table, which he hardly touched before asking to be excused.

In his room, he took out his hunting gear: torch, string, knife, and compass—the standard things that can get you through the thick of a wood or the dirty streets of Duraeston in the dead of night. He had to dig a bit more to find the map Cadman had given him last year—the Seven Woods covered nearly one fifth of Gaelastad, but the girl had been last seen near the border of Duraeston. Had she been on the east end, he doubted anyone would have spotted her at all.

He reckoned that if he left a couple of hours before dawn, it would take him three days to get to the Wood itself, then another day to bypass the guards. And then he would find her, as easily as he found his sister time and time again. Jonathan's guess was that she was in the center of that wood, living off the apples and pears that would be in season now. *And just what if she is a Terakhein?* The thought bit him with fear, for what was she doing so far from her forest if she indeed was one of the Guardian's children? Jonathan hoped the girl at least had a cloak for the night's chill. More than this he could not wish for, other than praying his father would not thrash him too badly for skipping out on the farm work, and that Jenna would forgive him for disappearing for a few days. He had planned to tell her, but so many plans had gone amiss today. Still, of all people, she would understand that he owed Jeremy this one adventure, this one rescue. And if all went well, then the dreams of being in the Order, which died the day his brother was buried, might be redeemed.

CHAPTER 2
THE STORM

Jonathan jolted awake when he heard a large crash and howling wind—how had he fallen asleep? Momentarily disoriented, the next thunderclap had him dashing out of bed, running through the house heedless of his father's shouts, and out into the night. He was clad only in his breeches, and a hundred icy shards stung his skin as he raced his way through the hail to the barn.

Once inside, he fared little better. Jonathan realized the sound that had awakened him must have been the roof tearing away in the wind; half the shingles were gone and several beams had fallen. The pigs were running mad with terror, squealing as they tore the flesh off each other. Most of the chickens were already dead, wings bloodied by hail and pieces of roof.

Neáhvalar help me. He stumbled over their bodies and grabbed two ropes off the wall. Within a few moments the hail had lightened, not by much, but enough. The cows at the far end of the barn shuffled back and forth, groaning in agony. One had already been blinded by a piece of hail, its left eye swollen shut. Jonathan's numb fingers fumbled as he tried to get the ropes over their necks. The blind cow pulled him forward, resisting. *No no no.* If they lost both cows tonight, they would starve. Wind whipped through the barn, cutting across his face as it howled. Jonathan spun around to see his father running into the barn.

"Put them into the house!" he yelled as he ran to the

horse's stall.

Jonathan slapped the cows' flanks hard enough to turn them around in the right direction, but then another peal of thunder shook the walls and one began to head for the corner.

"Try again." His mother's slight form appeared in the doorway of the barn, soaked to the bone.

"Merthenna, get back into the house!" his father yelled from the stalls.

She ignored him, instead tugging the cows' halter while Jonathan slapped their flanks and herded them towards the door. The wind took off another strip of the roof, spinning it out into the night sky. The pigs rammed themselves against their pens, breaking through two of the boards. In a few moments they would be out, tearing apart anything in their path.

Jonathan's skin burned from the assaulting hail, and he was vaguely aware of blood trickling down his arms, chest, and back.

"Silas, watch out," his mother cried.

Aisling reared and bucked against the stall door so that it burst asunder in hundreds of wooden shards. Jonathan's father dove to the right just before the horse charged out of the stall and straight through the open barn door.

"Aisling!" Jonathan ran out into the hail that was turning into rain, dimly hearing his mother calling for help with his father. He turned to go back when he felt all the air being sucked out of him. He knew what it meant, knew he should run, throw himself down on the ground, anything but stand there and simply look up. A loud *crack* reverberated through the night air as a stream of pale blue light broke through the sky in a myriad of dazzling branches, the main trunk of the bolt racing towards him in a crooked path. Suddenly, a line of fire, rising straight up out of the ground, white hot and sparking, rose to meet it, and shattered the lightning midair, creating an explosion of blue and white that knocked

Jonathan to the ground. Then all was dark again, and the wind came howling back through the rain.

"Damn it boy, what are you doing on your back!" Jonathan's father yelled as he drove the cows out of the barn and into the storm, a bright red gash in his forehead.

There was no time to be afraid. No time to even think about what he just experienced. Jonathan ran to take over the left cow, slapping its rump while his father herded the other one. A second glance skyward showed Jonathan just how low the dense clouds were hanging over them. Too low. *Neáhvalar, save us.* Rain could destroy with flood just as much as hail could with force. They were almost to the house when a fierce gale kicked up against them. Jonathan bent his head forward, slowly making his way to the heavy oak door. He grasped the iron handle, and with a fierce yank tried to pull it back, only to have it give a little, then snap shut.

"Together, now!" His father was there beside him. His mother wasn't far behind, driving the cows forward. If they didn't get the door open in time...

Jonathan placed one foot on the wall and heaved the door towards him. It was enough. His father caught the edge. Together they pried the door back open and held it in place while Jonathan's mother steered the cows one by one into the house. Another crack of lightning, and the land lit up, a blanket of ice pellets. His father stood there a moment, looking out at the devastation, until a clamor to the right signaled the last of the barn roof being ripped away.

Jonathan laid a hand on his father's shoulder, shouting over the din of the storm. "Come inside!"

Blood flowed down the sides of his father's face, but he seemed not to notice as he walked into house. Jonathan followed, keeping his full weight against the door until he let it slam shut at last. They cleared the furniture out as quickly as they could. His father was moving chairs and the table until he finally sank into a chair.

"Silas, you stay there until I can tend to that cut." In her sopping wet nightdress, she tended to his wounds while Jonathan corralled the cows to one side of the house. "Get him over to that comfy chair by the fire," she said when done bandaging his father's head. She left to change clothes.

"Here, lean on me." Jonathan looped his father's arm around his shoulders. Being four inches taller than Silas made it slow going. Step by step they limped across the floor while his mother, now dressed, fanned the fire until it blazed, and the whole room was washed in light.

Jonathan eased his father into the chair. Immediately his head sank forward onto his chest, revealing just how much dried blood had caked onto his thinning gray hair. A trickle still wandered down the side of his cheek. *Fear breeds the world of thorns,* he whispered, willing his face to look stoic. His father wounded, the barn almost destroyed. And Jenna...

Jonathan strode across the room, dodging the cows, and took the other cloak from the workbench against the wall. "Balfour's shop..."

"Will withstand both blast and wind," his mother said. "Put down that cloak and let me look at those cuts. First thing tomorrow you and Silas can go to Breithan and check on her, provided you don't move for the rest of the night, Silas."

"I'm fine," Jonathan said dismissively. Without another word he went into his room and threw on his rough work shirt. He was going to town tonight, with or without their permission. The scratchy wool stung as it dragged and caught on his torn skin, but the cuts were shallow. They would heal in time.

A loud crash in the other room. He rushed out to see the rocking chair smashed and the cows shuffling around, moaning and completely bewildered. Above that chaos was the bluster of wind and rain pounding in full force against the house.

He looked at his mother, half defiant, half pleading. "Balfour's candle shop wasn't made from the Fáliquerci…"

"Enough of it was," she said. "Our barn is still standing —it's just the roof that was torn off, nothing else, and the storm won't be as bad in the village. I need you here."

"It shouldn't have been this bad *here*."

His mother gave no answer to that, but they both knew it to be true. With the Fáliquerci on the south side of them, and the Ruaden Forest to the north, no great gusts had ever threatened to shatter their small farm into pieces before.

"We've seen worse," she said shortly. "And we'll see it again if we continue our foolery." She went over to the fireplace, and picked up their wereác from the floor. Gingerly she placed the branch back on the mantle, making sure that the delicately carved serpent intertwined was facing to the room. *To honor that which reaches towards the sky and crawls upon the earth*, the Terakhein saying went. "Now, don't you go frettin'," his mother said. "Our girl will be all right." She came back to hug Jonathan tight. "At first light, you'll go get her, but I'll not risk losing you in all that chaos out there." A quick kiss on the cheek and then she checked her husband once more before going to her bedroom.

Jonathan took a seat by his sleeping father and stared at the wereác on the mantle, trying to will away the gnawing doubt growing inside him. Of course his sister would be all right—did they not serve the Elementarí, especially the spirits of earth? How else could they have escaped the white wolf? But the storms that had swept upon them so suddenly…*fear breeds a world of bad dreams and thorns.* A momentary flash of Aisling running out of the stall and then the white hot flame that shot up from the ground to meet the lightning. That was no dream, nor was it like anything he had ever seen before, except in the forest. Two flashes of light amid a storm. He would tell Cadman and Widow Samsone about it in the morning after fetching

Jenna. And *then* he would make his way up to the Seven Woods to find the girl. For now, all he wanted was a moment's rest.

--◦-◉;◉-◦--

A rough hand shook him awake. "Come on, it's getting light." His father was already bundled in his winter cloak. His mother came out of the bedroom, hair disheveled like she hadn't slept a wink. "Take that bread over there—it was all I was able to find in this mess."

The house was a disaster of broken furniture, bandages, and cow dung, but at least the animals were gone. There was no time to wonder how they were going to clean up all that chaos, for his father had already gone out the door. A quick kiss on his mother's cheek, and then Jonathan followed.

"You sure you're feeling up to going?" he asked as they set out.

"Fair enough, I guess," was the only answer he got, for it was before dawn, and too damn cold to speak. After a mile, gray clouds crept up from the west, and a freezing drizzle pelted them from every direction. The dirt road that ran past their farm to Breithan was little more than a muddy path now. Jonathan looked over at the blue-green meadowlands that had been battered flat by the storm, hoping the village had fared better. The hilly countryside soon leveled out; up ahead loomed the Fáliquerci. But in the middle of the road they stopped in amazement as the freezing rain turned into a light snow.

"Damn my eyes," Jonathan's father said, as he held out his palm to catch a few flakes.

Jonathan squinted up into the bright gray sky. "It's better than rain."

"Perhaps," his father said, and kept walking. "But in summer?"

They soon reached the thick mass of ancient trees that began the forest proper and slowed their pace. His father's labored breathing made Jonathan glance more than once to make sure the wound on his head had not begun bleeding again.

"Stop looking at me like I'm a sick pup," his father warned.

"I was noticing how few branches were broken off," Jonathan lied. "We must have been hit with the worst of the storm."

"Could be," his father answered, his frown momentarily disappearing. "Least we got some cover from the snow."

Although the wood took on a ghostly hue in the gray light, the wind had not disturbed so much as a branch or leaf here. *Almost as if the wind had only swept into the far end of the forest, where Jenna and I saw the wolf.* Jonathan hadn't noticed it last night as he ran home. If there was anything amiss, it was the subtle silence that pervaded most of their walk. Whatever creatures had harbored here last night stayed quiet and out of sight. Towards the other side of the forest, the path was harder to traverse with all the broken branches, but Jonathan's father drove forward, wanting only to see his daughter. By the time they came back out on the open road, a dusting of white covered large patches of ground, but it was melting just as quickly. "Glad it's warming up a spell," his father declared as they crested a small hill. "Now what's that down yonder?" He pointed to the small gully that ran parallel to the road. On top of the ridge, this side of the road, lay scattered snow-covered mounds.

As they drew closer, the mounds took the shape of recognizable animals. Dead cows, horses, sheep, and pigs—anything unfortunate enough to be caught without shelter last night—had been picked up by the wind and thrown down here, in the open countryside. But that didn't explain how or why their bodies had been flayed open, blood still oozing from gaping wounds, turning the snow that covered the ground into a blanket of crimson. No wolf or bear, not even the legendary throcks could have done this. They saw

Aisling lying among the carcasses. A deep gash ran from his neck to hindquarters, laying bare the muscle underneath. Jonathan knelt down and looked closely at the foamed mouth.

"He's still alive," Jonathan said through gritted teeth, feeling dazed by all the death he had already seen.

"For the love of Neáhvalar—" his father cried.

With one deft movement, Jonathan pulled out his dagger and sliced through the main vein in the horse's neck. Blood bubbled up and poured out as Aisling took his last breath. Jonathan clenched his jaw even tighter, yet nothing could stop the overpowering stench. He retched and ran a few feet before the nausea finally took hold and he emptied his stomach. When he came back, Silas took off the scarf he was wearing. "Wrap it around your nose and mouth, and pray our village was spared this curse." His father took off at a run. Jonathan sprinted after him.

Within half an hour they entered the village. People ran about in freezing drizzle, calling out names, seeking the lost or injured. Jonathan and his father stopped and looked for Jenna.

"Do you see her?" his father wheezed, bending over and trying to catch his breath.

Jonathan shook his head. "Nor Balfour or Nellie. They must still be at the shop."

They walked quickly through the main square, where half a dozen animals had been piled like refuse; family pets lay among the livestock. They were not mutilated like the ones in the meadow. A few men were throwing carcasses into a wagon. To their left, the corner shop had its front window broken out and a collapsed wall, the wooden frame snapped in half. From its broken beam dark red sap flowed. On the other side of the square, the door to the town hall had been ripped from its hinges. One block down they found the door to Balfour's shop wide open, candles strewn about and broken glass everywhere.

"Jenna!" Silas stumbled up the stairs yelling.

Jonathan ran around the house and peered down the hill that led to the woods. No sign of anyone. He returned to find his father in the doorway.

"No one's here," his father said.

"Silas! Jonathan!" Cadman waved from across the square and ran over to them.

"We're trying to find Jenna," Jonathan said as soon as the smith reached them. "I let her stay with Balfour and Nellie last night," he explained in answer to the smith's quizzical look.

Cadman walked up to doorway and peered inside. "What happened?" he asked.

"Everything's smashed, and no sign of anyone."

Cadman's face darkened. "Riok's butcher shop's been changed into a physick's ward, and Sienna's coming with her herbs, so they might have—"

Jonathan didn't stay to hear any more. Gutted livestock and a smashed shop were all that was needed to turn his nightmare world into a real one. He ran through the spitting rain towards the butcher's shop, with shouts from Cadman and his father to come back, but nothing would stop him, not until he found her. Two paths to the right, one more to the left, and then he was pushing through bodies that were funneling through the threshold. The shop was full of wounded people: a few children, some mothers, and several men.

Riok lacked his customary apron, his shirt blood stained nonetheless as he tended the cuts and gashes of those who lay there or slumped against the walls. Sienna Samsone, her white hair sticking out in all directions, flitted from person to person, setting broken bones and applying poultices to their cuts. For a woman of sixty, she was as agile as someone half her age.

"Whad'ya need, Jonathan?" Riok asked.

"I'm looking for my sister."

"She's not been here," Riok growled. "Get to Lian's place; he might know where she is, and tell him we need more blankets here! We've got to keep these folks warm. Some of the wounds are deep, and more than a few might be mortal."

"We're trying to find—"

"Make way! Make way!" Balfour's large frame momentarily filled the doorway, his daughter Susanna unconscious in his arms. Nellie stumbled in after her husband, face pale and tear-streaked, her dress torn and covered in mud.

"Lay her down here." Riok pointed to a cleared space over in the corner. "Somebody get me some blankets."

"Let me have a look at her." Sienna swept past Jonathan and knelt down beside the little girl.

Nellie was about to follow, but Balfour held her back. "Now, Nellie, let Sienna look at her."

"Yes, move back and let me have some light, will you? Balfour, take Nellie outside please, and Jonathan—get out of my way!" Sienna ordered.

"Where's Jenna?" Silas bellowed as he entered, followed by Cadman. "She must have been with Susanna. Didn't you see her?"

"We checked on Jenna and Susanna when the hail started," Nellie's voice shook. "They were both gone. We've been trying to find them all night."

"Get out of my way or she will die!" Sienna's voice rang through the shop. Balfour drew Nellie back to the doorway, and Jonathan followed.

"I found Susanna by the hitching post in West Forest," Balfour said. Small gashes marred his face, and his mop of brown hair was matted with blood. "She was tied to it with some twine that Jenna must have brought with them. I looked all around for Jenna, but we had to get Susanna here or she'd have frozen to death."

"Like my sister will if we don't find her!" Jonathan yelled, and ran out of the shop. His sister was out there all alone, as was the white wolf...*Neáhvalar protect her.* He wouldn't let himself think more. Riok's horse was hitched to one of the posts on his right. He untied the rope and was in the saddle before Cadman came outside.

"Don't steal that horse, Jonathan!" he said quietly as he seized the horse's bridle.

"Let go," Jonathan said.

"Riok lost his father last night in the storm." Cadman scowled. "Damn fool ran out into the street yelling and shaking his fist at the sky. He was found in the middle of the square this morning amidst all the animals. Don't start something with this now. We'll get the men together and find her."

Jonathan kicked the horse's sides to make it turn and wrenched Cadman's wrist so that he had to let go. "She was out there all night, Cadman. How long do you think she'll last? And with the white wolf..." Without waiting for another word, he spurred the horse on.

He rode hard, straight towards the West Forest. He called her name, sometimes stopping to see if he could hear some kind of faint cry in response.

Nothing.

He could not cover the distance he needed to. Breithan itself was less than four hundred people, but the forests and hills surrounding it were vast. West Forest alone was a two day journey by horse. His father would rally the village soon, but would it be soon enough?

"Jenna! Jenna!" His eyes scanned the dense underbrush that covered the forest floor. Too many pines here were scant in girth. It was not enough for wind cover, not in a gale like last night's. She would have stayed low, crawled her way to some ditch and lay flat until the storm passed. For the rest of the afternoon Jonathan scoured the wood, calling her name, searching for any sign of her little footprints in the muddy terrain. He looked for wolf tracks too, but couldn't let himself imagine his little sister and that creature coming face to face. The rain had washed away any sign of footfall, but at least the drizzle had lessened so he could see.

Then, halfway up the steep embankment, he saw it. A glint of iron. His heart beat all the more quickly as he jumped off the horse and scurried up the edge, boots sinking deep into the mire. It was her dagger. Breathing came in short spurts now as he ran up the bank. What would have made her drop it? *You had nothing to protect you from that beast,* he thought, barely breathing. Up he crawled, grabbing bramble and bush until the forest plateaued slightly.

"Jonathan!" Alec's voice came from below.

"Up here." The ground was messy with pine needles, twigs, and broken branches, but Jonathan picked out a slight imprint in the flotsam. Twenty steps more, and it grew into a set of tracks. More voices. Some calling for Jenna, some for himself. Jonathan quieted all of them in his mind as he followed the trail of broken footprints to a narrow gulch. A flash of blue.

His sister's dress.

"She's here!" He turned his head and saw that Alec had just entered the gulch on horse. "Follow me!" He sprinted ahead, closing the distance between his sister and himself until finally, he reached her. She was lying face up in the mud. His hope grew, for there was still color in her cheeks. Then he saw the slow trickle of blood from the deep cut on her head.

"Jenna!" He drew up beside her, brushed her tangled dark hair away from her little face then felt her forehead and cheeks. They were warm. He put his ear to her lips for even a whisper of a breath. But her breath was still. "No, no, no." He listened for her heart and heard only the furious beating of his own.

"Jonathan, here." Alec ran up and covered Jenna with a thick woolen blanket then began rubbing her legs and arms.

"I can't hear her heart, Alec." Jonathan took her little hand in his. "I can't hear it."

"Let me." Alec leaned over and listened. "Neáhvalar help her." He placed his hand over her heart and massaged the area, turned her body over and thumped on her back several times. Jonathan waited for his sister to violently cough and spring back to life. He had seen that happen before.

Alec turned Jenna over so that she lay face up and listened for her heartbeat again. He stayed there for a long while, ear pressed against chest, waiting. Finally Alec sat back up, eyes already welling up with tears. "She's gone," he murmured, burying his head in his hands.

Nothing? There was nothing more to be done when they had searched so long for her, when her cheeks were still rosy? She had died out here, in the cold. She had died wondering where her big brother and father were—why they hadn't come for her yet even though she had called to him. Jonathan gathered his sister up in arms, kissing her hair, whispering in her ear to come back, that if she only returned he would make it all alright. He prayed as he had never prayed before to Neáhvalar, to the Elementarí, the Terakhein...anyone who would listen to his plea. *I'd die for you,* he told them. *I'd do whatever you asked of me, I'd even die for her. Take me instead.*

The rustle of leaves as more men came to join them. They stood by, heads bowed in respect, even as someone sent a messenger to tell Silas his daughter had been found.

CHAPTER 3
LOST CHILDREN

She was lost in the winter wilderness without a coat, running against wind and snow. Twisted trees with overhanging branches blocked out most of the moonlight, and what little slipped through only illuminated the dagger-like icicles that hung so precariously above her. The little girl was near Jenna's age, perhaps a year younger. Her dress and sleeves were ripped from the thickets, leaving scratches on her arms and legs. She stopped to shake the snow from her short dark hair while a whimper escaped her lips, then she bowed her head and sprinted forward. A blast of wind swept the white flakes side to side, making wispy snow snakes that followed her. Another gust and the snakes writhed, each piece blending into the other. Soon, one large serpent began to slither behind her. Its silvery body grew as it silently closed in, its tongue flicking. In one seamless move, it reared its head to strike just as the girl unexpectedly stopped and turned.

A burst of violet light, and when that purplish haze finally cleared, in place of the serpent a woman stood, dressed in white, hair piled high with golden ringlets around her face. Something was odd about her eyes. Almond shaped, slanting slightly upwards, the green within them was dazzling. Emerald green: the forest in summer.

"Stay where you are." The girl backed away, eyes darting all about for a place to hide.

"Now is not the time for such antics, love."

The girl turned and ran towards the trees. The woman laughed a little, then dashed after her, catching one little arm before the girl dove into a mess of thickets.

"No!"

The plea was not enough to stop the woman from clasping her head in a vice-like grip, nails driving into the girl's temple until droplets of blood appeared. "Stop," she commanded.

"*Nemari.*"

It was only a whisper, but the woman reeled back, struck by some violent force. She cursed in a strange language and snatched a fistful of the girl's hair, yanking her head back so that she had to look up at the woman's emerald eyes. The woman's pupils expanded, slowly eclipsing the iris until no color remained except for a strange slit of green in the middle. Reverse snake eyes.

"See here, love," she said, "you wanted your parents." Her voice sunk into a low hiss. "Guessss where they are."

The girl started choking, hands flailing about. She gasped again and again as the woman pressed her lips against the little girl's pale forehead, and then slowly slid her mouth down over the girl's eyes. Her little body convulsed one last time before her hands finally went limp. The woman barely seemed to notice, her mouth fixed in that strange kiss.

Run, damn it!

Jonathan woke up breathing hard within the darkness of his room. The blanket on his bed was drenched in sweat. Eight months since his sister's death, and still the nightmares had not abated. The day after they buried Jenna, the serpent woman had entered his dreams. Jonathan tossed the blanket aside and put on his clothes. He needed to get some air, feel the wind against his face and shake the intensity of the dream. The cloudless night showed the Hound of Tirial directly overhead—his sister's favorite constellation.

His mother hadn't screamed when they brought Jenna's body home that day; she only took her daughter from his father's arms and cradled her, crooning her name over and over. They buried her in the meadow by the lake. The sky had loomed black as night with the billowing smoke from the burning animal carcasses less than three miles away. His father, a man not given to tears, had fallen to his knees and sobbed, while his mother just stood as one struck blind and dumb. It was when they returned home that the rage in his father took over, for he had gone to the mantle and broken the wereác upon his knee and thrown the pieces into the fire. Jonathan thought his mother would have begged him to stop, but she only went into her room. She had taken ill after that, tossing in bed with a fever that made her mutter insensible things. Jonathan would sit by her bed, squeezing her hand tightly so that she knew he was there. But her eyes, open as they were, didn't see him. *My babies are all gone,* she would whisper until Jonathan could barely stand it. Sienna had immediately ordered him out of the room when she came, and did not leave her side until the fever broke weeks later. When at last she could sit up in bed, his mother had called for Jon and begged his forgiveness. "You're still here, my boy," she said as she kissed his brow and held his hand tight.

The final count of the dead from that storm wasn't as bad as many had feared: fifty-five animals had been killed, but Jenna and Riok's father were the only human casualties in Breithan. Other towns had fared much worse. Twenty people died in Klinneret when the river flooded the town. Ten others had gone missing and were never found.

Jonathan made his way to where their torn fields lay, ignoring his hunger pangs. Eight months of loss and unmet desire. Last summer had melted imperceptibly into fall then winter without any change in the raging weather save that the hail turned into snow. The year of storms, they called it now. Talks of the old winter coming back were whispered among the village gossips, but even the guildsmen had started to shake their heads and wonder if Ashyranna, Cadarn's holy flame, had helped slow down that first winter twenty five years ago. Tales of its power had expanded with each passing year, and now folks wondered if the Nemarons had been plotting to steal it all along. What if the Great War between the Cadarn and Nemaron had been but a ruse to allow the ice warriors to take the healing fire? Priests in Duraeston had sent messages to every village warning that the Terakhein would leave Gaelastad to the wrath of the Elementarí if Dormín continued to be transgressed, but what could they do now that they were starving? The Terakhein had yet to send any word about the storms or the breaking of their laws, and people were beginning to feel scared. Perhaps the rumors they heard after the war were true—perhaps there had been an invasion of the Terakhein Forest, its people, massacred. But what would that mean for Gaelastad?

Everyone had broken Dormín by planting in spring, believing the crop would take since the sun and sky had blessed them for four weeks straight with good weather. The storm that swooped in last week had killed those dreams, leaving a new hole in the barn roof and destroying two thirds of the crop Jonathan and his father had so painstakingly seeded. Meals kept getting smaller—it had already been a hard summer, and now fall held little promise of a true harvest.

Jonathan shook his head as he sat on his heels and gazed at the flattened corn and wheat. It would take weeks to glean what was prematurely threshed. They wouldn't survive another winter like the last one, not unless he worked extra nights at Cadman's shop and they sold their remaining cow today. And that meant walking through the Fáliquerci with its ghostly whispers. He massaged his forehead as a chortle of frustration escaped his lips. Everything had changed after they found the flayed animals last year. Rumors had quickly spread throughout all of Gaelastad that a wild herd was on the loose in the southern forests, and worse, a group of madmen with a thirst for torture and blood. The little girl who had been lost in the Seven Woods —the one he had been so desperate to go save—was later found dead in the center of the forest, her throat slit. Folk said it must have been the same butchers.

The surrounding villages had organized hunting parties to forage the woods and slay anything with claws and teeth. How many white-tailed foxes, brown bears, and wild boars were needlessly killed in the name of this quest, their pelts sold for copper coins up in Duraeston? Meanwhile, the Northern and Southern Councils, pressured by the priests, imposed rigorous restrictions on Breithan until the culprits had been found. Thanks be to Neáhvalar for Lian's crazed fanaticism, for he convinced Balfour and Cadman to threaten the Council with the influence of their guild alliances should the councils completely quarantine the village. Still, search after search produced no answers, and now the forest was too quiet. *Something* was out there, scaring beasts both great and small. The gray wolves had always denned farther east in the forest until last winter when they suddenly migrated south. Their howls rang in the sky night after night, and during the day, Jonathan heard only whispers. *Leave me be,* he sighed, and slowly walked back to the house.

--~-◉)(◉-~--

"You're not going into Riok's shop, are you?" Lian pulled Jonathan aside on the way into town and said he needed a word. "There's some bad news about his cousin Tarl. His body was found last week in a Duraeston alley, strangled to death."

"They catch the bastard who did it?"

Lian shook his head. "Riok's pretty shaken up about it. Tarl left two boys and a wife, so he's trying to get them to come live with him. There's talk that Tarl had a bag of gold stuffed in the wall. Not what you'd expect from a tanner's pay."

"Who knows what kind of politics they're playing up there; maybe the kind that's calling for blood. Meanwhile they still ignore us like we're a colony of lepers."

"Trade or no, it's almost the end of summer. The little ones in this village won't survive another winter like last year's. Last week's storm blew out all my windows and destroyed half my crops."

"We'll have more death yet," Jonathan muttered.

"Now, don't you be talking like that, Jon. I just wanted you to stay clear of Riok for the next few days. He's never quite forgiven you for riding his horse into the ground that day. I know, I know." Lian already had his hand up to Jonathan's protests. "I'm just saying watch your step and give him a little distance."

He was already late, and talking to Lian had just made him more so. Jonathan fumed; he hadn't appreciated Lian bringing up the debt he still owed Riok. There had been no way to pay back the horse yet, nor would there be in the foreseeable future if things continued as they were. That guilt threatened to sink his spirits into a dark sullenness. Jonathan shook his head, trying to snap out of the moment. Dusk had settled into twilight when he crossed the threshold of the smithy. Only one oil lamp was lit, and by it Cadman's wiry frame bent over a sword hilt he was polishing, hair pulled back in its customary tie. He glanced up as Jonathan walked through the door.

"You look awful."

The same could be said of the smith. Streaks of white now ran through his black locks where before there had been only a light gray, and the haggard expression he wore made Cadman appear older than his forty-seven years. "We had to patch up the barn again, glean what we could from the crops, and then I helped here when you were gone," Jonathan said as he sat down on the workbench. "Of course I look awful." He didn't feel like telling Cadman he had barely slept the past week.

"How's Silas?"

"Still plagued by that nasty cough. Sienna gave Mother some herbs that might help."

Cadman laid down his work and drew a small sachet out of the cloak that lay on one of the benches. "Give this to Merthenna. It's a tea I picked up in Duraeston, supposed to help purge phlegmatic blood. Worth a try."

Jonathan opened the sachet. Scents of cinnamon and ginger wafted up with a hint of orange spices from the south islands that must have cost the smith a day's wages. "Thank you, but I can't accept—"

Cadman waved away his protests. "Take it. Your father's been sick too long. How is Merthenna? I thought about stopping by."

"It wouldn't have helped," Jonathan said. The widow had cured her of whatever physically ailed her, but she had grown so thin and frail this past year, and her eyes were always red from weeping. Try as he might, Jonathan could not help feeling like his mother secretly blamed him for yet another death. He didn't want to talk any more about it. "What happened here?" he asked, picking up what seemed to be a mess of a bridle.

"It's Sienna's. Mind trying to fix it?"

Jonathan wasn't really sure it was possible. The bit was dented in such an odd fashion that he might just have to make a new one. "Sorry I'm late by the way. I ran into Lian and he told me about Riok."

"Did he now?" There was a note of irritation in the smith's voice, and Jonathan wondered if perhaps that information wasn't supposed to be shared. "That was bad business. Someone from Tarl's guild alluded to the fact that he might have had something to do with that little girl's murder last year."

"He didn't mention *that*."

Cadman's eyes glittered in the dim candlelight. "Because he doesn't know. I only found out through piecing together bits of information purchased, and some extracted through unseemly means and duress. Don't ask," he warned, when Jonathan raised a questioning eyebrow. He had not thought Cadman capable of any tactic involving the threat of physical harm. He wanted to know more but the smith kept talking. "It was a brutal crime, and one that I cannot even imagine Tarl having a hand in committing. What would be the point of killing some little girl lost in the woods? It makes no sense, and the inquiries I placed among several different groups up north have yielded few answers." He pulled the white-hot shoe from the forge and laid it on the anvil. "I've discussed it with Riok, and of course he maintains his cousin's innocence, but even he said Tarl's widow acted strangely afterwards. She has refused to come down and live with them, her last kin."

"But won't the Councils lift their sanctions off Breithan now if they suspect that her murder as the work of one man and not the butchers who killed our livestock?"

"Perhaps, but we still don't know whether it be beast or man which did that massacre last year, whereas now they are sure the girl's demise was orchestrated by human hands. Whether or not they remove the penalties will soon make little difference. There's a worse storm brewing farther north in Lailethas that will affect us more than we could have predicted—"

"The winter," Jonathan said automatically as he hammered the punch to form two new holes in the headpiece.

"Nemarons," Cadman corrected.

"How many?" Stories of the war had always fascinated him, and none more than those about the priestly soldiers—ascetics, really, who believed in nothing but serving the Elementarí of air. Their unprovoked assault on Cadarn had made them infamous, and had drawn Lailethas and Íarchol into the fray as allies to Cadarn. Stranger still was the vague rumor that the destructive winter preceding their attack a few years before was actually created by the Elementarí themselves.

"Only a few have been spotted, some say." Five quick bangs of hammer on anvil deafened all other noises. Cadman stopped momentarily to check his work. "But the uttermost northern passes in Lailethas have frozen over, and none can verify their number now. They come for trading, but since when does a Nemaron come to the west to trade when all the cities of Cadarn lay between us, eh? And now that Centuras is threatened, the Wood will be open to felling."

Of course they would come. Cadarians too. Who would not want timber that retained its strength? Still... "Centuras has not fallen *yet,* and I hardly think a few Nemarons on the northernmost edge of Lailethas is something for us to worry about. It would be easier for Cadarn to cross the Wild Lands and attack us than a Nemaron assault from so far north." Five narrow mountain passes in Lailethas would slow down any army wishing for a surprise attack, especially when they had sentry outposts at every pass. Gaelastad had no real army, but Lailethas and Íarchol had sent several companies of foot soldiers and their best archers to aid Cadarn in the war.

"There's been no word from the outposts or the villages beyond the uttermost northern passes for months now. Last we knew, the villagers were going to move south because the weather had grown worse, but no one in the southern towns has seen them." Cadman looked at Jonathan with such a fierce gaze that his pupils were mere pinpoints. The shoe on the anvil was beginning to cool, and the smith hadn't even seemed to notice. "The Lailethans sent five scouts up to see what happened, but they never returned. It's like they and the towns...vanished."

Jonathan looked disbelievingly at the smith. "Villages don't just disappear." Then again, trees weren't supposed to cry out in a strange language. He had never told Sienna or Cadman about the flame he saw that day—the year had held enough trial and misery without adding his own madness.

The smith thrust the shoe back into the flames, the dancing light turning the thick, ropey scars on his forearms into red snakes. "They can get slaughtered. Nemarons have been spotted, and I have never known them to travel in small bands, not unless they were trying to attack by stealth. What if the upper border of Lailethas has been taken?"

Jonathan thought a moment as he thinned the leather on the edges of the brow band. While Lailethas was Cadman's home country, he had not spoken about it but once or twice in all the time Jonathan had known him. He wasn't even sure how long Cadman had lived there, for he was missing the distinctive thick slur of the *r* that most Lailethans had. No, there was much he didn't know about his godfather and his past. Didn't the scars on his arms, which he refused to talk about, serve as a reminder of that?

"You know Nemarons could not take them in the rocks," Jonathan pointed out. Lailethans were legendary for their ambush techniques, especially among hard terrain. "And what would they be lords of? Two countries full of mountainous caves and wild rivers, Lailethas just has more snow. Even you left. And Íarchol's nomadic people are not known for their hospitality."

Cadman ignored the slight. "Both have jewels beyond count."

True, but Terakhein law forbade the mining of those jewels, just as the people of Gaelastad could not cut down the Fáliquerci and Ruaden, and had sentries to protect the Seven Woods. For centuries those laws had held, in part because natural boundaries made it difficult for armies to amass and cross over, but also because the Terakhein themselves had been a presence throughout each country. For years beyond count they had sent emissaries from their forest to each country, reminding them of their pledge to honor the Elementarí and be shepherds of land and river. But long had it been since any council in Gaelastad had received word from the Terakhein—upwards of twenty five years now, before the great winter, and five years before the war. And those rumors that these Guardians were no more...

"You yourself saw a white wolf shortly before the year of storms—does that mean nothing to you?" Cadman snapped, when Jonathan had remained silent.

"We never saw it again, so I don't see the point."

"Aye, I didn't believe it myself when you first told me," Cadman acknowledged. "We had assumed it had wandered down from Lailethas, but what if it had come with a band of Nemarons? They breed such monsters for war. Of course I did not put two and two together, not until I heard that Nemarons are on our northern borders. And have you forgotten the allies they bought with them to the Cadarn war?"

"It's not like you to believe such tales," Jonathan scoffed. "Cadarn told outlandish lies to cover the sting of losing that first battle, that's all." The priests of the Seven Woods had immediately condemned Cadarn for its sacrilege in claiming that the earth spirits were serpentine demons who fought for the Nemarons. The Elementarí were spirits, with no body to house them except the belly of the earth, where they slept.

"My mistake then, for bringing up such stories that are only told to scare small children," he said dryly. "I thought I had heard rumors that you were having bad dreams lately. Something about a little girl—not Jenna though, right?"

Jonathan's hands worked the reins more furiously. No, not Jenna. He hadn't dreamt of his sister since the day they brought her body home, and even that nightmare was hazy. Something about the wind calling her outside to come play on the night of the storm. "That's none of your damn business," he snapped. *And damn me for telling my mother about it.* Being low on both sleep and good temper, Jonathan was ready to leave his work right then and there if Cadman decided to push the matter. Sienna would have to wait for her damn bridle.

The smith wisely said nothing, and for a long time they sat there by the light of the candles, working in silence.

It had been quiet for so long that Jonathan began to wonder if Cadman was angry with him for the outburst. After all, they had survived a tough year, and Cadman was most likely acting out of concern for him. The moment Jonathan looked up, though, he saw that the smith was staring at him.

"You miss your sister."

"Leave it alone, Cadman."

"Jenna was the same age as that girl found in the Seven Woods. Same age as the little one you dream about, I warrant."

Jonathan threw down Sienna's bridle. "By the blood, what do you think you're doing?"

"I'm trying to figure out why two little girls have died mysteriously in the last year. I'm trying to figure out if the third you dream about is some kind of warning or actually a real girl in danger. Kindly don't treat the widow's things that way—we're trying to repair them, remember?"

Jonathan sat back down, resolving to have this out once and for all. He didn't need Cadman clucking after him like his mother. "She's a *dream*, and Jenna died in a hailstorm. End of story."

"And what if neither of those statements is true?"

"Stop this strange sport you wish to have with me—"

"I'm not in sport."

Jonathan looked hard at the smith. It was true that the humorous smirk Cadman usually wore wasn't there. But it made no sense. *Neither do whispers or flashes of light.*

"The woman in your dreams—she's beautiful and tall, taller than any man, no? With almond-shaped green eyes?"

Jonathan felt the room momentarily spin. He hadn't told his mother that part—not any of that horror.

"That's never been in the stories about the Elementarí—except for those tales that came out of the Cadarn war."

Cadman went over and closed one of the doors to his smithy. "Does she feed, your beautiful woman? Did you see her turn?"

"It's an abomination," Jonathan whispered. He shook his head and blinked hard to get the image of the serpent turning into woman, her mouth over the girl's eyes...

"What if it's a warning?"

"The priests will say it's sacrilege—"

"The priests weren't there that first day of battle," Cadman said, "but *I* was. As a Lailethan scout, I had been sent ahead to get the lay of the land and help, as we thought, to merely hold the border. The armies from Lailethas and Íarchol didn't arrive till three days later, when all the earth spirits fled. No one believed their tales because they had no proof, only Cadreyth and Evanna dead, their infant son taken, and no holy fire. But there are exiles in Duraeston who will swear they saw the earth spirits at war with their king, as Nemaron's ally. Now Nemaron is at the border of Lailethas." He leaned forward. "What if your dream is a warning about vengeance? I don't fully understand what the girl has to do with it yet—"

"She repels the earth spirit," Jonathan said, suddenly remembering. "She says a word that causes the woman to fall back—"

"What is this?" Cadman took a step forward, hands clenched into fists, as if ready for a fight. "At just a single word from the girl? Are you sure?"

"Yes, the woman momentarily retreats..." Such a strange, hungry look was in the smith's eyes that Jonathan didn't quite know what else to say. "What madness is this, Cadman?"

The smith slightly relaxed his stance as he fingered Sienna's bridle. "Sorry about that. Too much intrigue in Duraeston as of late. You see enemies around every corner." The beginnings of a smile played on the edge of his mouth. "This news about the girl—you know whom you are dreaming about, yes? Only a Terakhein has such power over the Elementarí."

"No." Jonathan shook his head vehemently, feeling somewhat queasy. "The Elementarí would never feed on their shepherds. They are spirits sleeping under earth and stone —"

"You can repeat that myth all you want, if it makes you feel safer," Cadman interrupted. "Yet I tell you, those spirits slinked to the surface in serpentine form and fed on Cadarn soldiers, no matter what the priests say." He waved away Jonathan's protests. "This changes things, my boy, and drastically so, given that we've had neither word nor an appearance from the Terakhein since the Great War. And," he added more gently, "two little girls killed who were roughly the same age as your sister."

Jonathan cringed at the word *killed*. He had never thought of his sister's death as a murder. How could that be, when it was the wind...To speak such a thing was more than profane—it was unforgivable, and it was even more disturbing that his godfather would believe the Elementarí capable of such embodiment and action. At the same time, if his nightmares *were* from the Terakhein, that would change everything. The priests would give him audience, maybe even ordain him as a sentry of the Seven Woods, citing special cause. And then he could take his parents to Duraeston, away from the farm that refused to yield any more crops and only taxed his father's health..."Can we go to Duraeston and talk to the Order? Or to your Iron Clads?" he asked, barely breathing. "They would commend me to the priests, wouldn't they?"

Cadman let out a short laugh. "The guilds?" He turned to stoke the fire. The renewed flame caused shadow and light to dance upon the smith's face, casting deeper lines of worry into sharp relief. "Dormín was erased, Jonathan. Soon other laws will be changed. Given that, how grateful would they be to hear that you've had a vision about a

Terakhein girl and the Law that she represents, the law that so many are now intent on breaking? The priests will call your dream about the earth spirit an abomination, just as you said." A pause. "Dreams aside, what if whoever murdered that little girl in the Seven Woods believed *her* to be a Terakhein?" Then more to himself. "That would mean that more people might suspect there exists...and if Tarl was involved—"

A slight thud came from outside. Cadman walked to the half-opened door, Jonathan following. To their left, they saw Riok closing the butcher shop and across the way, a townsman talking to Lian, gesturing excitedly with one hand while leaning on his crutch. Lian saw Cadman and flashed a grin. To their right, some older men were leaving the tavern and saying their goodnights, a few of them swaying as they did so. Balfour and Nellie were walking arm in arm. When Balfour saw them, he leaned over and whispered something in his wife's ear. She nodded, and he ran over to them.

"Evening, Cadman," he said, slightly out of breath. His wounds from the storm last year had healed, but his large face was slightly scarred. A full red beard now covered most of it. He often reminded Jonathan of a bear. Large, hairy, and just as slow.

"Good to see you and the missus out," Cadman returned.

"Jonathan, Nellie made some spiced apple bread yesterday. It would be mighty nice to share it with you all. Tell your mother we'll come calling on her the next few days."

"I'm sure she would appreciate it," Jonathan said, trying not to let the resentment show in his voice. He did not begrudge the fact that Susanna lived and Jenna died—no, was murdered. He could not think about it and meet Balfour's eyes.

The chandler seemed not to notice as a wide smile spread across his face. "Fine, fine. We'll see you soon, then." He lumbered back to Nellie, and they continued on their walk.

Cadman motioned for them to go inside. "Someone was out here," he said quietly.

Jonathan nodded, wondering if now he should tell the smith about what he heard going through the wood, if it had anything to do with his sister's death—

"You are to go home." Cadman's voice cut off his thoughts.

"Now?"

"Did you not just hear me? Someone was outside, and now other ears have possibly heard this new information. Yes, home. Best thing to do if we're being watched. I must stop by Sienna's place."

"That's it?" Jonathan snapped. "Nemarons to the north, the Terakhein coming unbidden into my dreams, and you tell me to run home, like a schoolboy?"

"You'll notice I didn't say it was a great plan," Cadman took ashes and began to extinguish the fire, "but I would not have you say anything more tonight about dreams—and tell your mother nothing! I will be by first thing in the morning—do not come here. We will find a better place to talk then."

Jonathan waited a moment, but the smith wasn't about to share whatever else he was thinking. At last he gave up and started walking out the door.

"And Jonathan?"

"Yes?" He stood there, on the threshold, waiting.

"Keep your dagger out."

CHAPTER 4
A WALK IN THE DARK

A ring of blue clouds encircling the moon promised Jonathan he wouldn't have much light soon. Despite Cadman's warning, his dagger remained by his side and sheathed. What good was a blade against forest whispers and dreams? And he didn't plan to meander through the Fáliquerci. It was still hard to believe that the serpentine woman he dreamed of was in actuality an Elementarí. More unbelievable still was the idea that the Elementarí were tied in some way to two little girls found dead in the woods: one north, one south, while winter crept towards them like a wild beast.

It wasn't until he entered the Fáliquerci proper that the clouds engulfed the moon, plunging him into darkness. *Nice time to become completely blind here in the middle of nowhere.* A faint sound behind him made Jonathan suddenly swing around, eyes darting from tree to tree as shadows seemed to jump between branches. Next he glanced over the forest floor—searching for a hint of silver-white, either creeping towards him on all fours, or slithering upon its belly. Nothing. He blinked hard. *Dreams be damned*, he thought, and broke into a run.

His lungs were on fire by the time he was out in the open again. A sliver of the moon's milky orb peeked through the dark, casting ghostly shadows upon the ground. Slowing down to a walk did not stop a shiver from running up his spine. It was cold, true, but that was not what caused his muscles to suddenly contract. Jonathan felt eyes on him, maybe even a multitude of eyes, intently staring at him. He pulled out his dagger even though he could see no one.

"Stay your path, little one. The blade will not be of much use." A cascade of voices. Jonathan turned around, and saw only the Fáliquerci. Had the forest suddenly erupted in speech, or was it some trickery from Nemaron? Jonathan had never heard a group speak together in such union. "Show yourselves," he said, backing up. *Give me a head count of what I'm up against, at least.*

A sudden gleam in the darkness appeared as a low flame waved about—surely it was an arm, or a leg? Jonathan retreated five more steps and brandished his dagger. "You're the fire I saw in the forest last year in the Fáliquerci," he declared, at once giving a swift survey around the meadow that bordered the forest—where was the white wolf?

Meanwhile, the flame had grown in size, illuminating the fact that it took no human form at all. Standing almost six feet high and equally wide, it looked like a fountain of fire— although the shape was still wrong. He had seen a leg. A claw. Something that belonged to a beast. "What are you?"

"Bryn." The ground seemed to tremble as the flame crept closer. "Of the Ogoni."

"I don't understand—" At least his feet seemed unstuck, and now he edged closer to the Fáliquerci.

The fire suddenly blazed. "How can you not understand that which you already know? You have seen an Ophidian, an earth spirit, with your mind's eye. We are both Element-arí."

"That...that cannot be," he stammered. There were no such descriptions given by the priests—not in Duraeston during the yearly festivals, nor anywhere in the scriptures they had recited back in those early school days.

White hot sparks flew from the fountain into the night and disappeared. "And yet your unbelief will not cause me to disappear, nor will the Fáliquerci protect you."

There was truth in that, he knew. There would be no escaping this creature, whether demon or Elementarí, but anger at Jenna's senseless death once more boiled up within him. "And are children your prey?" he countered. "The white wolf was tracking our steps, and you had us caught..."

"I was following he who was following you," Bryn said. "Although we have need of you as much as our Ophidian brethren, I dare say."

The fire seemed to *crawl* closer. Jonathan detected that each cascade of flame was one giant leg of some fashion, but he could not discern upon what kind of body such a leg would fit. A slight breeze stirred from the west, gaining strength as it swept over the plains of meadow grass. Was the Ogoni calling the wind once again? He was no match for lords of fire and air, for spirits who clothed themselves in flame and storm. "What happened in the Fáliquerci?" His mouth was so dry his words felt slurred. "The wind—"

"Wind cannot stop me, whether it comes mocking or wrathful."

"Then you did not call it?" Jonathan persisted.

"It was the Ophidian who brought the storm into your wood, not I." Bryn said softly, creeping nearer. "He had been hunting you for a long time. But not nearly so long as I."

"An Ophidian?" he asked, taking a step back. It was a slow, tense dance between them.

"You dream of one every night—an earth spirit—the serpent woman who is looking for the girl. Trapher was looking for your sister."

"I saw no serpent that day, only wolf, wind, and flame."

"Neither did you see it the day your brother died, but Trapher's fangs were just as sharp then."

Nausea swept over Jonathan when he thought of Jeremy lying in his arms, screaming in agony. Why were these creatures, these Elementarí, hunting down his family, one by one? "Did you kill Trapher, then?"

The fire subsided enough for Jonathan to see eight silver legs that bent out five feet in every direction, low blue flame dancing down each limb. Many eyes like melted glass stared at him unwaveringly, a red glow coming from deep within. A spider, monstrous and beautiful in form. Jonathan noticed one of its eyes looked damaged. Its light was not as bright as the others. "Trapher is strong, one of the oldest of his kind. He slipped through the fire bands I set around him. And the wolf went back to his master, no doubt. But it matters not, for twice already have I saved your life."

"Twice?" A momentary flash of the storm last year and the fire that shot from the ground. "You were there in the storm; you were the fire I saw then, too."

"Yes," the spider's chorus answered. "I did not know then, which of you was dreaming the vision."

"You could have saved her?" he whispered, horrified at the realization that he was the one who had been protected while his sister had huddled out there all night alone, crying for him. *I should have been the one to die.*

"Whatever my power, boy," Bryn said, "I cannot be in two places at once. I saw the storm clouds gather around your house and decided to stay there and do what I could. In the end, I was right, for she dreamed of winter coming, but you dream of a little girl dying." Legs moved in graceful unison to bring the massive body closer.

Instinctively, Jonathan moved back; the first trees of the Fáliquerci were less than five paces away. "So what do you want of me?" he asked.

"We are awake and hungry, as it should not be. The girl you dream of is Terakhein, and though you see her as one dead, I believe her to be alive. So do the Ophidians and the Agerathum, spirits of air. The girl's life depends on who finds her first."

Jonathan gazed into the Ogoni's many eyes. "What needs do *you* have of her, should she be found?"

The Ogoni hesitated. "To sleep. To walk above ground, clothed in flesh—we must feed. Ventosus preys upon the land with his winter, as he did before. Ophidians satiate their hunger with people, as you have seen."

A tense pause, wherein Jonathan once again considered trying to run despite the seducing warmth he felt. "And just what do you feed on?" he asked, remembering Aisling after the storm. "Was it you who flayed the animals open like that last year? We saw no tracks..."

"That was not me, not yet. But other things that have awakened now walk abroad. The Ophidians will not stop hunting the little girl until they are sure she is dead. If she dies, you all die, and the Elementarí will go to war—"

Bryn swung his massive body around and burst into a wall of blue and silver fire that blazed ten feet high. He stayed in that beautifully terrible form for a little while longer, and then the flame died down, so that all that was left was a shimmer.

"I won't show myself again tonight; it's not safe, for you or me. Continue your journey home. We shall meet again soon."

"No, wait! Tell me more about Ventosus!" Jonathan pleaded. It was the name the trees called out, and signaled that perhaps he wasn't just imagining voices. But the Ogoni's slight shimmer had already faded into the darkness. "Bryn!"

No answer.

Jonathan looked in the direction where Bryn was facing when he burst into fire. There was nothing but the meadow and the tree line where the forest began. Looking harder, Jonathan thought he detected a slight shadow blending into one of the trees. It didn't move as Jonathan stared, breathing hard at the thought of what that shadow could be.

He turned and ran the rest of the way home, not daring to look back. He ran to escape shadow and fire, his heart breaking once again over the death of his brother and sister.

I've lost all my babies, his mother had cried, over and over again till he almost thought he had died too. But no, blood coursed throughout Jonathan's body as he felt the wind on his face. The Ophidians were on the hunt for the little girl. Well, no one in all of Breithan could track like he could, and he would search for her, this Terakheini. He knew it as surely as if the trees themselves had told him.

When Jonathan finally reached his house, he turned around just in time to see one more burst of flame. He went inside, thankful that at least the embers of the fire gave him a little light by which to find his room. He stopped at the mantle and stared at the new wereác his father had made, the serpentine form carved so intricately into the Atreal branch. For a moment Jonathan gazed into the snake's eye. He no longer wondered whether he had gone mad with grief. The cold realization that he was being hunted, that he and his siblings had been tracked like prey, suddenly took hold. *I see you now,* he whispered. In one deft movement he took the wereác and thrust it into the dying embers.

－•－◉)(◎－•－

The murmur of voices woke Jonathan up. It could not be morning so soon. He listened, trying to figure out who was in his house, but could discern nothing. Flinging his blanket aside, the chill of the early morning air hit Jonathan as soon as he jumped out of bed to throw on his tunic. He walked out to find Cadman, Sienna Samsone, and his parents all huddled around the table.

"Good morning," Cadman said, as if this were just a normal morning visit.

"It'd be good if it wasn't so damn early," Sienna snapped and fetched a mug of ale. "We've been talking about you, my boy. Did you feel your ears burning?"

"My ears can't feel anything right now." Jonathan was unnerved by the sight of the widow in his house so early in the morning. He looked at his parents. "What's this all about?"

"Cadman's been telling us about a buyer up in Duraeston," his father said.

"Remember that intricate piece you helped with last year?" Cadman asked.

Jonathan vaguely recalled a sword that he and Cadman had worked on. What did that have to do with anything? "Last night—"

"I know we discussed it briefly then, but I've decided I want you to come with me to Duraeston. The buyer wants two swords this time, and is willing to pay twice as much, in advance."

"When would we go?"

"This morning," Cadman said. "With trade being so bad everywhere, I could use the money. And I would split half of it with you this time, for I need you to do more than just the etching."

"How much?" He was still confused about what game Cadman was playing, but at the mention of extra coins, he didn't care.

"Three times what I received for that other piece."

"I'll do it." If true, getting this work would be a way to survive winter, plain and simple. He would send the money to his parents, but continue on to find the girl.

The smith gave him a congratulatory slap on the back. "Good man. We'll be back in a week, two at most. Certainly in time for the harvest festival."

"Given that we have no harvest," Silas said, coughing slightly as he got up, "I doubt we'll have a festival celebrating one. Speaking of which, you know anything about this?" He went over the fireplace and pointed to the wereác on the mantle. The serpent had been burned off, but other than that, the wood was unharmed. "I found it among the ashes this morning."

All eyes were upon him now. He was about to tell them all about Bryn and the Ophidians and how the Elementarí they had foolishly believed in were in reality monstrous creatures who had been awakened somehow and were *hungry.* But a warning glance from Cadman held him back. "I must have accidentally knocked it into the fire last night. I'm sorry."

The answer sounded hollow even to Jonathan, but it was apparently enough for his father to blink away the transgression. "Next time be more careful, Jon. Took me almost two months to carve it; at least the wood is unharmed. Strange how only the snake was burnt off..."

"Nonsense!" Sienna interrupted. "It's the way of such things, especially of any wood from the Fáliquerci. Now go check on your cow, Silas. Breakfast will be ready soon."

A bustle of activity followed as she and Jonathan's mother finished preparing the morning meal, and his father went out to the barn. Cadman leaned in and spoke quietly to Jonathan. "That was smart of you, not to say anything. Now listen, there is no buyer in Duraeston. The same visitor you had last night came to see me as well."

"Bryn?" Jonathan whispered.

"Aye, that's what name he gave to me. About wet myself like a child when he first showed himself. We need to get you to Duraeston within three days. Another of his race can help you walk your dreams when awake, and perhaps we can find out where the Terakhein is hiding."

Such news was a surprising relief to hear, for at least this meant he hadn't imagined the whole encounter. That particular peace of mind was immediately replaced with the horrible realization that no buyer in Duraeston meant no money. "Why did you lie to them about the sword, then? My parents are relying on that promised money, Cadman."

"Don't you worry about that—you'll be able to send your parents your dues. But I had to tell them something they could readily believe. As much as Silas supports Terakhein law, I am sure he could not believe that the Elementarí killed his children, and are now hunting others," the smith said softly. "Go pack, we've got to get going."

So, the Ogoni had told him everything. *You wanted the chance to be important to the Order. Well, here it is,* Jonathan thought bitterly as he went into his room and stuffed two shirts into a sack, along with his winter breeches, some gloves, and his dagger. He remembered packing the exact same things almost a year ago to find a little girl lost in the forest. When he came out, the widow was spooning porridge into everyone's bowls. They ate without much conversation, although Jonathan noticed his father kept glancing at him, his brows furrowing. But he said nothing.

By sunrise they were ready to go. "Lian and Balfour are going to talk to Riok about that other business, Silas. It would be good if you went with them," Cadman said as he shook his hand.

"I reckon it's time." Silas nodded.

Jonathan felt a tug at his arm, and saw Sienna standing there. "Here, I brought this for your journey," she said, turning him around.

"Riok said he was willing—" He tried to listen to more of what Cadman and his father were talking about, but Sienna was pulling his sack away from him and babbling something about food. "You'll be thanking me for some of this later on, I can guarantee you that. Just stick it inside your own bag there. That's right. It's so light, you'll hardly notice it. There you go. Now try not to miss me."

Jonathan turned to look back at the men, but they had finished their conversation, and Cadman had already gone to get the horses. Frustrated, Jonathan didn't thank Sienna and began to walk away.

The widow pulled him to her in a fierce hug. "Listen to me, boy," she said in a low, serious voice. "Warmth for winter, and fire for darkness. Strong heart though you have, there are some things you just plain run from rather than fight." She gave him a soft, dry kiss on the cheek before turning to collect the bowls.

Jonathan stared at her, speechless at her strange behavior, until Cadman walked in, carrying a sheathed sword wrapped in velvet. Jonathan could only guess it was the one he kept locked up in the cabinet in his house. His father's blade. "Sienna, I'm leaving this in your keeping."

Jonathan walked over to his parents by the hearth. His father slapped him on the back. "Take care of yourself, son," he said gruffly.

His mother grasped his face with two hands. "You come back to me, you hear?" she whispered, her eyes already wet. "Promise to find your way back, no matter what."

Jonathan kissed her cheek. "I promise."

CHAPTER 5
WINTER COMES

They saddled Cadman's horses, two black palfreys named Hammer and Tongs, and took the northern path by the small creek out of the village, meeting only one or two people on their way. The wind was sharp and cold, the sun occasionally piercing the gathering clouds. Neither one said anything of importance to the other until they cleared the last farmhouse on the outskirts of Breithan.

"Now, Cadman, tell me what we are riding to," Jonathan demanded. He hoped that the Ogoni had at least explained more to the smith than what information he had received. What if this was all an elaborate trap?

"I barely know myself. That Ogoni came to me after he had seen you. I was in my smithy to finish up some work when a voice spoke to me out of thin air. I turned around so quickly I banged my head on a bellows hanging from the ceiling." The smith gingerly touched his forehead. "Bryn cut off your conversation last night because he thought he saw an Ophidian in the distance."

Jonathan's eyes immediately darted along the path they were riding, looking for any sort of movement. "Did he find it?"

"No, but he didn't want to take chances, which is why we had to leave this morning. I sent Jophil out before dawn to Klinneret to warn my friends Theo and Rose that we'll be staying with them—they're good people—Lailethans like myself who keep to themselves. Bryn promised to act as a rearguard of sorts, keeping Trapher and any others at bay until we left. I had not thought the Elementarí were awake yet, Jon. Otherwise, I would have been your guard last night."

Jonathan cast a dubious glance at the smith. "You knew they could wake, I mean really and truly take flesh? How was it you failed to mention that last night?"

"And would you have believed me? Such things are not talked about here in Gaelastad, but you forget that Lailethas went to war as Cadarn's ally, believing the winter that preceded it was due to the lord of air. Its scriptures never mention specific forms taken by the Elementarí, but they describe a time when the Elementarí walked upon the earth, clothed in flesh. I grew up on stories about how the wind whipped the oceans into towers of water that rose up hundreds of feet in the air, while flames spun around them like falling stars. Neáhvalar created the Terakhein race to put the Elementarí to sleep and be their guardians." Cadman looked over at him with a grin. "Makes for a great bedtime story, you have to admit. Your priests here say that they have always been under earth, tended by their shepherds; doesn't the Gaelastad wereác symbolize as much? Of course, you greatly transformed yours last night."

"And how does one take revenge on an earth spirit?" His face grew hot thinking about this Ophidian, Trapher, but that immediately turned into worry. "And what about my parents, Cadman? We should have moved them to the village for safety."

"You know Silas would rather die in his barn than leave his farm, which is why Sienna is staying with them. And Bryn said that the Ophidians would not attack so far from their ancient home. They come in stealth, like the winter."

"Like the one who killed my brother," Jonathan said through gritted teeth. "And the girl in the wood—you said Tarl had something to do with it."

"Aye, that. There is treason in Duraeston, and now certainly in Breithan, given our eavesdropper last night, whose identity I still have yet to discover. I do not understand who ordered the girl's death nor how Tarl was involved. Not yet, but that murder means someone in the guilds suspects that at least one Terakhein escaped. And so it appears that not just the Elementarí are out to find her, but there are human players in this game too. But let us leave discussing such matters until we are safe under another's roof."

—◦◦◦◦◦—

They rode hard as meadows turned into hill country and the sky became a blanket of grey until at last it began to snow. Such a thing had never happened during Jonathan's life, that snow should come in summer, down so far south. By midday they had reached the Ruaden forest, which covered half the land from Breithan to Klinneret. Only a small twisting road ran through it, wide enough for a wagon. It was the prize of Gaelastad, the Ruaden—the Red Forest. Its maroon leaves mingled with other shades of red —amaranth, rust, burgundy—dappled with orange and laced with dark green leaves. The snow drifted through the branches that arched over the path.

Helas nom, helas nom. Wera deáthen, Ventosus!

The howls burst from the trees the moment Jonathan entered. Jonathan, looking all around, stopped Tongs in his canter. In the distance, Jonathan heard screaming. A wild bestial sound that reverberated all around him.

Cadman reined Hammer back. "What's wrong?"

Jonathan scanned Cadman's face for any reaction. "Do you hear anything?"

Cadman stood still as he cocked his head, listening, his brows knitted together in concentration. He turned his glance to Jonathan. "There's nothing out there. What do you hear?"

The din of the roaring trees now drowned out the screaming. *Helas nom, helas nom. Wera Ventosus!*

Jonathan's eyes traveled from tree to tree, searching for

the cause of their cries. The maroon leaves fluttered in the wind. He watched, entranced and terrified, as they slowly floated to the forest floor. "Look!"

Cadman dismounted and picked one up, turning it over in his hand. "This forest has never lost its leaves in the entire time I've been here."

Wera Ventosus! Wera Ventosus!

"Ventosus is coming," Jonathan said softly.

Cadman paused, one boot in the stirrup. "What did you say?"

"Ventosus. Bryn said it is his winter that devours the land; it's how he must feed while awake." He did not want to tell Cadman about the voices. No sane person ever heard voices speaking to them. Visions could come in times of trouble, he supposed. But *this* was inexplicable. He could not even say what language it was. *Let's start with the small things.* "I heard his laughter on the wind when my sister and I were in the Fáliquerci."

Cadman swung himself onto Hammer. "Did you now? I have to admit, I've been worried about you for a while, ever since Jenna's death. I even consulted a physick when I was up in Duraeston."

Jonathan looked at him aghast. "You didn't."

"Merthenna only told me both you and Silas were yelling out in your sleep."

"My father?" His mother had said naught to him about this.

Cadman nodded. "Something about storms and the land; she was more concerned about you, though. She kept thinking you were dreaming of Jenna, and so was I, before I learned about the girl."

"And now?" The whispers were mere groans as leaves fell to the ground in clumps. It was as if the Ruaden itself was bleeding.

"Now..." Cadman hesitated, "I would have you back in Breithan under watchful eyes. Merthenna and Silas have lost everything but you, and I care for you as if you were my own son, Jon. To lead you to Duraeston where I am unsure of even *my* reception seems foolish, but sometimes it is the fool's path that is most true—what's wrong? You have that funny look in your eyes again."

"I told you. Nothing," Jonathan nudged Tongs ahead. The death gasps of the trees were too much for him. And what had been that screaming in the distance only a few moments before?

"You're keeping something back," Cadman said as he caught up to him.

"Funny," Jonathan said, realizing how many questions Cadman had failed to answer last night. "I could say the same thing about you."

Cadman slightly nodded. "Fair enough. But now's not the time to see who can outwit the other. Now we must outrun this weather and get to shelter!"

—◦—◎◦◎◦—◦—

Snow continued to fall for the rest of the day. Once they left the protection of the Ruaden, and began to navigate through the large rolling hills, they found more snow had already fallen—as much as half a foot in some places. The wind, thankfully, was no more than an occasional breeze, but signs of the previous storms remained. Smaller trees stood snapped in half, and branches lay scattered everywhere. Late afternoon brought no warmth, and by early evening, when they reached the outskirts of Klinneret, Jonathan could barely feel his hands and feet. Cadman yelled that they would go a few miles more to the other side of town and spend the night there. It was a grueling hour as they walked the horses through high drifts; around them villagers scurried about with heads down. Many were slowed to a mere crawl as they fought the wall of wind that pushed them back.

"There you are, Cadman!" A burly man wrapped in a bundle of clothes waved both arms at them. "We were expecting you hours ago. Then again, we weren't expecting this! Come, come, my wife has dinner all ready."

They walked a little ways more until they came to a spacious log home that had a strange, curved roof to it. "Jonathan, you go in; Rose will be expecting you. Cadman, help me put Hammer and Tongs in the barn," Theo said.

Jonathan's knock on the door was answered by a short, dark woman, hair as black as Jonathan's, and eyes the same color. "You made it," she said, and sighed in relief. "I'm Rose," she said, smiling at Jonathan as she ushered him in. "We've been waiting, but were worried that, with the weather..." Rose promptly gathered his cloak and scarf, eyes darting back and forth from him to the three children running and yelling everywhere. "Theo insisted you'd be coming soon though. Are he and Cadman in the barn?" She nodded without waiting for an answer. "You must be practically frozen stiff. Go over by the fire, and I'll bring you something to drink. I believe Theo has an extra pair of slippers you could wear, should you find the chill still creeping through your bones."

The children stopped their rambunctious play upon seeing him. A little girl of about five, with dark curls like her mother, came up to him. "Hello, who are you?"

"Jonathan, my lady," he said, bending down on one knee and kissing her hand. He had played this game with Jenna when she was this little. "And whose acquaintanceship do I have the honor of making?"

She giggled and blushed, but said nothing.

"Her name's Lyla!" one of the boys shouted.

She squealed and ran off to her room. "She always does that," said the tallest boy, who shared the curls of sister and mother. "I'm Tor, and I turn nine next month."

"So, you're the man of the house when your father's away."

"That's right," he said, beaming. "This is my younger brother Evan."

"How do you do?" Evan asked solemnly.

"Very well, thank you," Jonathan said, thinking back to how Jeremy and Jenna greeted any stranger at the door with howls of delight at the sport they would have. "How many years have you seen?"

"Seven, but soon enough it will be eight," Evan replied.

"Please sit by the fire. Mother will bring you refreshments."

Jonathan settled for a comfortable rocking chair by the hearth, wondering just how often poor Evan was pummeled by Tor and Lyla during playtime. He could see it being an irresistible urge for the other two.

"There's a pot of soup cooking right now." Rose put a mug of spiced wine in his hands, the scent of cinnamon and nutmeg already promising to warm him. "There's buttered bread too, and your room is over there to the left…"

Jonathan looked around the ornately decorated house. A few toys lay scattered on the floor—a finely crafted drum was in the corner with some blocks beside it that were formed into a chair. In it sat a doll with its head in its lap. *Jenna would approve,* he thought with a smile. Above the toys was a shelf with what he assumed where the heirlooms of Theo's house. He went over to look at them more closely.

On the shelf were two black river rocks, each bigger than a man's hand and polished so well that Jonathan saw his reflection. Beside the stones was an old open book that occupied most of the shelf. Jonathan looked at the writing but couldn't decipher the language, instead concentrating on the illustrations. Intricate pictures of white birds darted in and out of the forest that bordered the text, with the tree trunks forming many of the letters. Lovely, deep green leaves interwoven with gold flowers spread out to the very end of the pages.

Beside the book was an old chalice. Its emblem, a flaming sword held aloft by a silver hand that shot out of a gleaming pool of fire. The rest of the cup swirled with cerulean and gold writing traced around the silver hand, written in a different language, yet not the same as the one in the book. *This house gives their allegiance to the Ogoni, then,* Jonathan surmised, looking around the room for a wereác and not seeing one. That in of itself was odd.

The front door blew open as Theo and Cadman walked in. "It's getting worse out there with the wind, but at least the snow has stopped." Theo unwrapped the scarf around his face to show dark, smiling eyes and a neatly trimmed dark brown beard with mustache to match, both flecked with gray.

"Well, don't drag all of nature in with you. Take off your coat and things there," Rose ordered.

"Cadman!" Lyla yelled.

"Well, hello there, buttercup." He picked her up and twirled her around.

"And for you little ones, it's bedtime. Go on now. Cadman, sit down. You too, Jonathan. I'll bring out supper."

While they ate, Theo and Cadman talked about how trade was slowing down in the south, yet seemed to be picking up along the eastern coast. Polite conversation that meant nothing. Rose asked Jonathan questions of a domestic nature. Did his mother have a hard time making clothes to keep up with all his growing? What had she planted in her garden this year with the early frost? Despite her courtesies, every now and then, a haunted expression would cross Rose's face, just a flicker of sadness in her eyes, and an almost hungry look as she gazed upon his face. But then she would blink, and the expression would disappear.

"...you should stick to the main road that leads over the pass, rather than the one that goes around it," Theo was saying.

Jonathan's ears pricked up; the conversation had changed.

"It will be more treacherous because of the cold, but it

will keep you well hidden," Theo warned.

"There's more wine in the pot." Rose discreetly cleared the plates from the table. The fire smoldered in the hearth, but shadows still played on the wall as Rose took one of the oil lamps in her hand. "Take care you find some rest before you venture on," she said, giving Cadman a hug. To Jonathan's surprise, she kissed his forehead. "That goes for you as well, even though you're half their age and can probably run circles around them."

"I resent that," Cadman said.

"Of course you do."

They waited until she had shut the door to her bedroom before huddling closer, their talk reduced to whispers. The remaining lamp etched angular lines into their faces, throwing the rest of the room into half darkness. On the shelf, the river rocks took on a strange iridescent cast in the dim light.

"Now," Theo began, "how bad of a time did you have coming here?"

"Not terrible," Cadman said. "But the winter devours the land more swiftly than last time."

"Mother said that half of Gaelastad was covered in less than a year." Jonathan took a long draught of wine. She had lost her first son in that winter twenty-five years ago; they never talked about it. No one did. He took another drink.

"So it comes again," Theo said, "but this time there are no Terakhein to petition for help, no Ashryanna to warm the land. Am I right in that, Cadman? Tell me. So many of us have suspected for a while now…"

"Aye, Nemarons no doubt were the culprits, but how they found the Terakhein Forest, hidden as it was, still eludes me," Cadman said.

"You said the Terakhein were petitioned to help with the first winter," Jonathan pointed out. "Who was sent? It's been at least twenty five years or even longer since any Terakhein has come to Gaelastad."

Theo nodded. "Some of the exiles claim it was Evanna

or Cierdwyn that went in secret, but they don't go around spreading that information. It's best just to forget you ever lived in Cadarn. Folks here view outsiders with suspicion. Even coming from Lailethas, I've experienced it." He looked up. "But what of the girl, Jonathan? Who is she?"

Jonathan shot Cadman a withering look. He did not like the fact that his nightmares had been the topic of conversation among not only the Elementarí, but throughout the villages of Gaelastad as well. It was a wonder the entire council wasn't beating down their door, asking where the Terakhein child was. *Damned if I know—I only keep seeing her die, doesn't everyone understand that?* "She is indeed the last of the Terakhein, at least that we know of."

"One is enough," Cadman said.

"One is *not* enough to put Ventosus back to sleep," Theo countered, "not as his winter grows in power, and with no holy flame to aid us. And you *know* that we will not reclaim Ashryanna."

Jonathan sensed that there was some unspoken conversation going on between Cadman and Theo; some shared history they were referring to. He hazarded a guess: "You were a Lailethan scout with Cadman, weren't you? You saw the beginning of the war."

Theo nodded. "I didn't see it, but soldiers who tried to defend the hall that day swore they saw Adamara herself slay Queen Evanna and steal Ashryanna. Obviously, that gives me even less hope of its recovery."

Ashryanna. Adamara. One a flame and the other...? A cold chill swept up Jonathan's spine. "Who is this woman thief?"

"One of the Three," Cadman said. "Ophidians. Tell me that Gaelastad schoolchildren have made some kind of mad song about at least *that* fantastic tale."

"Sorry to disappoint you," Jonathan said. "Jeremy and I were too busy defending ourselves from Riok's boys to engage in song and dance. They always liked to set upon us five to two. Now, one of the three what?" he repeated; maybe the wine was starting to get to him. It was beginning to sounds like a bad riddle.

"The *Three.*" Theo said, and took a long draught. *"Three together, three as one*—the Ophidian triumvirate. Siblings, actually. The most beautiful and brutal Ophidians you will hopefully never have the horror of meeting."

"Adamara, Truculen, and Chalom," Cadman said in a singsong way. He leaned back in his chair, eyes shining from wine. "Put that in a rhyme."

"Holes, Jonathan." Theo poured himself another drink. "Giant rents in the earth that smoked and burned and into which fell half of Cadreyth's army that first day. You've never heard the high pitched screams men can make until you see them in pure terror. Nice trick the Three can do, isn't it?" He lifted his glass in a toast. "'Twas the most wondrous tragedy I have ever beheld."

"We would have all been dead men had it not been for Cierdwyn."

"Lady of the Poisoned Bow," Jonathan murmured, thinking back to that night in the meadow with Jenna.

Cadman nodded. "In that, the songs don't lie. Her arrows were poisoned, with what dark potion strong enough to harm an Elementarí, I don't know. But her shot rang true, for she wounded Chalom."

"And the Three went down to the Two," Theo said, smiling at the memory. "They can't open the earth without the third sibling, you see. Lailethas and Íarchol still hadn't come, but we had a fighting chance now. Until that afternoon when Truculen, the other brother, challenged Cadreyth to a duel. Take note, Jonathan. If an Elementarí ever invites you to duel to the death, say *no.*"

"Cadreyth was slain, as was his sister Cierdwyn," Cadman said. "Queen Evanna's body was found fallen over the altar where Ashryanna had stood, a Nemaron knife in her heart."

"And thus ended the second day," Theo drunkenly declared. "But on the third day, Jonathan, on that beautiful third day, when we had lost king and queen, hall and fire, the allies came."

"And the Ophidians?"

"Left as soon as they stole Ashryanna," Cadman said. "Adamara and Truculen took their brother back to Ophidia —"

"Bastard didn't die," Theo slurred.

"The other Ophidians followed the Three," Cadman added. "There had been no sightings of them since, so everyone on the battlefield that day thought they had, perhaps, been put back to sleep by the Terakhein. Of course Lailethas and Íarchol came later, and only saw huge rents in the earth, and blamed it on Nemaron war machines. Silly fools. They didn't want to believe their precious Elementarí could have come to fight against them."

"Aye, Adolan certainly didn't help with that when he took the throne." Theo spat. "A poxy fool that doesn't know his head from his arse. He refused to see the point in trying to reclaim Ashryanna, not with the possibility of another Nemaron attack. What's more, he sent only a handful of soldiers to search for Cadreyth and Evanna's son, whom the king's herald had taken during the sack of the hall. Word came later that their bodies had been found in the Wild Lands, barely recognizable. And now there are more creatures waking..." Theo suddenly seemed to be aware of Jonathan listening intently, for he shot a quizzical look over to Cadman.

"He might as well know whatever you're about to tell me," Cadman said.

"The creatures in the Wild Lands have awakened. An Íarchin shepherd saw throcks with his own eyes. They're beginning to roam again."

Throcks. Fang-mawed, and as large as a bear but twice as swift. All children had grown up on the legend, but no man had seen a living throck since the Second Dawn. Cadman got up from the table and walked to the window. "That means Truculen is walking abroad too. Those beasts didn't wake up just by themselves."

"Could they have been responsible for what happened to our animals last year?" Jonathan asked.

"It was not any *thing* from the Wild Lands," Theo said quickly, and his gray eyes flashed. "You would have heard them if they had descended upon your village." He stood up and Jonathan followed suit while noticing they were almost the same height. Theo was maybe half an inch taller. Theo laid a hand on his shoulder. "We have already talked much tonight, and dawn is only a few hours away. You both should rest. Although the journey is only a couple of days, I believe it will get harder. Let me know if you need anything." He showed Cadman and Jonathan to their room, then bade them goodnight.

Jonathan ached all over from the ride today, and the cold still clung to his bones as the wine dissipated into sleepiness. He was too tired to even ask Cadman more questions, and without so much as a goodnight, he tumbled into bed. In a matter of moments, he found himself walking along a road thick with mist; only a sliver of moon illuminating his path through the forest. The trees seemed slightly different this time: taller and thicker in the trunk. Perhaps this was in a different wood, then. Even a different country. But he saw them, up ahead. The woman was still cradling the little girl, rocking her, whispering something in her ear.

Stop that!

The woman started and looked up, her large emerald eyes growing wide when she spotted him. This was new—the woman had never so much as cast a glance his way, but now, clearly she was looking at him. Wordlessly she laid the child back down and glided towards him. Jonathan bolted forward towards the girl, but the woman suddenly swerved, caught his arm with the strength of ten men and threw him to the ground. *Hera stondelathhh,* she hissed, eyes black, and opalescent fangs extended. *Ictha Elementarí.*

Jonathan's shoulder took the full impact of his fall. An explosion of pain ran down his arm and side, but he jumped up to try the sprint again when a sudden pain in his left knee buckled his leg underneath him.

Hera stondelathhh, the woman hissed again, dropping down to crouch beside him. The air turned sweet, suffused with the scent of honeysuckle as she hovered close, sniffing him, her breath hot on the back of his neck. *Ictha Element-arí,* she whispered in his ear. Her fingers lightly traced the length of his jaw to his chin; she had glided seamlessly, almost imperceptibly to be in front of him, her hand tilting his face towards her.

Jonathan immediately cast his eyes down at her pink lips; the fangs retracted, but still his gaze could not rest there, and so he landed on the necklace she wore: a silver chain that held a single stone the color of honey. The center was hollow, as if something was to be inlaid there. *Now for it,* he thought, his eyes fixed and steady as he braced his right leg in order to thrust his weight up. But the woman's other hand came clapping down on Jonathan's wounded shoulder while the hand under his chin drew his face close to hers. *Ictha Ophidia,* she said, her voice musical, her scent intoxicating. He tried to shut his sight against such beauty, but her emerald green eyes had him now: almond shaped, slanted outwards and the color, like the forest in summer.

This is what the little girl saw before she died, the seduction of the earth. A slight smile spread across the woman's lips as her eyes shaded from emerald green to jade, then the dark blue-green of the Atreal trees, then finally to black, except for the slit in the middle. The slit stayed emerald green. Reverse snake eyes. *Quero que teraessa,* she said.

He was no longer standing on the earth but lying in it, mounds of dirt folding over him, falling into his mouth, his eyes and nose. Jonathan's hands flailed out to stop the deluge of soil and he choked, turning his head to gasp for air. His face was completely covered but that did not stop the scream that escaped his lips, his legs already paralyzed by the force of earth upon them. Only his arms remained free as the earth kept closing up.

Listhwall helas nom, Comtheras!

Something hard was thrust into his outstretched hands. *Listhwall helas nom, Comtheras.* The woman's voice echoed in his mind. He blindly fumbled with the object, lungs almost to the bursting point while he tried to understand what she had given him. A slim chain attached to a rock—the necklace. It was too late though; his lungs gave out and he opened his mouth wide to breath in only earth and darkness.

—◦◦◉◦◉◦◦—

He woke up to a hand covering his mouth. "Don't say anything." It was Theo, the sour stench of wine on his breath. Was he still drunk? "Come with me."

Jonathan got up and followed him into the main room and over to the window. Theo pulled aside the heavy linen curtain to reveal the moonlit snow. "Look, over by the barn."

Two slender shadows stood close together. One pointed to the house, and the other nodded. Slowly the figures glided towards them as howls and screams echoed in the distance.

Jonathan's first thought was to wake Rose and the children and hide them—whoever hunted him always wanted the children. His second thought was remembering where he had laid his dagger. But suddenly they dived into the snow, momentarily disappearing until they reemerged in serpentine forms, at least twenty feet long, their girth the size of a man's trunk.

A cry and a shout sounded as from around the corner of the barn Cadman appeared, a sword in one hand and a torch in the other. Jonathan rushed to the door, but Theo held him back.

"They're Ophidians, Jon!"

"I've—got to—help!"

They heard Cadman yelling outside.

"We can't," Theo whispered angrily, as he kept Jonathan in a tight bear hug. "Don't you understand yet? If they've come to fight, he won't win. If they come any closer, you must leave—Rose, the children, me—and escape out the bedroom window and run. Promise me. The Terakheini lives on only in you."

Jonathan nodded, just once, and Theo released him. They returned to the window. Cadman was still brandishing his sword and fire in front of the Ophidians, yelling in some strange language. The two triangular heads swayed, staring at him, still coiled in the strike position. Then without warning they turned around, and dove into the snow, disappearing in an instant. The howls and screams grew fainter once again.

Cadman ran into the house. "They're gone for now, at least." He was pale and breathing hard.

"What's all this noise? Theo?" Rose had come out, her hair disheveled, looking angry and frightened.

"Two wolves wandered close to the barn," he said. "Cadman saw to it. Go back to bed. I'll be there shortly."

"You sure?" Rose asked as she whisked by them to check on her children. She came out of their room to stand before the men, hands on hips. "Well?"

"They're gone," Theo reassured her.

"Aye, they'll be back, I warrant," she sighed, and went to her room. Cadman raised his eyebrows.

"We're getting used to…" Theo glanced over at Jonathan. "Never mind that now."

"The screaming and howls—I heard it too," Jonathan said.

Theo and Cadman stared at him in wonder. "What are you talking about? There were no howls."

"But...but I heard it. In the Ruaden as well," Jonathan faltered, unsure of himself now. Was the screaming in the same unreal world as the whispering trees?

"Why didn't you say something then?" Cadman demanded.

"You said you couldn't hear anything; how was I to argue against that?" His heart beat quickly, wondering if they thought him mad after all.

Neither said a word.

"Did you have any idea that you were being followed?" Theo asked, finally breaking the tension.

"We didn't see any sign of them on the road to Klinneret," Cadman answered. "And while they are stealthy, they're not invisible. There wasn't enough snow on the ground to give them that much cover, not until tonight. Yet, how would they know we were here?"

"No one in town knew you were coming here," Theo reminded him.

"They knew in Breithan, though," Cadman said. "At least, enough knew..." He scowled.

"Did someone betray where we were going?" Jonathan grabbed Cadman's arm. "My parents—"

"If you go back now, you'll just lead the earth spirits to them," Cadman warned. "The Ophidians are following *us,* remember? I made sure there were enough people watching over Sienna and your parents."

"Who?"

"Lian, Balfour, and Riok. Alec will help too."

Tarl might have helped kill a little girl who might have been a Terakheini, Jonathan thought. Who's to say that his cousin Riok hadn't followed suit? "And if one of them is a traitor?" Jonathan posed.

Cadman's face grew darker. "That's not possible."

"Riok's cousin was murdered," Jonathan said. "What if Riok was being threatened with the same as Tarl?"

"None of this will help you now," Theo said, already

moving about the room, gathering up Jonathan and Cad-man's gear. "The Ophidians know where you are—"

"And where we are going, no doubt," Jonathan said.

"Which is why you must leave and not take the open road to Duraeston. Dawn is only a few hours away. If you start now you will be well beyond the last house of Klin-neret by the time everyone is up. Get your stuff ready; I'll go fetch the horses." Theo gestured to be quiet as he went out the door.

Jonathan turned to Cadman. "I still think Riok—"

"Riok is not his cousin," Cadman said. "Nor was Tarl a bad man, from what I knew of him. I trust Riok just as you trust Alec with your life, and that's the end of it."

More like the beginning, Jonathan thought as he went into their room and stuffed all his things into his sack. When he came out, Theo was back. "Everything's ready."

"Good," Cadman said. "You'll need to send someone back to Breithan, Theo, to do some searching and find out who our spy might be. Find others to watch the border of the Wild Lands, but no one should alert Jonathan's parents to the fact that Jonathan and I are not safe."

"I will see that it is done," Theo said. "Wait here." He went into his own room and came back out a few moments later. "Take this," and he pushed something wrapped in a cloth into Jonathan's hand.

"What is it?"

"Only a simple stone. A wise woman once gave it to Rose and said it would bring good fortune to whoever kept it. It has blessed us enough, as you can see, with both home and family. You take it now."

Jonathan thanked him and stuffed the bundle into his pocket. Theo had some last minute instructions. "Remem-ber to stay on the road no longer than necessary. When you get to the river, don't take the path to the right as you nor-mally do. Veer to the left. The undergrowth will cover you as you make your way along the banks. It is a slightly longer road, but the land will help hide you, for it remembers the blessings of the earth and water when all were in harmony. Are we not known as the land of the undying trees?"

"We saw the leaves falling in the Ruaden on the way up here," Cadman said.

Theo looked out at the snow-covered landscape. "All the more reason to hurry now."

CHAPTER 6
MORGAN

They rode hard for a long while and were a good distance from Klinneret by the time dawn broke. The light brought a rich new landscape to Jonathan's view. Meadows slowly gave way to craggy hills on their right, now covered with snow. To the left of them lay a sloping field, with a small gulch in its center, punctuated with barren trees. Their great naked branches loomed ominously against a gray sky, yet what frightened Jonathan more was their complete silence. Not a whisper or a wail. He knew he had to tell Cadman about the trees, but not yet. They hadn't seen any signs of pursuit. *Then again, Trapher killed Jeremy in the blink of an eye,* Jonathan thought. One instant of looking the wrong way, and it was done.

"When will they come after us?"

"Soon enough, I warrant," Cadman said, slowing Hammer down to a canter. "They understand that we don't know where the girl is, I think, and so capturing you would do them little good as of now—at least, that's how the Ophidians might see it."

"I dreamt about her again." As Cadman drew up his reins, he quickly corrected himself. "Keep moving. It was the woman I dreamt about, not the girl. I was in an underground lake, and she *saw* me, Cadman. All the other times I watched her and the girl—they never looked back at me. More than that, she gave me the necklace she was wearing."

"A necklace?" Cadman asked, his voice suddenly on edge.

"What did it look like?"

"It appeared to be made of amber from what I could see. It was but a moment in a dream, though, Cadman." Jonathan frowned, unnerved by the smith's odd reaction. "What's gotten into you?"

Cadman dismissed Jonathan's question with a wave of a hand. "I don't trust this woman, but never mind about that. What else did you dream?"

"That's all, except that I was drowning in dirt. The woman, she looked the same, but she was different somehow…and the trees, too—I would almost say she was in a different place—that she had brought the girl to some other wood." If he bumbled about like this trying to describe his dreams to the Ogoni, they were all in real trouble. "The Ophidian wanted to help me, Cadman, I'm sure of it."

The smith was visibly shocked. "That can't be. If they're awake, they will have followed… No, she must have been there to trap you. Still, the necklace…" He refused to voice whatever other concerns he had, though, and merely spurred Hammer on.

The hills on their right grew as the field to their left began to slope downward, forming the banks of what soon became a small creek. Within a few hours it turned into a river. Finally they stopped to drink, and Cadman led the horses down to a shallow part of the embankment while Jonathan went farther upstream. After he had filled up his water bag, Jonathan drank a few mouthfuls—the water was almost sweet. He hadn't gone this way before, and wondered what made the water like this. A small splash startled him.

He looked down.

A ghostly pale face stared back at Jonathan from the water, with black hair fanned out all around it. A glimpse of dark eyes. Jonathan reached for his dagger and threw it spinning into the river. In a flash, the face was gone. "Cadman!" He looked wildly about and reached down to fish his dagger out of the water.

Cadman ran over, his sword drawn.

"What did you see?" he demanded, looking all about them.

"A face in the river."

Cadman frowned and peered into the water. "What were the eyes like?"

"Eyes?"

"Yes, damn it, eyes! What color?"

"Dark!" Jonathan yelled, irritated now. "Blue, maybe violet—certainly not an Ophidian."

"Sounds like a water spirit, unless you know of river nymphs in the area," Cadman said dryly as he lowered his sword. "That would mean more of the Elementarí waking. Never have I heard of such a thing, nor do I want to see more of them. Terakhein law in Íarchol, and even in some parts of Gaelastad forbids the people to build dams, yet I know this law has been broken by the millers guild up north."

"Just like we overturned Dormín in the south," Jonathan said.

"And Centuras is not far behind. If we allow the forest to be cut down..."

"Water spirits before us, and the Ophidians behind," Jonathan laughed. "And here we are, trapped in the middle like a fox in the hunt."

"Not trapped," Cadman countered, as he mounted Hammer, "not yet, at any rate."

They kept to the river's path just as Theo had directed, but their pace slowed as the snow started again and the wind whipped and chapped their faces. A furious gale blew against Jonathan, full of high-pitched wails. The cold sank into his clothes, and he was losing feeling in his hands. Jonathan stayed close behind Cadman, for the path along the embankment was narrow and now he could hardly see.

Then a sickening roar of wind, such as he had heard that

day back in the Fáliquerci, thundered all around him. Another burst of wind caused Jonathan to let go of Tongs' reins, and throw his hands up to protect his face. Gale upon gale crashed against him until one violent gust knocked him off Tongs and pinned him to the ground. It felt as if he were being pummeled to death by the very air. He rolled over on his stomach and forced himself up onto his hands and knees.

"Ventosus!" he shouted in defiance. The name was swept away into the howling wind. Jonathan brought his left knee up to brace his heel against ground, and with his other leg thrust himself forward.

"Ventosus...Nemari!" It was what the Terakheini in his dream had said to drive the Ophidian back. He yelled the word as he attempted to run against the wind, felt it momentarily give way, allowing him to take a few faltering steps.

Icometheru, a voice croaked. Laughter pealed through the whistling gales as something struck him from the side, and he fell. Then everything went dark.

~⊸◉⧉◉⧉◉⊸~

There is water both before and after you, above and bey-ond. Water in your dreams and in your eyes. Now wake and remember the earth as well.

It was the strangest voice, deep and layered, as if many people were speaking at one time. Jonathan tried to remember where he had been. The wind had been coming for him. Yet now he felt no cold. *I'm dead.*

No, but you were well on that journey before I found you.

Jonathan opened his eyes and stared into an odd face. The violet eyes were too large, and very round, widely spaced and framed by long black hair, a thin nose, and full mouth. She wasn't an Ophidian, not with those eyes, nor that raven hair that shimmered maroon and looked to be made out of a spider's spinning silk. *Alec would love you,* he thought. Alec always did have a taste for the peculiar.

The woman's eyes narrowed. *Who is Alec?*

She hadn't moved her lips, yet Jonathan heard her say it.

"How...did you..." His voice cracked.

She laid a slender white hand on his mouth and said out loud this time, "You are still recovering from the wind and cold sent to bury you."

"How did—" Jonathan began again, and then he began coughing violently. She motioned for him to remain quiet and gave him something to drink. It was sweeter than water and warmed his throat. "Thank you. Now where is— but the woman interrupted him.

Speak with your mind. You're still too weak to talk.

Who are you? How did you find me? Strange eyes... Jonathan's thoughts rapidly unfolded, yet he could scarcely make sense of them. He knew he should remember something about violet eyes. He panicked, unable to remember, and sat up—only to feel the world swing violently around. He was in a cave, speckled with thick milk-white stalactites; the "bed" on which he sat was raised limestone in a natural groove of the wall. Against the other side stood his packs and an odd-looking gourd. He lay back down.

"You're still weak, like I said. Why did you not listen?" She chided him. Her voice was low, almost musical.

She swept across the room to the gourd, and poured more liquid from it into the cup. The gems on her dark green gown sparkled with every graceful gesture. A flash at her throat showed a blue stone on a chain of silver. Tall and shiny. *Yes, Alec would love to get you alone and rolling in a haystack.*

"Is it considered polite to barter off one's savior as another man's plaything where you are from?" she asked. "I am Morgan, of the Delphini. Watch what you think as much as what you say to me."

The blood rushed to Jonathan's face as he tried to think of a way out of this scrape. How had she known what he was thinking? "I meant no offense," he said before another wave of coughing shook him.

"Did I not already tell you once to speak only with your mind?" She handed him the refilled cup. "What made you think you could dare defy a lord of the air?"

"He killed my sister," Jonathan whispered.

"And you would avenge yourself against the very sky? Are you so brave of heart, or merely a fool who believes in his own unassailable strength?"

There was logic in what she said, he knew. It was rash of him to try to challenge an Elementarí. *I have been pummeled by air and haunted by earth in dreams and journey. What else was I to do?*

Her look softened. "You need to keep drinking that, for you do not recover from such a battle so easily, as Cadman has discovered too. Do not worry! He is safe. He did not know you had fallen, for the wind had lied with your voice and said you were right behind him. I found him a little ways ahead, fighting a gale so fierce I thought it would take both him and horse away. He will have to tell you about the battle of songs Ventosus and I had." Suddenly she stood very still. "That is Hammer's footfall. Your friend will be joining us soon."

Why don't you tell me about that battle? he silently asked her.

I do not have time to tell bedside stories to wounded boys.

I have lost too much for that slight, my lady. And then, he saw himself get up and go to her, wrap his arms around her like any man would. Before he knew it, his lips were on hers, pressing softly, his hands at her waist. She tasted of salt and mountain lakes, and her mouth opened at the gentle insistence of his tongue.

The thoughts had come unbidden, although not unwanted, and Jonathan wondered if perhaps that was partially Morgan's doing, until he looked into her eyes, which had turned from violet to black. The room spun in earnest as he heard the roar of water before the deluge swept into the cave, white foam and salt spraying into his face. He tried calling out, but he could not so much as sit up while wave upon wave crashed over him, filling his mouth and nose, closing off all breath and life until he was under water, lungs almost to the bursting point.

"Am I interrupting something?"

Jonathan gasped for air as he blinked hard and saw Cadman standing by the cave entrance. Jonathan himself was sitting up, completely dry, still facing Morgan, whose eyes remained a smoldering violet. Had they been staring at each other the entire time?

Morgan collected Jonathan's cup. "Please enter, Cadman. Jonathan is recovering far more quickly than even I expected, but perhaps more wood on the fire is in order."

Cadman threw another quizzical glance at Jonathan before going to the small pile of sticks over by the other wall.

"Was it you we saw in the water earlier today?" Jonathan asked, slowly swinging his legs over the bed. Why had she let him dream of the kiss when all she wanted was to drown him? Damn women and their games; one moment hot and lusty, the next, cold as a stone. *Or was your drowning me repayment for the dagger I threw at your neck?*

That dream was yours alone. Salt and mountain lakes. He sensed her laughing at his thought. *I am of the Delphini, boy, not one of your village maidens, to take at a whim.* Aloud she said, "It was not my face you saw in the river. Bryn had sent word of two travelers to watch for. We did not know your journey would be so treacherous this soon; otherwise, I would have sent more out to watch the waterways." She turned to Cadman. "What were you able to discover?"

The smith's brows furrowed as he laid more wood on the fire. "There were no tracks, nothing to show we were being followed."

"I was struck from the side." Jonathan rubbed the back of his head where a nice knot had formed. "Someone hit me, I'm sure of it." He couldn't tell Cadman about the voice. It hadn't come from the trees, but it hadn't been human either.

Cadman shook his head. "I found a large rock beside you, and no tracks anywhere nearby where you fell. There was nothing but that stone. No branches or leaves, nothing else that had blown that way." Cadman hesitated. "An Ophidian could have caught up with us and made that rock fly at you. But they didn't want to attack us at Theo's house, so why here? Were they waiting for others to join them? Perhaps even Truculen or Adamara herself?"

"They would not be so reckless." Morgan's violet eyes momentarily shaded to black. "Neither of them would come alone and unaided, not here, where the Delphini rule the river ways. Only one or two Ophidians have been spotted, and they disappear just as swiftly."

"Trapher has been in Breithan," Cadman reminded her.

"Do not speak his name to me!" she commanded and drew herself up to a frightening height, so that she seemed, momentarily, even taller than Cadman. "That he has even dared to slink out of Ophidia is insult enough." She strode to the entrance of the cave and sniffed the air. Her hair fanned out, revealing the dark maroon stripes throughout, and when she turned around, her eyes flashed a darker violet. "You should camp here tonight. I must see what I can find out from others in the river—the wind brings a strange scent. I will return before you leave tomorrow morning."

"We'll be on our guard," Cadman said, kneeling down and blowing on the small flame.

Wait! The word echoed through Jonathan's mind before he could stop it.

Morgan stood in the entrance, her eyes piercing him as she searched within his thoughts, but he closed his mind,

willed it to go white as winter while he swung his legs over
the rock bed and stood up. The room tilted as he walked
slowly over to her. She was the same height as he, perhaps
half an inch shorter, if that. Perhaps it was only that he
wanted her to be smaller in some way. Instead she towered
there, her fragrance like the breeze over the ocean, eyes
darker than midnight.

"You showed me what you are," he said, in a low enough
voice that Cadman couldn't hear. "I'll be sure to return the
favor someday, my lady." What drove him to say such things
was beyond any of his understanding; he only knew her
beauty made his breath come up short. He wanted to talk to
her, hold her, kiss her...he tried to stop the flood of images
that came spilling forth into mind.

"I have no need of such antics," she returned, and
Jonathan wondered if she had seen the flashes of images he
had just conjured. "War is brewing, and you are caught in
the middle of allegiances beyond your reckoning. Find the
Terakhein and then return home where you belong." With
a slight bow, she left.

"That was an interesting goodbye," Cadman said as he
sidled up beside Jonathan. "I'd have thought you liked your
lasses a little younger, given your distaste for the widow's
advances, and Morgan's certainly older than her."

"Who is she?" Jonathan hadn't taken his eyes from the
mouth of the cave.

"She told you—a Delphini. But not just any water spirit:
she is the daughter of Morwenna, mother of the great
abyss."

"She almost drowned me."

"You look dry enough. A little red in the face, but then
again, she looked slightly flustered too," Cadman smirked.
"We'd be dead if she hadn't come along."

"So she said." *And was right smug about it too.*

The smiled widened. "Did she now? Her boast is well
deserved, no matter how much it might hurt your pride. If

others had seen such a fight, songs would be sung well into the next age. Certainly, I did not think to survive it. Remind me never to get in the middle of two fighting Elementarí again."

"Tell me what happened."

"I was lying flat on my back, having been knocked off Hammer by the fiercest gale I've ever experienced. Suddenly there's Morgan, standing on the river. Not *in* it mind you, or on the banks, but on top of the water, hair fanned out like a witch in the wind, yelling something in her language that sounded like a curse. The next thing I knew, a giant wave crested over me, and I half expected to be the only man to ever drown on dry land." A small shudder ran up Cadman's back.

"Instead, the wave froze in midair and formed a shelter over me so that I could no longer see the Delphini. Just as well I suppose, given the words I heard her cry out, which the wind answered. Dark voices and dark words from wind and sea, and there I was, thinking my bones would split apart from the very sound of them. Finally, the winds ceased their dark chatter. Morgan threw me on Hammer, found Tongs, and led us along the path to this cave. You were already here." Cadman looked him over. "You're looking green again. Let's sit you down."

Jonathan had been so intent upon listening to Cadman's story he had ignored the fact that he was feeling dizzy. The smith looped one of Jonathan's arms around his shoulder, and helped him stagger back to his stone bed. "It's time to make some supper. We won't leave tomorrow till late morning, provided you're well enough to walk."

"I'm fine." That wasn't true, though. He was cold. Not the kind of cold one gets from being outside; he was used to that. Winter hunting trips had exposed Jonathan many times to the bitter, wet chill that sank into one's bones. This was a different kind of cold, one that settled first in his heart and lungs then radiated outward in icy numbness.

"You don't battle Ventosus' wind and come out unscathed," Cadman said, trying to sound casual even as he felt Jonathan's forehead and cheeks.

"Stop that."

"Just making sure blood is still coursing through your veins. Here, let us have some dinner. Let me see what Sienna packed for us. Could it be? Of course." Cadman pulled out two biscuits filled with bacon, a lump of cheese, and a kind of fruitcake. Jonathan eyed the cake with concern. "She couldn't have messed up the biscuits that much."

Jonathan looked at the white milky towers hanging down from the limestone ceiling. "Cadman?" he said thickly. The stalactites lengthened, turned into blurry white towers dangling down, and swaying. Not swaying—he was running around them. A strange image of him turning a dark corner to meet—

"Here, drink this." A cup was brought to his lips, and the scent of spices wafted up in the steam. Jonathan opened his eyes to see Cadman holding it steady as he drank. When had he closed them? The drink was earthy in flavor, not sweet like its aroma promised. "It will calm the sickness you feel," Cadman said when he tried to stop drinking, "and help you sleep. Sienna's own recipe."

That explained the disagreeable taste.

"Cadman," he repeated, pushing the cup away. The entire cave seemed to lurch forwards and backwards, but still Jonathan could not remember the question he wanted to ask.

"No more talking," Cadman warned. "We still have to make it to Duraeston by tomorrow night without being waylaid by serpents or ice storms, and without your collapsing in a heap. This will give you a dreamless sleep." He handed Jonathan the cup again.

Jonathan took it, his hand slightly shaking. "What's happening to me, Cadman?"

Cadman turned his head so Jonathan didn't have the

chance to see his expression. "You tried to fight a lord of the air—just because there were no swords doesn't mean you received no wounds."

The smith's cryptic answer was hardly sufficient, and Jonathan was about to tell him so when he felt every limb grow heavy with warmth. He fell back into the bed and closed his eyes.

—⟶⟶⊙⟩⊙⟨⟵⟵—

When he opened them again, Sienna Samsone stood there, wrapped in a heavy blue cloak, her white tresses sticking out in wiry strands. Had she come to see that he drank all of her healing potion?

"Don't just lie there like an idiot," she whispered, looking furtively about her. "Follow me." She turned and walked toward the cave's entrance. Jonathan found he could finally feel his legs, and indeed, the warmth that had lulled him to sleep had stayed. He quietly slid out of his blankets and threw on his coat. In the fire's glow he could see Cadman fast asleep by the far wall.

"Stop dawdling," Sienna snapped. He hurried to where she was standing at the mouth of the cave. Beyond it, only a few shards of moonlight broke through the trees and neighboring rocks. "Now you must begin to see what has been kept hidden from you," she said, lighting a candle. "Far too much, I'm afraid."

She set off on the path along the embankment.

Jonathan wanted to ask how on earth she had found them, but Sienna kept her stride swift, and she remained a few steps beyond him. His legs, while warm, were still weak, and he could not catch her, but followed the light of her candle and sheen of her moonlit hair. They walked a long time, until the river narrowed into a stream, and then at last the waters gathered in a small pool. Sienna reached it first, but kept her back to him, and he wondered at this, until he caught up with her. Then she turned around.

It was no longer Sienna. Instead, emerald green eyes

watched him intently as the smell of honeysuckle flooded the air. Her white hair was really a very light gold. Jonathan froze and reached for his belt, where his dagger always rested. It wasn't there. *And just how would that help you?* he thought. *Foolish man that you are to follow a woman in the middle of the night.* But where was the girl? Surely she must be close by, if the woman was here. Jonathan's heart quickened in its beats, and he looked beyond her to the path they had just taken, expecting to see the child's crumpled form there by the side of it.

"I told you to watch where you were going," she reproached him, no longer in Sienna's raspy manner, but in a languid, sensuous tone. "Learn to see what is really before you—and that which is hidden among both darkness and light." Some outside force drew Jonathan to her side. He found that resisting it only caused unfathomable pain throughout his body, yet he could not stop his arms from flailing out in a desperate desire to get away from her. A flashback to little hands grasping out...

I believe her to be alive...her life depends on who finds her first. Bryn's voice suddenly echoed throughout him. The little hope that memory lent Jonathan allowed his muscles to relax, enough, at least, to bring him to the Ophidian's side without being torn apart from the inside out. His arms and legs were badly shaking, and he wondered how much longer he could stand.

The Ophidian didn't seem to notice. She pointed to the pool. "Look closely and tell me what is there."

Again he felt that if he did not gaze into the pool, his very head would burst, so sharp was the pain in resisting. He stared into the water. "I see the moon and the stars against the blackness of night."

The water slightly rippled, and the stars grew larger. He could see now they were indeed made of fire—large orbs of orange, blue, and red flames whirring around the sky like pinwheels. Then the image slowly changed. The stars disappeared behind large ice-covered mountains jutting out of a barren landscape. The moon sped across the sky until it met the sun and stood, it seemed, in the very center of it. The moon's silvery glow meshed with the bright bands of sun instead of blocking them out, and together the lights danced in all their brilliance until even the icy sheen of the mountains and lakes turned a warm gold.

A hand suddenly yanked him back. The woman took hold of his chin and turned his face towards her, just like she had the little girl. He tried to close his eyes, but it was too late; already, the green in the Ophidian's eyes was disappearing into black. *No, not black. Dark blue.*

"Remember what the sky and water have shown you," she commanded as he felt the earth drawing him inside itself. The next thing he knew, he was riding the night sky, eyes closed, with the wind on his face.

⟶⚫⚫⟵

Cadman was shaking him. "Morgan's coming."

Using the Delphini's name was a smart tactic for it made Jonathan suddenly sit up. He wanted to at least be out of bed by the time she arrived, but it felt like all the blood rushed to his head: flash of the dream he had wandered through last night. How had he gotten back to the cave? One minute he was riding the air with an Ophidian who could apparently enter his dreams at will. It had all seemed so real, and now he was here. Sienna's face drifted back into focus. Why had she been the one to lead him to the pool?

"You coming?" Cadman barked. "Or are you going to sleep in? This isn't the Three Sisters' Inn, you know." A pause as the smith looked again at him, keenly. "How are you feeling?"

"I'll heal soon enough," he lied, testing each leg. At least he could easily wiggle his toes now, although both knees felt stiff, like he had been walking most of the night instead of sleeping. But he still felt cold, like he'd never be warm again. That was not the most pressing issue though. "Cadman, the

Ophidian visited my dreams again, only this time she was Sienna at first."

"The widow?" Instead of laughing, like Jonathan expected, the smith's brows furrowed. "What nonsense is this? Tell me everything."

Jonathan quickly related the images he had seen: Sienna standing there, in the middle of the cave, the moon moving into the sun, and the Ophidian's eyes turning blue instead of black.

Cadman was silent for a while, long enough for Jonathan to feel like a fool for telling him. *He thinks me a boy, too, coming to cry with every dream I have. Just like Jenna used to do with me.* How he ached for his little sister just then. To think she might have experienced such nightmares alone! And that last night, when she had told him about the world of winter, he had been cross with her about his lack of sleep...

"Tell this news to no one," Cadman said, the frown still etched upon his face. "These things do not make sense, but I would rather Morgan not know that you dreamed of Sienna turning into the Ophidian. Her hatred of the Three and Trapher is great, but I have as yet to understand why. I would rather she not come to suspect our poor widow as being in alliance with her enemy."

"Aye, I've already experienced her wrath," Jonathan moaned. He was tired of these women all drowning him with dirt, sea, and abyss and yet with no scar or wound to show of it. If this continued throughout his journey, he'd be a madman before harvest.

"Just what is going on between you two?" A smirk played on Cadman's lips, but Jonathan could tell that the question was honestly given. That meant that even though Morgan could read his thoughts, and sometimes he could sense her feelings and hear her words, the smith could not. The thought was vaguely comforting.

"We had a rather messy first greeting," Jonathan said

shortly. "I will be on my best behavior, sir smith, do not worry about my conduct."

Cadman merely kept the wicked grin on his face as he toasted Sienna's biscuits over the fire. Jonathan slowly got up, dressed, and had eaten by the time Morgan entered the cave, followed by two dark-haired men dressed in blue cloaks the color of midnight. "My brothers will be your guides the rest of the way. You could not ask for better escort than the Lords Morvoren. This is Peran and Madron."

They were so alike that Jonathan thought he'd have trouble telling them apart, were it not for Peran's eyes being several shades of a darker violet than his brother's. The Delphini men each went up to Cadman and Jonathan and kissed them on the cheek while putting a hand on their heads. "It is the sign of welcome and blessing among us," Madron said.

"We thank you for your protection, my Lords Morvoren," Cadman said, with a deference Jonathan rarely saw in the smith. He pulled a map from his cloak while asking the brothers what path they would be taking to Duraeston.

Meanwhile, Jonathan turned to Morgan. "Will you be joining us?" He tried to hold back his desire to have her by his side for whatever else he had to endure. He would do anything—find children, fight a lord of the air even to the death, if she but asked it.

He sensed her displeasure at his thoughts, and once more her tone was high, queenly even. "I go back to the abyss, where no man or child can follow. My brothers have brought strange news that I must warn my mother about, and a watch needs to be set on the eastern and southern coasts. You promised repayment, and I expect no less than the Terakhein child as your due." *And do not presume to be a warrior born, when you are a farmer's boy bred and taught.*

Jonathan wondered at the tremor in her voice at the

mention of the child. "But of course, I will find her," he answered, looking straight into her violet eyes, "child though you still think me to be." *Let me show you what I know of children.* He opened his memories to her, then, of the little Terakhein girl running in the snow, crying; showed her Jenna's body lying there, bloody gash on her head and him, weeping over his sister; next was the nameless little girl found in the center of Seven Woods with her throat cut; and lastly, Jeremy's face, lips purple-blue and wide open in horror as he drew his last breath.

"Morgan," Peran's booming voice cut through the vision.

"In a moment, brother," she said, her gaze never leaving Jonathan. "You have your own quest in this matter, it would seem."

"It's not so much a quest as a promise to my sister." *To cut down a world of thorns.*

"'Tis a world of winter coming for you, Jonathan." Morgan leaned in closer, and Jonathan sensed her power, like the snap of air when lightning strikes. "Neither sword nor arrow will pierce the wind. Remember that the next time you dare defy one of the Elementari."

"Morgan," Peran repeated impatiently.

Without another word the Delphini walked over to Peran and they left the cave.

Jonathan grabbed his pack from the wall and followed Madron and Cadman outside to where the horses were waiting. The snow had stopped at least, but that provided scant comfort in light of the biting north wind that would be against them all day. Jonathan pulled the ends of his scarf more tightly around his throat. What he wouldn't give for a warm hearth and a full night's sleep. It had been days, weeks, even months since he had truly slept. Not since last spring...

Once on horseback, they followed Madron down the embankment to the river, where Peran was waiting for them.

"Where is Lady Morgan?" Jonathan glanced along the banks for any sign of her.

"She is gone to our mother," Peran replied. "Did she not already say her farewell to you?"

Morgan's slight made Jonathan blush. She had given him no such token of friendship. What had he expected from a woman—no, an Elementarí with that kind of power, who was as ancient as the rivers and oceans?

"Make sure to keep to the bank as you were doing before," Peran commanded. "In the river we can hear anyone approach, and we've let it be known that the brothers Morvoren are walking abroad once again."

"It is unlikely that we will encounter any enemy on this path, not after Morgan's duel with Ventosus," Madron added, the calm counterpart to his brother. "She should not have taken him on in such a rash manner."

"She did what I would have done!" Peran thundered.

"My point exactly," Madron retorted. He turned to Jonathan and Cadman "We have heard from the Feállí that the rivers in Lailethas have frozen over, and so we must part ways once we reach Duraeston. We should make the outskirts of the village by mid-evening."

The brothers then dove into the rushing river. Jonathan expected them to come up for air for one last greeting, but they did not resurface.

"What are these Feállí they spoke of?" Jonathan asked as they followed the narrow path along the bank.

The smith grimaced. "You don't want to know. What little Morgan told me of them was enough to unsettle my dreams for a week."

They stopped only twice during the day to eat, and, by dusk, they were still about three hours away from Duraeston. Peran and Madron stayed in the water and only once came to the surface to see if everything was all right. The riverbank was steep enough that they had to walk the horses. A question continued to nag Jonathan.

"Cadman, Theo said it is impossible to harm an Elementarí. He would not let me run out and help you that night."

"Your sword would have been of no use against them."

"Then how did Cierdwyn wound Chalom with only an arrow? What kind of poison would do that?"

"My guess is that she got that poison from the Terakhein—"

Peran burst out of the river, eyes black, his robe a giant wave rising all about him in his fury.

"Run! Run! Wild beasts from the north are here! Run on this path and do not climb up the banks! Do not stop until you reach Duraeston!"

He dove back into the water.

"We must help them!" Jonathan began to turn Tongs around.

"No! We run! Follow me!" Cadman shouted, and shot ahead with Hammer. They galloped along the banks as the howling in the distance grew closer.

Wolves, Jonathan thought.

But there were other noises. High pitched screams pierced the air over the howling and growls. The screams Jonathan had been hearing in the distance for months now were suddenly right behind them. A horrible crash, followed by more howling. Hammer and Tongs suddenly went wild and rode up the bank. When Jonathan and Cadman tried to rein them back down to the river, they bucked with such force that both men were thrown from their saddles. Jonathan felt himself flying through the air, and then with a thud, landed on his back as all the air was knocked out of him.

Cadman was the first on his legs. "Hammer! Tongs!" Cadman yelled as the horses galloped away.

Jonathan wanted to run after them but Cadman pushed him forward. "No! We can be seen up there. We must continue this way."

They sprinted ahead as the shrieking wails grew closer. The river beside them rushed in a violent torrent and soon overflowed onto the path, slowing them to a run until a hidden rock tripped Cadman.

"Keep going!" he yelled.

Jonathan turned around to see an animal running towards them, large as a bear, with a slanted snout, flat brow, and two fangs that extended well over its jaw.

Neáhvalar help us. Jonathan grasped Cadman's forearm with both hands and threw the smith past him.

Now he was between Cadman and the throck. Jonathan pulled out his dagger as the beast took a flying leap. At the same time a huge wave rose up, and out of it, Peran's head and hand emerged. The Delphini grabbed the snarling throck, which turned and sank its fangs into Peran's neck. They both fell back into the river. Another loud crash sounded from behind.

Cadman roughly pulled Jonathan away. "Go!"

Jonathan obeyed, slip-sliding through mud and rock as a burning pain in his legs traveled up into his heart. His lungs breathed fire, but the river was overflowing now as if in anger, its white currents threatening to overflow the banks and sweep everything away. Water rushed at their feet, and still they staggered on until at last they found themselves wading through mud, the river having finally subsided, and no sounds of pursuit behind them. Cadman finally let them stop, and they fell down against the sloping embankment.

"Stop...only a moment. Must reach...Duraeston before night." He bent over gasping for breath. "Never try...to save...me...again. I tell you to run, dammit...you flee."

"And leave you? Do you take me for a coward?" Jonathan had already recovered his breath but felt the cold reaching into every part of him.

"If it comes to that—you live. I die. You go on and find her. Promise me."

Jonathan closed his eyes, and saw her running on that

snowy path. Was she feeling the same freezing wind as the sun set? He opened his eyes to see Cadman standing up. "I'll find her." But he'd be damned if he was going to leave his godfather behind in any kind of danger.

The lines in Cadman's face relaxed a bit with Jonathan's answer. "Good. Now the problem is to make it to Duraeston before freezing to death. Let's hope the horses traveled back home safely or found some stable to house them. Ready?"

They began the last part of their journey—sometimes running to keep themselves warm; walking when they no longer had the strength to do more. Neither talked of the brothers and what might have become of them. If they were dead, Jonathan feared what Morgan would do in her wrath.

Cadman must have been thinking the same, for a sense of urgency seemed to overtake him. "Now for the last sprint," he said and took off at such a pace that it took Jonathan several moments just to catch up. Twilight quickly faded, and the sky was pitch black when they finally saw the twinkling lights of Duraeston, and came exhausted to the Three Sisters' Inn.

CHAPTER 7
DREAM WALKING

"Who are you?"

Jonathan heard the words through a long tunnel. There was a humming in his head that he couldn't stop, and when he tried to open his mouth to talk, he found his tongue was too heavy to form any words. A large blond woman eyed him with suspicion.

"Oh, Cadman, it's you. Ah, this young man's with you? Then I'm sorry. Come in, you poor dears. Why, you look frozen stiff."

More talk around him echoed then was swallowed up in the tunnel. He felt a tugging at his sleeves and slowly realized that someone was trying to take his coat off.

"As if you two didn't know any better than to go running around in wet clothes on a night like this, looking half crazed..."

Jonathan could no longer feel his legs, and wondered how it was that he remained standing. Someone put a small glass into his hand, and when he refused to drink, brought the cup up to his lips. Fire poured down his throat, and he sputtered.

"Wh-what is this stuff?"

"Something to bring you back to life. You looked like the walking dead." Cadman slapped his face lightly. "Here, take these and change in that room over there. We need to get you in dry clothes. Can you do that?"

The tunnel was getting longer; the words, more faint.

He could tell Cadman was worried, and that made the fear worse. Still, he brushed the smith's hand aside and stumbled over to a side room. It took a while to peel off his frozen breeches and shirt, with his hands shaking so. *I'll be fine. It's just the cold.* A bit more fumbling, and he was in dry clothes. That felt better, at least. He found Cadman a few moments later talking to the blond woman, who, when she saw Jonathan, rushed to greet him.

"Mirabel, two mugs of spiced wine for Cadman and...his friend. Give me those." She took Jonathan's wet clothes, pushing him into a big chair. "I'm Molly. Warm yourself, boy, and we'll have you feeling yourself again." She adjusted her round spectacles to get a good long look at him. "You need more than just wine, I warrant."

Jonathan watched as Molly went off to welcome other guests, her yellow dress swishing as she bustled about the room. Cadman had disappeared, but he was too tired to care. He closed his eyes, his mind blank like snow. *You'll be fine. You're just tired from running in the snow, and possibly seeing two Elementarí die.* The numbness kept crawling up and down his legs amid aches of feeling.

Another voice called him back into wakefulness. "No no no, you need to drink more of this."

Jonathan looked up to see a tall woman with such pale blond hair as to be almost white, wound in a giant braid on top of her head. "I'm Mirabel, and here's your wine." She handed Jonathan a large warm mug from which arose a light steam of berries and wood. He deeply inhaled the scent hoping it would help warm every part of him before taking a long draught.

Mirabel flicked her head around, sparrow-like, before asking, "Where's Cadman?"

"I don't know..."

She momentarily scowled, her pale eyebrows furrowing as much as they could within her round face, then spoke rapidly. "He should not have left you here alone; here, draw up that hood around your head. You'll catch your death of a cold. Marietta's just finished cooking up some stew."

Without waiting for an answer, she whisked herself into the kitchen. *She even hops like a sparrow,* Jonathan thought, amused. He stretched his legs out in front of him. The wine was working down his throat and into his limbs. A number of people sat in animated discussion at a long table while others ate at smaller tables, some leaning together and whispering. Someone kept calling for more wine, and over in the corner a few men had begun singing. Jonathan's eyes wandered over to the tapestries hanging on the far wall. The scenes were hardly beautiful: blue-gray caves hid amid a rocky valley, the overcast sky matching the blandness of land, a few brown-cloaked shepherds. *Íarchol,* Jonathan thought, for its caves were renowned as much as Gaelastad's forests. Briefly, he wondered if those famed Íarchin caves, like the forests, were also under threat of being exploited. Or invaded.

"Did the wine work? You have to climb stairs." Cadman was standing in front of him.

"Where did you go?"

"To check out our rooms." Cadman leaned closer. "I also wanted to see if anyone had heard reports of a rabid pack on the loose; so we might at least learn what happened to Peran and Madron. But no one coming from Klinneret saw any wild animals. A few heard wolves in the distance, but that is nothing new."

"They must have made it out safely, though," Jonathan countered, "otherwise we would have been pursued all the way here."

"I hope that is the case," Cadman answered wearily. Before he could say any more, however, Mirabel burst out of the kitchen with a tray laden with bread and stew.

"What are you still doing in the main hall?" She handed Cadman the bowls from the tray. "Up to your rooms, until you look more presentable, if you please. I'll send up more hot cider—drink as much of it as you can stand."

Was it just Jonathan's imagination, or was the advice to stay in their rooms more of a command? A glance around the room again—who here looked presentable?

But then the moment disappeared as Cadman laughed and took the steaming bowls out of her hand. "Bella, you're too good to me. Send up more cider when you have it."

They went upstairs to the fourth room on the right—not a large room but wide enough for one feather bed in the middle and a straw one on the floor by the corner. A small table with a pitcher of water and a bowl stood against the wall, a chair beside it. They washed the grime off their faces, turning the water almost black from the muck. Cadman had a cut just over his right eye that had bled very little but was already beginning to bruise and swell. "You look like you've been through more than just a long journey," Jonathan said.

"Speak for yourself," Cadman huffed. "They get enough tradesmen in here looking the worse for wear. And you'll be taking a razor to that face of yours before any sleep befalls you. You look half mad with those black eyes and throcky brows."

Jonathan didn't answer as he sat down on his bed and slurped the thick, steaming stew. His mother had also given him such commands, and Jonathan had ignored them, sometimes for months at a time during winter until a thick black beard had quickly covered his face. Even his father couldn't get such magnificent coverage, just wispy patches that made it seem as if he suffered from some unspoken illness.

The smith, for his turn, fell silent as he ate, but once in a while he would glance up at Jonathan with a worried expression.

"Stop looking at me like that. I'm fine." Jonathan had had to deal with those kinds of stares from his mother lately. *Father, too, come to think of it.* Well, he was done with worried looks and people whispering about him in corners. At last he stood up, catching a glance of himself in the small mirror on the little chest. The dark stubble was already beginning past his ears, creeping dangerously close to his neck. Black eyes, black brows—his mother said he'd inherited those particular traits from his maternal grand-father, who'd died before Jonathan was born. He certainly didn't look nineteen—more like a twenty-five or even a thirty-year-old man who had been out in the wilderness for two weeks instead of three days. How could Morgan still see him as merely a boy wanting to play warriors and throcks?

"Well," he said, catching Cadman's stare once more. "What is it?"

"The guilds here are wary of strangers—especially ones that looked like they've been on a month's march, and your name is scarcely known here—"

A knock. Cadman's muscles involuntarily tensed, and he walked quietly to the door. "Who is it?" It was a barking command more than a question.

"I'd be more gracious when sending for a barber at this godforsaken hour."

The smith's shoulders relaxed as he threw open the door. A bald, fat man stood there, wearing a plain black cloak, a leather satchel in hand. "Come in Jaxon. Sorry about the welcome." Cadman opened the door wider. "We've had a long night, but I don't know what tomorrow will bring us, so it's good you've come."

Jaxon took a surmising glance at Jonathan as he set down his bag on the bed. "I clearly see the issue. Those black locks will not do, my boy. Not at all. Especially with those eyes—a bit too striking a look, you know. You could stand a good run yourself, Cadman."

"Not this time, my friend; just my apprentice."

The word made Jonathan start. Cadman had journeyed with his apprentice, Jophil, on many a trip to Duraeston;

everyone would know Jonathan wasn't him. Jaxon pulled out some parchment and unceremoniously handed it to Cadman. "You'll want these papers then." From the satchel he also drew out a straight-edged razor, towel, and pouch. His eyes scanned the room and landed on the basin of water. "You don't expect me to use that."

Cadman smiled absentmindedly as he examined the papers. "Hmm?"

Jaxon had taken off his nondescript cloak to reveal a finely-stitched, long brown vest that came to his thighs, three blue emblems emblazoned on the breast. He was a master, then, in the guild of surgeons here.

"There's more water in the pitcher," Cadman said.

Jaxon immediately set to making a paste with the powder and water. "Have a seat in the chair please."

Jonathan had never had anyone shave him before. A good knife and some soap was all he needed to take care of the matter, and would have saved them both a coin. Cadman seemed to be thinking the same thing, for there was a glimmer of agitated worry behind his smirk.

"It's a good thing you're heading homewards within a day or two," he finally said. "Otherwise, I'd be spending a small fortune instead of making one."

Jaxon lightly massaged the paste onto Jonathan's jaw with soft, pudgy fingers. "If you wanted to make a fortune, Sir smith, I would support the miller's proposal to overturn Centuras. They've been trying for a year now to gain access to the Seven Woods, along with the tanners, and don't appreciate your meddling."

"You seemed to have implied several times that you support it too, Jaxon," Cadman said with a smile as he sat down on the bed.

"I do whatever must be done to ensure peace, even at great risk to myself. You heard what happened to Tarl."

Jonathan suddenly felt more alert. "Did they ever find the murderer?"

Jaxon lightly dragged the razor up the length of Jonathan's jaw. "So your apprentice has knowledge of such dealings. I suppose it's a sign of the times. Guild politics are dangerous ground, boy. It used to be very likely that you'd get your throat cut for being the opposition."

"Still likely, apparently," Cadman interjected.

"Only in extreme circumstances, such as the ones we presently find ourselves in." Another long sweep of the razor under Jonathan's neck. "Which is why I would suggest that you all stay *in* for the duration of your stay here rather than going outside for anything but your own business. The millers are holding court in the far end of town. They plan on bringing a motion to the Northern Council within the month to cut the Seven Woods sentries in half and form a standing army. Matters of state, they claim, but they changed their petition on Centuras so that they can thin the wood every twenty years, instead of one hundred, starting with the Harvest Festival."

The barber sighed. "While I do not deny the need for a standing army right now, I am already uneasy about the overturning of Dormín and this overuse of the land. This winter comes, and we believe our unseen Terakhein will save us like last time, even as we wipe their memory from our laws."

He wiped the remaining paste from Jonathan's jaw and rubbed some oil on his hands. "This will take the sting out of it," he said, massaging the oil into Jonathan's skin. "As for Tarl, they never found his murderer, but I could see one of his own guild brothers slitting his throat if need be."

"What else would Tarl have been willing to do?" Cadman asked, his eyes wary.

"To keep the peace? Oh, almost anything, Cadman. As would you, I'm sure. Our paths take us in strange directions, do they not? There my lad, you look good enough to eat," he said, with a tousle of Jonathan's hair. "Your hair could be trimmed, although I've no doubt the women find your locks simply ravishing."

"Leave it." Jonathan didn't like the look in Jaxon's eyes—it wasn't leering, despite the tone of his voice. There was confusion there. Fear, even. Just a flash, and then it was gone.

"As you wish," Jaxon said, packing up his things.

Cadman reached into his sack and pulled out a purse. He counted out five gold coins and placed them in Jaxon's outstretched hand. "This should take care of the shave, and ensure your discretion."

"My dear Cadman, you are generous to a fault." Jaxon gave him back a coin. "Do not expect to see me again for the rest of your stay here, but may Neáhvalar guide your path, wherever it leads. And Jonathan, keep that hair short, my boy. You have one of those faces people will think they've seen before, and quite frankly, you want to be forgotten as soon as possible." He signed a triangle in the air, and then folded his hands. Cadman did the same before Jaxon waddled over the threshold and shut the door after him.

"Does he know what we plan to do?" Jonathan asked.

Cadman shook his head. "I would say that quite a few people know we are here, but only Theo and Lian know *why.* Sienna suspects, of course, since your mother told her of your dreams. But Jaxon…Jaxon is a political animal. Always was. He helped keep Gaelastad out of the Cadarn war, so I assume that is his interest now."

"Then why do you trust him? Given that we've been followed all the way up here—"

"Because he believes in the Terakhein, above all else. Now I must sleep. You take the big bed." Cadman threw himself down on the straw in the corner. "I could sleep on thorns if I had to."

But could you sleep in a world of thorns? Jonathan thought as he threw himself down on the bed. It was feather-filled, and Jonathan immediately fell asleep as he sank down into that blessed softness.

—⟡⟡⟡—

Sleep eluded Cadman, no matter how much he bid it not to. There was so much at stake and so little the boy knew. *He'll eventually find out if we follow this path.* The thought made a small shudder run through his body—whether out of anticipation or fear, Cadman couldn't say. He was already on high alert when Jeremy died from the snakebite last year. He knew it wouldn't be long before they would have to leave Breithan, but oh, to leave for *this?* No, not what the smith had planned at all.

He let an hour pass, just to be sure Jonathan was asleep, and then slipped out the door. He slid the hood over his head so that most of his face was shielded—just another Iron Clad having a night at the Three Sisters' Inn. It wasn't long before he was standing outside the stables. One deep breath before he opened the door and walked in.

Bryn was already there, flames cascading down his massive legs. Cadman came forward and uncovered his head while he knelt before the Ogoni. "My lord."

"There is no need for that, master smith," many voices assured him. "Long has your house been loyal to my kind, and served the holy fire. Now, what would you have me do?"

Cadman slowly stood up, but kept his head bent low. "I would still ask that Jonathan be allowed to return to Breithan. It is too early to go on the longer journey, if one be necessary. I will find the girl, my lord." It was a slim promise, he knew.

"You cannot protect him forever, Cadman. We could not save Jeremy, nor Jenna. And Trapher suspects—"

"What he suspects and what he knows are two different things, and the tides are turning more quickly than anticipated. The boy isn't ready, and see how much resistance we have encountered just on our travels to Duraeston."

Bryn stood silently in thought, while Cadman held his

breath, barely hoping. The silver-glass eyes pulsated a soft glow. The Ogoni knew things, knew how to find him a few years ago, when he first awoke. Knew that the hunt was beginning. He would know now what to do. Cadman still couldn't see where the path led, except to impossible ends.

"Phlegon will decide the matter, when he comes." Bryn's musical voice interrupted his thought. "But more than what he is to you, Cadman, he is the dreamer who can see the Terakhein. For now, that is what matters most. Without the girl, our plight is lost, and even your hope will fail, in the end."

Cadman let out a long sigh. The Elementarí spoke truth, but sometimes the truth is not what we want to hear. He bowed low once more before the Ogoni, who had reduced himself to a mere shimmer. "Thank you, my lord, for even considering it."

—∗—◉⟩◉—∗—

"Where were they last? Did they say what it was?" A woman's voice woke Jonathan. He partially opened his eyes. Two people, cloaked and hooded, were standing in a corner talking to Cadman. Jonathan tried to get up, but his legs felt frozen in place. The world began to tilt again as a ring of light enveloped the figures. Just a dream after all. He shut his eyes again and slept.

—∗—◉⟩◉—∗—

He smelled sugar and apples. Hot cider.

"Morning." Cadman held a steaming cup under Jonathan's nose. He had already changed into a fresh tunic, scarred arms hidden well under long sleeves, and his salt and peppered hair was once more pulled back into its customary ponytail.

Jonathan rubbed his eyes and gladly took the hot cider. "What time is it?"

"Nearly noon. Bryn found me in one of the stables— almost made me piss myself again. Said that Phlegon will be here sometime, but refused to say when." He leaned forward, crossing one leg over the over. "Meanwhile, we will bide our time at the Inn. New guildsmen are here from Cadarn, asking for the Northern Council's permission to establish trade. Jaxon doesn't trust them, but he refused to say any more on it, only to watch what we do."

A sudden image of the cloaked figures from his dream. Or was it real? "Were there people in our room last night?"

"You were awake?" Cadman asked sharply.

"I tried to get up and speak to you. Only..." He shifted his legs and sat up, just to be sure he could. "I felt frozen to the bone."

"Then don't go challenging the most powerful of Elementarí," Cadman cautioned him. "Morgan warned me that you might feel the effects of your encounter with Ventosus for a while yet. No doubt our flight yesterday did nothing to help you either. But I'll try not to act as your wet nurse so long as you don't go headlong into any fight that presents itself to you."

Cadman stood up and went over to the washbasin. "The cloaked figure you saw last night was one of my Iron Clad brothers. Members from our sister-guild in Íarchol arrived here in secret two days ago, asking for help. Refugees from the northern part of Lailethas are fleeing in droves to Íarchol now. Whether they're running from Nemarons or Ophidians remains unclear, for the few who make it out of their villages alive are already half starved and almost mad with grief."

"And the other?"

"Morgan. She wanted to know about the attack, at least as much as I could tell her, which was precious little."

"Did she say where she was going?"

"I'm assuming to find her brothers." The smith sighed in frustration. "I am hoping we will meet Phlegon today, and he will provide answers. Meanwhile, I have made inquiries about sending an escort with you back to Breithan. Or I may get Lian, Alec, Riok, and Balfour to come get you."

"They'd be more a hindrance than a help. And who could help me get back home now? The Ruaden is bleeding to death, and beasts from the Wild Lands have crossed the river. Don't tell me that screaming monster was just a mountain cat from the northern caves. And it wasn't a throck either. What escort can protect me from that, if Peran and Madron were injured?"

Cadman's face darkened with a frown. "But you are no safer here—"

"I could join the sentries," Jonathan suggested, the desire to see even the outskirts of the forest so keen that it hurt his heart. "If they need more men to protect Seven Woods, perhaps the priests would let me—"

"With Centuras on the verge of being overturned? They will be sending away sentries, not inviting them into the Order."

"Then let me go with you to find the Terakhein."

"No, your place is in the southwest, away from Ophidians and guilds and winter. I had already spoken with your father and Lian about gathering the folks of Breithan and Klinneret to head toward the far south, close to the sea cliffs. This winter will soon bring storms of ice and snow that will not melt, and there are little ones to think about. Cadman sighed. "But first, let us go break our fast now. It's better to discuss such matters on a full stomach."

He strode out of the room.

Jonathan slowly dressed, the resolution to stay taking firmer shape inside his mind. The thought of being a sentry filled his heart with unspeakable hope. If Cadman wouldn't let him help find the Terakhein girl, at least he could defend her forest. Outside the room, Jonathan found Cadman slumped against the hall wall, waiting, and he suddenly felt a strange misgiving. How could one man go up against an army of earth and sky and expect to live? Didn't Cadman see the hopelessness of going into the wilderness alone?

He followed Cadman down to the hall. Molly was running around the tables, refilling people's mugs and making sure everyone's plate was piled high with food. "It's about time you were awake," she said, with the familiar tousle of Jonathan's hair. He would get tired of this ritual soon. "You clean up real good, though."

Lunch consisted of piles of roast beef and cabbage, with heavily peppered potatoes. Jonathan devoured his like it was his last meal on earth. "Here, take mine too," Cadman piled his potatoes onto Jonathan's plate. "You've not eaten enough in quite a while."

Aye, and it looks like I'll not be eating in the future, either. So why get me used to a full belly? After lunch, they played a few rounds of wolf and rabbit with some traveling guildsmen from the south. It was mostly a children's game that the men made more interesting with bets. Cadman's wolf ate, or at least mauled, all of Jonathan's rabbits. Jonathan finally decided to play with a ten-year-old boy in order to better his chances. But he became so tired that he couldn't concentrate anymore on the small stone pieces, and soon enough, he was beaten again.

"I'm just going to lie down for a moment." He saw Cadman's brows knitting together but turned before the smith could say anything and made his way back to his room, throwing himself down on the bed.

He woke up to the smith shaking him. "Come on."

"What time is it?"

"Past midnight. You slept clear through dinner." He waited as Jonathan achingly sat up and laced his boots. He had slept in his clothes. As Jonathan tied the final knot, he caught a shimmer in the air right in front of him.

"Bryn," Jonathan said softly.

"You have come through much danger, I hear." The Ogoni's voice belied a strange weariness; he had been walking on the surface of the world without feeding. *Just how long could Bryn deny his hunger?* Jonathan still wanted to know just what, exactly, the Ogoni fed on.

"Are the Brothers Morvoren safe?" he asked, ignoring the internal answer to his first question in order that he might satisfy the second. Nothing could shake the memory of the throck sinking its teeth into Peran's neck.

Bryn hissed, and the glimmer grew brighter. "We're still searching for them. Come, the night grows on, and I would not have you make your way back in the dark morning hours, when evil often walks."

Did that include the Ogoni himself? Jonathan felt an uneasy certainty that the fire spider had hissed not in answer to his spoken question, but to his unvoiced suspicion.

"Wrap your scarf around your face," Cadman warned, doing the same. Wordless, they followed Bryn's slight outline out their room door. The Ogoni's shimmer was barely visible; a trick of the light, nothing more. There were few people left in the main room, huddled around a table, talking quietly. Out-of-town guild members, most likely.

"Hail, stranger!" The shout came from a grizzled man wearing a maroon cloak and gold badge, his thick boots propped up on a table. "Where are you going this time of night? Join us for another pint."

"Keep your head down and follow Bryn," Cadman said in a low voice. Then he slurred, "I need a good piss in the wind and cold air to clear this addled brain!"

"He's drunk enough as is." A woman elbowed the grizzly in the ribs. "Let them be."

The moon was full high in the sky. Jonathan glanced around. A couple of men stood outside the brothel across the street, laughing and falling into each other's arms like they were lovers. *Darkness would be more a shield to us right now,* he thought.

"I don't like this, Bryn," Cadman said as they plodded through the snow-covered road. "Already people have noted our leaving, and will wonder at our return, if it's not soon enough."

The glimmer in front of them gave no answer as they walked past the stables and storehouses. The three sisters had picked a fine place for their inn, just at the edge of town where it was a welcome sight to a traveler coming from a long journey in the south of Gaelastad. But there was little else here. The Ogoni led them to one of the larger stables at the very end of the row. This one held thirty horses at least, Jonathan saw as low blue flames now cascaded down Bryn's legs, illuminating the cavernous length of the stable. They walked towards the back, where the bags of feed were stored. Jonathan breathed in the familiar smell of horses, hay, and manure. *No scent of honeysuckle here, and the horses are calm.* The Ogoni's blue flames did not appear to hold any heat, for no spark caught hold of the surrounding hay.

A horse whinnied, followed closely by another. It was Hammer and Tongs, both stamping the ground once in salutation. Cadman strode forward, a real smile now breaking over his face as he stroked their manes.

"They galloped all the way to Duraeston and found me," a man said, coming out of the shadows. He was tall, like Cadman and himself, except with a barrel-sized chest, and he had thick black hair and a full beard to match.

Cadman embraced him and brought him over to Jonathan. "This is Breoc, one of the best jacks of all trades I know, and a great guide through any wilderness."

Breoc took Jonathan's hand in a firm grip, and embraced him in Duraeston fashion, one hand clasped in friendship, the other slapping him on the back. "It is good that you both survived your adventure, although I can see why they ran to a kinder master such as me. I've a good hand with beasts." He grinned. "Lasses too."

"I won't contest the second, but with the animals you're a cheat. I warrant Hammer and Tongs remembered all the sugar you fed them last time," Cadman said dryly. "Gave them a stomachache, from what I recall. Still, that's better than dying in the jaws of a throck..."

Like Peran might have, Jonathan thought. He could not look Morgan in the eye ever again if Moran and Peran were lost protecting him.

"Aye, I'll be sure to slit its throat if I have the fortune to meet it." Breoc grinned. "I've not had the chance to go hunting for a nasty beast in a long while. My blade's getting dull."

"Not this one, Bree. We are about to meet an Element-arí," Cadman said, as he peered around in the darkness. "Phlegon, are you here?"

"I am," said a deep, sonorous voice from the back of the stable. It was more powerful than Madron's or Bryn's, like it belonged to something ancient, from the beginning of time itself. Yet none of the horses showed signs of distress.

The Ogoni slowly crept out of the darkness. Phlegon's many eyes were each the size of a man's head and ruby red, with a brilliant fire burning inside them. It was like looking into the center of the earth itself. Four times the size of Bryn, the massive spider took up the entire width of the barn, with low blue flames cascading down each of his massive silvery legs.

"Come closer, boy," Phlegon commanded. "But not too close, for I am weakened in this state unless I feed."

Jonathan stepped forward a few paces so that he stood directly in front of the Ogoni, which now had its silver fangs extended. Cadman started to come to his side, but Phlegon said, "Stay back, master smith. I can hold my hunger long enough for a dream, but no longer than that. Now, boy, look into my eyes. Where do you walk when the night has come upon you, and your heart is heavy with sleep?"

Jonathan gazed into the many eyes of the Ogoni and fell not into the darkness, but into the sun. A blinding white light surrounded him until he was tumbling through the sky and then into the very center of the earth where there existed only fire, and throughout it, legs upon legs and giant, round bodies—the Ogoni sleeping in their den. Then a rent appeared within the fire, and through it, Jonathan saw a horizon of dark clouds and steep mountains. Perhaps the Akrates? He walked through the rent into a new land. He turned around. Phlegon was behind him.

Let yourself walk the path.

He began following a stone road wide enough for an army. It wound up a hill populated with forests of pine and other evergreens, then another, ascending what must be the foothills of a mountain range. The air grew thin and cold the higher he climbed. Finally the road widened into a plateau, and there he stopped and took a deep breath. A great city lay before him, with silver and white towers high enough to block out the sun. Amid the spires and elaborate turrets, Jonathan could see numerous soldiers moving among the walkways. Was he in Cadarn or Nemaron? No houses were scattered among the fortresses, only lesser towers of gray that still rivaled any castle. The townspeople must live in those, unless they were housed in the three black obelisks that formed a half circle in the center of the capital.

Suddenly, the corners of the city folded in and the entire landscape began to crumple. Great citadels toppled into each other and were split asunder from the sheer force of the quaking ground, thundering as they fell. A massive black cloud of dust and mortar rose and spread out like a mushroom. *I can't breathe,* Jonathan thought as he tumbled forward into the debris. He clawed at the ground that was slanting upright like a wall, gasping for air as he tried to hold on.

Phlegon! he cried. A bridge of fire suddenly stretched over the collapsing city from one end to the other. Phlegon's voice boomed over the thunderous din. "Run."

Jonathan hesitated, wondering how he would traverse the flames and not be burned, but it was better than the pit

waiting for him. Flames licked the sides of the bridge, singe-
ing his clothes as he ran over it and stepped off into a new
terrain. He was at the edge of a forest. It wasn't the Fáliquerci, he was certain of that, for these trees were older
than those, twisted in trunk and branch. Jonathan forgot his
concerns as he looked out onto the meadow. There, surrounded by a pack of wolves, was his sister.

He turned to Phlegon to ask what they should do, but
the Ogoni was no longer there.

Neáhvalar take back his fire and wind, he cursed and
crouched down amid the tall grass that bordered the wood.
Dream or real world, it mattered not. Jenna was within a
hundred yards' reach. A pack of about twenty wolves circled
her, sniffing and uttering low growls. His sister seemed not
to notice them as she stared at the setting sun, one hand
shading her eyes from the glare. Beside her stood the largest
of the pack. As tall as Hammer and thickly muscled, its coat
was black as midnight. Beautiful, terrifying, majestic. Jenna's
wolf. The creature directed its gaze in Jonathan's direction,
as if it sensed a disturbance in the wood.

"Jenna!" He was a quarter way across the meadow
before she turned. Jonathan saw not his sister but a girl with
a heart-shaped face, a surprised look of recognition in her
eyes.

The shock of it stopped him cold. It was the Terakheini
girl from his dreams. She stood there, as motionless as he.
Only the wolves kept circling in unbroken speed. But where
was the Black? A sense of terror filled his heart upon realizing the wolf had left her side, and that he was now visible
and unprotected in the middle of the meadow. Suddenly the
Black broke from the circle of wolves and bounded towards
him. *It's just a dream.*

"Stay there!" Jonathan yelled to the Terakheini as he
whipped out his dagger. He only had to reach her, find out
where she was hiding. So swiftly did the wolf run that within a moment it was already within a hundred feet of him,

growling words Jonathan didn't understand. *It can't be speaking. Wolves don't talk.* He tried to throw the dagger, but his arm was paralyzed, even though every muscle was tensed, ready for battle.

Ictuneri heracth norifram.

The wolf stood only five feet away now, its eyes smoldering like burnt rubies. Just like Phlegon's eyes.

I can kill in the shadows of your mind; no dream can stop me. I am the One who froze you to the ground, for I outrun any man. Nor upon waking will you wake.

Then Jonathan understood. It could vision walk, just like the great Ogoni. Between waking and dreaming, the world of thorns trumped all.

Ictuneri Truculen! It growled and sprang.

Terah chi thero Hecthrax! The Terakheini was suddenly in front of Jonathan, arms thrown up and wide. *Nemari alin clath!*

The Black dropped to the ground, snarling in pain. The girl sprinted to where it lay. *Nemari Hecthrax!*

Immediately the wolf winced again as if struck and bounded back to its pack, which still circled the empty area where the girl had stood. She turned around again, her eyes wide and sad as she smiled at Jonathan. She was older, he suddenly realized, perhaps ten. "I'm Samara," she said, turning her little heart-shaped face up at his as she took his hand.

Immediately Jonathan felt all his limbs unloosed from the power of the Black. The wind howled and whipped against them in its fury. Large branches broke off and spun high in to the air. He didn't have much time. "Where is this place?" He bent down so she could hear. "How can we find you?"

She pulled him closer as she whispered, "Not yet. Find Kei and Kayna first."

"Who? Wait!" The wind surged in between them, picking Jonathan up off his feet and blowing him back into the forest. He slammed into a tree and then fell down onto his face. He slowly rolled over, but when he tried to get up, a sharp pain in his neck and ribs paralyzed him.

"Samara!" There was no answer.

Instead, he heard the rustling of leaves, and there appeared two faces peering over him—a boy and a girl, older than Samara but a few years younger than himself, with shocking red hair that stuck out wildly from both of their heads.

"Help me, please," Jonathan asked.

The boy whispered something to the girl, which made her laugh, and they began to sing. It was a beautiful, sad song that Jonathan didn't understand, but his pain subsided, replaced with warmth that gently washed over him. They kept singing until he finally closed his eyes. He was almost asleep when he felt a tickle in his ear.

"Find us." It was the girl. "We live in the valley where the waters are parted by Morwenna's voice." He heard her laugh again, as if she found him a very funny creature.

Jonathan opened his eyes and found that he was back in the stable, looking at Phlegon. "Where did you go?" he whispered, backing up. "The wolf can walk through dreams, just like you!"

"What wolf is this?" Cadman frowned.

"One that does not dream-walk unless his master Chalom bids him to," the great Ogoni said. "That sibling slips ever deeper into fever. Therefore Truculen would be his master now, none the kinder, but more vigilant than Chalom ever was."

"Why did you leave me there alone, knowing what he was?" Jonathan tried to control the shaking in his voice. Just how many of these Elementarí could find him, and possibly kill him in his dreams?

"The wolf was not searching for you, and only as a shadow in his mind he saw you. But my appetite grows, and I would have devoured the both of you if I'd stayed. Even now my patience wears thin. Tell us what you saw."

It felt like the walls of the stable had suddenly constricted as the flames dissipated and the Ogoni loomed in front of them, a giant creature ready to feast on its prey. Jonathan instinctively stepped back to where Breoc and Cadman stood, and quickly relayed the entire dream to the rest. *And pray believe everything I tell you,* he thought.

When he was done, Phlegon stayed silent, and for a moment Jonathan thought perhaps the Ogoni doubted his vision. Then the spider's eyes flickered scarlet. "Samara's parents were of the house closely tied to the Agerathum, the air spirits. Even so, none were so great as her mother and father, who led the first charge against Ventosus when he had set winter against the land years ago. But we must find the other two children first, for they are in the greater danger now. The brother and sister Samara spoke of are twins. Their father belonged to a house loved by the Ogoni, their mother was of those most closely tied to the Ophidians. Truculen and Adamara will hunt for whichever sibling has the power of the earth, for that Terakheini will also have the power of healing."

"They'll take the twin to wake Chalom from his fever," Cadman said softly.

"Then the power of the Three will be restored." Breoc bowed his head.

"Three together, Three as one," the Ogoni chanted.

"They will bury men alive again," Cadman said, laughing bitterly. "What spirits of Neáhvalar are you all to make the earth a coffin for us?"

"Stay your wrath, master smith," Phlegon's voice echoed, crimson eyes pulsing. "We are Elementarí, and it is not for you to judge our lust for sustenance; Neáhvalar has only given that authority to the Terakhein. Now, where is this valley that will lead us to the twins?"

"It's a very general description," Breoc said at last, shaking off whatever thoughts he had been lost in. "Íarchol's

Animur River divides into two rivers—one leading north, one leading south—once it hits the Sulath Valley. The Valley of Eyes, they call it."

"Then that is where you shall go." Phlegon extended on long leg towards Jonathan. "We will send word to your parents that you and Cadman are still needed for your services."

"My lord, I wish for Jonathan to return to Breithan," Cadman said. "His parents are old, and his father has yet to recover from an illness."

Jonathan balked. "As far as I can recall, Cadman, the Terakhein talk only to me." Finding the Terakhein would mean being appointed to the Order, and then he could hire more help with the farm, and his father would finally get better.

"The boy speaks true, Cadman," Phlegon said, extending yet another leg towards Jonathan. The Ogoni was slowly getting ready to pounce, but still Jonathan couldn't back away; its ancient eyes were just as hypnotizing as Hecthrax's. "A direction to take is all the twins gave you, nothing more. The vision might change as you travel, as visions often do, you will see. But leave now before I forget my place and take my fill."

"Run!" Bryn's voice commanded.

Cadman grabbed Jonathan's arm and jerked him forward. He pumped his legs hard into a run, despite the chill that was beginning take them.

"Don't look back!" Breoc yelled as they finally cleared the door.

Cadman stopped them once outside. "It will not do to go running willy nilly down the street; the jailers will come for us quick. The Ogoni will not pursue us outside, I think."

"What's to stop them?" Jonathan panted.

"Nothing, should they choose to follow suit like the Three and feed themselves on those who have begun to devour their goods," the smith said, urging them to walk on. "But Phlegon will hold on, as will Bryn, since they have come here to aid us, and partly because they fear what Neáhvalar might do, perhaps, should the Elementarí go to war. However, we must make plans to leave soon. I will only let you come as far as Íarchol, Jonathan, and only if I have your word to go back to Breithan when I send you."

"Aye, whatever you say," he promised. *But we'll see yet how matters play out on this journey.* The smith was obviously displeased with the Ogoni's decision to encourage him to find the twins. The motivation behind Cadman's disapproval—whether it was out of overprotection or fear that he would fail—Jonathan couldn't as yet decipher. There were enough problems to turn over in his mind, enough riddles to answer.

At least the inn was quiet; no one seemed to pay attention to them as they entered, and the main hall was dark except for the soft glow from a wall torch. Jonathan didn't even bother undressing as he crawled into bed, hoping that true sleep would come, without dreams. Cadman blew out the candle, and Jonathan lay there, thankful for the complete darkness.

"You know...I will keep them safe," Cadman said quietly

Jonathan was confused by the smith's almost tender tone. "Who? The Terakhein?"

"No, your parents. No matter what you and I have to do, others in Breithan are watching out for them."

"You think they're in danger?" Hadn't they been leading the Ophidians and enemy eyes away from his village? The smith didn't answer right away. "Cadman?"

"There is more power in Breithan to defend it than you know," the smith said softly. "But it will take everything in my power to protect *you.* I swore an oath to them as your godfather on the day you were born." He sighed and rolled over, as if not expecting a response.

Jonathan didn't answer. He had already lost two siblings to the Elementarí, and here they were, seeking out the very prize the Ophidians wanted. *What an oath to try to keep,* Jonathan thought, as fear bit his heart. *Safety in a world of thorns.*

--❀--◉--◉--❀--

He was running though a meadow thick with blue-green grasses that waved in the wind like the sea. He was looking for someone, although he could not say who, or where he would find them, but soon enough he realized it was no longer grass he was treading on, but the backs of wolves. Wolves upon wolves that covered the land completely, so that Jonathan's feet didn't touch the ground. He kept running, not looking down until, suddenly, he stepped on one that howled. It was black as midnight, with red eyes that burned like rubies...

"Phlegon!" Jonathan sat up, panting. A vision of the Ogoni, waiting for him in the stables—he couldn't shake the feeling that the fire spirit had one last thing to say to him, and there were still too many unanswered questions. Cadman was snoring loudly; *like a pig in heat,* Jonathan thought, wondering how the smith didn't wake up the entire inn. He doubted Cadman would let him approach the Ogoni again, and so with great care he crept out of bed and opened the door. The smith stirred slightly, but did not wake. Once in the main room, he took note of its occupants. Only a few traders sat at the tables, guzzling the last of their ale; two had giggling women on their laps. Grizzly was wrapped in his maroon cloak, slumped in a chair in the corner, passed out. Jonathan had almost made it to the door when a slurred voice yelled out, "Now wherrres' you goin' this late at night, friend?" Jonathan turned to see the man with one eye open, looking suspiciously at him. *This won't do; he'll remember.* And Jonathan stupidly had not wrapped a scarf around his face, a striking face that few forgot once they saw it. "I gotta get me a woman now; my friends just want to sleep. Heard there was a place down the road for such late playin'" he stammered, hoping that he sounded more drunk than nervous.

The grizzled man nodded and waved him on. "Get yer money's worth," he cautioned as Jonathan closed the door behind him.

Clouds had swallowed up the moon, promising more snow. Jonathan slowly made his way in the darkness. A few men stood slumped against a shop, heads down and waiting, perhaps, for a game to begin in the tavern down the street. Jonathan watched to see if anyone was following him, but the bowed heads stayed down. He finally made it to the stable and opened the door.

Phlegon was sitting near the entrance, silver fangs extended, each the size of a dagger. "Well met on a moonless night, boy."

Jonathan knew he couldn't risk being seen standing outside the stable, but how to risk coming closer? "You called me, and I came." He bowed low, hoping this sign of deference would stay whatever lust or anger the Ogoni was feeling as he slowly stepped over the threshold.

"Shut the door; we must not risk being seen, and I am too weak to reduce myself into a shimmer," Phlegon's voice croaked. Jonathan reluctantly did as the Ogoni requested. Now they were shut in, the two of them. Low blue flames that dripped down the Ogoni's legs illuminated the barn with a ghost-like hue. "Good. Now listen. Greater I am than the Three, but not the One who dwells in the Akrates. I am no match for Ventosus, even as Morgan could not defeat him, so would I lose if I went into battle. Ah, yessss... Morgan." The Ogoni's eyes pulsed vermillion. "You hunger for her—"

"No, my lord! At least not in the same way the Elementarí hunger, it is..." Now was not the time to ask him about his feelings for the Delphini. He tried to keep his mind blank lest Phlegon see images of his arms wrapped around her, his lips on hers. "It is..." Certainly not love. What was it?

"No matter," Phlegon rumbled. "She searches for her

brothers as she did her sister so long ago. Pray they are found. Their mother Morwenna will only stay in the abyss for so long. Awake, our appetite grows, unsatiated, and only the Terakhein can put us back into a sleep that lets us forget, and instead nourish the earth."

The Ogoni's eyes dimmed. "It was I who saw Ventosus first wake twenty-five years ago, and yet I stayed in the belly of fire deep in the heart of the world, for I thought he sensed a disturbance he wished to warn the Terakhein about. Then I felt the Three arise from their slumber, and I could no longer see them, nor could I find Ventosus. The Terakhein were still strong in power then and went to the Akrates Mountains and hemmed Ventosus in, putting him back to sleep. The winter was stayed, but I still do not know how Ventosus was first awakened, nor do I understand his probable alliance with the Nemarons. You saw their capital city in your vision for a reason. Something has awoken him and the Three once more. Find the answer, for there is treachery afoot."

"Do you think Samara is hiding there—in Nemaron?" Jonathan asked, now very afraid for her.

"Perhaps. The Terakheini children have not reached out to me, despite all my searching, and I cannot see within their dreams. You, on the other hand, seem to be connected to not just one, but three of them."

"Ophidians too," Jonathan murmured.

Phlegon jerked one of his enormous legs in surprise. "What is this?"

Jonathan quickly related the dreams concerning the Ophidian woman. "Why would she want to help me, when in my other dreams she's killing Samara?"

"Why indeed…" the Ogoni pondered the question. "Take heed to what she shows you nonetheless. I do not understand…"

"But you guess—something."

"Child, my guesses could cost you your life." The spider

crept forward. "Know this, you have already lost much, more than you know. But what you have lost will be found again. Be ready to seize truth no matter which face presents it."

Jonathan immediately thought of Jeremy and Jenna. But no, they were buried in the ground. "What kind of promise is that, my lord?"

"One that will come to pass, for good or ill."

Suddenly, voices just outside the stable—a group of five men or more, talking. How had they not noticed before now?

"You'd better watch your step, Tobin. Someone came around asking about Tarl's killin' today."

"Aye, why you didn't slit that cur's throat I'll never know. Now we've got to keep an extra eye out."

"What fer?" a higher voice chimed in. "Plenty asked about the murder at first, it being discovered in the alley right outside Three Sisters. Sloppy work, that. Leave well enough alone, and be done with it. Things'n place now, knowing anything more ain't going to stop what's been done."

"But still," the first man wheezed, "keep an eye out for that one—didn't see what guild he was from, but he had scars running all up his forearms. Shouldn't be hard to find with enough prying."

"Don't you worry about that, love, I'll get right on it." The last voice was distinctive, low and smooth. A chill ran up Jonathan's arms. He turned to see what Phlegon thought, but the Ogoni had retreated into the inky blackness of the stable, and Jonathan wasn't about to venture after him alone and without a light.

Just then the stable door cracked open. Jonathan pressed himself up against the wall; there was nothing to hide behind here. One of the men held aloft a lantern as he stepped inside. "Could 'ave sworn I heard somethin'."

"Well, hurry up then, but we're not waiting around. My

missus will be wondering what I'm doin' out of bed."

Jonathan heard the other men take their leave. A young man, slim and red haired, perhaps thirty-five years or less, stepped further in. He hadn't seen Jonathan, who had wedged himself as far into the corner as possible. Not yet.

Clang. The sound of a bucket being knocked over in the back of the stables, and then rustling.

"Now who's there? Show yourself; I ain't going to hurt you." It was a dog-faced lie, of course, for Jonathan could see the sharp knife the man had pulled out and now held in his left hand. Jonathan reached down for his own dagger and felt nothing. *Serves you right for half sleepwalking your way here,* he thought. It would be a matter of speed—the stable door was still cracked open, and the man was cautiously walking midway down the stable now. Jonathan sidled along the wall towards the door when he accidentally stepped on something that let out a *crack.*

The light swung around as the man smiled. "Well, now, it's late for you to be out and eavesdroppin' on talk not meant for young ears. Don't move or I'll send this dagger flying at you, boy, and my friends are just outside, don't you worry." The accent was thick on the *o's*—not from any country this side of the Wild Lands. Cadarn?

"I didn't hear anything. Now let me go, for my father knows I've come to check on our horses," Jonathan lied, hoping it would be enough. "Hammer hurt his foot today."

"Not at this hour, lad," the man laughed. "Not—" He had come close enough that the light swung full on Jonathan's face. "Wait. Not *you.* Oh no, this cannot be. Tobin!" he shouted. "Tobin!"

A massive flaming body rose up behind the man as the silver fangs pierced his neck. Before Jonathan could even cry out, Phlegon was on top of the red-haired man, feeding, even though he was still alive and screaming.

"Phlegon, stop!" Jonathan begged.

"I must feed; he must not live and tell the others he has

seen you. He knows more than you understand, boy. Go!" With that, the Ogoni went back to feasting on its prey, fangs piercing the man's convulsing body.

Jonathan took off running, out the stable door and down the street, praying to Neáhvalar he wouldn't meet any other members of that party, not daring to look around and check, so terrifying was the image burned into his memory.

Once inside the Three Sisters, he breezed through the commons area. "That was mighty quick!" The grizzly called out, laughing. Jonathan only saw a blur of maroon and gold as he swept past, up the stairs and to his room. He went over to the smith and shook him.

"Eh, what's this?" The smith sat up, rubbing his eyes. "Wait, where have you been?" he demanded, once he had noticed Jonathan's cloak.

"Phlegon called me." *Called you? No, you only sensed it. The Elementarí cannot summon you at will. That is why they stalk you in the forest and at night.* "I mean I sensed he still needed to tell me something. Yet I heard and saw more tonight that I wanted." With that he launched into the events that had sent him running to his room, like a child. *There are some things you simply run from, just like the widow warned.*

Cadman's face grew more worried as he talked, and by the time Jonathan was done, he had already dressed. "That was careless of you to go without waking me—everything could have been discovered from that one mistake. Do you understand? *Everything.* No, of course you don't," Cadman growled. "I told you not to go headlong, or headless, apparently, into situations you have no place in."

Jonathan had never seen the smith so angry. "So where are *you* going at this hour?"

"That is none of your concern—I had hoped to wait a day or two and let us rest, but I have been careless as well, it seems. We must leave in the morning, and to that end, I need to make arrangements. Pray take off your cloak; you'll not be coming too."

"It was strange, what he said, don't you think?" Jonathan couldn't help but ask. *This cannot be.* "His accent proved he wasn't from around here—I thought Cadarn maybe?"

"Eh, what's that?" Cadman seemed not to be listening. "I warrant he thought you safe in Breithan still, is my guess. Think no more on this. You are already wounded and need to sleep. A longer journey awaits us within a few hours." Without another word, the smith blustered out.

Jonathan couldn't decide what had the smith more spooked: the fact that the Ogoni had fed on the man so brutally, what he had said to Jonathan just prior to his death, or what the group had discussed about Tarl's murder. In any case, Cadman seemed...besides very angry, actually *scared* for once, and that gave him no great sense of comfort. If they knew Jonathan by sight, did they know where he was from, how his father was sick and not strong enough to defend his house as well? *Cadman promised he had taken care of their protection. Yet the man recognized me by sight, and they didn't know Cadman by description.* More perplexing still was how they were going to get out of Duraeston while escaping the notice of whoever was watching for them. A hundred different scenarios flashed through Jonathan's head, threatening to steal what little rest could still be snatched from the night, but it had been a hard two days' ride, and finally sleep quieted all thoughts.

—◦◉◖◉◦—

"Well, now, someone's still looking a bit peaked," Molly said as he came down the stairs the next morning. The commons area was full of customers, some of whom Jonathan had seen last night, except for the grizzled man in maroon, markedly absent. *Most likely sleeping in his own vomit,* Jonathan thought, given how drunk he'd appeared last night. Cadman was already at the table, gulping down a huge mug of yaré.

"That looks tasty," Jonathan smirked. It was the only tea

that looked just like piss, and many claimed it tasted like it too. But if you had a long night of drinking and needed to work the next day, it was what you drank. The smith looked like he sorely needed it. Jonathan hadn't heard him come back last night. "You'll both be needing a warm drink, if you hope to make it through the day," Molly said as she filled their mugs and shouted to the kitchen, "Henrietta, one more plate of ham and eggs."

Jonathan had yet to meet the infamous cook, and remarked upon it.

"She stays in the kitchen usually. I should have had *her* keep an eye out for you, apparently," Cadman chided. "But they'll make your day about as comfortable as a summer picnic if you let them. Isn't that right, Molly?" he added as she returned with a plate.

"Now, don't you go on flattering me like this, Cadman." She laid Jonathan's food in front of him and then promptly deposited herself on Cadman's lap. "You always promise roses and sunshine, then take off in the next moment. When are you going to settle down and let a wife take care of you?"

He grunted at the unexpected weight and the ruffles from her dress that almost smothered him. "Why…Molly," he gasped, "it's the absences from here…that make…my heart grow fonder. How about…some more of those…little cakes."

"It'll take more than just a few cakes to put some meat on you both," she smirked before hoisting herself off the smith's lap and swishing back into the kitchen.

"Don't you just have all the women after you," Breoc said as he came up to their table.

"I can't feel my legs."

"Serves you right, pulling heart strings like that." Seeing Breoc's mock grin, it suddenly struck Jonathan how much he resembled Theo. Somewhat similar in girth, but even more so in the eyes, the same shape and slate gray. The trader leaned in. "Everything is ready; it took some doing, but I found a caravan going to Cúrmhangon, which is close enough to where we want to be." He pointed at Jonathan. "Keep your midnight wanderings to a minimum please, I would like to actually sleep at night instead of being your nanny."

That meant Breoc was coming with them to Íarchol. "Sounds more like a guard than a nanny." A pause as neither man had any retort to that. "Is it really so bad as that? At least tell me you were able to find out something about the men I overheard talking last night." Jonathan wished he had glimpsed faces, or heard more names that just Tobin's.

"That has not been as easy to discover," Cadman said. "No body was found in the stable this morning, and I've not heard of anyone looking for a missing friend. At least, not yet."

"Maybe they came back to the stable and took...what was left?" It suddenly occurred to Jonathan that Phlegon might not have left anything to discover.

"Nay, lad, I've had people keeping an eye on the stable all night, and there was nary a visitor for the rest of the night unless they tunneled in," Breoc said. "No, our Ogoni feasted last night on a tasty morsel. Be thankful it wasn't you."

"We'll hear yet of this Tobin if he keeps making inquiries about me, especially now that his friend is gone," Cadman added. "Keep a sharp eye out on this journey, for who knows what we will find. Breoc, you packed two good swords for us?"

The trader nodded. "Then it really is that bad," Jonathan said.

"Let's just say we'll be practicing our swordplay once again as we travel," Cadman replied.

CHAPTER 8
THE LADY IN GRAY

Within the hour, Jonathan and Cadman met up with sixty or so people. Some on horseback while others loaded down their horses with sacks and saddlebags, and still others drove wagons. It would take a week to reach Cúrmhangon with this miserably slow caravan, but it was better than attempting the road without any escort.

"I told them we sometimes trade with Íarchin nomads who live in the valley," Breoc said. "They will be expecting us to leave them once we cross the border."

The roar of the Animar River grew quiet the farther they ventured north. The landscape was changing, too: the beginning of a long craggy outcrop on their left signaled they were at the end of the outskirts of Duraeston. To their right, the ground unevenly sloped as the brown tufts of grass gave way to rocks. In the distance loomed blue-gray mountains, massive and dark amidst the gray sky, their snow-capped peaks hidden by thunderous clouds.

They traveled far that first day and night to get ahead of the weather. It wasn't until they set up camp late into the second night that most gathered around the big fire in the center of camp, and Jonathan could see some of his companions. The guild members grouped themselves together in small bands, talking quietly—but Jonathan could sense there was news afoot. What had Jaxon heard but not told them? One could almost see two camps forming, with the goldsmiths, iron workers, and masons on one side of the fire, and a various assortment of artisans on the other. Two men in maroon cloaks with the yellow badges—Cadman had said they were drapers—stood slightly to the side, observing everyone. It occurred to Jonathan that the grizzly who had camped out in the main room last night was wearing the same garb. Over to the left, almost outside the warm reach of the fire, five hooded women in gray cloaks banded together in a tight circle. One looked over in their direction, and Jonathan was startled to see how gaunt her young face was. She would have been lovely had she not looked so hungry.

"Do women often travel alone in such bands up north?" Jonathan asked.

"If they do, I haven't had the pleasure of meeting any," Cadman answered, averting his gaze from the tallest of the women in gray, who was now also looking intently in their direction. "Seems they've had a rough time of it, but we need not meddle. We have our own worries, remember?"

"Yes, but surely we could give them some of our food later, when no one will see, and call it vulgar charity," Jonathan said, knowing full well what hunger felt like—the gnawing ache that kept you from sleeping.

"Aye, we might, if they've not found some men who are willing to share a little bread for a little company. Don't give me that look, I said *company,* nothing more. Now pull up your hood a bit more, like so. Your hair stands on all ends once it's wet, doesn't it? Makes you look half mad. Now, to the left are a few of the River Goldsmiths. I told you about their proposal to dam the Animar, so steer clear, less that hot head of yours starts talking off the cuff about a certain beautiful Delphini—"

"Watch how you talk about Morwenna's daughter," Jonathan warned.

Cadman's eyebrows shot up in surprise. "Well, well, you really do like her. Fair enough, now do your part and help me find out what's going over there. I do not like the look in the tallest one's eyes."

Jonathan wandered over to where the weavers were talking as three or four men began to raise their voices.

"I'm telling ya it's not decent, them thinking about disbanding the Order."

"It'll not happen, not with the girl's murderer still at large."

"Tarl—

"Tarl be damned. He couldn't hurt a flea and you know it. Anyway, look how *he* turned up. Now's not the time to be lettin' people with larger purse strings buy out the priest's vote."

"Too many crops failed because of this damn cold. The poor are clamoring for more food and dying quicker than they can be buried—they'll take whatever coin the guilds throw at them."

"But the girl in the wood—"

"Damn it, son, there's not been another killin' since that one last year. Now steel yourself with another drink..."

Jonathan tried to match the voices he heard now with those he'd heard last night outside the stable, but with no luck. Cadman finally waved him back to their blankets, where dinner awaited him. It wasn't much—just some dried meat, bread, and pickled eggs. Still, he was starving and would have eaten far less appetizing fare. Breoc joined them too, his plate full of steaming food. "I love traveling with people that can actually make a decent meal."

"I am an excellent cook," Cadman retorted. He reached out to pull a big chunk of bread off Breoc's plate.

Breoc flicked the smith's hands away. "Get your own." He glanced over at a flustered mother who was trying to feed the baby in her lap. "Been observing our neighbors?"

"I know some from the River Goldsmiths, but they'll not likely want to talk to me after last month's court. There are too many new people here. Jaxon would know who they all are. Damn me for not asking him more news on what has transpired recently in the council."

The women in gray walked by them quietly in a tight group, with heads down. As the last one passed, she briefly touched Jonathan's shoulder.

"I think she's taken a fancy to you. Too bad she looks half-starved." Cadman half smirked, but Jonathan had noticed how he'd adverted his eyes as the woman walked past. Almost as if he were ashamed.

"Go give her some of your food," Breoc cajoled. "Feeding them helps."

"Do all Duraeston men treat such ladies as beggars?" Jonathan couldn't believe Breoc's insolence. "I didn't know traders were so charitable."

Breoc turned to Cadman. "You're right, he does have a temper. Settle down, lad. She's thin from some other worry besides becoming a beggar. They have money, at least from what I've seen. Certainly enough for the trip and food, but I don't take it upon myself to make sure everyone's rightly moneyed."

"Your eyes were certainly checking if they were corseted tight and high," Jonathan added dryly.

"A temper and a wit," Breoc chortled. "We shall have good sport yet on this trip."

—◦◦◉◦◉◦◦—

That night Jonathan felt a hand on his shoulder. At first he thought he had entered another dream when he opened his eyes to see large blue eyes framed by a hood. The tallest woman in gray held aloft a candle, the light throwing her thin face half into shadow. She was around his age, maybe a few years older, but she had the worn look of someone who had lived long in fear. She silently peered at him for a moment more then blew out the small flame.

"I have come with a message. Here is my signet." She put something in his hand. A ring.

Jonathan sat up, rubbing his eyes while turning the ring over in his hand. It wasn't just any ring—it had a gemstone in it that glinted in the faint moonlight. She was from some highborn family. "I'm sorry, my lady," he said, "there must be some mistake—"

"But I thought..." She seemed at a loss for words, suddenly fearful. "Surely you and your companions...."

"You did not guess wrong, my lady." Cadman sat up. "I may guess correctly that you are from Lailethas?"

"From Kendrick. My father is lord and master there. I am Keira."

"I've heard of your father—Jocelin, isn't it?" he said. "What are you doing so far from home and without a proper chaperone?"

"We were attacked three weeks ago," Keira whispered bitterly. "Nemarons invaded our hall, and we had but one day's warning. Even then, we could not believe it, not with the northern passes covered in six feet or more of snow. Who would attack in such a strange winter as this? Curse those Nemaron dogs! My father sent the women and children to the southern part of Lailethas, but our party was ambushed on the way." Her voice choked as she struggled not to cry.

"I escaped while our escorts fought, and then I hid among the hills. After days of searching, I found these few maids of my house. Together we rode down into Íarchol, where families gave us shelter. We'd heard that a remnant of the King's house lives in Duraeston, and my mother is of the House of Felast." It could have just been Jonathan's imagination, but it seemed that the smith's jaw clenched at the name. "I thought I would find allies there. I was wrong; none would help us."

"There are Cadarian exiles in Duraeston who would indeed come to the rescue of any person from the House of Felast," Cadman said, measuring his words. "Yet these are troubled times, and you might not have gone to the people with Kendrick's safety in mind. Let us go take a walk amid the night air and discuss this more. Where's Breoc?" he asked Jonathan, looking at the empty space beside him.

"He had the third watch tonight."

Cadman nodded and stood up but motioned for Jonathan to lie back down. "Stay and fix the space beside you so it looks like someone is sleeping there. It will not do to have the three of us gone and wandering the camp. I'll return shortly. Come, my lady. Don't be afraid. See?" He drew something out of his shirt and held it out in the darkness. Keira momentarily held it in her hand.

"Ah, yes." There was a sound of happy recognition in the young woman's voice. Enough that she linked her arm through his as they walked away.

They were gone a long time. *He had better make for a kiss, else someone will be asking questions on the morrow.* Jonathan turned over, too aggravated to sleep. He was getting tired of secrets, of finding out that everything he thought was true—wasn't. Keira believed Cadman would help her because she was of the house of Felast—where had Jonathan heard that name before? And Cadman...well, what exactly did Cadman show her that secured her trust?

The moon had sunk low in the sky when the smith returned. Jonathan, unwilling to show his frustration, kept his eyes shut. Cadman, however, leaned over and whispered, "I'll explain everything tomorrow." Then he fell down on his blanket for a snatch of sleep.

—⋄⊛(☉)⊛⋄—

"Ah! Where is it? Where did you put it?" Keira's shrill voice carried throughout the camp that morning, interrupting everyone's breakfast preparations.

"I do not know, my lady. I had it yesterday morning when we started out!"

"You'll be punished such as has never been seen, if it's lost or stolen," she threatened. "What shall I do? We must go back and get it."

Jonathan pushed through a crowd of folk to see that Keira had slapped one of her maids, the bright red handprint still visible on the girl's cheek. She was kneeling before Keira and sobbing. A few other women tried to separate Keira from her maid, for the lady was about to strike her serving girl again. "I must have it, do you hear me! It was my great grandfather's knife and worth more than any other heirloom. If I lose it..." Keira's shouting dissolved into sobs and coughs. One older woman tenuously tried to approach her, murmuring soothing answers, but there was nothing to be done about it. They all had to be in Cúrmhangon within the week; there could be no turning back.

Breoc strode into the cluster of women. "Aye, stop your wailing, my lady, this need not be such a bosh and blunder as all that. I'll take you back to Duraeston, if you must have it. My journey was not of such great importance that it cannot be detained for a day or two. We'll ride within the hour and can be in town by nightfall."

The trader played his part exceptionally well, looking half cocky and somewhat greedy—one could easily surmise he wanted a reward, and that Keira, in her situation, would happily compensate for services. Most of the guild folk looked grateful that his offer had stopped Keira's crying, and they quickly dispersed.

"He's leaving?" Jonathan asked as they walked back to where their belongings lay.

"You wouldn't expect her to travel alone, given the amusing time we had going from Gaelastad to Duraeston" Cadman retorted.

Jonathan felt a sudden stab of fear for Breoc and Keira, remembering all too well the creatures that had pursued them from Klinneret to Duraeston. They had barely survived, even with the help of three Delphini.

"Don't look as if I'm going to my funeral." Jonathan glanced over to see Breoc leading Hammer and Tongs, the customary grin on his face despite the serious tone. "We will not take the slow, grandmotherly route this caravan took, but ride hard through the pass. I am not the keeper of dreams, so I doubt we'll get much notice."

Cadman took his packs off Hammer. "Still, be careful, my friend. The pass was cold enough when we passed through a little while ago. Should you feel the breath of Ventosus upon you, go east to one of the smaller villages and send word to our friends." He handed one of the packs to Jonathan. "We'll be walking into the valley, so we'll keep our load light."

"I'll send word as soon as I can." Breoc embraced Cadman, then Jonathan. "May Neáhvalar guide you to the children swiftly!"

They were soon packed and ready to leave. After a courteous farewell to the camp, Keira and Breoc rode off. As the caravan moved forward, Cadman and Jonathan stayed mostly in the middle, near the artisans, who kept to themselves. The two drapers were slightly ahead, just out of ear's reach.

"I will tell you some of what transpired last night." Cadman cast a cautious glance over at the drapers. "We made up that story about losing her family's heirloom so she and Breoc could go and gather what Cadarian exiles are in Duraeston and any Íarchins who would help. They may get enough to take back her father's hall at least.

"Don't hold a grudge against me for leaving you out of our conversation, and don't tell me you weren't fuming that I did. I saw that look you gave me. But any prying eyes would have due cause to alert the camp if they noticed three people gathered in the middle of the night. Two people taking a walk around camp might be explained with enough cunning. Now converse with our fellow travelers and find what news you can about the little girl, but keep away from Keira's women. We don't want to draw any more attention to them."

Cadman shifted to the back left of the group, where the River Goldsmiths were, apparently to make what amends he could concerning last month's scuffle. Jonathan increased his pace so that he was soon near the front of the caravan.

A few masons were talking low, but their deep voices still carried. "They said the Northern Council will call a special vote if the snow is as bad this winter..."

Jonathan inched closer, trying to hear more.

"Aye, it's about time we shortened Centuras. The Wood grows too big and needs not another seventy years' protection, but our borders need it."

"How many Nemarons did you hear were seen in Lailethas?"

"Some said as many as fifty!"

"Pshaw. I heard only twenty. Where are you getting your facts, Samuel?"

"What matter is that? All I know is that Íarchol and Lailethas have standing armies, and we have only sentries for our wood, what sense does that make?"

"Perfect sense," another man now joined the conversation. "Their trees die. They have no need to protect them. Think, man, how many Cadarians and Nemarons we'd have overrunning us if they knew they could, with impunity, chop down trees with incorruptible wood. It would be a bloodbath."

"Pardon, lad, but I heard you're from Breithan."

Jonathan turned his head to see a woman beside him, cheeks flushed from walking so quickly. He remembered dimly that her name was Martha.

"My cousin lives there. Married a tanner by the name of Pieter. Do you know him? Second cousin to Balfour the candle maker..."

"Yes." Jonathan increased his gait. *Now get back to the other prattling women and leave me be.* The men were still talking about the possible overturn of Centuras, but he hoped they would bring up the little girl.

"And how is little Susanna doing?" Martha prodded, still keeping up with Jonathan's long gait.

"Was that the little one hurt in the storm?" another voice

asked. It was one of the drapers, a tall man with a shock of blond hair that swept over his clear-blue eyes. Jonathan thought someone had called him Parth.

"She was caught in the hail, yes, but her father found her in time," Jonathan said quickly.

"But surely there were other deaths?" Parth asked. "We didn't see such a fury up here, but many were hurt."

"Two died in Breithan. But other towns had it worse." He prayed to Neáhvalar that Parth would not bring up his sister, or the flayed animals. He didn't want to relive those nightmares again.

"I heard one of them was a little girl, though," Martha said. "Or was that the one they found in the Wood? I'm so confused."

Jonathan was quite content to let her remain in blissful darkness and merely shrugged his shoulders. Oddly enough, Parth did not seem to want to further discuss the matter either.

"Been bad luck all around, I reckon, with the hail and crops and all," Martha continued, apparently oblivious to the strange silence she had created. "Now my husband Robert says it's all a matter of timing, what with sowing and reaping. But really, if you ask me it's all just..." On and on she droned, finally driving Parth away, but the men talking about Centuras had hurried ahead and out of sight.

—◦◦◉◦◦—

Clouds began to roll in from the east, casting a gray hue upon the entire landscape. The day only grew longer, and Jonathan was ready for night when it came. The next morning they woke to light rain, the kind that was at times more mist than anything else. Breakfast was a short affair, and they were on the road before dawn. In a couple of hours, the semi-pleasant drizzle turned into freezing rain and hail that pelted them from every angle. Everyone walked with his or her head down. Soon the sleet would turn to snow.

"That poor girl won't be able to catch up to us if this

continues," one of the artisans said, a hulking man of about fifty. "What about your friend, Cadman? He said he could be detained for a day, but the day is gone, and we have seen no sign of them. What will he do?"

"No need to worry. He was not as set on this journey as I, nor did he require as much convincing to go back. I wouldn't be surprised if he used the weather to convince the woman to stay in Duraeston beside a cozy fire."

"Did he not have anything to sell or trade up north?" a raspy voice asked. Jonathan turned to the other draper standing there, almost as tall as his guild brother, except he had brown hair and eyes almost as black as Jonathan's. "'Tis a long journey to leave such an investment."

Cadman smiled politely. "I've found that Breoc can trade anything to anyone, anywhere. He has a special talent for finding out what it is people really want."

"Does he now? That indeed is a gift, especially when traveling with such a beautiful woman." The draper gave something between a laugh and a snicker. Several joined in, and Jonathan found himself wanting to defend the trader, who reminded him so much of Theo. But he kept his mouth shut and head down. Cadman had warned him not to draw any undue attention to himself. Towards midday sleet had turned to heavy wet snow. They all bundled up more. The talking grew less.

⟶⟞☙⟨☺⟩⟞☙⟵

It took a day or two before Cadman and the others realized Parth and his fellow draper were gone. They must have quietly left camp during the night. No one had seen them leave; only one of the River Goldsmiths said he had overheard them talking about a "sudden change in plans due to the infernal weather." The news of the drapers' leaving did not seem to trouble the rest of the guild folk at all. The terrain had changed, with steep rocky hills on both sides of the road, creating a much narrower pass. Boulders jutted out from the base and overhead and, with the current rain, the possibility of rockslides was high, but the caravan would stop for no one.

Cadman pulled Jonathan to the very end of the caravan so they could talk.

"Do we go back?" Jonathan asked, feeling a deep uneasiness gnawing at his stomach. "The grizzled man that night in the commons room wore the maroon cloak of the drapers. What if he was watching us? You didn't recognize these two from the guild, and now they're just a day or two behind Breoc and Keira."

"Aye, but for that reason we don't know if they are going after Breoc or getting ready for us up ahead. I say we press on. They have horses, remember, and Parth and his man set out on foot. I took note of the grizzly, just as you, but I could not check up on everyone who sat in the commons area that night."

"Fair enough, but what if Parth and his friend are meeting others?"

Cadman frowned, as if he were working out all possible scenarios. "Time is still on Breoc's side. It is less on ours. We'll set out for the valley soon, and finding the children is the charge Phlegon laid on us. Still, it's time that we practice sword play."

They trained that night, despite the rain that hit them sideways and blinded Jonathan half the time. If other people thought them mad or simply trying to make the best of bad weather, they didn't say. Most just huddled close to a fire or sat underneath the wagons. By the third day, when at last the rocky hills grew into small snow-capped mountains, Cadman surprised Jonathan with a "well done" at the end of their session. They had finished for the night, and Jonathan sat on the ground, bruised and tired. "We're only two days from Cúrmhangon," Cadman said. "Tomorrow, we'll break from the caravan and head east, towards the valley." He knocked on Jonathan's head. "Any more visions in there of the twins?"

Jonathan smacked Cadman's hand away. "Neáhvalar take your knuckles. No, I haven't."

"Just as well," he said lightly, in part, Jonathan thought, to take their minds off Breoc and Keira.

But the lady in gray was at the forefront of his mind almost as much as the twins. Would they be able to help take back Keira's hall from the Nemarons once they found allies in Duraeston? Jonathan tried not to think about the missing drapers, for his heart misgave him the most when he thought of the blond Parth, and his questioning about the "little one" lost in the storm. Not that it wasn't common knowledge, but to bring it up and then disappear…no, Jonathan didn't like it. Not one bit.

—⁕◦❀◦❀◦⁕—

Gray clouds hung low and promised snow again, but they were only a few hours from the border and half a day from Cúrmhangon. By noon thick white flakes fell as they climbed the narrow pass, allowing less than ten feet of visibility.

"Is this normal weather?" Jonathan asked one older weaver who had been trading up here for the last thirty years.

The old man shook his head. "Not even in Lailethas does it snow so soon in the year. Only in the Akrates Mountains to the uttermost north does the land stay blanketed in perpetual winter."

The wind began lashing fiercely around them, making their voices lost in the air when they tried to speak. Those with horses or carts carried the children so they did not have to labor in the snow. After trudging up the pass, the snow stopped, allowing shards of sunlight to peek through the clouds. Before them lay the plains of Íarchol, with the city of Cúrmhangon jutting out to their left and the Sulath Valley to their right. Jonathan had never seen such an expanse of land, with its blue-gray rocky terrain shifting into green pasture at times and then back into the stone mountains, with the Animar side-winding its way from valley to city. Snow covered the ground in many places, but, even so, it was melting. Phlegon's warmth from the belly of the earth, Jonathan guessed. He shuddered when he thought of the monstrous spider sleeping in a den of Ogoni. What would happen if they woke up, hungry and ready not to feed the earth, but to feed?

Goats roamed on one of the rockier hillsides, and farther west, packs of elk grazed on the valley floor. It was a shock to see the animals there so casually grazing, when in Breithan they had all fled. Jonathan wondered what predator could have scared them away from the very forests that gave them life, when here, all was well.

The group descended the pass and soon came out onto the plain, where they stopped to eat. Although it wasn't as warm as it should have been, the snow had quit falling. If it wasn't quite summer, at least it wasn't all-out winter. Not yet.

Cadman was talking to one of the goldsmiths. "Good travels to you both," the man said as he shook their hands. "Do not worry about Keira's maidens. We'll make sure they arrive safely in Cúrmhangon until Breoc meets them later. But take care where you go in the valley, Cadman. While you know some of the Íarchins, they are a people distrustful of strangers, and I have misgivings about just the two of you going to the caves without horse or escort."

"Do not worry about us, friend, for this is not our first time here and people are expecting our wares," Cadman lied. "But trust that we will be on our guard nonetheless. Why else would this place be called the Valley of Eyes if someone wasn't always watching?"

—⁓◉⸰◉⸰⁓—

As they walked east, the talking and laughter of the caravan faded and the pasture land disappeared. Rocky outcrops spiked up on their left, forming a wall that jutted out overhead and elongated strange shadows made by the setting sun. Soon the valley truly began, and small blue-gray stone plateaus rose up on either side of the brownish green pasture on the valley floor. It was rough terrain to travel through without even a horse to hold one's gear. Rougher still if you had Nemarons pursuing you, like Keira did.

"The House of Felast," Jonathan said, now that they were truly alone and beyond prying ears. "Where have I heard that name before?"

Cadman's face remained tense as he continued to peer to the left and the right. "Queen Evanna came from the house of Felast," he said slowly. "When she married Cadreyth, it sealed the alliance between Cadarn and Lailethas."

"But then why did Keira come to you and me for help?"

Cadman walked on for a few silent steps until finally he reached into his shirt and pulled out a braided leather strip, on the end of which hung a ring. "I don't know why she asked you for help, but this is why she trusted me." He slipped off the leather necklace and handed it to Jonathan. The ring was plain silver, with no gem or emblem, only a very faint ornate etching of a letter. Still the silver was pure, with no evidence of taint or defect, and was worth all the shops and farms of Breithan. Jonathan gave a low whistle.

"It's a C—my mark on any work I do," Cadman explained. "I did quite a bit for the high House of Kendrick years back, although not specifically for Keira's father. The ring was payment from my employers, and it allows me to trade anywhere in Lailethas. She recognized it."

"It's beautiful." Jonathan gave him back the ring. "Will they find enough exiles in Duraeston to help them fight?"

"Perhaps. Many will remember their old allegiance, especially to the houses of Felast and Kendrick; Keira just didn't know where to find them."

"And Breoc does?" He remembered the bowed head of the trader on hearing the possibility of the Three restoring their power. "He was in the war, too, wasn't he?"

"We all were. That should not surprise you by now. But,

more than that, he's lived in Duraeston long enough to know everyone who left Cadarn when Adolan took control of the throne."

Finally it was time to ask. "Is that how you received those scars on your forearms? During the war? You've never talked about them."

"I'm not about to start now. Suffice it to say that I received these—" he ran a hand over the thick, snake-like marks on his right arm "—after the war. It is a story you will hear some day, I assure you," the smith said quietly, keeping his gazed fixed upon the uneven ridge behind Jonathan.

"Neáhvalar's blood, Cadman, what is has gotten you so spooked?"

"The people in these mountains are excellent archers and are not known to be friendly to strangers. Let's make camp over there." Cadman pointed to a medium groove in the rock—not quite a cave, but rounded enough so they would have a kind of shelter, and could make a decent enough defense, should they need it. "Bryn is supposed to meet us here after he escorts the messenger to your parents, and it will be none too soon. We come with no guard, no announcement, and no mediator from their clan. Even when we find Kei and Kayna, I am unsure of where to lead them. They can't stay here in the valley, not with the Nemarons at Íarchol's doorstep. Nor will they be ready to face Ventosus."

They set their packs down in the dirt, unrolled their blankets, and ate a scant dinner of black bread, which could last for a week or more. Jonathan thought he would crack his teeth on it with every bite. The dried meat wasn't as bad, but Henrietta had under salted it, and now it tasted like old leather.

"I'll take the first watch," Cadman said.

Jonathan lay down, surprised by how tired he was despite the precariousness of their situation. He couldn't sleep, though, and for a while he silently gazed at the stars while

Cadman sang.

> *Black stones in the night, deep seas of the world,*
> *The Water Ones delight, set their voices in this pool.*
> *The dark stones call us back to the dreams*
> *Beneath the ocean floor, where Morwenna sleeps.*

"What is that you're singing?" Jonathan asked.

"Sorry, I'm not known for being any kind of bard."

"No, no, it was beautiful," Jonathan said. There was something in Cadman's voice, a hint of sadness, of longing, that had filled the words.

"It tells the story about the pool of Lestár. Cadarn's first king had a pool built in his courtyard. The Delphini came and placed six stones from the sea in it so that anyone who came near it heard the voice of the ocean. Legend has it that Morwenna herself sang a blessing over it, to be a memorial of her."

Cadman began to sing again as Jonathan finally fell asleep.

> *At night we gather, our fires gleaming*
> *And gaze into our pool to hear the singing*
> *Of Delphini love for waters wild, Ogoni flame*
> *For the stars above…*

—◦⊙⊙◦—

"Don't move or make a sound," a voice whispered in Jonathan's ear as a cold blade pressed against his neck. His arms and legs automatically tensed, and he visualized where his dagger was, just a few inches over to the right. Damn it, why had they not scouted out the place more thoroughly?

"I said not to move," the gruff voice repeated.

Jonathan opened his eyes. The person's face was shadowed by a hood, but he could tell it was a boy, not a man, who held the blade so tight against Jonathan's neck he could feel the iron cut into his skin.

"What are you doing here? Be quick about your answer!" he demanded.

"We are looking for two children," Jonathan blurted out, at once regretting his decision.

"There are many children here in our valley, but we would never sell our little ones into slavery."

"Not just any children. Twins. We are looking for them, *not*," Jonathan said quickly for the boy had pushed the knife further into Jonathan's skin, "to make them slaves. We've come to ask for their help."

"We do not give help to strangers here." Yet the boy seemed to relax his grip on the knife, for the pressure slackened. In that moment, Jonathan reached up and twisted the boy's hand hard so the knife fell. Jonathan rolled left and brought his knee up to thrust the boy away. Just as he stood up, his assailant rammed his shoulder into Jonathan's stomach with surprising force for one so small, knocking Jonathan off his feet. One deft motion, and the boy had Jonathan's left arm pinned underneath his own body. A sharp pain shot up his shoulder with every breath.

"Do you yield?" the boy rasped.

"Not quite," Jonathan jerked his legs up high enough that the boy momentarily loosened his grip and allowed Jonathan to flip his opponent on his side. His hood had fallen off to reveal a shock of red hair and a very young face. Jonathan's right hand slid down to his dagger.

The boy, undaunted, leapt upon him before could draw it out. "Yield!" he cried, with a sneer on his lips.

Jonathan dimly heard the sound of heavy boots. Real soldiers to come help, no doubt. He drew his dagger out of its sheath, thinking that holding the boy hostage might be the only way out of the scrape.

"Kayna, get off of him!" a voice yelled.

Kayna? Sheer amazement made him let go of the dagger's hilt. He looked up at the face again. *This boy...is a girl?* His other hand relaxed its grip on her arm.

"I'd like to introduce you to the twins."

Jonathan turned his head left to see Cadman standing beside a red-haired boy. "You've obviously already met Kayna. This is her brother Kei."

CHAPTER 9
THE VALLEY OF EYES

"Get off me before I throw you off," Jonathan warned, having half a mind to flip her over to the side anyway.

Kayna did not lose her smile at the threat, but lightly leapt up and went over to her brother. Cadman reached out a hand to help Jonathan to his feet. "Remember that they are Terakhein, and as such, show them due respect."

Kei was tall and lean like his sister, but with more freckles and his eyes were such a dark blue that they looked gray, whereas Kayna's were almond-shaped and bright green. She bore a distinct resemblance to a cat both in face and form. Her snipped curls did nothing but add to the effect, sticking out in odd little tufts. "I am sorry my sister met you in such a manner on our watch," Kei said. "We had received word to look out for three strangers but were perplexed when we saw only two wander into our valley. We waited to see if a third would join you. There have been other sojourners traveling through the valley in pairs or small groups, so as to avoid detection.

"Nemarons?" Cadman asked.

"We couldn't say. Now you tell me that you traveled here to find me and my sister, yet you have kept back the larger purpose of your journey, Cadman, or am I wrong?"

"Given the nature of our journey thus far, I am less comfortable talking out here in the open air than I would be in shelter. Can you take us to your family?"

"It is approaching dawn, so our relief will be here

momentarily, then we may go."

Kei's voice had a musical cadence to it, and reminded Jonathan of Bryn's chorus of voices. Would the Ogoni come soon? The twins offered them a slab of bread and a hunk of cheese, which they gladly took.

Within the hour, a new watch relieved the twins. Cadman and Jonathan followed the twins on a stony path through the valley and up into one of the many caves that permeated the rocks. The cave they entered was larger than it had first appeared and turned into a great hall with a rounded roof. For a moment Jonathan thought they were under the sea, so dazzling were the green jewels embedded in the dark blue-gray stone above.

About ten or more families were gathered around a long stone table for the morning meal, each dressed in simple tunics of gray, blue, or brown with heavy brown leggings. Some had short black vests made of fur, but not many. Jonathan felt uneasy with their unsmiling stares. An older woman with long silver hair and slate gray eyes greeted them courteously with a kiss on both cheeks. "I see our watch has found guests for our morning meal. You were not entirely unexpected, although we had heard there would be three." She motioned for all of them, including Kei and Kayna, to sit at the end of the table where they might have some privacy. This would be tricky, with the twins sitting right there.

"We had another man with us—Breoc," Cadman said quietly, "but there has been trouble up in Kendrick. The hall was overrun and—"

"But what news is this?" A man about the same age as the woman had walked in and immediately sat down beside Kei, white eyebrows furrowing. "Is Jocelin alright? We heard nothing about such an attack."

"You know him?" Cadman's surprise was no less than Jonathan's.

"You forget, being from Gaelastad, that we went to war

with our northern brothers," the man admonished them. "While your country stayed neutral."

"Aye, but I lived in Lailethas at the time, so I marched under its banner," Cadman was quick to point out. "And now the colors of Íarchol and Lailethas might fly again on the field of Camholch soon enough." He leaned in closer, not wanting to be overheard by anyone this time. "Nemarons on the border—not enough for an army but more than we suspected. Our third traveling companion escorted Jocelin's daughter back to Duraeston, to seek aid from the king's exiles. But we are worried, for two guildsmen also left the group in the dead of night, and we are not sure whether they have gone for reinforcements to follow us here or pursue them. We have journeyed long, from Breithan, to ask you for help.

The man looked surprised. "You've come from so far south? The Lady Morvoren did not mention that, only to give three strangers safe harbor for they were on a mission from the Elementarí themselves. We have had no such visitation from a Delphini for years beyond count, and now you tell me that part of Lailethas has been overrun…"

The Lady Morvoren. That meant Morgan had been here, and from the way they had been treated thus far, she hadn't mentioned that he and Cadman were coming to take the twins. It would have been better had Morgan at least prepared them for it, but knowing her, she would enjoy the thought of Jonathan stumbling over his explanation—

"…allies from the east." Wait—what had he missed? "But we have forgotten ourselves," the man said. "I am Jory, and this is Bree." The woman tilted her head in another greeting. "And our twins you have already met."

Jonathan's stomach dropped even as Cadman told them their names, for while he had envisioned telling a group of Íarchin tribesmen they needed the twins, he had yet to account for telling a mother they needed to steal her children, adopted though they be, and take them into certain danger. He wondered how much the twins had told their tribe about that fateful day when the Nemarons and Ophidians massacred their people in the forest. Did they have any idea that these two were the last of an entire race?

"…The council is ready to see you." Jory was standing up. It was much too soon—he and Cadman hadn't had a chance to talk, and they needed to factor in this new information. But Jory was already leading them, along with Bree and the twins, to a stone doorway at the back of the main hall. Here they entered a smaller corridor that was wide enough for only two to walk side by side. Jonathan and Cadman soon found themselves climbing up a gentle slope, their way lit by torches in the wall. The dim light sparkled with green among the dark blue-gray stones. Jonathan thought the gems almost inspired as much awe as the Atreal trees of the Fáliquerci. "Jory, how many of your people live here?"

"Over sixty of my house abides in this hall, but there are ten halls in this valley alone since the caves are plentiful. We have more kin up in the far northeastern mountains." Jory opened a door to reveal a spacious area lined with maroon tapestries, and filled with many chairs and small tables. Twenty shelves had been carved into the wall opposite the door. Over half were taken up with large leather-bound books. "This is the teaching room where we instruct the children during the day, and the room on the right holds the scriptures of our forefathers, as well as all Terakhein Law."

"You keep your Terakhein Laws here, where anyone can get them?" Jonathan asked. Only the Holy Order of the Seven Woods had access to those decrees in Gaelastad.

"The laws were made for the people to learn their place in nature," Jory said. "Our people are encouraged to come and study them at their leisure."

"And do you share these scriptures with the guilds that meet in Cúrmhangon?" The smith couldn't quite keep the edge of sarcasm out of his voice.

"We are cave dwellers," Jory replied calmly. "You'll find no guilds in Kaelest, nor anywhere else save on the border of Gaelastad and Íarchol. It would seem the responsibility was laid on your own councils then."

Cadman said nothing in response, and Jonathan wondered just how Jory and his people were going to believe that Kei and Kayna were the very Terakhein of their scriptures. Had the twins told them anything of their forest, of their past life? They continued up the hallway until Jory stopped in front of a ladder. He went up first and then threw open a door at the top. Bree, Cadman, and then Kei climbed up next. Jonathan followed, and Kayna closed the door after them.

They were on a plateau that overlooked the entire valley. Sheep and goats were grazing where the Animar split into two smaller rivers, with Íarchin shepherds keeping watch. The clouds had sunk just below the mountain peaks, the humps of monsters lost in a thick soup of fog.

"This is the Sulath Valley. Few have ever seen it from this high place, for it is where the council meets," Jory said, and directed Jonathan to turn around.

Twelve chairs were in a half circle, and seated in them where the elders of Kaelest, dressed in dark blue. Kei and Kayna stood at each end of the half-circle while Jory and Bree took their seats. Jonathan and Cadman were left standing alone before them. Jonathan felt that the elders were waiting for them to speak.

"We have a charge from the Ogoni Bryn and Phlegon," Cadman said. "They believe that some Terakhein children are alive." Excited whispers among the council.

"No one has ever seen them," one woman said.

"Quiet, my friends. Let us hear him out," Jory admonished.

"Although it's true that very few have ever seen one of the Elementarí's Terakhein," Cadman admitted, "the Elementarí are now rising in their wrath over our breaking of

Terakhein law, and we believe that Adamara and Truculen are once again preparing for war." Cadman talked over their excited whispering. "Eight years ago, the Terakhein forest was attacked by Nemarons and Ophidians, yet the Ogoni believe that several children were sent away by a Delphini using the Avexi Celarise. A little girl, Samara, has been guiding Jonathan, and during his dream walking, he saw two Terakhein children. They were twins, with red hair. Kei and Kayna."

Everyone erupted into speech. Kei looked at Cadman without moving, his head slightly tilted to one side as he listened. Kayna's eyes met Jonathan's and he could see she was angry. Bree called the council to order.

"What do you want?" Bree's voice trembled, and Jonathan couldn't tell whether it was from great anger or fear; so tightly did she grip the chair that her knuckles were white. "What is it you expect them to do?"

Cadman looked steadily at Bree and Jory as he told them how the children were needed to help fight Ventosus and stop his winter. It was only a matter of time before they were tracked by the Ophidians, even with Bryn and Morgan working to waylay the earth spirits.

Jonathan listened, glancing up at the sun and back down again to find he was no longer in front of the council but instead on a hill above a field. He turned around, remembering how in his dream walking he could see Phlegon. But no, he reached down and felt the grass, heard the sounds of war. To his right, scores of men on horseback waited as two captains rode through their ranks. Could *they* see him?

"You boy!"

Jonathan froze, but the red-haired captain was shouting at another soldier. "Tell Jaromír to send out his sortie now, mine shall follow after the first assault."

The name was unfamiliar; he couldn't tell if it was Cadarian or Nemaron; it was wartime, and Jonathan didn't even know which damn country he was in. He looked at the vast field below where tens of thousands hammered at each other with maces and swords. The acrid stench of burnt flesh was so strong Jonathan thought he would choke. Over to the left, the armies fought around a giant sinkhole, three hundred feet wide and deep enough that Jonathan could only see the heads and shoulders of men trying to climb out. Black smoke rose from the center of the pit. Screams as well. What was he here to do? If this was Nemaron, maybe even Samara was here, hiding.

"Neáhvalar's mercy save us," a soldier swore as he came to survey the field.

"Neáhvalar can go piss on himself," the captain shouted. "Launch my sortie and get them out."

"Yes, Lord Marek."

But Jonathan could see that was impossible, for the enemy had now created a wall of guards around the monstrous rent to keep inside whoever had fallen. From the other side, a fireball suddenly hurled through the air and landed dead center in the abyss. Flames rose up from the center of the pit, along with shrieks and black, tarry smoke.

"What devilry is this?" Marek screamed and charged down the hill.

Jonathan turned around to see a woman with long blond braids shoot her bow into the tumultuous mass of flashing armor.

"Pray it hit the brother and none else!" said the soldier who held the reins to her horse.

"Aye, Calon, we'll soon see. Now, take your men and reclaim the rocks!" she shouted over the fighting. "Make sure the Three do not come together again, no matter what mark the arrow found."

Jonathan felt the knot of fear in stomach suddenly tighten. *I am not here, not on that day. The pit, the Three…*

More shouting from the other side of the hill. Jonathan ran over to see two men engaged in single combat, their swords flashing as a circle of thirty Nemarons and Cadarians gathered around them, cursing and jeering. No one entered the circle where the men fought, even as war still raged on the field. It was lunacy. The raven-haired man was the taller of the two and wore no armor save a white cloak. The blond warrior at least had chain mail, covered by a breast-plate, yet he had already been wounded in the side and the gash bled heavily. Jonathan felt sick to his stomach. *This* story he knew.

The shouting increased from down on the field. There were men still alive in the pit, clawing at the edges to pull themselves out, but the Nemarons stood guard, hacking off any limbs that reached out of the sinkhole.

"Send in more men. Break through that cursed leaguer!" the other captain shouted as he passed, his face completely covered by a silver helmet except for his mouth and eyes.

A collective cheer and cursing from the other hill. The golden-haired warrior was on his knees; his sword had been wrenched from his hands. He struggled to rise while the dark-haired prince circled him. One violent thrust through the warrior's back, and the prince's sword point traveled straight through the warrior's chest. A clean stroke. The blood didn't begin to gush until the prince lifted his foot and pushed the warrior off his blade, like a piece of carrion.

"Cadreyth!" The woman's cry tore through the air as she jumped on her horse.

The king. I just saw the Sun King of Cadarn die.

Jonathan ran at Cierdwyn, throwing up his hands. "Stay your challenge, lady, do not—"

But Cierdwyn had rammed her heels into her horse's flanks, charging the scant ranks that lay between her and her dead brother. Jonathan ran after her. "It's Truculen you fight!" he screamed. "You cannot defeat him!"

The ranks parted and allowed her to pass for, as the king's sister, she had the right of challenge. No, not the right, but the duty to avenge her king's death. *It's just a memory. There is nothing you can do!* The refrain kept running in a loop through Jonathan's mind but still he followed. By the time he reached the other side of the small hill, Cierdwyn and Truculen were in full combat. Jonathan pushed his way through the men, but the final guard around them would not let him through.

"She is lost if you let her do this!" he yelled at the two giant men who had barred the way with their pikes. Cadreyth's men.

"The challenge has been made for kingship, boy," said one gruffly. A fierce shove sent Jonathan sprawling to the ground. "We must honor it; now get back into the bloody fray like the rest."

Jonathan leapt up. He had to get in between Cierdwyn and Truculen; damn their honor, why did the Cadarians not start a melee? Stepping close to the man on his left, Jonathan crouched down. He could start the chaos if need be.

A cry went up as Truculen nicked Cierdwyn's shoulder. She was quick, but her skill was in archery, not sword fighting. Jonathan remembered that much from the stories. Still, she brought her sword down hard upon Truculen's steel and cried out in an ancient language. Flames shot up either side of her blade, forcing Truculen to stumble back.

"Oh, my pretty little thing," the Ophidian laughed, "where did you learn that trick? Know I will remember the secret allies that aided you today."

"Neáhvalar judge your betrayal to both man and Terakhein then." She swung again as flames licked her blade. Truculen did not retreat this time, but pressed on as he brought his sword under hers and locked them. "Can you best your own brother's sword?" Truculen asked.

Jonathan inched forward. Just another foot and he'd slide through the pikes that barred his way. Cierdwyn's mouth was grim even as tears rolled down her cheeks. *Nemari, Truculen re verath!* she cried, and Truculen suddenly staggered back as Cierdwyn regained her balance. She lurched forward and brought her sword in from the side, aiming for Truculen's neck. But a woman dressed all in white with golden hair broke through the pikes as if they were twigs. In but a breath, she reared up behind the king's sister. *Moon-stone,* Jonathan thought, as he saw the purple blade come down to slice Cierdwyn's sword arm.

Cierdwyn's stroke suddenly went wide, allowing Truculen to bring his own blade up, straight into her chest.

"Now, go take the Hall," the Ophidian woman ordered, her voice sensuous and deep, reverberating over the din of war. "I want Evanna brought to me alive. The fire too." She turned so that her face was fully visible to Jonathan.

It was the same Ophidian hunting Samara!

Then chaos.

The Cadarians formed a rout, trying to withdraw, while the Nemarons from below finally broke through the rear-guard and came charging up the hill. Jonathan dodged man and horse to get to Cierdwyn. Someone was already at her side, a man who had foolishly taken off his helmet, reveal-ing long blond hair and a very young face. He wiped the blood from Cierdwyn's fingers "Hold on," he said, then glanced over his shoulder. "Ulric, bring me a physick!"

Cierdwyn turned her head and saw Jonathan. A look of surprise flashed in her eyes, which were beginning to close. "Tell them to remember...the holy fire," she whispered as more blood trickled from her mouth. "Warmth for winter and the door...he must tell them about the door..." Then she drew her last breath.

⁓⊶◉⦆◉⊷⁓

"Jonathan? Jonathan!" Cadman was shaking him.

"Don't die! Don't die!" Jonathan was lying on the ground, tears still streaming down his cheeks while the entire council hovered over him. He tried to get up, but the smith kept his hand firmly on Jonathan's shoulder.

"Stay still," he said sternly. "You're safe in Kaelest. No one has died."

"Quickly. Get some spice for him to smell and stir awake," Bree said.

"No, no, I'm fine," Jonathan protested, realizing where he was.

"Tell us what happened," Cadman said as he helped Jonathan stand up. But damn it, the circle of adults didn't back away to give him space. No, it felt like they were drawing closer, and the air was disappearing again. *Give them what they want.*

"I saw…" No, he had really been there! He had smelt the burnt flesh, felt Cierdwyn's hand in his. Jonathan tried to swallow. "I was with King Cadreyth when he fell in battle, and his sister too."

Cadman's fingers suddenly dug into Jonathan's shoulder. "You had a vision of that day? Who else was on the field? Be quick!" The smith's hands gripped Jonathan's shoulders so tightly it hurt. "What of the Five Captains? What did you see?"

His thoughts were all jumbled but it was Cadman's fierce stare that made him look away. "Marek…" Yes, he had distinctly heard that name. "Jaromír." Yes, and who else? "There was another whose face was hidden under a helmet. That is all. What does it matter? You were there, remember?"

"Everything matters now," Cadman said vehemently.

His head felt like it was about to split open. With one hand he pushed Cadman aside. "Then you should know that the Ophidian woman who stabbed Cierdwyn's arm is the same one hunting Samara in my dreams."

"Neáhvalar's blood." Cadman whispered. "Adamara."

"What was she doing *there?*" Kei broke through the circle of elders.

"She stabbed Cierdwyn's sword arm so Truculen could kill her. But Cierdwyn's last words were to *me*—"

"That's not possible!" Cadman gripped his arm again. "The dead cannot speak—even in dreams."

"But she did, Cadman," Jonathan had to practically shout it over the council murmurs. "Her last request was to remember the door. Warmth for winter and fire for darkness. A man knows where it is…" And there he faltered, for Cierdwyn hadn't said who knew that secret.

A very old man raised his hand to quiet the council. " It is best to discuss these matters in our chambers. Kei, Kayna, make sure our guests are well cared for."

It was a quick dismissal as one by one the council members went through the opening in the floor and down the ladder. Jonathan and Cadman went after, followed by the twins.

—⁘—◦⟨◉⟩◦—⁘—

"By 'well cared for,' does that mean we are to be kept under lock and key?" Jonathan asked as they walked down the narrow hallway.

"You're not prisoners," Kei said. "Yet neither are you free to wander through our caves unattended. Here, let us talk more." He led them to the room of tapestries and cushions, where a small fire was crackling in the center pit. His manner was calm as he sat down on one of the pillows, and motioned for Cadman and Jonathan to do the same, but there was a tremor in his voice. "You had not said before that Adamara was hunting a Terakheini."

"Nor that the dead could see you," Cadman said, his eyes now refusing to meet Jonathan's.

"I have not seen Adamara pursuing Samara in my dreams of late," Jonathan assured Kei. *She's been hunting me instead.* "Samara is hidden somewhere safe, I believe."

"But for how long, if Adamara is searching for her?" Kayna asked. She looked more catlike than ever, cross-legged on top of a high pillow against the wall. She jumped off and scuttled up to Jonathan on the floor. "Do you know what she can do?" the Terakheini whispered. Her green eyes flashed emerald, almost Ophidian-like in their intensity. "Do you know, when she is really hungry—"

"Kayna, stop!" The command sounded odd coming from Kei, who was more courteous than his twin. "Forgive my sister, Jonathan—it comes from an old grief we both share."

Kayna jumped back onto her high cushion. "Grief would not be the word I would use, brother."

No, it is hate that I see in your eyes, Jonathan thought. *What did Adamara do to you, little one?*

"We should have waited to hear Jonathan's vision, given the nature of what he saw," Cadman said, staring deep into the fire. "You did tell us all that you saw, right?"

What had the smith so worried? *I will remember the secret allies that aided you today.* Jonathan vividly remembered Truculen's face as he said those words. "The Ophidians invaded your forest out of revenge," Jonathan said to the twins, suddenly understanding. "Truculen knew the Terakhein had taught Cierdwyn some of their chants—"

"We do not chant," Kayna said. "Nor would our parents and Elders have been involved in a war of men; it is against our laws."

"But her arrow wounded Chalom," Cadman countered. "No human weapon could have sent an Elementarí into fever save one imbued with Terakhein power. Otherwise, Cadarn would have been lost."

"Lost or found, still you expect my sister and me to fight the Elementarí on your behalf, whether it be Ventosus or one of the Three," Kei said.

"War is coming on many fronts, Kei," Cadman said. "The Nemarons—"

"We need no lecture on what the Nemarons can do, Cadman," Kei said, and Jonathan could see that the Terakhein was very angry. "We have never, ever spoken to our parents about this, but we remember the day we fled our forest, when it was overrun with them. Against a defenseless people they brought their maces and swords. No one was to be spared. And the Ophidians fed on the wounded." The Terakhein's voice shook. "We hold no power over men—otherwise, our families would still live. Nor could Kayna and I alone send all the awakened Elementarí back into deep slumber."

"Not alone," Jonathan said. "Samara's alive—"

"You do not know where she is," Kei cut him off. "And the Ophidians have hidden servants other than just Nemarons."

The door suddenly opened, and a man around Cadman's age stepped in. He had a striking appearance, with a hawk nose and deep-set eyes. Two blond braids tied back with a bright-colored band highlighted the large scar running from ear to chin on his left cheek. Jonathan found something oddly familiar about him.

A smile immediately flooded Kayna's face as she bounded over and gave him a hug. "Nylen, what are you doing here?"

"The Council sent me." He nodded at Jonathan and Cadman as he drew an old parchment from the folds of his cloak. "I am to show you the lands that lie between here and Ophidia."

Nylen unfolded the paper to reveal a map of the greater countries: Íarchol, then to the south, Gaelastad. To its north, Lailethas. The east was hemmed in by the sea, and bordered by the Wild Lands to the west. For the first time, Jonathan saw where the Ophidian Desert lay, a vast expanse of land to west of the Terakhein Forest, and south of Cadarn.

"Cierdwyn said to get the fire, which is here." Nylen pointed to the center of the desert. "It would take you well-nigh into next spring to get there, and that's only if you survived the months of travel in the Wild Lands. But we will go in by stealth. Here, just a day's journey into the Wild Lands, is a cave that holds a door blessed with the Avexi Celarise, a Delphini spell that allows one to travel great distances in but a breath. Hawks on the winds of Ventosus could not out-fly anyone who used it. The door lies deep in the Dorlíhein

Forest, but it will take you immediately into the Terakhein Forest. From there it is but a week or two's journey."

The face was more chiseled now after twenty years, and no longer was there any hint of softness around the mouth, but Jonathan finally realized why he recognized Nylen. "It was you who was by Cierdwyn's side when she died, wasn't it?"

"Aye," Nylen said. "I have kept this information a secret for almost twenty years, and have broken my oath only at the request of Cierdwyn herself, it would seem." A crooked grin pulled the corners of mouth. "She would have appreciated the odds of this rag tag group going in, stealing the fire, and coming out alive."

"Maybe, maybe not," Cadman said.

"But think about it, Cadman," Kei reasoned. "By taking the fire, we finish the deed Cierdwyn attempted that day when she wounded Chalom. Chalom dies, and Cierdwyn is avenged against the two other siblings who caused her death. And then, we have a way of stopping the winter—for a while."

"Until we find Samara," Jonathan sighed. Two tested warriors, one sometime smith's apprentice, and twins who could...well, it remained to be seen what Kei and his sister could do. Not good odds. Not good at all.

—⟨⟩—

Jonathan woke hours later to find that Cadman and Nylen were gone. They had spent much time talking of the guilds and whether the erasure of other Terakhein laws might wake up more Elementarí. At last Jonathan had sat down on a few cushions and fallen asleep.

He rubbed his eyes and looked around. The room was dark except for two candles, so he didn't know if it was even still daytime. Kayna had curled up in the corner and dozed off before him, but she, along with Kei, had left as well. He walked out into the corridor and was wondering which way to turn when a little girl running down the hall barreled into him. "Come with me." She took his hand. "Papa says it's time for the evening meal."

Bree was already in the main room, gathering children and telling them to sit down. A number of people introduced themselves, asking about his journey. It had been so long since any of their kin had visited Gaelastad. Was the Ruaden still blooming as always? A hand clapped on Jonathan's shoulder. "So you made it in time for dinner." It was Cadman, smiling but looking more tired than he had that morning.

"You don't look so good," Jonathan observed.

"I've been talking to the council."

"And?"

"Not now. We'll talk after dinner."

They took seats next to the twins, who were now careful about their conversation in the presence of others. Their questions were courteous and shallow, which was fine with Jonathan, who was trying to enjoy the lamb and vegetables before him. Eventually someone called out for a song, and Jory stood a young girl of about nine summers—the age Jenna would have been—on the long table in front. The room grew quieter as she began her lay of the Delphini. The song was surprisingly sad, recounting the journey of their forebear Kaelen and his house, from the sea to the west beyond the green hills and the Peragrond Mountains, until at last they came to this valley. Here they settled in the rocky caves and multiplied into a truly great people, but they were now sundered from their kin on the coast. When she was done, the room erupted into clapping. Jory tapped Cadman on the shoulder. The smith rose to follow him, and Jonathan did likewise.

"Please, stay," Bree motioned for Jonathan to sit back down. "We only need one of you."

Cadman nodded slightly. Jonathan took his seat again as the three of them walked away, then leaned across the table. "Have you any idea of the council's decision?"

Kei shook his head, but there was a quiet apprehension in the Terakheini's eyes. "They've been in their chambers most of the day. They know the need you have of us, and the old allegiance, but will that be enough to convince them? I cannot say."

"I am weary of this talk." Kayna frowned, but the down-turned corners of her mouth seemed less angry than the fiery gaze she had cast upon Jonathan earlier that day. She seemed resigned, almost sad. "We'll not know anything till morning, anyway. And if these are to be our last days here at Kaelest, I want to remember them well."

Jonathan understood—had he known that he would be gone for so long, he would have spent more time with Alec and his parents; even the widow Samsone deserved a better goodbye. He didn't feel like eating anymore, or being social, but an older woman to his right began asking about Breithan and had any of the animals come back? He answered her questions as vaguely as possible until dinner was over. Immediately after, he excused himself for the evening and headed to his room.

Sleep wouldn't come, not until he had some answers, but when Cadman finally returned a few hours later, the smith didn't want to discuss his conversation with Jory and the council. He simply fell into bed with all his clothes on, and within moments was snoring heavily. Jonathan, however, restlessly turned from side to side on his bed, wishing he were home. The harvest festival would be happening now, torches and lights all around the square while music played till dawn. Alec would have a gaggle of girls trailing him for a dance when he wasn't plotting some stupid trick to play on some poor, unsuspecting bastard.

He wished, impossibly, to be both here and there. Or what if he could just bring up some of the Breithan villagers to the Valley of Eyes? Alec would come in an instant. Lian too. *'Tis a storm we bring to save the land,* he had warned that day. Well, he and his father would be the Brothers

Storm to replace the Brothers Morvoren they had possibly lost. Balfour would join them. His daughter had almost died at Ventosus' hand; surely he would want to avenge that. They would send for Breoc and Theo, who had already seen what war could do. Together they would become the Order of the Terakhein, sworn to protect the children. His mother would be taken care of in Duraeston by the priests, for if he was the great dreamer of the Terakhein, then surely his mother would be revered. The picture unfolded slowly, beautifully...

—⁘⊙⁘⊙⁘—

Jaxon's man was performing his part quite well, explaining to Merthenna and Silas how the buyer asked Jonathan and Cadman to stay on in Duraeston for two more weeks to finish the sword work. Bryn tried to keep out of the moonlight, lest anyone notice a distinct shimmer outside of the Breithan smithy, but just how long did Phlegon think he could survive on the surface without feeding? The Harvest Festival filled the town square with lights and music, but it was the smell of the parents and little ones, the young ladies and their ardent lovers that threatened to overwhelm him. He crept from the smithy down the street towards the lights, trying to contain his hunger, when he suddenly stopped and listened.

A pounding in the earth. Not of stomping feet or dancing girls, but a thundering of hooves and claws. *Aduram èxuro, veraláqueth neafás!* Bryn burst into giant flames while rushing towards the square, where the children were gathered playing in a circle. He would, at least, save them.

He barely heard the rush of throck, bear, wolf, and winged creatures descending upon the Breithan; as a wall of flame he continuously circled the little ones while screams filled the air. More blood in the air. His appetite unhinged. He caught glimpses of bodies being torn asunder, then buildings catching fire from the heat of his wrath. He wondered if anything would be left by the end of it, even himself.

—◦◦◦—

Someone was shouting Cadreyth's name over and over again. Men yelled to retreat, that the hall was on fire. Then the sounds turned into something less human. Growls and animal sniffling, then howls as a mass of dark creatures rushed up a green hill towards a village…

"Neáhvalar save them," Jonathan screamed.

Cadman jumped up from his bed, went over and shook him. "Wake up…wake up."

Jonathan gripped the smith's arm. "Animals from the Wild Lands—"

"Another vision? We will warn them—"

"It has already happened." Bryn shimmered before them.

"Those beasts….whose village did I see?" Jonathan's voice was hoarse. He couldn't swallow.

"Your own."

Jonathan jumped out of his bed and ran to the door. Cadman grabbed him in a bear hug.

"You can't…help…them now," he said breathlessly as Jonathan struggled to get out of his grasp.

Jonathan threw Cadman against the wall, "Just try to stop me." He was about to run out when Bryn fully materialized in the room as his spider form.

"Stop." Jonathan froze. "Your village is gone, Jonathan. Where will your run?"

Jonathan began shouting. "Why didn't you protect them? You let them be devoured…torn apart! You are Elementarí!" He spat the word out with disgust. "You were strong enough."

"The children?" Cadman's voice broke as he let go of Jonathan and fell to his knees.

"Them I was able to save, and only just. It took all of my power to create a wall of blue flame that would not harm them yet could also burn anything that tried to break the circle. Your entire village would have been consumed had I chosen to fight, boy. The beasts bore Truculen's mark and would not have fed my hunger, only increased it."

"Was it Breithan only then?" Cadman asked. "No other village? Klinneret?"

"No." Bryn burst into such giant flames that Jonathan and Cadman had to stand back. "I sent out word inquiring what other towns had been massacred. Breithan was the only one attacked before the beasts fled to the Wild Lands."

"Why?" Cadman put his hand over his eyes as he shook his head. "They knew we were headed north, why attack the village?"

"That question must be solved before long, Cadman, for treachery is closer than we thought," the Ogoni warned. "I was eventually able to lead the children to Theo and Rose's house. But that journey took more time than it ought."

"I left them. I put them in danger!" Jonathan cried.

"You were already in danger. Look at me, Jonathan," Cadman said.

Jonathan could barely stand to meet Cadman's eyes, which were bright with tears that he refused to shed. "I had people watching all the time. Had we stayed, everything would have been lost." Cadman's face was ghostly white. "Do you hear me? You'd be dead too if you had stayed."

"Stay away from me!" he yelled and stormed out of the room.

The smith started to go after him, but Bryn stood in his way. "Let him go, Cadman. It is not your job to save him anymore."

--◦-◉-◉-◦--

No one stopped Jonathan from running down the corridor and out of the cave. He kept running until he found a path that followed the river farther east. He slowed to a walk and kept going until his legs started to hurt. It didn't matter where he went. Finally, he fell on his knees and dropped his head to the ground, hands covering head. Tears refused to come. "Don't go, don't go," he whispered over and over again even as their images began fading away. Closing his eyes didn't help. He could barely see his father and mother anymore, nor Jeremy; even Jenna's smile was blurred when he tried to picture her. In their place was a strange blankness, and a haunting song that floated into his mind. A lullaby Sienna used to sing to Jenna when she had one of her nightmares. A song to cut through the world of thorns.

It wasn't his imagination though. Someone *was* singing. Jonathan looked up and saw a figure sitting on a rock only a few feet away from him.

Jonathan squinted in the darkness. "Who's there?"

"Kayna," she said as she jumped off the rock.

"How long were you there?" he growled, wiping his eyes as he stood up. That this tomcat of a girl should see him so vulnerable...

"Not very."

"I didn't hear you follow me." He turned away from her, hoping she would leave him to grieve on his own.

"I wasn't following you," she said, her voice gentle, which unnerved him even more. "I was out for a walk on my own. And no one hears me when I walk."

"Is that a trick all Íarchins know?"

"It's not a trick. My Terakhein parents taught me."

Jonathan turned to face her. He didn't want to think about Breithan anymore. "What happened to them?"

Kayna shook her head. "Hearing about my forest being invaded will not ease your pain, Jonathan. Kei told me about your village."

Had Bryn told the entire tribe already? "I don't want your pity."

"I'm not giving it." When he didn't respond, she continued. "The council will be meeting with us in a few hours. See? The moon is starting to set. I wanted you to know that Kei and I are going to go with Cadman."

Jonathan tried to picture his house, but only saw its dim

shape within a mist, and the outline of his parents and Jenna. No real image came into focus, except a flaming sword shooting out of a sea of fire. The etching on the cup at Theo's house—and a sign of loyalty to the Ogoni. That he could see, perfectly. Inexplicably, he felt strength return to his limbs as he threw back his shoulders. "I am going too." He was surprised by the confidence he heard in his voice. "The massacre of Breithan demands a reckoning."

"Through dark dreams and winter you've traveled here." Her cat eyes seemed mere slits under the shadow of the rock, but they were fixed on Jonathan in an unwavering gaze. "Yet we have all lost something of great worth; there's no magic in that."

"I found you, didn't I?" Jonathan challenged. He remembered how she had appeared in his vision. Dirty-faced and laughing.

"That is but a small thing compared to what lies before us." She jumped over to another rock, her lithe body landing square on feet and hands, just like some woodland beast. "This war will not be won with swords and steel. Only you can find Samara, and only with her can we defeat Ventosus. But if you want vengeance, join the Íarchins when they fight alongside Cadarn in the coming battle. What good will your sword skills prove in any other quest?" Without waiting for an answer, she turned to go back to the hall. Jonathan did not try to stop her, the sting of truth having rendered him speechless.

CHAPTER 10
THE HIGH COUNCIL DEBATES

Jonathan sat, staring into the dark early morning sky. Nothing stirred except for the dim shadow of a vole or mouse that occasionally ran up and down the rocks. A snake slithered past him, on the hunt for a nightly meal. "Finally, a serpent I could kill," he muttered. Reaching down, Jonathan picked up a small stone. He turned it over and over again, feeling the smoothness between his fingers before sending it whistling through the air. A distant thud as it fell among the other rocks.

Ventosus was their greatest threat, and Jonathan held the key to destroying his power. Yet his visions of Samara had been scarce for so long now, what good was he to anyone? Lost in thought, Jonathan didn't notice that a shepherd was quickly scaling the small hill in front of him.

"Who's there?" Jonathan jumped to his feet.

"It's my watch right now."

The man's voice was low and musical, like one of the poets Jonathan had heard the previous night, and for a moment, he relaxed. But the soft pink light of dawn had just crept up over the valley, and Jonathan could now see that the man was too tall for an íarchin. He backed away. "Who are you?"

The man smiled, a beautiful, dazzling smile as he threw back his hood to reveal long silver hair. "Did I not introduce myself? I am Trapher."

The name resonated within Jonathan like a thousand

clanging swords. Immediately, he pulled out his dagger, knowing it was useless to try killing an Elementarí, but surely the body could be wounded? Hadn't Cierdwyn done as much when her brother had fallen? A sudden light appeared behind Trapher.

The Ophidian turned to see Kei standing there, a torch in his hand.

"What, is this Master Kei that I see before me, all grown?" The smile grew wider. "Does that mean your sister is around here as well? How lovely to see old friends. Although, I already saw an old friend yesterday. Good old Breoc, whom I've dearly missed. Seemed to have landed himself a lady. Both tasted rather delicious, if you must know." Then he redirected his gaze towards Jonathan. "Much like your brother. Jeremy, was it?"

"Neáhvalar curse you for such lies!" Jonathan shouted.

Trapher looked amused as he drew out of his robe a gray traveling cloak. "Recognize this?"

Jonathan felt the blood leave his face, and even Kei looked stricken. But in one fluid motion the Terakheini threw his hand out towards Trapher. *"Aduram èxuro, neafás!"*

The Ophidian winced at the words, but laughed. "Almost," he said. "You forgot the middle part. Haven't you been keeping up on your lessons?"

Dropping to the ground, Trapher morphed into his serpent form. He whipped past Jonathan and, in the blink of an eye, had returned to human form, with a knife pointed at Kei's neck.

"I don't want your death, love. Just your sister." He leaned in to whisper something into Kei's ear. At those words, Jonathan thought of Jeremy, and ran straight at the Ophidian.

Aduram èxuro, veraláqueth neafás! A roar as if of fire. Trapher yelled as his cloak burst into flame. Bryn appeared just above them on the rocks, and rushed down, white hot in his wrath.

"Not tonight, Bryn," Trapher hissed and immediately slunk into his serpentine body, leaving his burning cloak on the ground. Then he was gone.

Kei and Jonathan ran to Bryn, but the Ogoni retreated from them. "Stay back!" he ordered, giant fangs extended and dripping venom. "My hunger is great."

They froze in place. Bryn's fire had dwindled to small orange flames that cascaded down his monstrous spider form, but his eyes burned like coals. The ground shook beneath them, and some of the rocks from the valley wall fell. "Our interaction is beginning to disturb the land," he warned. "Hurry back to the hall and call your council. Now events will turn quickly, and we must act or suffer grave misfortune. Go!"

They turned and fled back to the cave, careening through the crowd in the main hall preparing for the morning meal. They finally found Jory.

"We must gather the elders," Jonathan said breathlessly. "Trapher was here."

—◦—◎—◎—◎—◦—

Within the hour, Jonathan was once more in front of the twelve Íarchin elders, with Cadman, the twins, and Bryn, who had finally come, cloaked in his fountain of fire. Jonathan felt as if he were underwater: everything was blurry, slow-moving. At Bryn's request, he related his encounter with Trapher. When he told of Breoc and Keira being waylaid by the Ophidian, Cadman's shock was visible as all the color drained out of his face, but he kept silent. His rage dissipated, Jonathan now only felt numb.

"So now the Ophidians know that some Terakhein do indeed live," Jory said, his face pained by what they would discuss next. "What needs to be done, Bryn?"

Orange-red flame cascaded down the Ogoni's legs, and his body glowed white hot. "Kei and Kayna must go to their desert and recover Ashryanna, then take her back into Cadarn. Truculen and the others would not expect us to be so foolish as to enter the heart of their realm with two untrained Terakheini. They are not safe here anymore, for they will be hunted no matter where they go, and Ashryanna can only be carried by the Terakhein—it would consume any human that tried to touch it." Bryn turned towards the twins. "I will teach you as much as I can while I'm with you."

Jory sat, still as death, until he finally turned to the twins. "Eight years ago we found you by the river, with no idea how you arrived here, and we never pushed you to tell us what happened that day. You escaped a terrible fate, one that still pursues you. Now it is you who will go on the hunt, and we will prepare once again for war. Last, but not least, Cadman has given us one last request concerning Jonathan."

Jonathan felt his face flush as he looked around him. Obviously the smith had discussed some matter with the council, and he tried not to let his anger rise in guessing what it was.

"You have just lost your family and village, Jonathan," Jory said. "Cadman has told us that you are the only son of your father. You have fulfilled your task in finding the children; therefore, should you wish, you may remain with us and be adopted into our tribe. The house of Kaelest would gladly welcome you."

"Although I recognize the generosity of your offer, and thank you for it," Jonathan said quickly, "my place is by the twins."

"You are not ready," Cadman insisted, meeting Jonathan's glare with his own hard stare. "Not with this new grief, and the dead who speak—nay, even see you—as much as the living. Did you hear that, Bryn? What would happen if Nemarons surrounded us and he was paralyzed with a vision?"

"Let the dead speak if it is their time," Bryn's voice boomed. The Ogoni crept closer, yet Jonathan resisted the impulse to back away from the vermillion eyes pulsating with hunger. "You know that the Terakhein's power has no effect on men, only the rising Elementarí. Kei's fire would not guard you against a score of Nemarons, nor could you single-handedly defeat them, as skilled a swordsman as you are, Cadman. Jonathan should be given the chance to enter into this journey with you; he has earned the right."

"And I choose to go." Jonathan looked around bracing himself against any further objection. Cadman was staring at the ground and refused to look up; many of the council seemed lost in thought. Then he met Kayna's cool green eyes. In her gaze there was neither pity nor admiration, just a challenge. Beside her Kei slightly nodded.

Finally Cadman looked at him, his eyes unreadable. "That settles it, then." Turning to the council, he said, "The Ophidians may return, and next time they'll bring the beasts of the Wild Lands with them."

"Have no fear for us, sir smith," a tall and stately woman answered. "We have many shelters throughout these mountains. We also will be gathering our weapons and men to help the Lailethans and to take back Kendrick. But the main strength of our force we will send to Cadarn, when you call us, for our pledge to Lady Cierdwyn remains true."

"Then let us begin," Jory commanded. "There is not much time."

⚬⁓⦿⧉⦿⁓⚬

For the next week the Íarchins who dwelt in Kaelest and the neighboring halls gathered what was most needed and began to travel farther north in the mountains towards Lailethas. Jonathan avoided Cadman as much as possible, instead spending most of his time in the reading room, looking at maps of where the Ophidian desert lay and books about the Elementarí, of which there were many. Their scriptures were mostly about the Delphini in the ancient days, particularly Morwenna's children. Jonathan discovered that besides Moran and Peran, Morgan had a sister as well—Branwynne. It was she who was closest to the Terakhein, traveling to their forest via the river ways while her siblings stayed in the abyss with their mother. The descriptions of the Feálli bordered on nightmarish, so grotesque were their punishments on the humans who soiled the shallow seas with their first ships. They would make human gardens, taking the bodies of those they drowned and planting them on the ocean's floor, so that they swayed in the current, invisible as a warning but always the last thing a drowning victim would see.

What stories he found about Morgan where usually in relation to battle, for the Elementarí had gone to war with each other often in the first few years of human life. She was described as a towering woman, with fins for arms and eyes black as midnight. The Delphini and Ophidians fought for ownership of *Tera*—what the Cadarians called this world—creating huge chasms and violent land shifts so that the first peoples could barely survive. That was when Neáhvalar created the Terakhein, a race between the humans and the Elementarí, to be the stewards of Tera. Neáhvalar gave them the power to put the Ogoni, Agerathum, Delphini and Ophidians to sleep and stop their petty wars.

The passages about the Agerathum lacked any adequate description, only referring to monstrous wings and a large golden eye. *We think Ventosus is at the heart of this crippling winter, yet how can that be when he was known as an ally of the first peoples?* one scribe had written in a shaky hand. *Why indeed?* thought Jonathan. *And what is your connection with Nemaron?*

—◦◦◉◦◦—

Cadman called him out on the second night to spar, and though Jonathan felt like he couldn't look the smith in the eye without accusing him, a refusal was out of the question, knowing what lay ahead. The twins had been spending most of their time out in the valley being trained by Bryn.

Conversation was sparse between the smith and Jonathan, except for the short commands or reproofs barked out by Cadman. By the fourth night, Jonathan could offer Cadman a worthy riposte.

"You're...getting better," said Cadman. He was almost out of breath.

"About time," Jonathan grumbled.

"Yes, it is." Cadman threw his stick down. Jonathan's fist flew up and hit Cadman squarely across the jaw. Surprised, the smith reeled back as Jonathan swung again, but Cadman swerved just enough to the right so the punch only grazed his cheek.

"Coward!" Jonathan said through gritted teeth. "You want to just toss me off? You filthy coward! We let them die, you won't let me avenge their death, and now you wish to hide me behind any mother's skirt!"

Jonathan swung again, but Cadman ducked and threw his shoulder into Jonathan's stomach. They both fell to the ground. One right hook to Jonathan's jaw at close range did little damage except a cut lip, but it settled him down plenty. He glared up at the smith who hovered over him, holding on to his shirt with a balled up fist.

"You lose things in war," Cadman cried hoarsely. "Your home, your family. The earth is at war with itself; don't you understand that yet? Don't you know what drives the Ogoni's hunger? What fuels the Ophidian's desire? These are no dark overlords wanting only power; they fight for their very essence—earth, water, fire, and air—to remain unfettered and to dream within the earth. Amid all that are the politics of kings and armies, and yes, even small villages like Breithan. I loved your parents as much as I have ever loved anyone." He suddenly looked down at his hand and unclenched his fist, releasing Jonathan's shirt. The hand blindly went to his forehead and stayed there, shadowing his eyes. "If I had known that danger was so near, I would have sent more people to protect them. I didn't know that it was so close...I didn't know, Jonathan. I've spent...I'll spend my life trying to find out who did this...someone was working with the Nemarons. Someone knew those creatures were coming."

He shuffled aside, unpinning Jonathan, but remained kneeling. "I lost everything too, you know. My closest friends and allies—Lian, Balfour, Riok, Sienna, Breoc." At the last two names, his voice cracked.

"Then what is there for me to go back to!" Jonathan shouted. *Except the Order.* That was his goal now, and he must make Cadman see it. "How could you just leave me behind *again* after all I've already sacrificed?" He let that sink in. "They'll follow me, those things, just as surely as they follow you, so stop acting like I'm a bastard pup whining to be fed. You need me."

At that, Cadman stood up with that old glint in his eye. "Well, it seems you're very much like your father. Stubborn to defend your honor—to the point of idiocy."

He had never thought of his father in such a way. Silas had always defended the land, but his honor was seldom on the chopping block. "He was a brave man, though," Jonathan countered, and wiped the trickle of blood dribbling from his mouth.

"One of the bravest people, Jon." For the briefest of moments, there was a faraway look in Cadman's eyes, some distant memory. Jonathan wanted to ask him about that, for he suspected it had something to do with his father's honor, but there had been enough talk for now, enough fighting. He accepted Cadman's extended hand and pulled himself to his feet. Together they walked back to their room, a tense understanding now between the two of them, one that perhaps would work its way to forgiveness.

—◦◦◦◦◦—

"Bryn had no word of whether or not the Cadarian exiles were able to expel the Nemarons from Kendrick," Cadman told Jory on their last day together. The people had packed up most of their belongings and were now ready to make their way along the valley to other dwelling places. "I still advise you to go farther south and east rather than north."

"We will travel through a narrow pass between the high mountains that border both Lailethas and Cadarn. If we must fight, we can reach Camhanaich from there within a month." Jory stood outside the entrance to their hall, and Jonathan was reminded how, from the outside, it just looked like a simple cave. Nylen walked out with Kei and Kayna, who were both wearing gray-green tunics over brown pants, with a warm brown traveling cloak over that; they blended into the very landscape.

"Where's Bryn?" Nylen asked, wearing much the same garb as the twins, except he was dressed all in brown, with high black boots.

"I am here." The Ogoni partially materialized in front of them. "I will not completely show myself; the land is still healing from the hurt that Trapher and I caused."

Cadman turned to Jory. "Send scouts out before you. Are you certain that the halls you will go to are defendable?"

"Our mountains are not easy to traverse, even for an Ophidian," Jory reassured them. "Morwenna herself spoke strong protection into the Animar so that it can beguile any traveler who does not know the way. The myths about this being a wild land where people get lost are not entirely untrue."

"The last are now going," Bree said as she came out, holding two cloaks in her hand. "We made these for you since it will get colder as Ventosus' winter overtakes the land. They're lined with fur for mountain travel."

"Thank you," Jonathan said, swallowing hard. His mother would have done the same for a guest.

Bree and Jory embraced Jonathan and Cadman, then held each of their twins one last time. *You come back to me, you hear?* Jonathan remembered the words his mother said when he was ready to go. He had promised her he would find his way back. *Damn it, don't you cry. Not now.*

At last Jory and Bree let the twins go, and then quickly left to join the remainder of their caravan. Neither of them looked back.

A shimmer appeared to their right. "Be watchful, for the Wood sleeps, but only just," the Ogoni warned. "And Jonathan, listen to all who speak to you—living or dead, human or otherwise."

Then Bryn disappeared.

Cadman turned to Jonathan. "That was cryptic."

"When is he not?" Jonathan retorted, not wanting to explain forest whispers.

Cadman began securing his pack. "He's been more so today." A pause. "I wonder if he is more worried about Trapher than he lets on."

"Let him come," Kei challenged, holding out his palm, from which emanated a small blue flame. "I will not forget the words of that chant again."

Nylen joined the group. "Everyone ready? We'll head south and then cross the border into the wilderness. We should enter Dorlíhein Forest within two nights."

They descended the rocky terrain in single file, with Kei and Nylen leading them and Kayna keeping guard at the back. That first night they reached the edge of the Íarchol and Gaelastad border, now no longer in the valley but truly in the mountains.

Even though it had not snowed for the past week and the sky was blue with few clouds, the air was icy, and their breath puffed steam as they walked. They camped for the night in a small hollow in the side of the mountain, naturally protected by a few boulders that they'd had to climb.

The next day they began their descent. The terrain was rockier, with fewer foot- and handholds. The paths were narrower, and there was a sheer drop on the right side.

"This is what has protected Íarchol from those which

inhabit the Wild, and over there you see the source of the Thraelis River," Nylen pointed out. "It is called the Dark River, for its waters are murky and deep. It is what protects Gaelastad from the Wild as well."

"Not all of it," Jonathan muttered.

Cadman looked at him but said nothing.

By noon they had cleared the mountains and were walking a hilly landscape with sparse patches of brown grass and large, low-lying shrubs that offered no shade or shelter. A few birds flew overhead. Hawks maybe, or íarchin eagles, whose feathers, according to some folk, were a gray blue in honor of the Delphini.

As the afternoon sun began its descent, a dark mass of trees rose up to line the horizon.

"Let us keep going until we are under the cover of the forest, as unappealing as that may be," Nylen said. They increased their pace and were only a short distance from the trees when Kayna motioned for them to halt.

"Everyone stay still," she said, peering up into the sky. A flock of birds were flying high in from the south. They circled around, descending, and Jonathan caught sight of bright blue feathers, the color of the sky on a summer's day, streaked with brown.

"Run! Run!" Kayna suddenly cried, fear in her voice. "Keep low until you reach the forest!"

Everyone broke for the trees as the birds circled twice, and then swooped down. Jonathan heard nothing but the thundering of wings and mad cawing all around them. One monstrous creature, three times larger than any hawk or eagle, bore down upon Kayna, each curved talon as long as a small dirk. Jonathan was just to the left, but circled around as he pulled out his dagger and threw it straight into the bird's belly. With a thud it fell to the ground.

"Keep going!" he cried when Kayna turned to see what had happened. He sprinted to the carcass and yanked out the dagger—just in time, as another damn creature dove for him. He swung around, slicing up. The bird's entrails spilled out as it dropped to the ground. Dashing forward, he looked up to see five birds circle him and start to descend. A searing pain in his shoulders caused Jonathan to stumble. Another bird flew in front of him, and became a wall of talons, blocking him from any escape. He threw his arms up instinctively, lost his footing, and fell. Before he could get up, something heavy landed on his back and then all he felt were talons plunging into his flesh.

Morgan—help! Jonathan cried out for the Delphini as he tried to crawl away. In front of him, two more creatures swooped down, their beaks open to reveal razor sharp teeth as they fixed their eyes on him. They fell over dead in the next instant, an arrow spitted through their necks.

Kayna ran to him. "Get up!" she yelled as she threw his arm around her shoulder and half-dragged him towards the forest while Cadman and Nylen brandished their swords at the other birds. Kei sprinted over to Jonathan's other side, and together they carried him to the first line of trees.

"Farther in!" Nylen shouted as they reached Jonathan and the twins. "We must risk the forest now in hopes they will not follow us in there!"

The birds flew up to the branches of the first few trees, cawing frenziedly. Nylen took the lead, hacking at the dark undergrowth that barred their way. Their pursuers did not follow, as Nylen had predicted, but the forest sensed them now. Thorny branches closed in and ripped their faces and hands while new thickets grew to meet them. Jonathan thought of nothing but how his back was on fire and that the sticky wetness meant he was bleeding badly.

"Hold on," Cadman said and put one of Jonathan's arms around his shoulder so he could lean on him. Farther in, the forest grew dark as evening though dusk was at least an hour away. Still they fought against branch, stick, and stone, until at last they found a clearing, about six yards long and wide.

On the other side of the clearing, a staggered row of trees grew up partway and then curved back down in a graceful arc, their branches digging into ground. With bark striped gray, green, and black, they resembled grim rainbows. Before all stood one large tree. It grew straight for about four feet, then turned horizontally, then turned again toward the sky.

"The bent tree," Kayna whispered. "It's a Terakhein warning. Father told me about this forest once when I was little." She frowned, trying to remember. "Something about an ancient spirit that did something so terrible…but I can't remember. Kei?"

He shook his head. "Father never told me any such thing."

Nylen gazed suspiciously at the bent trees. "We should camp in the clearing tonight before attempting to cross what might be a powerful barrier. And we must finally see to your wounds, Jonathan. Kei and Kayna, prepare something easy for us to eat—so we can pack up and fly if we need to."

"Let's have you lie down here," Cadman offered his arm, which Jonathan had to use as he kneeled, then slowly eased down onto his stomach. Gently, he inched off Jonathan's coat. "I'm going to have to cut your shirt off. The blood's dried to the cloth." Wetting Jonathan's skin with a little water, Cadman pulled away pieces of his shirt. "Kayna, come here." The smith's words were even, unemotional. That meant it was bad. Really bad.

Spokes of fire shot through Jonathan's back as he tried to twist his head around to catch a glimpse of his wounds.

"Keep thrashing your head like that," Cadman's rough voice was suddenly right up against his ear, "and we'll leave you for whatever else needs feeding."

Jonathan heard the fear behind his godfather's threat. He kept very still.

"Cralen wounds this deep are often incurable," Kayna's

voice sank into whispered awe. "I'm amazed you were even able to run with us like you did."

Jonathan scoffed at that, even though his back hurt so badly he didn't think he'd ever be able to stand up again. "I was mauled every day by the village boys until I was ten," he said thickly, as the pain began to spread throughout his body, followed by cold. "I could run black and blue, cut and cracked, if the day called for it."

"Aye, those were boys you fought." Kayna's voice was oddly subdued. "These were the Cralen, the birds of Ventosus—you'll be feeling these wounds for a long time to come."

A flash of purple caught Jonathan's eye. Kayna had pulled a few flowers from her sack, and he shuddered as she placed the petals in the deepest of the cuts. "I'm sorry. These won't take away the pain, but they should stop the bleeding." He felt multiple stings as she filled his wounds, but still wondered at the strange fragrance now in the air. Not a sweet smell, but something that reminded him…of Morgan. Of the sea.

"Close your eyes," Kayna said softly. "And think not of home nor forest nor river nor stars." Then she began to sing, and as the world faded away in a fog of pain, Jonathan recognized it as the same song she had sung to him in his vision back in Duraeston.

--⊶⊚⊙⊷--

"How do you feel?" Nylen was beside him, examining his back to make sure the bleeding had stopped.

"Somewhat better." His throat was dry and swallowing felt impossible. "How long have I been asleep?"

"The better part of the evening. We wanted to see if you were hungry. Can you get up?"

Jonathan rolled to his side and tried to prop himself up with his arm, enough to bring his legs underneath him without bending his back. It didn't work. The pain was so bad he bit his lip until a spot of blood appeared.

"Lie back down, and I will bring you something," Nylen said quickly, and made to help Jonathan lie down again.

"Kayna says he should try walking tonight, at least a little." Cadman came to Jonathan's side and placed his arm beneath Jonathan's right. "Think you can do it?"

Jonathan silently nodded, afraid of the pain his voice might reveal as he hoisted himself up, bracing his arms against Nylen and Cadman's so as to avoid using his back. The world spun, and Jonathan imagined whispers telling him to die while, step by step, they crept over to the fire.

"You're looking better already," Kei said solemnly, handing his sister a few more carrots. "But this soup will give you more strength to sleep tonight."

Strength to sleep. Now that was an odd truth that Jonathan completely understood, and he threw the Terakheini a smile of appreciation. Meanwhile, Kayna had prepared a few blankets where Jonathan could lie down on his side while he ate. He was settled soon enough, Nylen beside him. Although there was little talking, Jonathan slowly realized that he was hearing voices.

The forest was speaking.

The sprawling, dense branches reached so high that most of the evening sky was blocked out. Soon, it would be full night, and then what things would come out, what monsters that should have remained asleep but were now prowling a forest that reveled in their madness?

As if in answer to Jonathan's silent question, a wolf howled in the distance. No one said a word as they waited to hear any answering cries. None came.

"We should be able to rest without trouble tonight," Nylen said, breathing a visible sigh of relief. "We are still at the outer edge of the forest proper, which is why I allowed the fire."

"What about the Cralen?" Jonathan's skin prickled even as he said the name. "Doesn't that mean Ventosus knows we're here?"

"I don't believe so. Here—I want you to finish this." Nylen passed a tin cup of stew loaded with roasted carrots, onion, and meat to Jonathan. The rest sat down in a circle and immediately fell to eating. "Those birds arrived here with Ventosus' winter twenty-five years ago, looking for prey," Nylen continued. "The winter left, but the Cralen stayed; sometimes they search farther than the Wild Lands, but not often. Our archers have orders to shoot them on sight. It only takes a few moments for them to rip an animal's flesh from their bones, and then they're gone, as quickly as they'd come."

"It must have been them," Jonathan said, trying a bite of carrot. Suddenly famished, he wolfed down the rest of it. Only after did he notice that everyone was still waiting for an explanation. "Last year our livestock were torn apart just after a storm. We've always wondered what did it."

"We looked for an animal pack, or for a band of desperate men," Cadman added. "We never thought about birds."

"How much of your livestock was lost?" Nylen asked.

"At least a third," Cadman said. "Aye, they were easy prey, lying wounded out there in the open."

Just like Breithan, Jonathan mused.

Kei nodded ever so slightly at Jonathan, as if guessing his thought. Then he turned to Nylen. "You never told us how you know about the Delphini pool."

Nylen stirred the fire. "Most of what I know I learned from Cierdwyn."

"She told you about the door that leads to our forest?" Kayna said, disapproval in her voice. "Our forest was to remain hidden and secret. Why did she tell you?"

"That's always a tricky question," Nylen smirked, "unless by some magic you can decipher any man or woman's heart. Suffice it to say that she thought it necessary, and she never explained just *why* or *how* the Terakhein took her in when they kept everyone else out. They allowed her to visit more than once, which explains how she was able to wound

Chalom. No other poison could have sent an Ophidian into twilight; the Terakhein taught her that knowledge."

"They knew about the war between Cadarn and Nemaron then," Cadman said, and Jonathan saw that his knuckles had turned white, so tightly did he grip the spoon.

Nylen nodded. "Cierdwyn asked the Terakhein for help. I'm not sure even Cadreyth knew his sister had gone to beg for their aid. She didn't foresee the Nemaron alliance with the Ophidians, and as such, the Terakhein told her they did not engage in the battles of men. They did, however, show her the Delphini pool that would take her to the Wild Lands. From there she made her way to Kaelest." He smiled briefly.

"I was the lookout for the southern wall when I first saw her. Tall she was, and proud. She told me her name straight-away and said that she needed to see our king. I laughed and told her we had no king but led her to our council, and there she asked for our aid. That is when Íarchol formed an alliance with Cadarn, and we gathered ourselves together with the Lailethans for war." Nylen continued gazing into the fire. "She left me in charge of the archers when she went to fight Truculen. I vowed to avenge her and Cadreyth's deaths, for it was dishonorable the way Truculen challenged them both to single combat, knowing neither had a chance of defeating him. At least Cierdwyn brought down Chalom."

"She seemed a worthy opponent for Truculen too," Jonathan said, bitterly remembering how Adamara had snuck up and stabbed Cierdwyn from behind.

"All were overcome that day," Nylen said. He pointed to the deep scar on the side of his cheek. "An Ophidian gave me this before the battle was over."

Kei looked at him. "You never told us."

"It was long ago." Nylen shrugged. "Everyone thought that with the Cadarian victory, peace would soon return. I returned home and continued the life I knew." He leaned over Jonathan. "You don't look well."

The pain in Jonathan's back had been getting worse, and a cold numbness had entered his legs. "I...I'm not sure I can walk."

Nylen motioned for Kayna. She had Jonathan lie back on his stomach and with expert care examined his wounds. Then she pulled Nylen away and talked quietly to him out of Jonathan's earshot.

Cadman brought him Sienna's drink mixture. "Remember this? You know how it works—better than three mugs of wine without the after effects in the morning. Drink up."

Jonathan rolled onto his side so he could sip the hot tea. Familiar warmth quickly spread through his arms, yet his legs remained cold and numb. Still, he was feeling more relaxed and wasn't minding the numbness as much when Kayna came back with Nylen.

"The Cralen's wounds do not fully close." Jonathan heard Kayna's words through a long tunnel. "The purple flower has staunched the bleeding, but I don't know how to stop the spread of the freezing numbness. Normally, I would use whatever healing herbs I could find around our camp, but the plants here are bitter in their roots, and they would poison rather than heal him. Yet there is one more thing I can try." She knelt down put her hands on Jonathan's back. Surprisingly, her touch didn't hurt.

"*Haleth fortheis quielath argo.*" She repeated the words several times as her hands skimmed his back and shoulders, radiating warmth. Jonathan waited expectantly to feel something in his legs, but there was nothing. "Try walking anyway," Kayna said, and Cadman helped him up.

Jonathan leaned on Cadman as he limped around. After a few moments, he felt a sensation of warmth in his back that eventually spread into his legs.

"I think it's working," he told them, relieved. Cadman kept him walking until the limp became less noticeable, and then brought Jonathan back to his bed.

"The numbness is due to Ventosus," Cadman whispered. "But remember that Sienna's drink also packs quite a punch, so even as Kayna's trying to heal you, that drink is making your legs heavy. Sleep well, and call if you are in pain."

—◦—◉◦◉◦—◦—

Throughout the night, the violent whispers of the trees mingled with Kayna's healing words. Jonathan briefly woke up and saw Cadman and Nylen talking together. Then he drifted back into dark dreams. When he opened his eyes again, Kayna was stirring the fire, her head tilted to one side, as if listening. Jonathan gingerly tried moving his legs. He was still very cold, but found he could at least get up.

"You need to rest," she said when he sat down beside her.

"I know that." He was getting tired of being such an invalid. "What were you listening to?"

She looked around. "The trees. They whisper to make men get lost in these woods."

"You hear them speak words—out loud?" Jonathan barely whispered the question. He scuttled closer to her.

Kayna regarded him warily. "They speak Ophidian. Many Terakhein can hear the forest, but few understand its speech. Only the houses trained by the Ophidians, such as my mother's."

The world began spinning again. Jonathan put a hand on the ground to steady himself. It made no sense. "I hear them too."

Kayna's eyebrows rose. "You? That cannot be."

"I can't understand their speech like you can," he added quickly. "Their whispers only started eight months ago, just before the storm that killed my sister."

She was quiet for a few moments, and Jonathan waited, hoping she did not notice how fast his breath came, how red his face turned.

"Tell me what they say," she said at last. "Perhaps I can interpret it."

"How am I to remember such a strange language? It was gibberish to me...except for Ventosus. The Ruaden—as the red leaves bled to the ground—cried something out about the winter lord, but I remember no other word except for his name."

"Did you tell Cadman about this?"

"How could I? Trees don't speak to any save madmen."

"What if this means you are—"

"I was busy in the fields with my father when your forest was taken," Jonathan said shortly.

"But what if—no. No Terakhein would ever give their child away to one of the Keep."

"The Keep?"

"Those outside our forest—we are your Terakhein and you are our keep. Except, perhaps you are something else?"

The question held more power than she knew, for it explained Cadman's unyielding desire that Jonathan not accompany him on any journey beyond Duraeston. Perhaps there was another reason for the smith's strange behavior, some underlying motivation that no one, not even Morgan or Bryn, had guessed at.

"It's my watch."

Jonathan jumped and twisted his neck to see Kei standing there. Instantly, a searing pain traveled down his back but he suppressed a groan.

"You need not have startled us like that," Kayna said, eyes narrowed in reproval.

Kei looked unmoved. "You should have been more on guard, sister, and Jonathan, it is time you went back to sleep—we must travel long tomorrow, and you will not be fit."

"Give us a few moments more, Kei. We are just trying to —"

Kei cut her off. "You know the rules. You watch until your time comes to sleep, and then you sleep. Who knows when you may have the chance to rest again?"

Kayna sighed, and stood up.

"Can you...can you both help me?" Jonathan tried to keep the rising panic out of his voice. "I can't feel my legs."

"That would be my sister's fault for having not ordered you immediately back to your bed," Kei said.

"And just how could I have made him do that?" Kayna glared.

"You're the watch," Kei admonished. The twins instantly flanked him, with Kayna grabbing firm hold of his elbow with one hand, while bracing his neck with the other. Kei mirrored her, and gently they lifted him to his feet. It was odd, how easily they did it, since he could barely hold his own weight up. But then, after a few steps, he began to feel his feet, and then warmth traveled up into calves and thighs. Still, he leaned heavily on Kei, who was lean yet muscular. A few more steps into the clearing, then he was lying stomach-down on his blanket.

"Do not move again for the rest of the night," Kayna warned, once Kei had gone back to his post. "The flowers will work their salve into your skin, but true healing will only come with rest."

"What about—"

"We will see what the morning brings."

For the rest of the night he swam in a shallow sleep, as the trees whispered words of sorrow and fear.

CHAPTER 11
IN THE WILD LANDS

"We need to make the Terakhein door today," Nylen said as soon as they all were awake. "I'm not sure how long we can survive once we are deep within this forest. Is it just me, or does it look like the trees have crept closer together?"

"If they have, it's not by much," Kayna said while examining Jonathan's wounds. "Their roots are deep here, and their thoughts bitter and hateful. Last night they kept whispering to me that there was no way out."

"You heard them?" Cadman asked.

Kayna nodded, avoiding Jonathan's eyes. "They speak the language of the earth spirits."

Cadman gave a low whistle. "Then warn us if they're about to do something nasty."

The bent trees were slightly staggered, one in front of the other, so they formed narrow doorways with their arcs. Kayna walked forward and stood by the tree, listening for a moment, before she tentatively placed a hand on the bark. "We'll have to run through them. They sense us but don't know what or who we are. Not yet, at any rate."

"You have sustained the most injury," Nylen said to Jonathan. "Do you feel ready?"

"Of course," Jonathan said, a familiar stubborn smirk cropping up. "Neáhvalar knows I don't want to slow you down like I did with the Cralen."

"In truth, it was Kayna's fault, since you were just trying to save her," Nylen said, just as smoothly, ignoring Kayna's glare as he surveyed the invisible line they were to cross. "We should each choose a tree to run though."

They spread out, about ten feet apart, at the point where the bent trees crossed.

"On my mark," Nylen said. "One, two, three!"

They dashed forward through the arcs, diving between low-hanging tree branches that snagged their hair and cloaks. A low-pitched moan went up from the line, like some ancient thing being awakened from the dead of sleep. The cry increased its intensity with their every step, as if the forest floor was in dire pain.

"This way," Nylen ordered, perhaps seeing some invisible path through the dense tree growth that none of the others could. Taking a short ax from his sack, he quickly hacked off the low branches that barred their path.

Immediately, a thousand screams reverberated in Jonathan's ear, drowning out all other sound. With a shout he doubled over, causing the wounds in his back to reopen. Beside him, Kayna moaned, falling to her knees.

"What has happened?" Cadman looked every which way and drew his sword. Nylen kept his eyes peeled on the outer wall of wood. Kei drew his bow.

"They cry when you cut them!" Jonathan shouted, rubbing his right ear to get rid of the ringing. It felt like someone had boxed his ears twice over.

"There's no other way through," Nylen said. "You will both have to bear it until we clear the undergrowth and get into the forest proper, where perhaps the trees might still slumber. He cast a troubled glance at Jonathan. How is it that you hear the same sound that Kayna does, and we do not? That should not be."

"That matters little right now." Jonathan reached for Cadman's pack. "We can't run through them like this—we won't be able to hear you over the din." He rummaged through the pack until he found a candle and tinder.

"What are you doing?" Nylen barked. "Do not light a fire

here—"

"Not fire, just a flame." Jonathan lit the candle and dripped wax onto his finger. "A trick Balfour once showed me," he explained. The candlemaker's round, blue-eyed face momentarily came into sharp focus. *Remember the dead later.* He molded the wax into little balls and gave two to Kayna. "Fit them in your ear."

"How is it?" Nylen asked and Kayna nodded. Jonathan did the same. The forest cries were muffled as they cut their way through thick clusters of branches, pushing apart limb after limb. Deep scratches marked everyone's hands and faces by the time the forest finally began to thin out. By noon they no longer had to cut apart vine-like branches and dense undergrowth, for the trees had grown in girth and stature, almost twice the size as the Atreal trees of the Fáli-querci. However, instead of blue-green leaves, the bark of these trees was lined with long black hair.

"We walk through here," Nylen said. "Have your arrows and dagger at the ready. I am wary of this part of the wood, even more so than what we just encountered."

They continued on for several miles, with Nylen leading and Cadman acting as rearguard. Jonathan's back became sticky with blood from the reopened wounds. "Nylen, how far till we get there?"

"It shouldn't be much longer, I hope."

"Then let us not stop until we reach the pool," Kayna said, glancing behind them. "Something sees...senses us."

Nylen drew his sword. "The trees?"

Kayna closed her eyes, sniffing the air. Jonathan had seen Morgan do the same thing at the cave on their way to Dur-aeston. "No, not the forest—you are right that they are still sleeping. But something lurks here. The wind is too contrary for me to tell where it is."

They doubled their pace. Jonathan's back burned, and the cold was beginning to creep into his legs once more. The forest grew denser as the trees continued to increase in size, although now they were more varied in appearance. The thickest trees had mats of brownish-black fur as their bark, interlinked like puzzle pieces while others were gray and wrinkled in texture, their branches sporting leaves of a dark olive green with blue-red veins running throughout. They stood, sullen and sagging, as if about to die but refusing to let go of life in the hopes of one last act of vengeance. The forest now completely blocked out the sun so that Nylen slowed their pace, searching the grounds for some invisible trail he had followed years ago.

"I don't remember this," he said, a scowl on his scarred face. "We should have come to a tree that was split, with a river beside it."

"Do you want to double back?" Kayna asked. "I think something is still behind us. I say we continue moving forward in the same direction."

Jonathan was glad they had stopped. A strange heat had crawled up his back while the cold continued to trickle down his leg, making it feel like the spirits of fire and ice were at war in his body. He focused his eyes on a tree in the distance to get his mind off the pain. For an instant, it almost seemed as if the bark were breathing, the fur slightly rising and then settling down again.

Suddenly, snarls and howls erupted behind them. Jonathan and Cadman recognized the sound at once.

Throcks. They took off running.

Jonathan saw the trees beginning to shed their fur, the hair slowly peeling away from the trunks and falling to the ground. It took a moment to realize what the fur actually was. Within the next moment, grotesque animals stood up on two legs to sniff the air before dropping on all fours and, grunting, began to give chase. They ran like throcks, swift of foot, but their faces were man-like, grossly misshapen with no eyes and only a flap of skin for a nose.

"Go left! Left!" Cadman shouted. They all swerved aside and saw a river. "Quick, into the water! Perhaps they are afraid of it, for even here the Delphini may still have some power." Falling back, Cadman drew his sword.

Nylen did the same. "Onward you three. We'll follow!"

Jonathan began running and stumbled as his left leg went completely numb. Kei and Kayna quickly grabbed him, and half dragged, half carried him to the stream. The men followed, flanking them on their right and to the rear. The tree creatures sprinted alongside the banks but did not enter the water. They were the size of men, but hunched over so far as to walk on their arms as much as their feet. More creatures dropped from the surrounding wood, howling, as if they were dogs leading a hunter to a quarry. Then, a screaming in the distance—Jonathan recognized it as the thing he had heard in the Ruaden, the thing that had possibly wounded the Brothers Moroven. Something that was neither throck nor tree beast. And it was gaining on them.

Soon the river was up to their knees. The trees now formed a canopy over the river, and the beasts crawled out onto the limbs and dangled upside down, their arms grasping for them. Jonathan found himself face to face with one that grunted loudly, only a seared line where its eyes should have been. It opened its mouth wide and bared its jagged teeth, but before Kei or Kayna could reach for their knives, Nylen's sword had sliced its head clean off.

"Keep going!" Nylen shouted, as the creature's body dropped into the river.

Two large wolves appeared and sped around either side of the stream, jumping into the middle of the river and barring their way. The tree creatures around them grunted and cried in delight, for they heard the wolves' howl and knew their prey was caught.

Nylen was in front of them with his sword drawn against the wolves. "What now?" he shouted back to Cadman.

A monster crashed through the trees on their right, running on all fours. When it reached the river bank, it stood up and revealed itself to be three times the size of a bear, with

long, sinuous arms that ended in talons. Its skin was interwoven with snake-like scales, and it was blind, only two
dark sunken grooves where its eyes should have been. It
shrieked again, turning its lips inside out to reveal two rows
of jagged teeth and a forked tongue that flicked the air as it
smelled them. It had hunted Jonathan and Cadman before
and knew their scents.

"Neáhvalar help us," Cadman whispered.

"*Exuro!*" Kei yelled. The chimera only screeched louder
as it stepped into the river, its misshapen head thrust forward at an unnatural angle from its body as it crept toward
Cadman. Kei let go of Jonathan and ran up beside the
smith. "*Exuro!*" he repeated, raising his hand towards the
sword.

"*Terah Aceri!*" Kayna added.

Cadman's sword blazed. The chimera's massive tail
whipped into the air.

"Damn it, Kei, run away!" Cadman shouted, never taking his eyes off the demon. "We've got wolves on this side,
remember?" Nylen shouted from the front.

Kayna released Jonathan to stand behind the warrior and
repeated the spell so that his sword flamed like Cadman's.
The wolves did not withdraw. Kei pulled out a knife and
Kayna strung her bow.

The chimera was still five feet away from Cadman when
its tail wrapped itself around Cadman's sword and wrenched
it out of his hands. Flames singed its skin, making it howl in
pain as it dropped the sword into the river.

"Don't do it!" Kei yelled as Cadman dived into the water
for his weapon. Meanwhile the wolves closed in on Nylen
and Kayna.

His legs numb, Jonathan floated in the water, now
caught between Nylen, Kayna, and the wolves in front, and
Cadman, Kei, and the beast behind. He reached for his dagger in his pack, but it wasn't there. Instead, his hand found
something hard. He drew it out to find himself clutching an

amber necklace, just like the one the Ophidian woman had thrown them.

"Cadman, look out!" Kei shouted.

The smith had found his sword and was stumbling out of the water, but with one swipe of its claws, the chimera knocked Cadman down, causing the sword to fly out of his hand again. It lunged at the smith, its talons ripping open his chest. Cadman stumbled back, screaming, and sank into the river.

"Cadman!" Jonathan yelled.

"*Exuro!*" Kei shrieked. Blue flames sprang up along the edge of his knife as he stabbed at the thickly scaled leg. The blade sank in deep, causing the creature to thrash in rage and pain. The chimera's tail slammed against Kei's chest, knocking the Terakheini into the river. Kayna turned in time to see her twin stunned in the water, the shrieking demon bent over him with one long arm extended to rip open his throat.

Jonathan tried to get up but fell again, and out of his pocket tumbled the white stone that Rose had given him.

Suddenly Sienna's voice rang in his head. "Now, boy! Remember what the sky and water showed you. Do it now!"

A vision of the moon moving into the sun. He placed the white stone inside the hollow of the amber necklace.

Everything slowed as the necklace glowed with amber light that started at its center. A low melodic note began to emanate from it. Jonathan looked up to see Cadman, bloody and torn, stab the claw that was reaching for Kei. He heard Nylen cry out as one of the wolves leapt towards Kayna, just as the blond warrior threw himself in front of her, flaming sword swinging left and right.

Time sped up again. He heard the monstrous beast screeching while its tail lashed around Cadman's legs and pulled him under the water once more. The wolf had swerved aside from Nylen's sword. Now its brother had arrived and both closed in on the warrior.

Jonathan heard singing. Kayna's voice grew louder as her song harmonized with the music coming from the necklace. Kei cocked his head, listening, and then, drawing himself up, threw both hands out and uttered words that were both beautiful and terrible to hear.

"Nemari!" The screaming beast was thrown back, but its tail still held the smith underwater.

"Aduram èxuro, veraláqueth neafás!" A wall of fire sprang up between the chimera and themselves. The beast clawed at the fire and withdrew, hissing, but the smith still did not surface.

"Kayna!" Jonathan threw her the necklace. "Save Cadman. Call him out of the river!" He began swimming towards the wall of fire. It was the fire of the Terakhein, and could not harm him. He must find his godfather.

Kayna's voice grew more powerful as she sang. The tree creatures stopped running. Some fell to the ground while others swayed side to side in a trance. Even the trees were silenced. The wolves, however, were not affected, for there in the heart of the forest, nothing could quench their hunger.

"Kayna! Call Cad—"

But Jonathan looked back to see the wolves had turned from their pursuit of Nylen and were dashing towards her.

"Kei!" Jonathan pointed to his sister.

The Terakheini shot his hand out and another wall of fire sprang up. The wolves landed within the blaze, their howls rending the air as their flesh was slowly consumed. In answer, other howls tore through the air, both in front and behind them.

Jonathan's legs were totally numb. He started sinking. *Neáhvalar help me. Give me my legs, give me the warmth of the Ogoni. For Cadman's sake, let me walk.*

Hands roughly yanked Jonathan up just as his head went under water. "Fool, you can't go after Cadman!" Nylen shouted.

"We can't leave him!" Jonathan screamed. "He's not dead! He's not dead!"

The warrior shook him. "If you die, Samara dies. Now follow the damn river to the cave, before I knock you out and carry you there."

A scream peeled across the forest. The chimera had climbed up over the river bank to find the end of the fire wall.

"Kei?" Nylen shouted.

The Terakheini's face was streaked with tears as he swam up to them. "I can't throw the fire that far, not yet."

"Then it is a race to the door. Help Jonathan," Nylen commanded.

They swam towards the cave. The howls grew closer. Two wolves stood in the distance on either side of the river.

"We're almost there! Straight ahead!" Nylen said.

Suddenly three more wolves appeared at the top of the left bank, running parallel to them. The deafening screeches began again, signaling that the demon had found its way around the fire. Jonathan tried using his legs as the twins carried him. The wolves to their left had disappeared.

"We will need you to defend us as we try to get inside, Kei," Nylen gasped. The mouth of the cave was partially hidden by an outcrop of rocks, within but a moment's reach. Twenty feet, maybe less.

One of the wolves reappeared on the rocky outcrop above them.

"Look out!" Kayna yelled, but it was too late.

The wolf hurled itself onto Kei, partially pulling Jonathan under with him. At the same time, two wolves to their left had climbed down the banks and were now crouched by the edge of the water. Kayna let go of Jonathan to use her knife, but the wolf and her brother thrashed so violently in their struggle that she couldn't help him.

Nylen brandished his sword in front of the wolves.

"Kayna, get Jonathan into the cave!"

"Kei needs me." Her brother and the wolf were still entangled under the water in a foam of white.

Jonathan seized her roughly. "You're coming with me! Your duty is to live. My duty is to find Samara. If we die, the world dies!"

She blinked hard, nodded, and they half stumbled, half swam towards the mouth of the cave. Nylen still kept guard in front of the wolves, his sword flashing every which way. As before, the wolves did not attack, but now the screaming was very close. Nylen dared not look away, but he heard less splashing where Kei and the wolf were. There was a churning of water, followed by silence.

"Kei? Kei!" Nylen shouted.

No answer.

The chimera galloped into view. Nylen began backing towards the cave as the monster careened down the bank and into the water. Twenty feet high when upright on two legs.

Just as Nylen turned to run, a spiral flame shot out from the water and a hand grabbed hold of him. Kei pulled himself up, coughing and spluttering. One wolf howled as it caught on fire, and the chimera momentarily retreated from the blue flame. Nylen and Kei swam the last twenty feet to the mouth of the cave. A brief look of joy flashed over Kayna's face at seeing her brother alive.

"We can't go inside," Kayna shouted. "It's filled with snakes!"

Nylen climbed through the cave's small opening and lit a flame to see that in the midst of the giant cave—filling it almost entirely—was a whirlpool, its black water raging. Across it he could detect the faint outline of a rounded silver door. Small white snakes lined the shallow edge of the whirlpool, and one was almost eye level with him, sitting on a rocky shelf. But none of that mattered now. The monster and wolves were coming. Kei helped Kayna get Jonathan inside just as the wolves charged the entrance.

"*Comburo!*" Kei threw out his arm.

At the same moment, the snake sitting on the shelf struck out and sank its fangs into Kei's hand. A burst of flame larger than anything they had seen before shot out of Kei's palm and exploded into the cave's mouth. The hill of rock above the cave shuddered, and the entrance collapsed. Nylen pulled Jonathan to the side just in time to avoid getting hit by falling rocks.

Kei ripped the snake off his hand, cursing.

Kayna lit a torch. "Kei, your hand."

"No time now..." Kei's breath came in spurts. "The snakes...they're poisonous."

The chimera began to pound on the rocks outside the entrance. The door at the other end of the cave was at least a hundred feet away. Kayna began singing, hoping to lull the serpents to sleep, but they seemed only to be angered, furiously writhing back and forth, some rising to strike at the air.

"I don't know what else to do!" she cried. Her brother was dying, and her Terakhein power seemed useless.

Nylen pulled a rope out of his sack. "We'll have to cross the pool. Take a torch, Jonathan, and keep the snakes at bay."

Kayna peered across the whirlpool. "I see a small stone by the door."

"Guide it well," he said as he handed her the rope. It required a few tries before Kayna was able to finally catch hold of the rock on the floor. She tied the other end to a large rock that had fallen by the entrance.

Iieeeeee. The screaming thing was beginning to break through the rubble.

"Go first," Nylen told Kayna. "Then we'll tie Kei around me. Take him through the door right away. Don't wait for us—you should end up in the Terakhein forest. Heal him and wait for Bryn to find you. Then go to the Ophidian desert." Nylen had rigged another rope around the first one so if they fell it would act as a second support. Kayna lowered herself down, then hand and over hand she pulled herself across the whirlpool. The snakes sensed the disturbance and began slithering towards the other end of the pool where Kayna was heading. "Curse these things!" Nylen lit a few sticks he had pulled out of his sack, but the fire was strange—of greenish hue and it emitted no heat. He threw two or three over to the door, enough to scatter the serpents and give Kayna time to reach the other end.

However, the snakes were already looking for a way around the small emerald flames. "This won't hold them long," Kayna yelled.

Nylen picked up Kei, who had now sunk to the ground, and lowered him into the seat. "I'll return soon," he said to Jonathan as he swung down with Kei.

Jonathan closed his eyes as the numbness in his legs now spread up through his chest and arms. He saw a winter landscape in the distance, and a little girl running.

A chink of light broke through the caved-in entrance. The beast thrust its nose into the small hole, smelling for them. Then it roared a guttural and undulating yell that echoed through the cave.

Nylen's head and shoulders appeared as he climbed back up from the edge of the whirlpool.

"No, Cadman first," said Jonathan, as the warrior tried to stand him up.

A slap upon his cheek. "Cadman's dead. Come on, Jonathan, damn it! The twins are on the other side of the door."

The hole widened as the beast clawed its way through the rock. Nylen got Jonathan into the rope seat, sat behind him, and pulled them both forward. The monster finally forced its body halfway into the cave, and let out a shriek of delight. The snakes were sent into a frenzy at the sound, and now they slithered through the flame to bite at the rope. Nylen and Jonathan were three-fourths of the way across when it snapped. Nylen fell as Jonathan swung across the wide expanse of the whirlpool.

"Nylen!"

The warrior was able to grab hold of Jonathan's feet, but he had slipped out of the seat, with the rope underneath his shoulders, cutting into his armpits. Pain exploded in his back where the rope had raked over his wounds. He gripped the rope with numb fingers while Nylen tried to climb up his legs, far enough to find some hold in the wall to grasp, but the rock was too slick with moisture. Looking down, Jonathan saw a green light growing within the churning black water below them. The monster had cleared the hole and now it was at the edge of the whirlpool. It seemed to peer down at Jonathan and Nylen with sightless eyes, while flicking its forked tongue, tasting the air. It reached out one long sinuous arm and caught hold of Jonathan's cloak.

The light from the center of the whirlpool grew bright. *Please, not Adamara, Neáhvalar help us, not that—*

"Watch out!" Nylen shouted.

A great rush of wind and water, and then Morgan the Delphini sprang up from the whirlpool in a fury that shook the entire cave. With one hand, she caught hold of Nylen and Jonathan and hurled them up and onto the cavern floor.

"Avexi Celarise, Abscida lunali!" Her voice thundered, and she threw her arm towards the creature. A maroon light enveloped the beast and pinned it, thrashing, against the wall.

"Afflictalen estani!" The cave shook again, causing another rockslide that blocked the entrance. Morgan's hair fanned out, a brilliance of red and black, and her face was white with rage. Her darkened eyes were so large that she looked like an Ophidian ready to feed. The snakes slithered out of her way, hissing furiously.

At least Nylen will be saved, Jonathan thought...

"You're not dead yet," Morgan said, lifting him up. "Everyone else is already through the door."

Golden flames now danced on the edge of the whirlpool. For a moment, Jonathan could have sworn he saw Bryn's eyes staring back at him. Rocks fell all around them. They were at the door.

"It will be easier if you shut your eyes." Morgan said as she glanced back into the cave. "Now," she commanded and pushed Jonathan over the threshold.

He closed his eyes and was suddenly weightless, as if submerged underwater. It was warm, and the blood surged through his body again. Jonathan wished he could stay there forever, in that life that wasn't really life but only the in-between. A surge of cold air hit his face, and the numbness crept into his legs and back again as his feet touched solid ground.

"We're here," Morgan said.

CHAPTER 12
THE TERAKHEÎN FOREST

They were in a small clearing, about fifty feet wide, sur-rounded by great trees with emerald-colored leaves edged with gold. Almost as green as an Ophidian's eyes. Nylen was bent over Kei, who was lying on the ground, his head in Kayna's lap.

"The Terakheini needs healing, my lady," Nylen said.

"Both of them do," Morgan said as she brought Jonathan over and gently laid him down on his stomach.

And you had to carry me to safety, damn it, Jonathan thought, even as Nylen and Morgan's voices faded into bliss-ful silence. He was drifting among waves of snow, and a blinding white began to fill his eyes, though they were closed. Two enormous outstretched wings flapped foul air as large claw-like hands beckoned him further into a winter landscape.

Ichecthu. Caphecus evistorath Cadman.

Jonathan let all other voices go as he sank into that world, felt the strength return to his legs and all cold disap-pear as he rose from the snow-covered ground. He was going to find his godfather.

⁻᷄⁓᷅(ᴏ),(ᴄ)⁻᷄⁓᷅

"Winter is in his veins," Morgan said as she finished tend-ing Jonathan and went over to Kei. She knelt down and placed her hands on Kei's face, checking his cheeks, chin, and forehead. "But it is different with the Terakheini," she said, frowning as she glanced around. "Where is Cadman?"

"He fell back in the Wild Lands," Nylen answered.

"Can you help my brother? One of the cave snakes bit him." Kayna pleaded, her face streaked with tears. "I tried to bring him back with the music," she added as she pulled out the necklace. "But it isn't helping."

"How did you come to have that?" Morgan asked sharply. "Never mind. I will need your help for this, for my own power is weakening. Can you remember the way to your home?"

"I...I haven't been here for so long, I don't know..." She angrily wiped her tears away.

Morgan laid her hand on Kayna's forehead and whispered a few words in her language. Then she gently asked, "Can you see it now?"

A blurry image of their door and the path to it. "In part, my lady."

"You'll remember more as we walk to it. Your mother would have kept what we need to heal your brother."

"We can't leave him!"

"We will only be gone a little while. You, sir—" Morgan turned.

"Nylen, my lady." He bowed low.

"Keep them warm until we return." The Delphini hesitated a moment, her eyes growing hard. "Use a flame on Jonathan if you must. Whatever it takes to keep him conscious." She reached for Kayna's hand. "Come, there's not much time." They set off to their left, between two of the giant trees.

Jonathan's cheek and hands were icy to the touch. It would be better to lay the boy on his back, but his skin was too torn. Nylen slapped him on his cheek. "None of that!" he shouted. "You have to stay awake." He called Jonathan's name several times, but there was no response.

Nylen pulled out tinder and flint, and within moments had a small fire going. He slid Jonathan's dagger out of his belt, and laid the blade in the fire, then went to check on

Kei. Instead of getting colder, the Terakheini was growing hotter to the touch. Nylen brought his water pouch to Kei's lips as he elevated the Terakheini's head, but the water merely dribbled down the boy's mouth and chin.

Returning to the fire, he pulled the dagger out of the flames. *Neáhvalar forgive me* he muttered, signing a triangle in the air. Then, lifting Jonathan's hair, laid the blade on his neck.

"Cadman!" Jonathan cried out.

Nylen frowned. The boy's cry had held no anguish, only welcome, and he hadn't even flinched from the heat of the blade upon his skin. What dead land was Jonathan walking?

A sudden crash of branches nearby and the neighing of horses had Nylen reaching for his sword before he was even on his feet. He crept over to the trees where Kayna and Morgan had gone.

There was a yell, coupled with a bit of swearing.

"That was a woman," Nylen found himself saying out loud from the very shock of it.

"Given the head I lack below, I'd agree." A woman came into view, slight in frame, hidden within a heavy cloak and hood. "Although the one on my shoulders can outwit either of yours on any given day."

What little Nylen saw of her face was so caked in dirt he could not place her age. The accent was slightly western. Cadarian? She was followed by a barrel-chested man with a wide jaw and shoulder-length black hair. The lines around his eyes told of forty years lived, maybe forty five. His right hand held the reins of two horses—chestnut coursers, at least sixteen hands high—while his other hand steadily gripped a drawn broadsword.

"Put your weapon down," the woman ordered Nylen. Her eyes darted from Jonathan to Kei, then back to the warrior. "Or you'll join the dead you already have."

"They live still," Nylen growled, and raised his sword higher.

"Then state who you are, before I take your head," the dark haired man threatened. "This forest belongs to Cadarn now."

"I am Nylen Eris, captain of the Íarchin archers who came to succor Cadarn in the war, and now am guard to this last Terakhein and his companion," he ventured. "Both were sorely wounded in the Wild Lands and are on the edge of death."

"Stand down," she barked at her escort. The man lowered his sword and the woman hid her knife in the folds of her tattered cloak. "You have no others with you?"

"No more," Nylen said warily. "The demon monster of Dorlíhein took our only other companion."

The woman's escort didn't move, but Nylen saw his hand grip the hilt of the sword so tightly his knuckles turned white.

"Now tell me your name and purpose for being in a forest so long hidden from human eyes," Nylen demanded.

"My purpose, for the moment, is to save the life of that Terakhein and his friend, apparently," she rasped, as she retrieved a small pack from the saddle of one of the horses. "There's a blanket on the courser to the left. Please cover the young boy with it, and I will be there shortly."

"I would have your names," Nylen demanded once more.

"Fool! Your Terakhein is dying and you would question me for nothing more than a lie. Well, then, you may call me Lady Widara," she said bitterly, "for that is what I am now, a widow both in soul and body. This is Master Coerb." She turned to her companion. "Restart Lord Eris's fire, please."

"Yes, my lady," Coerb grunted.

Nylen looked over at Kei, whose forehead was dripping with fever. The lady was right; there was little choice. He lowered his sword and, with a curt nod, grabbed the blanket from the chestnut courser and laid it over the Terakheini. Nylen's water pouch was almost empty, but he poured the rest of the cool water onto a strip of cloth and bathed the boy's face with it.

The woman kneeled over Jonathan's body and peeled away a piece of his dressing. Her face grew more serious. "You lied, Lord Eris. Where's the little lady who wears this?" she held up the necklace Kayna had left behind.

"There is a Terakhein girl as well," Nylen answered slowly.

"A sister? And where did you let her wander off to, seeing that her brother is in such peril?"

"More than just a sister," Nylen said, wondering how to work this knowledge in his favor. "His twin. Therefore, be careful how you treat him, for she has gone off with a Delphini to find medicine. They will be back shortly."

"Do not lecture me on how to treat the wounded," she said, pointing to the burn on the back of Jonathan's neck. "Did you do this?"

"The Delphini said to use fire if necessary," Nylen explained. "He was attacked by the Cralen, the birds of—"

"I know what the Cralen are and what they do," she snapped. "Master Coerb, bring more tinder over here and make that fire as big as you can. We must keep him warm."

Coerb broke off some of the dried undergrowth and fed the fire, while the Lady Widara pulled a vial out of her sack. After spreading a white ointment onto her hands, she rubbed them together until the white paste became as clear as water. She smeared the balm on Jonathan's forehead, cheeks, and arms.

Coerb stood guard over them, one hand on his sheathed sword. The great coursers stood off to the side pawing the ground. Yet neither was hitched to any of the surrounding trees. *Horses bred for battle and burdened with a Lady and her servant,* Nylen wondered.

The woman continued to massage the clear salve into Jonathan's arms and face, singing his name, but nothing happened. She sang loudly at first, and then more softly. But there was still no movement, barely even the rise and fall of his chest. The lady finally leaned down to his ear and whispered something. Jonathan stirred slightly. She sat back on her heels and stared at Jonathan for a moment more, then sighed. "Keep watch over him," she told Coerb and went over to Kei.

She removed the wet rag from his forehead and placed her hands on his face much in the same way Morgan had done. She kept shaking her head; in anger or despair Nylen could not tell. Loose dirt sprinkled off her cloak and hair onto Kei so that she had to keep dusting him off. When she pulled back the blanket, both saw little pink spirals all over the Terakheini's neck. The woman threw off the blanket and began to pull off his shirt.

"What do you think you're doing?" Nylen cried as he seized her wrist. "Morgan said to keep him warm, not to strip him."

"Unhand her!" Coerb drew his sword.

"Stand down, Master Coerb." She twisted her wrist out from Nylen's grasp. "This venom," she pointed at the marks, "will kill him before the Delphini gets back if I don't help him. You burned your other boy to keep him alive, now trust that I know something beyond how to embroider handkerchiefs."

Against his better judgment, Nylen let go of her. Coerb had not lowered his broadsword, and Kei was dying. There was little else he could do but let her finish removing the Terakheini's tunic. They found more spirals on his chest and shoulders, which were beginning to darken.

"Once they begin moving…" Widara rasped, getting up for her sack. She pulled out two large black river rocks and placed them in the fire, and, when they were hot enough, placed them directly on Kei's chest. His body shuddered and began to convulse.

"Hold him down," she ordered as Kei thrashed back and forth. It required all of Nylen's strength to keep the boy still.

Soon, though, he stopped struggling and began to moan for water.

"No," she said as Nylen rose to go refill the water pouch. "He must not drink. The venom is taking over his body and only fire can drive it out—if he's strong enough."

"When will we know?" Nylen asked irritably.

"Soon enough," she said and sat down. Coerb stood next to her, his sword still unsheathed.

"How do you know of such a cure?" Nylen frowned. "Those snakes were of the Wild Lands, which the Ophidians have stirred awake once more."

But the lady merely drew hood and cloak more tightly around her, and answered him not a word.

⁓⚬⟨◉⟩⚬⁓

Jonathan slowly limped through a barren landscape, turning every once in a while to peer through the blur of ice and snow at what might be stalking his steps. The wind's frigid touch seemed not to affect him, although an odd weariness was spreading through his limbs. In front of him stone-gray mountains jutted into the sky, their purple jagged peaks forming the turrets of an impenetrable fortress. Above, grotesque birds circled—like the ones that had wounded him in the Wild Lands—but they did not attack now, nor did they swoop any lower. Jonathan felt certain that something within those mountains was drawing him forward, but he cared not. His godfather was here, somewhere.

He staggered on, thankfully numb to the deep scars the birds had left on his back. How many times had he run from this winter world in his dreams, only to wind up here once more, and this time for real? There were names for the birds above him, but his mind fled from the cruel sound of it. Nor could he remember what creatures had pursued him here. Even his godfather's name had disappeared from memory; only his face—half moon hazel eyes, the thin nose and half-cocked grin, with his long salt and pepper hair pulled back

—only that image remained. A distant scream echoed above the wind that stung his face. Was *that* what hunted him now? For the first time since he came to this place, he felt terror. It propelled his legs towards the mountains, where either his godfather—or something monstrous—awaited him.

—❦—

Nylen sat unmoving beside Kei, watching for any sign of improvement while Widara tried to wake Jonathan. Coerb stood between them, fetching whatever they needed. Nylen heard a slight rustle in the trees and instinctively reached for his sword. Coerb did the same.

Moments later, Nylen could make out the figures of Morgan and Kayna walking though the underbrush. Fresh scratches ran down Kayna's cheeks, and Morgan had a long cut on her left arm. "Did you find a village?"

"Yes," Kayna said, rushing to her brother. The numerous spirals were now slightly underneath Kei's skin and had darkened so completely that they now looked like baby serpents. Kayna fell to her knees. "Is he...?"

"Not yet." Morgan looked at the stones lying on Kei's chest then noticed the hooded woman sitting beside Jonathan and the man standing behind her.

"I brought them," Widara said, throwing back her hood to reveal a cropped head of hair so dirty one could not tell the color of it. She was older than Nylen expected, yet he still could not place her age.

"Those rocks alone kept him alive," Morgan said, and emptied the bag that Kayna had brought with them.

A shriek tore from Kei's lips as the spiral on his shoulder began to slowly move; Nylen instinctually took a step forward, but held his tongue as the Delphini made a salve and smeared it on a very thin leaf. She laid it on Kei's shoulder, then put Kayna's hand over it. "Keep it there," she said.

The Delphini smeared more salve over her hands and held them over the fire. Soon they began to glow from the heat, like a sword inside a white-hot forge. Her mouth was set in a pained grimace as she kept them over the heat. Finally, she placed her white-hot hands directly on Kei's chest. Nylen yelled out, for surely she would burn the boy and destroy him in the very act of trying to save him.

"Stay back!" Morgan's voice echoed like the ocean during a storm.

The Terakheini's shrieks turned into screams as the raised spirals curled up into tight little circles and began to wriggle out through his skin. Snakes, each the length of a man's little finger, fell to the ground. The Terakheini screamed and thrashed more violently as they continued to bore through his flesh. Some were already dead, but others tried to slowly slither away, until Nylen sliced them in half with his blade. The holes in Kei's skin closed up almost as quickly as they opened; Kayna wept as she helped hold her brother down. Morgan smeared the salve over Kei's chest, arms, and legs until all the serpents had fallen out, including the one on his shoulder.

A few moments passed, but the Terakheini didn't stir.

Morgan leaned down and said softly, "Come, little one. Do not fall away into strange voices." Kei lay once again in deep sleep, and Morgan's face at last relaxed a little as she stood up. "He must fight his way out of this fever on his own. The snakes are gone, but some of the venom is still left."

"What are you saying?" Kayna almost shouted.

"We can't do anything more. Not right now."

Nylen and Kayna watched over Kei while Morgan went to Jonathan. Widara and Coerb stood by, helpless. The Delphini met the other woman's eyes.

"He's almost gone," Widara said quietly. "The river is over to the left."

Morgan nodded, lifted Jonathan in her arms, and disappeared into the forest.

A soft sound of movement behind Jonathan caused him to glance back to see an enormous white wolf padding through the snow, its eyes as dark as ebony. When the beast had begun following him, he couldn't say, but there it was, tall and powerful as a warhorse. No curses came from its mouth to paralyze his gait; it merely followed a little distance behind as he continued towards the jagged range of precipices. He was close to the base of them and soon would begin his ascent.

Another scream pealed across the land, nearer now. Jonathan saw out in the distance to his right, perhaps half a mile away, a man-like creature barreling towards him. It must have been of horrific size to be seen from so far away. A jolt of terror rippled through Jonathan, prompting him to turn and sprint to the nearest icy foothill that lay before him. His godfather was farther up in the ring of mountains. The godfather with hazel eyes and no name, who had drowned with his heart spilling out into the river.

Jonathan had gained good ground when a sudden force smacked hard against his chest, knocking him clear off his feet. He lay there, stunned for a moment. Lifting his head slightly revealed no assailant. Slowly he climbed to his feet, looking around to make sure the wolf had not ventured any closer. It was pacing back and forth, sniffing the ground. The creature in the distance continued to run, swiftly closing the distance between them.

Jonathan took only a few steps before something rammed against his body, throwing him once more onto his back. The birds above broke their circling pattern as they darted chaotically about, their high-pitched caws a frenzied cry. Jonathan rolled over to see the wolf sprinting towards him, its massive paws kicking the freshly fallen snow behind it into a whirlwind, its dark eyes glittering. *Ictuneri heracth norifram.*

The curse froze Jonathan just as his right leg came forward, his left bent and braced against the ground, ready to spring up and flee. Flee to what? A thundering of wings behind him, but there was no time to register their source, for out of the snow-covered ground, between Jonathan and the wolf, sprang four flaming legs. A massive spider body followed, only partially revealed as it snatched the wolf with fangs and claw and dragged it, screaming, back down under the snow.

The wolf's curse still held Jonathan rooted to the spot, and all force and resistance ebbed from his limbs as a foul gust knocked him once more onto his back. The sky was suddenly darkened by wide wings.

Ict thei utic, Cadman, the thing above him croaked. *Ict thei utic Caphecus.*

Its face was obscured by the maelstrom of ice and snow, all except for its golden eye, which gazed down with all the malice of a lord long-chained in darkness, its pupil neither completely bird, reptile, or human, but all three at once. Beautiful and terrifying.

Urt Ventorasura.

Monstrous talon-like hands reached for Jonathan's throat as he instinctively flipped back onto his stomach and tried to crawl away, his fingers digging deep into the snow, reaching for something solid.

The ground cracked all around him. A long fissure began to widen just to his left. It grew so wide that Jonathan thought he was on an island of ice, for water began to splash up the sides of the fissure. Something gripped his arm. Not the talons above, but a hand from the water. A woman's hand. It pulled him off the ice and down into the icy sea, so far down that Jonathan knew he was never to come up again.

⚓

It had taken Morgan a long time to find him. When she pulled him down off the ice, he had immediately sunk into the depths of the ocean, for Morgan could not catch him so easily. She was holding another body in her arms. He opened his eyes and saw her above him, and the man that she held looked vaguely familiar. It was himself.

Morgan took the hand of the Jonathan she was holding and placed it in his own. The next thing he knew, they were moving through the water—he was holding the other Jonathan's hand, and that Jonathan was holding Morgan's hand. She kept swimming further down to avoid the large masses of icebergs blocking their way. She dragged the other Jonathan down into the darker abyss of the ocean, and that Jonathan kept a hold of him. Finally, they stopped on the ocean floor.

"Luminathia." A soft glow spread through the water, and Jonathan found himself face to face with his other. Between them was Morgan, her eyes like onyx, hair fanning all around her. The Delphini's gown was no longer a mere dress as she spread her arms wide as if to embrace them both. *Almost like fins,* he thought, just as her hand clapped onto his back.

"Illia profundum vita!" Morgan's voice thundered as she heaved the two bodies into one another.

Pain seared from head to foot as lightning crossed his eyes. *I'm being ripped open!* A flash of the smith's torn chest, the Caphecus' head burrowing deep into his godfather's flesh. *Neáhvalar's blood, let it end!* he cried as something crawled into his skin.

"Breathe."

Jonathan struggled for air, and felt a burning ache as he gulped only water. He kicked his way off the ocean floor, swimming in a body that didn't quite feel like his own. A sudden wave hurtled him upward until his head and shoulder broke through the river's surface. He immediately vomited up water.

An arm was around his neck now, drawing him to the riverbank. Once on the ground, he finally he opened his eyes. The land of ice and snow was gone. Instead, he was back in the Terakhein forest, looking up into Morgan's eyes, which had finally returned to their normal shade of deep violet.

He turned over and coughed up more water. "What happened?"

"Ventosus' cold had crept into your veins from the Cralen's wound, but your spirit left to wander his realm earlier than I'd expected."

Jonathan remembered the talons and the wings, the stench that had hovered over him. "How did you find me?"

"The water and the sky, does one not reflect the other? I used the river to lead me to you. I kept calling, but I didn't think I would find you." Her face softened as a smile played on her lips. "You held on longer than many seasoned warriors would have if they were lost in that world."

He closed his eyes. *Cadman's still there.* "The wolf," he whispered. "It was bigger than Hecthrax."

"It wasn't a *he*; it was a *she*. Hecthrax's mate, Tréasa." She pulled him up into a sitting position. "You cannot sleep yet. When we get you to camp, then you may rest."

Jonathan tried to keep awake. "Was that Bryn who brought him down?"

"Phlegon."

"He fled the last time I dream walked and saw Hecthrax."

"Ventosus called you into his land. You were in *his* vision this time, not your own. Think you can walk if you lean on me? Here, put your arm around my neck," she ordered, forcing him to stand, but then buckling under his weight.

"Morgan?" He had never seen her weak before.

"I'll be all right," she said, straightening herself.

Every muscle in Jonathan's body hurt, and a mist was beginning to shroud the green of the forest. He shuddered slightly. Morgan wrapped her already dry robe around him. Jonathan wished he could enjoy being this close to her, but the world was disappearing into the mist. Only her scent—a clean breeze over the river, faintly sweet—kept him moving.

By the time they entered the clearing, the ground was tilting dramatically. Other hands led him to a roaring fire and covered him with a blanket. He immediately lay down and watched the glow of the flames slowly fade to black.

—◦—◉)(◉—◦—

Jonathan slept for two days by the heat of the fire. When he opened his eyes, the mist was gone and in its place was afternoon sunlight. Kei sat beside him, looking tired but ever thoughtful. "How do you feel?"

Jonathan was lying on his side. "Better." His back burned less, or, at least, it was a duller kind of pain. Most of his chest was still encased in dressings, and he had an itching desire to pull them off. He tried moving his legs. Relief poured through him as he felt the muscles contract when he bent one knee, and then the other. Though it had been only a few days, it seemed like forever since he had any real feeling of warmth in his legs. Noting how badly Kei looked, Jonathan pointed to the scarlet spirals covering the Terakheini's bare chest and shoulders. "What happened?"

"The snake venom devours you from the inside out," Kei said quietly. "Morgan healed me in part, but the Lady Widara had a hand in it too."

"Who?"

"The widow of the Wood." Kei pointed over Jonathan's shoulder.

Jonathan slowly turned to see a little rocky enclave that held a fire pit where a woman stirred a pot. He blinked a few times. Surely he was still dreaming. Bryn was quite sure everyone had been killed. Everyone.

"How did you…" Jonathan whispered.

"Time enough for storytelling later," Sienna Samsone declared unceremoniously as she brought him and Kei a bowl of stew. "It's no morning meal, but it'll do."

She looked so small now without her long white tresses, the purple cloak in burnt tatters. "Lady Widara?" Jonathan looked quizzically from Kei back to the widow.

"My name when I was a maiden," she said, running a hand through her cropped hair. "You needn't look so awestruck, for certainly I was once an innocent lass who lived under my father's roof."

Jonathan couldn't get over the shock of seeing her alive, not after seeing Cadman's death. "Bryn said—"

"Enough questions," Sienna said. "You were near death before Morgan brought you back, and Ventosus will call you into his haunted realm again if you don't eat."

"Ventosus is not death, Widow Widara," Kei argued.

"*Sienna*, if you please, Kei."

"The Elementarí belong to Neáhvalar, Sienna," he continued. "No matter what. None evil nor good, but all hunger when they walk abroad."

She gave no answer to this, which was strange, since the widow always seemed to have a retort to everything, no matter the circumstance. Jonathan rolled over onto his hands and knees so he could sit up, but his back spasmed in pain from the sudden twisting movement.

"I wouldn't do that just yet," Sienna warned as she walked over to the fire. "Keep on your side till we're ready to move."

Jonathan did as he was told. "Where are the others?"

"Morgan took Kayna and Nylen to scout out the land," Kei said. "They found a village to be our camp."

Jonathan paused, then asked, "Yours?"

Kei shook his head as he looked at Jonathan with cool, emotionless blue-gray eyes. "Kayna and Morgan tried to find it after we came through the door, but many villages have been razed to the ground with fire."

Jonathan tried sitting back up, more slowly this time; he did not like feeling that he was completely immobile. "Then we are as unsafe here as we were in the Wild Lands."

"Because my village was destroyed?" A deep blush colored Kei's cheeks as an edge crept into his voice. "The Nemarons would not have found this forest were it not for the Ophidian's betrayal, but that does not mean they forever broke Neáhvalar's protection set around it."

"But even Sienna was able to find it, despite such protection."

The widow looked singularly unimpressed. "Humph. *Found* it my arse. Stumbled into it is more like it. Now give me your bowl if you're not even going to try to eat—"

The whinny of a horse made everyone turn. "Who's there?" Jonathan shouted.

"One who expects a more courteous greeting, given the morning he has had," a man barked as he rode a large chestnut courser through the trees, another one of its like obediently following. His face was clean-shaven, revealing a strong jaw and nose, familiar widely-placed gray eyes.

Jonathan blinked hard. "Theo?" No, another whose resemblance he had seen back in the barn at Duraeston. "Breoc."

The trader dismounted and clasped Jonathan by the hand. "Well met, after a long journey."

Joy and panic immediately filled Jonathan's heart. "Where's Keira? Trapher said you both were taken."

"Trapher's a lying dog trapped in a snake's belly," Breoc growled. He bent down and immediately began putting out the small fire, making sure it did not smolder. "We were almost overtaken by a small band of Nemarons going in the same direction. Only five of them, but they were disguised in Duraeston guild garb. They brought one of their damn throcks with them, too."

"Did you kill it?" Kei asked softly. His voice chilled Jonathan to the bone, for he had never heard the Terakhein speak so coldly.

Breoc shook his head. "The throck had already caught our scent and was leading them straight to us. That's when we cast off our cloaks and sent them down river to divert it and rode northeast, far away from Duraeston and into the smaller hills. Luckily, Keira's used to that terrain, or we would have become lost ourselves. It fooled the throck for a little while, but then we heard their horses, and knew the beast must be leading them back, curse its black snout.

"Outrunning a throck in the hills is like trying to outrun a bear in the woods—you've got something twice your size leaping after you on four legs with fangs for teeth. As we kept climbing, we discarded things from our packs. Then, during the dead of night, we found another little creek, and led the horses through it. The Nemarons gave up searching for us by morning next, but we had to beat them to Duraeston, for I wondered just where and how they acquired those guild badges. Plunder from Kendrick? I didn't know, neither could Keira tell if any of the cloaks were from her hall. We waited a day, huddled close since we dared not make a fire—"

"Must have been nice," Jonathan laughed.

"We were too damn cold," Breoc snapped. "She didn't stop shaking till we arrived at Jaxon's house in the dead of night. I searched Duraeston inquiring after the men, but none had seen them. How you hide a throck in the middle of a city, I don't know. It'd drive any barn animals mad with terror."

"Then there's an alliance between guild members in Duraeston and Nemaron," Kei said.

"Never!" Jonathan exclaimed. "The Order of the Seven Woods is there; the priests—"

"The Terakheini's right, Jonathan," Breoc said. "That's the news I discovered. The Council has ordered the disbanding of the Order to make a standing army, and they've already started felling the Seven Woods."

CHAPTER 13
TRAITORS

The news fell on Jonathan like a thunderclap. There had been talk, of course—he had heard it on the way to the caves of Kaelest. But to disband the Order that protected the most ancient of woods…"The priests," he stammered. "They would not support such a thing."

"The priests were overruled, at least those that argued against it." Breoc's voice quickly turned to bitterness. "But the priesthood has long been tied to the purse strings of the guilds. Those with crops ruined by that damn hail that's plagued us for a year now want to get into trade. And the guilds need more tinder for their fires, and bigger places to hold both shop and house. Don't be ready to run back just yet. Centuras hasn't been overturned, but without the sentries, already there's been 'thinning' of some of the boundary trees."

"Enough news, Breoc!" Sienna said. "We'll figure this out more later. We should get moving before the sun sets, if you please."

The widow gathered their meager belongings while Breoc helped Jonathan and Kei onto Hammer and Tongs. Jonathan gritted his teeth in pain as he hoisted himself into the saddle, but he doubted he could have walked very far.

Slowly they made their way through the most ancient of trees. Deep gashes scarred many of the wrinkled trunks and badly burned branches revealed blood-read bark beneath. Others were smooth, made of thick vines that snaked around each other to form a thin trunk, but the vines had been slashed, and thick sap had poured out and hardened.

"Can you hear them?" Kei asked.

Jonathan shook his head, not wanting to look any more at the devastation around him. A memory of walking through the Fáliquerci with Cadman came unbidden into his mind. His last words to the smith had been angry and short, and the week before that, Jonathan had dared to strike him. Now there was no chance to tell Cadman that he had always been a second father to him, that the smith had been the one to inspire Jonathan to seek to join the Order. But what use was any of that now? Wouldn't the Seven Woods eventually be reduced to mere skeletons, like this forest? The path Tongs walked was overgrown with vines, the trees no longer merely scorched but completely charred, tall, dark ghosts against the noonday sun.

"What are the names of these trees, Kei? The emerald ones tinged with gold?" They seemed to have sustained the most damage.

"They're Auréa, Terakhein trees," he said. "The sentries of our forest."

Dead sentinels of a dead land, Jonathan thought as they began to see other signs of Terakhein life. Kettles and shattered dishes, broken swords and scattered toys, chaotically littered the sides of the path. Jonathan wanted to ask Kei about it, but the Terakheini's face was set like stone.

Eventually they came to a grassy expanse, with more of the same flotsam they had seen along the path. In its center, large white stones encircled a wide fire pit. A mass of Auréa surrounded the clearing, amid other smaller trees with large dark green leaves. Looking more closely, Jonathan saw that the foliage partially concealed houses nestled within the branches, a broken ladder hanging midway down. Small dwellings on the ground blended into the trunks of the trees. They were circular and looked to be woven out of the thick, dark vines of the tree Jonathan had seen earlier. Yet everything was in shambles: walls broken out, trees torn in half, and the roofs partially burned.

"Over here!" Kayna was standing in the doorway to a house and waving. She had bathed and changed into a dark green tunic. For a moment, she even looked like a girl as she sprang forward and gracefully ran to her twin. Kei leapt off Hammer and met her halfway. "We were beginning to worry," she said and embraced Kei in a fierce hug.

"Careful, I'm still sore," Kei pulled away, laughing.

"Which is why you're not to be doing anything at the moment," Sienna ordered. "You and Jonathan get settled by the fire. We'll sleep in the house, though, away from the breeze and chill of morning."

Jonathan doubted the house could keep out much of either as they crossed the threshold. It was spacious enough for a large family, but there were great rents along the wall where the foundation met the ground. *As if something had tried to burrow underneath,* Jonathan thought with a shudder. Burns scarred the opposite walls in crisscross patterns, and the dome-like roof didn't cover the house all the way, but opened up to the sky.

"Jonathan, stop milling about," Sienna ordered. "Still wounded, and you trek across the forest like you're on a summer walk."

He didn't think the slow shuffle he had managed across the clearing counted much. "Isn't that to be expected, having been healed by an Elementarí and a Terakhein?" Still, he obediently sat down by the fire, disappointed at not seeing the one person he expected. "Where is Morgan?"

"Wipe that mopey look out of your eye. Your Delphini went to the river, but will return soon enough, I'll warrant." Sienna busied herself making the stew. "Bringing you back from death was no small matter."

"She's not my Delphini," he said, even though he could feel a blush rising in his cheeks. Kei raised an eyebrow, perhaps in puzzlement. Or in amusement. "But it would be bad manners if I did not thank the one who battled a frozen waste to save me."

Jonathan thought back to the day they met, how he had promised her he would find the children, and how much he had wanted to prove that he was a man worthy of the Order, worthy of her respect and...what? Desire? The Elementarí certainly felt hunger, were driven by it, even. But did they feel the need to be loved?

I'd been torn asunder and frozen along the journey. He looked over at the twins, sitting close by each other. *No, it was her duty to save me. I am the only link to the Terakhein. No other reason.* He took a few mouthfuls of stew, though not really tasting it. With Sienna's cooking, that might have been for the best.

The twins conversed in low voices, while Nylen, Breoc, and Sienna discussed inconsequential things they had found in the forest. No one talked about Cadman. As they finished dinner, Nylen looked at the widow. "Now, strange woman, tell us how you escaped the sack of Breithan."

"Actually, I would like to take a walk with Jonathan, if you all don't mind."

He took a deep breath. He wasn't ready to hear it, not so soon after losing his godfather, but there it was.

"Do not wander far," Breoc warned. "Stay within shouting distance, and come back before dark."

They walked across the clearing to a dark house, half of which had been burned away. There was still a log bench and the remains of a table in the center of it. Jonathan offered his hand to Sienna as they stepped over the broken house frame. "I'm not sure I should even tell you all this," she began.

"I have already dreamed much of it, and Bryn told me a good deal more," Jonathan said. "So tell me what you will, if you think it necessary."

"You want to know how I lived while others died." She sat down at the table across from him. "I'll tell you. Your folks and I were at the smithy to see if there was any news of you. When the beasts came, it was like hearing the world die. I made a firebrand of sword and cloth and tried to find the children in the chaos. The stores were on fire, and smoke filled the air so thick nothing was visible. Riok ran into me, flailing his arms and shouting something. He had no sword or any weapon that I could see—damn fine time to have gone crazy like his father. In the town square I found a few men gored by a wild boar, and Susanna lay dying on the steps of the candle shop, Balfour just a few feet away. I finally spotted Lian on the other side of the square." Her voice cracked, and Jonathan thought she might lose herself to tears, but she set her face hard as flint. "He was fighting off a bear and two throcks that were attacking the children.

"I went to help him when three wolves suddenly sur-rounded me. I was keeping them at bay with my firebrand when your father appeared out of nowhere, wielding one of Cadman's swords. He killed two of the wolves while I used the sword end of my firebrand and finished off the third." She paused. "Never have I seen Silas in such a fury before, and his swings kept many of the wolves busy while people fled to the river. I lost sight of him in the smoke. Nathan's apothecary store had not burned yet, so I went in and cobbled together some powders and oils that can make a quick blast. I ran back out and started explosions where I could—that drove many away. Unnatural or not, beasts don't like fire." She grinned ruefully. "And then just as quickly as they came, they left. I stumbled across the square to find the children gone. The throcks finally took down Lian. Most of the town was on fire."

"Your hair…" Jonathan said.

She nodded. "I pulled Alec from under a burning shelf in his father's shop, half his body blistered so badly you'd barely recognize him. He died that night."

A wave of nausea overtook Jonathan, and he dashed over

to the trees and retched. Nothing came up, but he stayed there, bowed over and shaking, thinking of Alec's burnt body, his best friend and almost-brother dying in such agony. He did not want to hear any more. He could not.

Jonathan stood up and slowly walked back to her. Sienna laid a hand on his arm.

"I found your mother two days later. She had a long knife still clasped in her hand, slain animals all around her. Obviously, she fought so that others could escape, although I doubt many did. When I could not find anyone alive in the village, I set out to Klinneret to tell Theo and Rose what had happened—"

"You know them?"

"Everybody knows them," Sienna chided. "But Breoc found me in the Ruaden on my way. I was easy to spot since all the leaves had fallen—"

"All—"

"Not one branch had its leaves; the ground looked like it had bled to death. Our forests are dying. *Our* forests, which never die. All the foliage gone in one fell swoop, and our village, dead." Her voiced cracked. "Breoc had been coming south to find some damn throck. Together we headed back to Breithan and looked for survivors. Now your father..." She paused, as if trying to find the words. "...he wasn't found among the dead. He was carrying a distinct sword, which wasn't around any body we found, mangled or not, and animals don't despoil their victims after a kill. I know what Silas' marriage band looks like. There was no such ring or sword found."

"Are you telling me he's still alive?"

Her hand squeezed his, hard. "I'm saying Silas didn't die in Breithan, that's for sure."

Jonathan disengaged himself and jumped to his feet. "He could be out there, wounded and wandering!" he said, at once elated and terrified. "Did you send out a search party?"

She nodded. "Theo and Rose did, I'm sure. There is

more you must hear, but the rest I need to tell the others as well. Come, let us go back to them."

The other four were talking animatedly until Jonathan and the widow returned to the small fire. The silence was sudden and awkward. "I have finished the story that was only meant for Jonathan's ears. But the rest of you must know that two others escaped Breithan besides myself." She turned to Breoc. "Tell them."

"Two sets of footprints went towards the Wild Lands," Breoc growled. "Who would dare pursue their attackers in such small numbers? We decided to go and see. Four days we followed the trail to the Thraelis River. The footprints were lost amid the muddy bank, and we didn't know if they had crossed the river into the western border of Cadarn or walked north along the river up into Lailethas."

"Then how did you find us? Is all the magic gone from this place that now anyone can come here?" A blue ball of flame had formed in Kei's hand. He looked down, as if surprised to see it there.

"The power of the Elementarí still holds here, Kei," Breoc said. "A voice from the river told us to cross and find this forest; we both heard it. Although Sienna led the way."

"Second sight," the widow said dismissively. "I'm old enough to see unseen things, like forgotten paths. Extinguish that flame of yours, Kei. There are no Nemarons here."

The Terakheini slowly closed his hand over the flame.

"They could have been my father's tracks," Jonathan blurted out. *'Tis a storm we bring to save the land,* Silas had said the day they came back from the Southern Council. The memory circled in Jonathan's head, unbidden and cruel. The law of Dormín was broken so the land could not rest, and soon the Seven Woods would be desecrated. Had Silas foreseen their coming doom, and formed an alliance with spirits of the earth, no matter what sacrifice they demanded—including that of the last Terakhein? He might have known all along, might have heard Jonathan cry out in his sleep and guessed the same things Cadman had about the girl. And what if Trapher had come to him, promising that the land's honor would be restored if he only gave up his son, who held the key to the Ophidians being put back to sleep.

Jonathan still remembered the man in Duraeston who seemed so shocked at discovering him in the stable. *It can't be, no, not you.* There was a piece to the puzzle he still didn't have. Neither did such knowledge explain why the beasts had destroyed Breithan though, unless they were looking for something, perhaps *someone* else. Jonathan stared hard at the widow. She had somehow escaped a massacre, when everyone else died; what other secrets did she keep?

"We don't know, boy, what happened there," Sienna rasped. "Remember, Riok's cousin Tarl was murdered almost a year before—all that Seven Woods business. There was treachery, no doubt, but no use wondering about it all now; you cannot undo this riddle of politics and kingdoms and strange creatures like me in one night." Her eyes glinted a bit, much like Cadman's, and just then it hit him how alike they were. "Our course is set—for the desert or Cadarn—but first bed for all of you. The journey behind us is nothing compared to what lies ahead."

"Aye, and do not worry, Jonathan," Breoc said in an even tone. "If Silas lives, we will find him."

Jonathan couldn't tell if that was a promise or a threat.

⚬⚬⚬

Everyone slept badly that night. Once, Jonathan opened his eyes to see Nylen and Sienna walking in together, whispering. The next time, he jerked awake to find Kayna sitting up, her back to the wall, staring at nothing. He was considering talking to her when he drifted back into dreams. Then voices again, this time real and solid. Jonathan woke and saw through the open doorway that everyone was breaking their fast with stew. His heart skipped a beat when he saw that Morgan was among them. Sienna was flying around cooking and refilling people's plates. "It's about time," she said, peering in.

"What hour is it?" he yawned.

"Past morning. You had better get up if you want to break your fast before noon."

Jonathan's back stung more than it burned as he stood and tried bending to the side. It was a relief to feel less pain at least, given how little time they would probably stay here. He ran a hand through his thick mop of black hair, wishing for once that he had a mirror and comb.

Morgan turned from her conversation with the twins as he entered the clearing. "You seem to be in less pain."

"Yes, thank you." Despite not wanting to act like an invalid, Jonathan let her help him sit up as Sienna filled his bowl.

At the mere touch of Morgan's hand, Jonathan's thoughts almost betrayed him, but something had happened on his journey through the winterscape—sure, he had almost died, but he had regained some part of his mind that before had been so easily penetrated by the Elementarí. Morgan couldn't sense everything he was thinking now, and that was key, since there was so much more between them than just a young man's desire or heartfelt appreciation. For that alone, he was grateful for the frozen journey he'd taken. Instead, he focused on the monster he'd seen in Ventosus' kingdom, just as he had back in the Dorlíhein forest. "The monster you killed, the one that," a catch in his throat, "that tore open Cadman's chest? What was that?" Seven times worse than any throck or beast he had ever heard about.

Everyone turned to hear her answer. "We call it the Caphecus; I'm sure Truculen has a more tender name for it. And I did not kill it, for it was his creation, and as such, has some of the life of the Elementarí, like Hecthrax," Morgan said.

"Seems a cruel jape, then, to make it blind," Nylen

barked.

"It had eyes, once. Nor did the Caphecus always look as you have seen it, naked and twisted. But that is a story none of you need to hear now."

A shudder ran through Jonathan. The Delphini's eyes had shaded to a darker violet—whether from anger or hunger he couldn't tell, nor did he care. She was so beautiful.

Feed I must, like all Elementarí walking these shallow lands. Morgan's thoughts invaded his own. He tried to close his mind to her, but a question slipped out.

And just what is your *prey?*

"What about your brothers, my lady?" Breoc's voice seem to thunder all around Jonathan, so intent was he on discovering what satiated Morgan's desire. "You haven't mentioned them."

"Nor will I," Morgan scowled. "The Caphecus wounded them so badly they required my mother's healing." She stood up and walked over to Kei, who finishing the last of his biscuit. "May I look at your shoulder?"

One raised spiral remained on the Terakheini's left shoulder where the serpent had begun moving. "I wish we could have burned that one in time," the Delphini said, "but don't worry, for it's dead. Still, the scar might cause you pain." She sat back, looking at the twins. "I cannot see what is in your minds, yet I sense you want something of me."

"You remind us of someone. A Delphini who visited us every once in a while, and on that last day..." Kei paused as his voice shook. "That last day...she was at the river and sent us away using the Avexi Celarise. You...you look like her."

"Branwynne," Morgan said softly.

The name sounded vaguely familiar to Jonathan, and suddenly the song that one of Jory and Bree's girls had sung came back to him. Was this the very Branwynne who had led the Íarchins from the coast to the Caves of Kaelest?

"Do you know what happened to her?" Kei asked. "She

sent us to the Valley of Eyes, and we waited by the bank thinking she would follow..."

"Trapher killed her. She was weakened from the Avexi Celarise, otherwise he would never have dared come so close to a daughter of Morwenna."

"She was your sister." Jonathan immediately thought of Jeremy dying in the forest. Two siblings dead due to Trapher's blood lust. And yet here was another bond that drew him closer to Morgan.

Kayna's lip slightly trembled as Kei put his arm around her; in his right hand, a blue flame appeared. It was becoming second nature now, to ignite the flame when his thoughts were troubled.

Morgan drew herself up. "Feel no guilt, my Terakheini. Branwynne gladly sacrificed herself for you, as would I, and so now we will continue the training that Bryn started. You will not be able to storm Ophidia—"

She extended her hand to Kei, who dropped the blue flame onto her palm.

"But neither will you be so defenseless again." The small flame spread out until it became a brilliant lake of fire in her hand and, shooting out of it, a sword. Jonathan blinked. The familiar image on the cup from Theo's house once again disappeared. It was a sign of allegiance to the Ogoni, but also a sigil of someone's house that belonged to neither Lailethas nor Íarchol. And Theo had said he was from Lailethas.

"Kei, Kayna, gather your belongings; your lessons begin now." Morgan crossed the clearing and disappeared amidst the Auréa.

"Did you see that sword?" he asked Kayna.

"What sword? There was only a lake of fire." Her eyes were shining as she quickly gathered her things. Then she frowned as she stopped to stare at him. "Are you alright?"

"Never mind. Just tired." His legs were heavy, and a strange weariness was upon him now. "Go," he waved, and she ran to join her twin and Morgan.

"Let me see to your dressings, Jonathan," Sienna said, gathering an extra blanket from the house. Jonathan wondered if she would leave him be if he feigned sleep, but it was no use. "Off with your shirt, boy, and don't dally so. While it might be warmer here, it's still not summer."

It was no longer painful for Jonathan to lift his arms all the way over his head, but Sienna insisted on helping him pull his shirt off. Quickly she unwound his dressings with a deft and gentle hand. Then she looked at his back.

"Well?" he asked, when Sienna remained quiet. "How is it?"

"The scars won't be pretty, but it's healing," she said at last, her words coming from far away. "Leave the dressings off for the rest of the day, and let's see if that doesn't help. You won't be moving, of course, for most of the day."

"And just how do you plan to stop me?" Jonathan laughed although he felt like someone had hit him over the head with a sack of grain.

"I didn't trust you to keep still, so I thought to give you some aid with just a little of the sleeping powder in your food. You might want to lie down."

The world was beginning to spin a bit as the widow helped him lie down on his stomach, but he kept his eyes pried open just long enough to see Nylen walk into the clearing.

"Breoc has the south watch," Sienna said, through a long tunnel. "Now I must go too." He heard Nylen reply but couldn't understand the words. Then he closed his eyes, and all voices disappeared.

⁓◦◎◦◉◦◎◦◦⁓

"Keep an eye on him," Sienna warned as she gathered her things. "I gave him just enough to keep him down for the morning and most of the afternoon, but there's a fine line between not waking and not breathing."

"A wise precaution, my lady," Nylen said, smiling. "But

you?" He took her hand in his. "Where are you going with that sack? You're to be the watch, not a hauler of wares."

"We need firewood," she replied, "and there will be plenty along my path."

"Aye, that there will," he said, kissing her hand. "Still the good nurse."

"Always." She kissed his cheek in return. She looked into his eyes, long enough to see the love that was still there for her. *The others need not know. Not yet.* She hurried out of the clearing and down the path. There wasn't much time.

—*◦◎◉◎◦*—

It was a sad forest, Sienna thought, as she picked up sticks here and there and put them in the bag over her shoulder. Now and then she would stop and listen, hoping to hear some sound, some twitter of life. But there was nothing. A tear slid down her cheek as her eyes grazed the ground once more for firewood amid all the debris. There, a broken doll, its head burned completely black, and next to it, a smashed wooden flute. She had wandered off to the left of the center clearing, and found an almost invisible path, overridden with groundcover and wayward vines. She followed it, cautiously pushing aside the dense foliage that covered the path so as not to startle any life that might be hidden beneath the massive vines. *Even a snake would be a welcome sight.*

The trees grew thicker the farther she walked, and whatever light the sky held was blocked out by the numerous branches, bare as they were. "I need a torch," she muttered as she searched her pockets. She could scarcely see more than ten feet in front of her, nothing but murky shadows of leaf and limb. The foliage underneath her feet had turned to such a deep shade of blue-green that it almost looked black, and was joined by thick vines snaking their way across the path.

The branches dipped to the ground, and smaller limbs sprouted dark red leaves, with sinewy green veins that flowered throughout. Another clearing lay up ahead where the daylight was allowed to settle unencumbered. The shadows that gathered at the edge of the clearing lengthened as she entered the circle, but her sight rested on one particularly strange shape. It was a ladder, not going up into the trees as they had seen before, but rather, sticking out of the ground.

Kneeling down in front it, she peered into the narrow square whereby a person could climb down into the home. All she could see was darkness below. She turned and scanned the forest floor—surely there was something she could use. A few feet away she spied a few small stones.

"Well, I guess that'll do." She gathered some of the rocks and sticks, and then pulled a small sachet out of her pocket. Pouring out a little white powder, she coated the rocks then struck them together until they sparked. After a few strikes, the spark caught hold of the sticks. Taking one of the larger branches from her sack, she lit the end of it and stared into the dark hole, thrusting the torch in as far as she could.

It was a gloomy sight. The chairs and tables were all smashed, and books and clothes were strewn about. Sienna pulled herself up, shaking her head. She went over to another hole and peered in. Then another. Finally, she sat back up and listened for any sound. Still nothing. She gingerly tried the first rung on the ladder. It seemed strong enough. Another rung. Then another until her feet hit the dirt floor. She held the torch out so she could see.

This home was more damaged than the rest. Sienna couldn't even tell what the splintered pieces of wood and stone once were—whether a table or a chair. There were ashes scattered about and burnt marks on the wall. The Nemarons had been sure to set fire to this place. Sienna walked slowly into one of the other rooms.

Crack.

She froze, looking around the room. Nothing.

"Damn," she said when she saw that she had only

stepped on a twig. She relaxed her shoulders, shook her head, and went into what she supposed was the parents' bedroom, searching among the debris. Then she went into what must have been the children's room, and held the torch closer to the ground, peering intently.

"Don't tell me it's not here," she muttered. She bent over to get a better look as she moved pieces of burnt toys and clothes aside, moaning a bit as she did so. "I'm getting too old for this—ah, there you are," she said.

There in the rubble something gleamed by the firelight. The old widow knelt down, picked it up, and wiped the ashes off of it. It was a very old broach, shaped in the form of a tree, with deep green leaves made of emeralds and golden flowers made of crystals. She smiled as she blew the dust from its crevices so that it sparkled. Then she drew out a cloth from one of her pockets, placed the broach within it, and tucked it away in her pocket.

"Well, that's that." Back in the main room, she looked around one last time before heading back up the ladder.

Once outside, she could tell the afternoon was getting on. She had better hurry. Sienna moved in the direction of the path, but stopped. That sound again, as of a twig snapping. She lifted her torch high. "Who's there!" she yelled. No answer. She moved slowly towards the path when she heard another crack.

To her left, two yellow eyes peered out from the deep shadows.

"So, you've found me again," Sienna said as she backed away. A deep growl emitted from the trees. "Come on then. We've not got all day," she baited, reaching inside the folds of her outer cloak.

Slowly the white wolf crawled out of its hiding place, teeth bared as it continued to snarl.

The widow pulled out her dagger and brandished it with one hand while holding the torch in the other. "Remember this? It gave you that nice little scar. I'd be happy to give you another," she said, almost growling herself.

The wolf sprang.

"Nemari!" She was able to get out the word just as the wolf fell upon her in one leap, howling as it knocked her to the ground, sending the torch flying out of her hand. Its teeth grated against the widow's white head as together they rolled over and over until they stopped, the wolf on top of the old woman. Neither moved as evening came, and darkness filled the place.

CHAPTER 14
WIDOW, WOLF, AND WARRIOR

The widow had been missing for half the day now, and it was after dusk. Breoc had waited to meet her in the south, but she never came, nor had she answered his calls. They had to find her before night set in. Someone needed to be at base camp in case she returned, and given that his back was still as Nylen put it, "shredded like a piece of carrion," Jonathan was told to stay. Breoc and Kei headed south on Tongs while Nylen and Kayna rode Hammer to the north, leaving Morgan to circle the rest of the river. Jonathan sat by the fire, Cadman's sword by his side lest any man, spirit, or beast came upon him unawares.

The golden flames danced high while deep red coals glowed from the fire's center, reminding Jonathan of Phlegon's eyes. Eyes of truth. He tried to focus on those red flames, to forget how he'd felt the day he went in search of Jenna, how he'd believed he would find her in time. How her body was still warm when they tried to get her heart beating again.

Jonathan shook his head and blinked hard. *None of that.* No use dredging up a dead memory. *Tell me something I need to know, Phlegon. Dream walk with me.* Then he willed his eyes to unfocus so that the red and the gold blended together into one lake of fire. But, try as he might, all he saw was Jenna's face, eyes closed and cheeks blush red, as if she were asleep.

Dusk turned to midnight, and then the robin's eye blue

of dawn slowly cracked the sky. A whistle suddenly pierced the air, sounding far away. A little while later he heard voices —Morgan's was among them. Breoc appeared on Tongs, the widow's body cradled in his arms. Behind him, Nylen, Kei, and Kayna were dragging an enormous white wolf.

"What took you so long?" Jonathan took Tongs' reins as the trader carried Sienna into the house.

"She was in the southwest end of the forest where there were underground houses," Kei explained. "She must have been exploring when the wolf found her. Good thing she had this." He held up a dagger covered with dried blood. "She certainly would have died without it. The wolf's body must have kept her warm, for she still breathes, although it's faint."

They quickly crowded the small house until Morgan ordered them all out.

"But will she be all right?" Nylen demanded. With his thick golden braids undone, Jonathan thought the warrior looked the same as when he ran to Cierdwyn's side almost twenty years ago, the scar across his cheek being the only difference.

"Perhaps, if you leave me be and let me work," Morgan flashed, indicating just how worried she was. "The wolf was one of Hecthrax's brood."

Breoc spat on the beast as they passed it outside. "May Neáhvalar damn it to burn in darkness for all eternity."

Jonathan saw a resemblance to the wolf that had followed him and Jenna. Had it still been hunting him, but had found the widow instead? He tried not to think that he might have caused another death.

—◦◦◉◦◦—

It was well into mid-morning before Morgan slowly walked out of the house, her face almost alabaster white. "She's awake at least, and asking for you, Jonathan."

The twins exchanged glances but said nothing. As Jonathan passed Morgan on the way to the house, she laid a light hand on his arm. "I still don't know that she'll make it through the day. Try to keep her awake and talking if you can. She has fought one of the Elementari's creatures—sleep is not welcome after such an encounter."

Where are you going? he silently asked, seeing how exhausted she looked. He knew her hunger must be great, being awake and walking instead of in the abyss and dreaming.

To the river. It took much to bring the widow back and I must rest again.

Return soon. He sent the thought with a flood of emotions he couldn't show earlier. The bleak memory of Jenna and then grief and rage over Sienna's assault all dissipated in his desire for her. It almost seemed to him that the Delphini smiled, but so quickly did she turn back to the river that he couldn't be sure.

Jonathan steeled himself as he walked into the house and knelt down by Sienna. Her eyes were closed, and, for the first time, he noticed how many deep lines laced the widow's face. He wondered about her age, before gently nudging her. "I've had dreams about you."

"About damn time," she answered, a smile spreading over her face. But she still kept her eyes closed.

"You turned into an Ophidian."

"Really?" Her eyes fluttered open. "Was I beautiful and young?"

Jonathan smiled. "You were breathtaking, although you scared me quite a bit."

"My dear child, when *don't* I scare you?" she whispered and then her eyes closed again.

He shook her shoulder. "Haven't you heard that the Seven Woods is being felled? And my dreams, Sienna. You have no idea what I've seen." *What I've heard and felt.* The cry of the Ruaden, the hate-filled railings of the Dorlíhein and the pain of the Cralen in his veins. "The wrath of the Ophidians is great already from the broken laws, and how shall we stop this madness?" Even this question failed to rouse Sienna. Perhaps a memory would wake her. "Come now, woman, and spin me a tale. Tell me a story about when you were young."

She stirred slightly. "I remember your father stealing blueberries from my garden..."

"Blueberries don't grow in the southern Gaelastad, silly woman." Jonathan playfully squeezed her hand. "You were dreaming."

"Blueberries..." She mumbled. "And his sister was just as bad, even worse. Always wandering into strange places, finding strange people."

"My father had no sister," Jonathan corrected her, gripping her hand tightly now. More family secrets? Had he lost an aunt during the great winter? There had been a son—born that year and lost. His parents only spoke of him once, and then never again, until his mother had cried out about losing all her children. Did that fuel Silas's anger, and perhaps his betrayal?

"Twins of fire, twins of earth," Sienna whispered in a singsong voice. "Cursed in death, blessed in birth."

She was starting to scare him now. Was she walking a deathless land like he did? "Sienna!" he cried, and shook her.

The widow's bright blue eyes opened wide. "What's this?" She stared at Jonathan for a moment as if seeing him for the first time. Then her lids closed as she shook her head. "Sorry, dear. Wrong place and time." She looked around like she had misplaced something. "Where's my cloak?"

"Over there. Don't worry, we even brought your dagger back."

She seemed to become more peaceful once she saw the cloak, but more alert as well. "Well, don't just kneel over me like I'm on my deathbed. Help me to sit up."

He gently lifted her, wondering how someone so small could be so tough. Yet as soon as he sat her up, she snuggled against his shoulder. "This is better."

A shadow from the doorway suddenly blocked the light. Kayna stood there, a smile spreading over her face. The first real smile he had seen since her triumphant cat grin while sitting on top of him on their first meeting. "It's good to see you awake!"

"Aye, girl, you think a little pup like that could stop me?" It sounded like a challenge—another good sign that the widow was returning to her senses.

"I think it would take a lot to kill someone like you." Kayna laughed, a sound like water upon the rocks in the dark, war-torn house. "Can you eat something?"

"Depends on what you have in mind," the widow said. "If it's good for me, it's sure to be on the less tasty side, and I've had a rather rough day."

"It's not so foul tasting as that, but you'll drink it regardless. And I think it would be better to have you in the sun rather than darkness."

Sienna offered no retort to this, and merely acquiesced to Jonathan's carrying her outside to the soft grass in front of the fire.

Nylen and Breoc arrived a little while later, having swept the perimeter once again for any sign of the wolf's pack. Both rushed to Sienna's side, but it was Nylen who held her longest. "You had us scared senseless, old woman," the warrior said, finally letting her go.

Breoc's tone was oddly more reprimanding. "We know how much you like the hunt, but damn it, woman, next time do not wander—"

"You can stop your lecture, Master Coerb. Although I don't mind giving chase, this beast followed me—picked up my trail after his brothers and sisters had done their damage in Breithan. I was glad to meet up with you in the Ruaden since all I had was a dagger and a few things that could, in the right mixture, create a fire in a pinch. Seeing as we were on Hammer and Tongs for the rest of the journey, I didn't give another thought to it. I was, as everyone can see, quite wrong."

"Where did you meet it again?" Jonathan asked.

"The same place you found it," she snapped. "On top of me. Barely had time to unsheathe my dagger before it attacked."

"But the houses?" Kayna asked, frowning. "How did you find them? I had forgotten they were there."

"While gathering firewood," Sienna explained, "I was surprised to discover that little path and found myself in another little clearing like this one. Are there many more like that?"

"Hundreds," Kei said. "Although this was one of the main places where the elders would gather." He looked up at the ragged Auréa around them. "I wish we had time to explore the forest. There is so much to remember, and if we could but find the old books—"

"Time is the one thing we no longer have, Kei," Breoc cut him short. "Morgan said that Nemarons are amassing on the Cadarn border in great number now, and that Hecthrax has been spotted roaming the countryside. Should Adamara and Truculen come to the battlefield, our armies will not have the victory. The Nemaron assault will be the greatest in the east near the king's city, and then along the Lailethan border where the mountains start. We need willing warriors on both lines of defense. Cadreyth's outposts are spread throughout the land, but Adolan has only ordered half of them to be manned, damn fool. But if we find one sentry willing to start the beacon, then the alert will spread throughout Cadarn by two week's end."

"It takes time to muster an army," Jonathan said. "And you are no lord from Íarchol or Lailethas. Gaelastad stayed out of the war, so there would be little reason for the king's sentries to believe you."

"Aye, I am little more than a trading man now, but in my younger days, I served under Cadreyth as the king's man."

Jonathan had thought that nothing could surprise him anymore. "You were one of the Ausels?" The king only appointed fifty at any given time, to protect the hall and lead his army.

"Did I not tell you that I knew where to find the exiles in Duraeston?" Breoc's voice sunk to a growl. "My loyalty was always to Cadreyth; Adolan never earned it. When I failed to retrieve the fire after the war, Adolan dismissed me, citing cowardice. It was best to disappear. Others, like Jaromír, were outright killed, although no one could prove it was at the king's—"

"But I saw him!" Jonathan said. "Back in the caves of Kaelest, on the day of Cierdwyn and Cadreyth's death, I saw Jaromír, and Marek, another of the Five Captains."

"You saw Marek?" Breoc's voice turned even harder. "Who else? What else did you see?" Hadn't Cadman asked the same question?

"No name that I recognized." It was hard to remember that vision with the smoke and blood, teeth and blade scraping against skull and bone. "And since you went into hiding, would any Cadarian soldier be willing to listen to you?"

"There are enough who remember me and will follow, should I muster them. Adolan hasn't bought out all his men. In a few days' time Sienna will be my guide out of this forest. Jonathan, you should go with us."

He hadn't been ready for that offer, and for a moment, he considered it. To ride into Cadarn with an Ausel, thundering on Hammer and Tongs and alerting the outposts to rally the army was the closest he might ever attain to being a servant of the Elementarí, given that the Order of the Seven Woods was an empty promise now.

"That would not be wise, Breoc." Morgan glided into the circle. None had heard her approach the clearing. Her face had more color than an hour ago, yet Jonathan thought she still looked weary. "Jonathan hears the land in a way only the Terakhein could rival. Kayna will be bearing Ashryanna, but it is a mighty burden to carry through the desert, and for that alone Jonathan should go with twins. Kayna, perhaps it is time to show them the vessel that will hold the holy fire."

A slight blush crept into Kayna's cheeks as she drew Jonathan's necklace out of her cloak. The white stone was intact, yet it no longer emanated the low melodic note.

"The moon piece was given to your people by Adamara herself, but we thought it had been destroyed in the great winter," Morgan said as she turned to Sienna, who began to fidget.

"Don't look to me for illumination," she murmured. "I found it one day in a field, and it brought me good luck—at least, I'm convinced it brought me Mister Samsone. I passed the charm on to Jonathan. I had no idea there was another part to it; I usually don't give broken things to other people, you know."

Jonathan smirked. "What about that hacksaw you lent Balfour two years ago?"

"I'd like to have it right now," Sienna said.

"It works in our favor, however you found it." Morgan laughed, but Jonathan felt the Delphini's thoughts earnestly reaching out to the widow even as Sienna pointed at Jonathan.

"How did you get the stone? I had no idea there was another part to it."

"Theo gave it to me for luck. Said some old wise woman had given it to Rose."

"It's the way of most things, to find their way back, whether they will it or no," Breoc added, with a note of bitterness.

While the necklace seemed to hold no more magical qualities, the milky white amber produced its own glow that radiated onto Kayna, making her cat-like features softer. Almost pretty.

She is very pretty, and only a scant few years younger.

Jonathan almost jumped as Morgan's words pierced his thoughts. Her eyes, though, were looking at everyone but him. "I must be in Íarchol by the end of the week to warn Jory's people. My brothers will lead the Lailethan and Íarchin allies to the western border if they are healed in time. For the next few days, the Terakhein will be with me, except for meals and what chores you need them to perform. There is still much they must learn."

Which is why I fancy the teacher and not the student, Jonathan shot back. Morgan turned without even acknowledging him and disappeared once more amid the trees, the twins following.

—⁌⦁⦅◉⦆⦁⁍—

"We must bury that *thing*." Breoc pointed to the lifeless wolf, its gaze angry even in death. "Sienna, you're off to bed for the rest of the night. Don't argue with me, woman," he fired when her mouth opened to reply. "The trek to Cadarn won't be an easy ride and you're—"

"Old, and a woman. Thank you for the reminders, Breoc," she said, getting up. "Despite both drawbacks, you'll not find your way out of this forest without me, nor will you get Ashryanna to Cadarn without Kayna. Remember that, please, when you confine us to our sex and age."

Jonathan found it heartening to see some of the widow's spark back.

It took a good hour for Nylen and Breoc to bury the wolf, and they handled it guardedly, touching it as little as possible. The rest of the afternoon and night, Jonathan and the two men discussed routes to Ophidia and Cadarn. Their conversation was often interrupted by a burst of blue light that illuminated the trees around them, followed by loud cries. They would look at each other with raised eyebrows, but no one remarked upon the matter. It was enough to see the flashes and hear the ancient words to know that the tide in the history of mankind was turning. The Terakhein were preparing for war.

CHAPTER 15
A PARTING OF WAYS

They stayed together for three more days. Jonathan and Sienna were ordered to rest, except for light, short walks. Jonathan tried to do as he was told, mostly because Morgan was working day and night with the twins, but also because he found himself mourning Cadman more than he could admit to anyone. His godfather was the only thing he really had left in the world, the only real tie to Breithan besides Sienna. He wanted to tell Morgan all this, wanted to hold her and feel the warmth of her breath upon his neck. He even attempted to engage in more conversation with Sienna, but she seemed to avoid him, claiming that she needed to rest whenever he tried to ask her a question.

So instead he tried to distract himself by listening to Breoc and Nylen discuss how to send emissaries back to Gaelastad to stop the destruction of the forests. Here Jonathan felt somewhat useful, since Breoc often enlisted Jonathan for help when listing out who might be sympathetic to their plight. Lian had admonished him to figure out how politics work, and so he had paid attention to marketplace chatter about Dormín and Centuras. He knew which guilds were secretly afraid of breaking Terakhein law and who felt that Gaelastad's neutral position in the war long ago was a mistake.

All this activity, however, did not abate Jonathan's desire to be with Morgan. Yet by the fourth day, when Morgan was set to leave, he still had not managed to get one single moment alone with her. Sienna's slight he could take, but Morgan's avoidance of him was inexplicable, after all she had done to save him. Well, if that's how she wanted it. After a night of neither dreams nor sleep, he had finally dozed off when a voice called him.

Wake up.

Jonathan sat up. Everyone was still asleep except for Kayna, who was on watch. He looked up through the domed roof at the indigo sky.

Come outside.

He followed the voice inside his head, but it was only when he saw Morgan standing next to the fire pit that he realized she had been calling him. Drops of moonlight fell like silver upon her sapphire gown. *She's changed her dress.* He had only seen her wear green thus far.

"It is the garb I wear when entering my mother's abyss." The Delphini glided towards him. "Green is for the shallow waters of sea and river."

"I thought you were going to Íarchol," Jonathan said. She was close enough for him to catch a whiff of her scent— river, wind, and sea.

"That will take but a few days. Meanwhile, my mother's wrath grows at the insolence of Ventosus and the Three. I must persuade her to stay within the abyss, neutral in this war except for what I and my brothers do."

Jonathan took a step closer. "And just what is that, *beautiful?*" The last word he had only thought, not said.

She swept past him. "My beauty will not avail us in the war, nor should you keep pondering it. Come, walk with me."

He fell into step beside her as they traveled a small path that led to the river, wondering what she wanted to say to him. The Delphini had closed her mind to his, and a sidelong glance at her profile revealed nothing of her motives. Soon enough they came upon the banks, and Morgan turned to him. "I have a request of you."

He smiled. "Just ask, and I'll do it. You know that." *You sense it.*

Morgan's face remained grave. "I'm afraid you will not find it so easy to fulfill, unless you get these friends to help you. Even if they don't, still, you must find the Terakhein of water first—if there is one left alive—*before* you find Samara. When Trapher murdered Branwynne, my brothers swore they would bring the heads of the Three, along with Trapher's, to our mother. Now Madron and Peran have returned, wounded, inciting her to stir up the Feállí—"

"Feállí—I read about them in Íarchol, but didn't understand what they were."

"Lesser Elementarí of the rivers and seas who control the shallow tides. Untamed and unbridled, except for the obedience they give Morwenna. But she will let them wreak havoc on your coasts and waterways if she believes the Ophidians and Nemarons are winning, and the Terakhein lost. Find the Terakhein of water and you may stem her wrath." Her gaze faltered. "I'm not sure I can."

Jonathan took a step towards her, close enough to feel her desire for him, whether she willed it or not. He paused, knowing full well that he would find the children—they would never let his dreams be until he had done all he could to discover where they were hidden—but the human element was tricky. "Tell your mother we'll go to the guilds and warn them of abusing Dormín and Centuras," he said. With two Terakhein at his side, the priests would at least listen to him, and perhaps correct the mistake of letting the Order be disbanded. Jaxon could help him. The barber knew the underbelly of Duraeston, Jonathan suspected, enough to sway the guilds.

It was all politics, was it not? And once the Iron Clads learned of Cadman's death...

"You can't turn back that tide, Jonathan." Morgan's stern eyes glistened with tears as she clenched her fists. "You think your guilds will give up their power and Adolan will stop building his mighty fortress?" Her voice grew hard. "Even in Íarchol too many rivers have been dammed, diverting their water. You may win against the Nemarons, but at terrible cost to yourselves, should your countries continue on their path to wealth and greatness, and forget *us.*"

"I hear the music and the murmur of the forest," he said. "I dream-walk in a world of fire spirits and wolves and will dare to enter the Ophidian caverns in hopes of rescuing the holy fire." He leaned in, wanting only to take her in his arms and hold her at least once before she left yet again. But something wouldn't let him. "Why won't you believe in me?"

Even in the dim moonlight he could see Morgan's eyes had darkened. "I want—"

The crack of a stick made them both turn with a start to see Kayna.

"I've just come from my watch," she said, looking uncertainly at them, her gaze darting down to the ground.

"Then dawn is not far off," Morgan said, taking a step back. "And I must leave."

"Now?" Jonathan asked, frowning at both of them. "Surely you will want to say goodbye to the others—"

"I told Breoc and Nylen I would leave before dawn's light," she said, turning from Jonathan, and Kayna, who stood but twenty feet away, unmoving and silent.

Yet you didn't tell me. The words flashed out of his mind before he could stop them.

I brought you here to say goodbye. Morgan walked halfway down the riverbank, refusing to look at him.

"Then say goodbye, damn it!" he shouted, not caring who heard. "Don't call me out in the middle of the night to tell me I'll fail in the end, and look as if killing me or loving me were up to the toss of a coin."

Her hand came up and caressed his cheek before he could even comprehend it. *I believe in you,* she said as her lips lightly grazed his before she leapt into the cold water.

Jonathan waited for her to come up. *Just one more time to say goodbye.* But the moment dragged on, and the Delphini did not appear again. Slowly climbing the bank, Jonathan tried to swallow his anger and disappointment. When he reached the top, he saw Kayna with that same half-angry, half-hurt look in her eyes, arms crossed, like he had broken some law. *Perhaps I have,* he thought, eyeing the Terakheini's almost haughty posture. "What is it?" he asked in passing, not caring if she answered.

Kayna waited until he was a good twenty steps ahead of her before she answered. "She must stay in the abyss."

Jonathan kept walking.

"You know," she said, running up to him now. "You know Morgan cannot stay here with you as a woman. Her place is by her mother and brothers in the deep."

"Her place is wherever she decides it to be." *Even to search for me in Ventosus' realm.* "Nor should you berate her actions, seeing as how she rescued us in the Dorlíhein. Or do you think yourself to be mightier than one of the Elementarí?"

"What I think," she said, jumping into his path and forcing him to stop, "is beside the point. What I *know* is that the role of the Elementarí is to sleep in the earth and under the sea, not to go to war with men, whether out of love—or pity."

The cut sank deep. "How would you know the difference?" he spat. "Now get out of my way." He shoved her aside and kept walking.

—◦◉◉◦—

Sienna was the first to greet him back at the camp. "You hungry? There's a little bit of food left, so you had better hurry."

"Why?" Jonathan snapped. Too many emotions were at war within him—frustration over not being able to kiss Morgan goodbye, exhilaration at her last words that had promised something more than just loyal duty, anger at

Kayna's slight, but even more so, at the hurt look in her eyes when she'd come upon him and the Delphini. He did not understand what he had done to deserve such a look.

The Terakheini entered the clearing. "Where's Nylen?" she asked the widow.

"To the west of the trees over there," Sienna pointed. "I believe he's with Breoc."

She stomped away without another word.

"What did you do to make her so angry?" the widow chortled. "And of all times, when Breoc and I are about to leave."

Jonathan knew he should go after Kayna, wanted to explain...what? What would he say to that look in her eye? But he couldn't let Sienna go without getting a definitive answer to a question that had been bothering him for the past weeks—no, past months. Since his sister had died, in fact. *I've lost all my babies,* his mother had cried. What did that make Jonathan? "Sienna, before you go, tell me why I hear the trees. If this be a gift only bestowed upon the Terakhein, then I—"

"You are not a Terakhein, Jonathan," she said. The widow took a deep breath. "I was by your mother's side when she gave birth to you. A full two days' labor you were."

"Then why—"

"Why anything?" Sienna tossed back, growing irritated. "Why was our village smashed into rubble, why is Cadman's body lying at the bottom of a river? Of all things, stop trying to figure out *why.*"

Jonathan wanted to warn her that this is exactly what he wouldn't do. He had grown up too much in the past eight months, lost sister and parents, only to find out that his father might be a traitor, and his godfather had a whole secret history. The widow, too, remained an enigma. But even more so, Jonathan felt the currents of history and struggles for power alive in the stories of the people surrounding him, and felt caught in the intricacies of their quest. Yet no one was telling him the full story—not even Breoc and Nylen. Oh no, there were a good many things still to figure out.

"You still haven't explained how I hear—"

"Your mother could hear them too," the widow snapped. "She never heard words the way you do, so stop with that look. She had me swear to never tell anyone; thought people would take her as a madwoman. Called it a family gift."

"Aren't you ready yet?" Breoc led Hammer and Tongs into the clearing. Kei came out of the house just as Nylen and Kayna returned.

"Don't hurry an old lady," the widow said and embraced the twins. "Goodbye, my Lord and Lady of the forest. Someday, you'll return to this place. You will rule again. Nylen—"

The warrior took her hand and kissed it.

"Take care of my charges, friend," she said tenderly.

That was an odd goodbye for strangers, Jonathan mused. But then the widow was hugging him tightly in one quick movement, her mouth to his ear. "We've lost him," she whispered. "He protected you all your life, and now you must live, no matter what the cost." She pulled back with tear-misted eyes.

Jonathan blinked back tears at the mention of his godfather. "He never told me how he got his scars." *What an odd thing to say.* But it was one of the last things Cadman had promised him.

"Ah, my boy, someday *I* will tell you that story. You will have deserved it." Sienna turned to the burly Ausel. "I'm ready. Breoc."

"That's Master Coerb for the rest of our journey, my lady," he said, and helped her into the saddle.

"We will see you in Camhanaich!" Nylen held his hand aloft in farewell as the two disappeared into the forest.

—⚬⟨⊙⟩⟨⊙⟩⚬—

Ride now, while you can. It was a woman's voice, low and musical, but not Adamara's. Certainly not Sienna's.

No, come with me, a man argued. *I can bear both of us on my horse. There's still time.*

He saw them as through a mist. No real faces, nothing but vague outlines. Then light, so blinding white that he couldn't see. *Remember, warmth for winter, and fire for darkness.* The voice kept repeating the phrase, but it was Sienna who walked out of the brightness, and stood before him. She, too, repeated the words. *Warmth for winter, and fire for darkness.*

Then Cierdwyn emerged from the light, not as Jonathan had seen her in his last vision: a dying woman, eyes closed and mouth bleeding. Here she was young and strong, standing next to Sienna and holding her hand. The three voices repeated the phrase once more, and then Sienna and Cierdwyn suddenly changed into Adamara, two exact copies of the Ophidian woman, their emerald eyes drinking him in...

He woke with a start. *Damn it.* Sienna had left the sleeping powder as a precaution, but it was beginning to lose its potency. Kei, the lucky bastard, was asleep in the corner, and there was no sign of Nylen nor Kayna. Wondering which one was on watch, he quietly got up, ignoring the dull throb in his back.

The glen was dappled with scant moonlight, only enough for him to make out a faint silhouette on the other side of the clearing. The shadow was holding on to the tree, almost as if in an embrace, its palms laid flat against the bark. Jonathan glanced at the dying coals in the fire pit, knowing at once they would not combust into a flame strong enough to deter an Ophidian. *But Kei could do something.* One small step back landed his boot on a twig that snapped in half.

The shadow turned its head, and Jonathan saw that it was Kayna. He still couldn't tell what she was doing with the tree, other than…talking to it. He went over to her. Her eyes were closed as she whispered, "*Wetha helasme. Haleth fortheis quielath argo.*"

"What are you saying?" Jonathan asked in a low voice.

Kayna jumped as her eyes opened wide. "What are you doing here?" she whispered.

"Couldn't sleep," he lied.

"You were asleep when I left," her cat-like eyes narrowed. "Did you have a vision?"

"No," Jonathan lied again, as he placed his hand on the burnt, wrinkled bark, its cavernous grooves allowing his fingers to sink in. "What are you doing?"

Kayna fixed her gaze at Jonathan, measuring him. "I'm trying to wake him up."

Jonathan turned his head. "Who?"

"The tree."

"Do you really want to do that?" Jonathan asked, gawking at her. *Perhaps they can tell us where the Terakhein bodies were taken. What a world of thorns to wake in and find your entire race dead, your skin charred off—*

"Will you help me or not?" Kayna whispered.

"How?"

"That's what I'm still trying to figure out," Kayna said impatiently. "They are lost in deep water. I keep calling but I don't know if any of them can hear me." She leaned against the great Auréus once more, running her hands up and down the bark, her ear pressed to the trunk, as if trying to find its heartbeat. "*Wetha helame, haleth forthis quilath argo,*" she whispered.

"*Wetha helame, Haleth forthis,*" Jonathan repeated as he walked around to the other side of the tree, closed his eyes, and ran his hands along the grooves. "*Quilath argo.*"

No sentry of the Order had ever tried to wake a tree within the Seven Woods; it was a forest already on the edge of consciousness, not alive with malice like Dorlíhein, but certainly imbued with as much power. For that reason alone the Seven Woods was the only forest in Gaelastad with sentries to guard it, and it was three times the size of the Fáliquerci and Ruaden forests put together. Each a scion, perhaps, of the ancient wood Jonathan now stood in.

Jonathan laid his ear to the tree. *"Wetha helame."* He said it at the same time as Kayna, and felt the rhythm of the words pulling him towards the tree.

"Haleth forthis." His hand pushed into the grooves, the bark growing over it.

"Quilath argo." The trunk suddenly became soft, almost spongy. Jonathan sank into it, not feeling any pain in his back as the tree closed over him and a heartbeat pressed up against his. He sank deep into that warmth and sound.

A flashing vision of a girl he had never seen, lying asleep in a corner bed of a dark room. Dark haired, and not unlike Jenna or Samara. He sank farther in. The picture changed to a section of forest he did not recognize. Everything was blurry, as if seen through a windowpane during a storm. He could make out that the trees were twice as tall as the Atreals of Fáliquerci, with golden bark and snow white leaves shaped like coins. Could it be the center of the Seven Woods, rumored to have housed the golden palace of the Elementarí in ancient days?

Jonathan let out a breath as the Auréus squeezed him more tightly still, and the scene came sharply into focus. On a small patch of ground thick with grass lay the girl, sleeping. No, she was dead, for Jonathan suddenly noticed the thin line of blood across her slim throat. What blade could have made such a precise cut through the flesh in which a wound could be hardly seen? Jonathan exhaled to squeeze himself farther into the heart of the tree. *Show me.*

But a hand, cold and rough, grabbed his arm and began pulling. *No, do not take me yet!* Jonathan tried to resist and felt the Auréus clutch even more so that his breath came in short gasps.

"Auréus amitta!" a muffled voice said. The hands

renewed their grasp and pulled with such vigor that Jonathan was certain he would be ripped in two as his head and shoulders popped out while his legs remained captured in the tree's trunk. The Auréus now fought to keep him, and there was bone crushing pain as the wood tightened around his thighs and calves.

"*Comburo!*" Kei yelled. A small blue flame appeared in the Terakheini's hand before he placed his palm flat against the bark. "*Auréus amitta!*"

The pressure went slack, and Jonathan's legs came free as Nylen yanked him out. Jonathan fell to the ground and rolled over to see Kayna lying beside him, her brother now hovering over her.

The warrior kneeled down between them. "What in Neáhvalar's name did you two think you were doing?"

"We were trying to wake the tree." Kayna's entire body shook. "Didn't you hear it, Jonathan?"

He nodded, more bewildered by what he'd seen than what he'd heard.

"You were *in* the tree. That is not waking the forest," Nylen argued. "That is being devoured by it. You should have known better, Kayna, especially after what we encountered in the Dorlíhein."

"I helped too," Jonathan said indignantly.

"You are not Terakhein!" Nylen countered.

"They speak to me anyway." Jonathan's anger rose, even though he knew Nylen was right, knew it had been a foolish thing to do. "It let me into its heart and showed me another vision—about the little girl whose throat was cut a year ago. I saw her in a room—I think at the Three Sister's Inn—and where the sentries found her in the Seven Woods. I saw her, and the Auréus was about to show me the person who did it, I think, when you jerked me out." He slowly stood up, his limbs very stiff, as if he had just run for miles.

"I have never heard of such a thing," Kei said, regarding the tree with a frown. "And I would suggest both of you sleep while you can now."

No, we have to figure out why the tree showed me the little girl. There was treachery—deep, deep treachery in the heart of Gaelastad. "But—"

Kei cut him off. "The Auréa are sentries. If you woke this one, you might have woken them all."

"We will all stay in the house for the rest of the night," Nylen said with a sigh. "And none of you shall wander again without my leave first, even if it's to take a piss."

Jonathan and Kayna slowly walked side by side back to the house, strange allies now. While Jonathan felt exhausted, a plan was unfolding—a vision of what could be—in conjunction with what the Auréus had shown him. Kei and Nylen were closely following them, but in the morning, Jonathan would pull Kayna aside and ask about the possibility of waking up the Seven Woods. If after all this mess, the Order was going to stay disbanded, then perhaps they could get the forest to really wake up and defend itself and never need sentries again. Perhaps those trees would at last reveal answers about the little girl's death.

And just who in Duraeston was responsible.

⸻⊛⊚⊛⸻

A hand over his mouth woke Jonathan.

"Say nothing, and collect the packs," Nylen said softly. "We need to leave now."

Jonathan sat up, listening for whatever disturbance outside had caused such alarm in the warrior. He heard nothing. *Don't let it be Hecthrax's brood coming to look for its missing brother.* But whether it was wolves, or Nemarons, or the wood, *something* had come for them. Feeling his way along the wall was not easy, given the tears in the wood and vine. Twice he scratched himself while grappling with their provisions.

"I've got them," he whispered. Three packs instead of four. They had each taken a portion of Cadman's supplies.

"Take this." Nylen passed a thin rope to Jonathan. "Wrap

it once through your belt and then pass it on," he ordered, "but allow yourselves enough slack to leave about five feet between us. We go out one at a time. There's still a small path left."

"What—" Kayna began.

"Quiet," Nylen barked. "You have done enough." He tugged once on the rope, and stepped out of the house.

The clearing had given way to the forest, thus little of the moon's luminescence could guide them now. The Auréa that had stood at the edge of the clearing had either moved in, or else their sinuous branches had laced themselves across so that the entire wood now barred their way. As black as wraiths, they loomed over what little of the glen was left. Jonathan could still see the fire pit, but the table had been swallowed up. Only one narrow exit remained where Kayna had tried to wake up the old Auréus.

"Are they saying anything?" Nylen asked her.

"No." Kayna's voice trembled. "Though they're *very* awake now."

"Let them know you are Terakhein." Nylen's voice was hard, like sword on stone. "You woke them up, send them back to sleep long enough for us to escape."

Jonathan could make out Kayna dimly shaking her head. "It's too late for that."

"Then we'll go slow and quiet," Nylen ordered, "and pray the forest does not lead us farther in instead of letting us out."

They took a few steps to where the old Auréus stood when Kayna suddenly yanked the rope. The path between the trees was, as Nylen warned, wide enough for only one person to go through at a time. Kayna put one hand on the ancient tree, listening. "Go!"

Nylen pulled them into the dark opening. Jonathan's sight was plunged into blindness as they stumbled through the trees that immediately closed in behind them. All around, the Auréa had gathered, waiting. Thick branches pulled at Jonathan's cloak and clawed at his cheeks, prompting him to throw up his hands to protect his face until the rope yanked him out of Auréa's grasp.

Helas Nom, Ophidialatha. Morte ethu walas, the forest softly moaned.

"They call for our death," Kayna choked out.

Their path became waylaid with vines that tripped Nylen and wrapped around Kayna's feet. Kei laid his blue flame to both, weeping brutal words that caused the Auréa to shudder and withdraw in pain. Nylen gave a hard yank, and they broke into a run, their retreat becoming a rout as branches pummeled them from every side. Kei's fire spread everywhere in his panic, and the Auréa responded in kind. Kayna received a gash on her forehead from one thick limb that smacked against her face. The forest moans turned into hateful cries, so that the Terakhein wood sounded as cruel as the Dorlíhein. Jonathan couldn't help but wonder what dark creatures it could call to in its distress. Over to their left, a soft rushing sound. What was it? Jonathan tried to listen more closely.

The river! He pulled on the rope, but no one stopped. He yanked it again, and now he felt everyone slow down, but not completely stop. A resounding crack drove them right just as a branch crashed to the ground.

"Jonathan, what is it?" Kayna asked, not daring to look at him as she staggered forward.

"Follow the sound of the river."

"We can't go that way—the forest has blocked off the paths to it," she said irritably.

"I didn't say to go *to* the river—but make sure it's always on our left. Morgan said it leads into Ophidia. If we must be caught like prey between forest and desert, why should we not trust the waters of the Delphini?"

Kayna was quiet for a moment then said, "I'll tell Nylen."

--~·◉·◉·~--

The morning sun at last fell in dappled swathes of gold through the canopy, creating more shadows than light. Were the vines truly creeping across the path like Jonathan thought, or was it but a trick of the eye? The old numbness crept up his right leg as they stumbled over the trailing foliage.

"How long before we are out of this, Nylen?" Jonathan asked.

"A day's journey still, from the way Morgan described the layout of the forest."

"Then let's cast the rope off so we may run more freely," Jonathan said.

"Leave it on," Nylen said. "Should one of us fall, I doubt these creeping plants would let us up again." At least the path was now mostly canopied by lesser trees that resembled the Fáliquerci's dark blue-green Atreal. More Auréa shadowed the lane ahead.

The warrior glanced down at Jonathan's leg. "Is it troubling?"

"I can still run." He'd not be the one to slow them down like in the Dorlíhein wood.

"That isn't what I asked," Nylen cast a quick glance past Jonathan. "Kayna, how are you, dear heart?"

"Same as Jonathan," the Terakheini said in a flat voice. "I can still run."

"Then get ready," Jonathan said as they approached the line of trees. "Kei."

Jonathan saw a blue flame shoot past him as a loud cry rang out, and they charged forward to where the Auréa were waiting.

CHAPTER 16
JOURNEY INTO THE DESERT

They were bloody by the time the trees began to thin out. By then it was late afternoon. *We tried to give them new life,* Jonathan thought bitterly, *and they nearly took out my eyes.* A violent shove from Nylen had sent him sprawling to the ground so that the Auréa had merely split open his brow instead. But the vines had immediately crawled over his neck, cutting off all air until Kei's fiery hand flooded the entire floor of the forest with blue waves of flame. Everything after that moment was a blurry mess of limbs, blood, and the cries of the forest.

Jonathan thought the path had grown a hairbreadth wider since they'd left the wood. Perhaps it was simply that the branches no longer reached out with such frenzy to attack their hands and faces. He turned his head to Kayna. "Do you hear them now?"

"Faintly," she said as she stumbled behind him.

It wasn't until they felt a fresh breeze on their face that Nylen let them remove the rope. After a few miles the dense undergrowth gave way to patches of thick brown grass that sprang out of rocky soil. Scrub brush and sparse wildflowers dotted the new terrain as an outcrop of stone rose on their left, trees dwindling to an occasional pine.

They decided to camp where the land dipped into a thin shelf beside the outcrop; dark knoll blocked the horizon ahead. Jonathan gratefully threw down his pack and looked at Kayna. Small red scratches crisscrossed her cheeks, but worse was the deep cut across her forehead where dried blood now matted her hair.

"They're gone," he said in a low voice.

"I know." She quickly brushed away a single tear that had escaped down her cheek. Was she crying from relief, or from a broken heart at having to flee in terror from her forest once again? Jonathan wondered.

Nylen came back from the river with a full water sack. "Kayna, let me see to that cut." He ripped a small square of linen into strips. "The rest of you get yourselves cleaned up."

"Can we risk a fire?" Kei surveyed the dark mass of trees behind them.

"A small one." Nylen gently wiped the dried blood from Kayna's forehead. "Although you have already given us enough blazes for today. Pray the wood does not remember it."

"Would you rather I had let us be devoured?" Kei asked, gingerly picking up some scattered twigs. For the first time Jonathan noticed how the Terakheini's palms were pink and raw, as if he had scraped them repeatedly over stone. One of his knuckles was ripped open—the work of some Auréus he hadn't turned away in time.

Nylen noticed it too. "I'd rather both of you exercise more control over the power you have gained of late," he said, tearing a new piece of cloth and handing it to Kei. "Bandage that finger tightly so it doesn't fester."

"Would a soldier from Cadarn's army have fared better?" Jonathan tossed back, scowling in turn as he wiped the gore from his own wounded brow.

"We should have been guarded by twenty of the king's Ausels on this quest. Ashryanna was theirs to protect," Nylen said. His smooth cheek was now etched with two deep scratches that ran from nose to ear. "Instead we enter Ophidia with you wounded and two young Terakhein," he said quietly. "I would have us more prepared to meet an army of earth spirits."

Kei fixed a cool gaze upon the warrior. "And how does one prepare to meet those who fed on your people?"

"With such stealth and skill that we are felt but as whisper on skin. Not running blindly like we have been, torn from foe and friend alike."

"We need more tinder," Kayna said shortly, and, without another word, scaled the small hill perpendicular to the outcrop.

"One of you go with her," Nylen said.

Jonathan turned to Kei. "Take care of your hands—use the widow's salve. I'll watch over her."

The hill was rocky and steep, but Jonathan kept climbing despite the growing ache in his back. He should have rested and let Kei look after his sister, but he had wanted to get a lay of the land.

Once he reached the top, he only saw more rocky hills that blocked any further view. *Just as well,* Jonathan thought, sitting down to ease his back before going to find Kayna. The top of the hill sloped dramatically to the west, where he assumed she had gone. He gazed up at the sky darkening into twilight, trying to ignore the increasing sting of his wounds. A group of birds were flying in the distance —the first animal life they had seen since the Wild Lands. Jonathan froze as the birds swerved right and began to circle around.

A hand on his arm. "They're not Cralen." Kayna was suddenly beside him. She smelled of earth and sweat, a musky fragrance so unlike Morgan's or Adamara's.

He looked back up at the sky. "How can you tell?"

"They don't fly this far south. At least, when I lived here there was no report of such a sighting." She had kept her hand on his arm, but turned red as she quickly withdrew it. "Does your back hurt?"

"No," he lied.

"Let me put some salve on it anyway." Then in a kinder tone, "Remember those tears take time to heal—sometimes years. If you had been with us in Kaelest, our physicks would have kept you in bed for at least two weeks."

Jonathan found himself unnerved by her tenderness and turned away. "I'll remember that," he said, slowly trying to get up, but the pain had suddenly become unbearable.

"Stay here," she ordered. "I'll be right back."

Jonathan reluctantly remained seated, taking shallow breaths while cursing the erratic nature of his pain. One hour he would be walking with nothing more than a dull ache in his lower back; the next, half his left leg would go numb. Kayna soon returned and gently lifted up his shirt. She warmed the salve with her hands and spread it onto his wounds, singing, "*Halan argo quiesa.*" Slowly the pain ebbed out of Jonathan's back, and where there was cold and fire, healing warmth crept in.

"That's much better, thank you. Now, we must come back with at least some proof that we were working," he teased.

"That's only to save your reputation, lazy bones," she retorted, but a blush slowly crept up her cheeks. They collected dried scrub for kindling in a comfortable silence, as if, at last, some truce had been found.

--❖⟨❖⟩❖--

The stench of Kei's stew hit them before they even saw the camp. "You don't expect us to eat that," Jonathan said, as Kei spooned a gelatinous substance into his cup.

"Go hungry if you prefer," the Terakheini said with a wicked grin. "Íarchins are not known for their cooking, but you can live off this stew with only one cup a day, and little else."

I'd keep little else down, Jonathan thought as he slurped the bitter mixture.

Nylen didn't seem to like it much either, and he took a long draught of water. "We'll stay here a few days until you heal, Jonathan. Kayna, start teaching Jonathan what you remember of the Ophidian language."

"Why?" Jonathan asked. "There are no forests here to listen to."

Kayna leapt up onto a small rock, and perched there, grinning like cat. "You'll have to call me Master Kayna."

"Then our conversations will be very short," Jonathan smirked.

"No one is 'Master' but me," Nylen said, for the first time allowing a small smile to spread across his face. "Forest or desert, you can hear the land like a Terakhein, so for a while a Terakhein you'll be."

⟶⟨ʘ⟩⟨ʘ⟩⟵

"It's your watch now," Kei said as he shook Jonathan's arm.

A cold snap of air hit Jonathan's face. He wrapped his outer cloak around him and pulled the hood over his head along with another scarf. With his blanket and sword, he took his position up on the hill. Looking out over the dark landscape, a sense of loneliness crept over him. Where was Morgan now? He wanted her, more than ever. Wanted her in his arms rather than rallying the armies to begin their march to Cadarn. *And how is it I never dream of you?* Daydream, yes. He conjured up Morgan's image many times a day, pulling her towards him until he could taste her lips. A soft fleeting kiss before moving to her eyes and cheeks, then slowly tasting her delectable mouth again, his tongue even daring to slide between her lips.

His fantasy always ended there, in the moment of longing when he pressed his body against hers. Morgan's eyes would flutter open, black as onyx and naked in their insatiable desire for him. And then, no matter what his will, his mind would go blank in the enveloping darkness of her pupils. Jonathan reached for a rock the size of his fist and hurled it in frustration. *Why won't you come to me in the dead sleep rather than all these other women?* Samara had ceased to visit him, but Adamara was appearing in his visions with alarming regularity. *Do you know I'm coming to your lair? Have you dreamed of me too?* he thought, unsettled by the unvoiced answers.

The sound of footsteps made him turn to see Kei's head bobbing into view. "Can't sleep?"

Kei nodded, and sat down beside him, humming. With a blanket wrapped around him and his wavy red hair mashed down, the Terakheini looked like any sixteen year old boy. Jonathan vaguely recognized the song he was humming.

"What are the words?" Jonathan asked him. "It reminds me of something Sienna used to sing to me."

"It goes something like this:

> *In dark mountains the wind dreamt of twilight,*
> *its ice meeting sky, sank through the star-filled night,*
> *where flame awoke in waters swirling,*
> *traveled in dust through a serpent's skin*
> *and in caverns deep dreamt of dawn."*

Kei sighed, perhaps remembering too much. "It's only one verse of a longer lay."

Sienna knew it. "Did your elders teach the people of Gaelastad that song?" Jonathan asked. Terakhein law was as old as the First Dawn, when the Elementarí had lain themselves down to sleep and the Hidden People had taken up their Terakheinship.

Kei shook his head. "It's a lullaby," he said softly. A long pause. "Does any of that matter? You are a part of the Terakhein now, just like Nylen. Sentries who watch over the last of our kind."

"It matters," Jonathan said. *Two girls dead, two traitors, and the village widow singing Terakhein lullabies.*

"You think it will be easier if you can define your role," Kei said. "Traitor's son, Terakhein, sentry of the Seven Woods, smith's apprentice. You may be all or none of these. Will any of them aid you in our journey?"

Jonathan didn't answer. *I am good at dreams and dag-*

gers. Tracking too, and forest talk, but neither would be useful in the desert. *There is no true place for me*, he thought, but it comforted him when Kei lay down and drew his blanket snugly to his chin. Soon the Terakheini was breathing heavily, and the soothing sound of that company made Jonathan's watch pass all the more quickly.

—◦◦◦◦◦—

They spent five days in the shadow of the outcrop. The wounds on Jonathan's back began scabbing over with the help of Sienna's balm. Every night Kayna would massage it into Jonathan's back, singing Terakhein songs of healing over him until he could do simple things—rise from bed, walk, reach for his dagger without acute pain. He assumed the dull ache that ran from his shoulders to his waist would remain for some time. If Kayna was right, possibly for the rest of his life.

The morning they set out for the desert was bleak and gray. A night of cold, unrelenting drizzle had robbed them of any good sleep, and the bad weather continued until noon. They were traveling in between realms, neither sheltered nor pursued. Not yet. Jonathan wondered what memories would be stirred for the twins once they reached the Ophidian's desert lair. Would it trigger them into vengeance or paralysis?

The next day, the land shifted from semi-grassy hills into a flat, arid world. The soil changed from a rich dark brown to a deep rust color that crumbled easily beneath their feet. Sage and yucca thrust themselves defiantly through the cracked earth, surrounded by silver bristled plants with fierce pink blooms that none of them had ever seen before. Lizards and desert rats darted across their path, chased at times by small snakes that slithered around the brown scrub brush and disappeared into burrows. Nothing else. No flash of silver white or the faint tracks of throck or wolf.

By the third day the hills died completely away and the river shriveled into a small creek. By the fourth, it was gone.

In Gaelastad, the forests had always given relief to Jonathan from the sunniest of days. Here there was no shelter.

In the distance, a dark canyon stretched out before them. To the right of it stood five giants: massive rock formations carved by years of wind and water into tall, grotesque bodies, their heads bowed toward one another. They formed a haphazard ring around the entrance to the caverns where the Ophidians slept. As the sun slowly settled into the horizon, the giants took on a bloody hue, living ghost-guardians of the spirits.

—❧❦❧—

"I don't like being out in the open like this," Jonathan said as they moved to the side of the camp to practice their swordplay. Cadman's wasters had been in one of the packs saved from the Dorlíhein. If only it had been a true sword instead.

"We'll be in the canyon soon enough," Nylen said as he swung a massive blow, nearly knocking Jonathan off his feet. "See how close we are to the five giants?" He struck from the left again, then hammered in from the right, blow upon blow that Jonathan could barely deflect. "Just to the north of them lies a canyon that leads into their caverns."

Jonathan grunted in response. Sweat drenched, and with his back muscles aching, he tried to keep up with Nylen's unrelenting pace. Cadman had never been so brutal in his fencing; hard yes, and once he had even broken Jonathan's arm during a particularly grueling session. Nylen stood a few inches shorter than Jonathan, but his arms and legs were twice as thick, and no force could stop him once he began moving. Two more strikes and the warrior had Jonathan tumbling over an unseen bush behind him.

Nylen lowered his sword. "Your skill is improving."

Jonathan ignored the familiar throb in his back as he climbed to his feet and dusted himself off. "I am being pummeled."

"Then mind your form as much as you do my strikes."

Nylen straightened and lifted his sword again.

Jonathan lunged and brought his sword into a hard right. Nylen blocked it easily and offered his own riposte. "Side step when I attack you at an angle from your left, otherwise I'll slice right through your kidney," he shouted. Jonathan did a neat pirouette and launched a second attack, this time with accuracy. "Good show!" Nylen said as he stepped back momentarily then renewed his assault. "Are you faring so well in your lessons with Kayna?"

"She's impatient," Jonathan panted. *Haughty too.* "And she's forgotten the meaning of several words—I can't even string along a sentence."

"Then learn enough to babble something coherent," Nylen said, thrusting his sword down and center, forcing Jonathan to once again stumble back. "By Neáhvalar's name, be aware of *everything* around you!" he shouted, with a cut across Jonathan's waster that sent it flying from his hand. "This land might not speak, but it can kill you all the same unless you mind your footing."

It might get us in the end, Jonathan thought as he glanced at the five colossal stones. What good would his wooden sword do against such grotesque monstrosities? He picked up the fallen waster, reminding himself that he only needed to get through the next hour's battle with Nylen, and let the morrow take care of itself.

The next day Nylen veered their path north, so that by the evening, the dark canyon loomed up ahead with the five giants now on their right. It was almost midnight when they reached the edge of the gorge, where Nylen decided they would camp.

"Surely we would be safer under the protection of its walls?" Kei asked.

The warrior stared at the gorge with furrowed brow. "We will wait for what the dawn will show us of this gulch, for I trust it not."

Within the hour, everyone was asleep but Jonathan, who

had first watch. The moon's glow threw elongated shadows against the canyon's sandstone cliffs, yet Jonathan's eyes were drawn to the endless horizon, searching for any movement. *Why am I more worried about an attack coming from the open land rather than a fortress provided by those walls?* He cast a long glance back at the canyon. What if something lurked there that even the Ophidians feared? *Then enemy or friend they may turn out to be,* he thought, and returned his gaze once more to the land still as death.

—◦◉◎◦—

Before the gray light of morning had filtered into the edge of the gulch, they had gathered their gear and were ready. "There is a weariness here," Kei warned, before they set out, "as if the land itself were in mourning."

"Aye, I can hear neither trees nor feel the land, but even I sense that," Nylen said as he slung a leather quiver across his back. They walked down the rocky slope, loose gravel cascading in mini rockslides as they shuffled onto the canyon floor. A very small stream ran through it—not deep enough for fish, but enough to allow a little vegetation, surprisingly green amid the sand and stone. The morning sun hit the west wall, illuminating the deep red and beige rock strata layered throughout. By noon they reached the middle of the canyon. At times, Nylen or Jonathan would stop them, thinking they heard something move, whether from the top of the canyon or just around the bend. But there was nothing.

They stopped only to eat some dates and a little bread. Uncanny shadows crept across the vast expanse of rock as the sun began her afternoon descent. Then Jonathan heard the cries. He stared at the dark shapes slowly moving on the sandstone. Oh, he knew it was the sun on the rocks, nothing more, yet the cries....

"Do you hear them?" he whispered to Kayna.

She nodded, her eyes scanning the valley.

"What's wrong?" Nylen asked.

"Can't you hear it?" Jonathan's heart beat quickly as he looked around. "There are people crying out for help. Kayna hears them. Can't you?"

Nylen and Kei stood very still, listening. "I don't hear anything," the warrior said.

"Shhh. Listen. They're not....the cries of the living." The Terakheini's eyes filled with tears.

Jonathan stood very still.

Wara deáphen, Neáhvalar, hialeth.

The language was similar to Ophidian. He caught the words *we're dying* and *Neáhvalar help us,* but he couldn't discern any more amid the screaming.

"Look!" Kei suddenly cried as he pointed up farther to their right. Embedded in the valley wall were the remains of a few clay houses. The crumbled windows and doors looked as if at one time they'd held a notch for a ladder.

"They died horribly." Kayna choked on the words. "I can't translate all of what they're saying, but I think...they were buried alive."

"Then the legend is true," Nylen said, his eyes wide with wonder. "Morgan warned me that this canyon could aid us or be our worst peril." He gently touched Kayna's brow. "It is the Alaini-Nah you hear. The story went that when the Three awoke, they sank the village into the canyon."

Kayna merely stared at the ground as if trying to bore holes into the dirt with her vision. Kei had his back to both of them. What old memory were they seeing? Jonathan remembered Cadarian soldiers falling helplessly into that smoking pit on the battlefield of Cadarn. His thoughts went to Breithan and the wild creatures that tore his village apart. Now they were to walk upon a nation that had been buried alive. *A world of thorns.*

"Their pain will be their justice." Nylen lifted Kayna's chin. "Morgan believes that the cries of the Alaini-Nah, who revered the Ophidians even more than the Terakhein, will haunt their executor. That is, unless they drive you two to madness first."

Kayna and Jonathan flashed an unspoken agreement between them, and his heart felt a surge of protective love for the Terakheini, for she was hearing the dying of her people all over again, just like he was.

They continued down the canyon. Above them more crumbled clay houses hung, broken in half, barely having two walls. Below only piles of clay and stone remained. At least in the Terakhein forest there had been some furniture and houses left, some kind of memorial; here, there was nothing.

After a half hour, Jonathan thought he would go mad listening to the wails of pain and fear: cries of a mother's despair when her child dies, and screams of children torn from their parents. They were walking over an entire nation swept silent by the very earth itself. Tears streamed down Kayna's cheeks, and every once in a while she couldn't hold back a sob, animal sounds that erupted from deep within. He had yet to cry for Breithan and the people he had lost: his mother, Lian, his best friend Alec, Balfour and Susanna —even Riok, with his sour disposition. He couldn't even think about his father, possibly still alive and hurt, or hunting him.

Finally, when the unending moans and howls became unbearable, Jonathan made them stop so he could melt the wax off a candle for Kayna and him.

"Now I hear them," Nylen said. "Although only as a faint whisper. We are a little over halfway through. Here," Nylen said, handing Jonathan and Kayna the wax. "Is that better?" the warrior mouthed to them.

"Yes," Jonathan said, not realizing he was shouting until Nylen signaled to him to be quieter.

They walked in the same formation, stones and dry earth crunching under their feet. The high canyon walls protected them from the worst of the afternoon blaze, but no breeze wafted along the canyon floor. It was like being trapped in a giant oven. With dusk, the sun shifted the color of everything to a deep orange red, and in that hazy light they saw the end of the canyon in front of them.

Large, misshapen boulders rested against the walls that abruptly ended. Beyond them rose pink and brown sandstone dunes that would eventually lead them into the Ophidian caverns. Within two hundred feet of the widening mouth of the canyon, Nylen motioned to Jonathan and Kayna that he wanted to talk to them. The two slowly took out the wax with a look of apprehension.

"How is it now?" Kei asked.

"I can still hear them," Kayna said quietly, "but it's not the deafening sound that I heard in the middle of the gorge. What about you, Jonathan?"

"Same."

"Good enough," Nylen said. "We have an hour of light left, so set up camp. I need to go examine the caverns. All of you will remain here," he said, before any of them could protest. "Cadman and I had planned to scout the area, so you cannot dissuade me now. We don't know what Ophidians use to watch for them, whether that be Hecthrax or some other creatures worse than Cadman's bane."

Cadman's bane. Jonathan pictured the Caphecus tearing open his godfather. *I'll find you,* Jonathan thought. *Even if only in my dreams, I'll find you and kill you.* Phlegon had said it was possible to destroy someone while on a vision walk. He would test that, someday.

The twins said nothing to Nylen as they found a little nook in the sandstone wall where they could remain comfortably hidden until he returned. All three of them watched the warrior disappear down the canyon, his brown cloak blending into the landscape. They waited as dusk turned to twilight, bringing a cooler breeze to bathe their faces.

At length, Kayna spoke. "He's been away too long."

"Jonathan or I will search for Nylen in the morning, if he

has not appeared by then," Kei assured her.

"And what do you expect me to do?" Kayna asked angrily. "Smooth out my skirts and fix up the house while you're gone? I'm not some serving woman to stay behind."

"But you are the one Terakhein who can heal Chalom," Kei retorted. "If they capture you, the Three return to their full glory. And just how many men do you wish to be buried for the sake of your pride?"

"*I* will go tomorrow if Nylen doesn't return by morning," Jonathan interjected. "You are both more precious than all the armies and nations put together."

Neither twin said anything to that, but the deep blush on Kayna's cheeks diminished as she shot him a grateful look.

Twilight gave way to darkness, with the rising crescent moon illuminating only the ambiguous shapes of rock and scrub. Behind them, the rest of the gorge resembled a dark gaping mouth, but Jonathan tried to focus his eyes on the other end of the canyon, where Nylen would appear. *If he returns.* Jonathan shook the thought away. The warrior would come back. Jonathan had first watch, but Kayna relieved him an hour early. "You can go now; I can't sleep anyway," she said.

"You know the rule: sleep when you can, take the watch when you must. Go back to bed," Jonathan ordered, though not unkindly, for he'd heard the weariness in her voice.

"The voices are softer here," she said as she sat down beside him.

Jonathan could barely see her outline in the darkness, but he sensed something in her tone. "What is it?"

"I...keep wondering...if this is what my mother sounded like when they came for her. I heard so many screams that day, and the bodies..." She brushed something away from her cheek.

Jonathan reached out and took her hand. "This was not the Terakhein's fate," he said. "Your mother fought. The Alaini-Nah never had a chance to defend themselves. None of them escaped." *A world of thorns that won.*

"And what chance do we have, of all of us coming out of this alive?" she asked with a bitter laugh.

"Fair, I'd say," Jonathan said, but he couldn't meet her eyes since he didn't believe a word of it. Cadman had died, his father had lived, but only Neáhvalar knew if he was a traitor or not. "I'll watch for Nylen with you," Jonathan said.

Kayna unclasped her hand from his. "You know the rule —"

"I know that we are trapped in a canyon full of dead voices and restless spirits," Jonathan said.

She turned to stare into the black horizon. "That is reason enough."

CHAPTER 17
ASHRYANNA

As a gray dawn broke out over the sky, Nylen returned, covered in mud and golden dust. His braids were caked in dirt, and his cloak torn.

"I have found a way in," he said. "The tunnels are confusing and more than once I lost my way."

"Did you find the lake?" Kei asked.

"Aye," Nylen said, but the furrow in his brown belied the good news. "From a distance, at least. There's rough terrain ahead, but it will be easier once we are in the caverns." Jonathan brought him bread and figs, which he wolfed down at once. "At least I saw no Ophidians or other creatures."

"I have concocted a light camouflage for us," Kayna said when he had finished eating. She led them to a large hole she had dug and filled with water early in that morning. "We need to smell less human, and look it too."

They smeared the reddish brown mud onto their arms, necks, and faces and waited for it to dry. Nylen's thick blond braids resembled dirty ropes. It seemed a foolish thing to do; no amount of camouflage was going to deter the Ophidians once they took the fire.

"Should our plans go amiss today, and one of us falls, we leave them, just like we did Cadman," Nylen said, his voice hardening at the name of the smith. "Whoever is left alive gets Kayna to Cadarn with Ashryanna, no matter the cost. When you make it to the capital city, ask for the house of Taralin. She will provide you shelter. Breoc will get you into the king's hall. Understood?"

Jonathan and the twins exchanged looks of stony agreement. The warrior took a deep breath. "Good. Now let us visit the Ophidian's lair."

Below and farther away stood another canyon with tall, jagged, golden walls wide enough to house an entire city. To get there, they would have to scale large stone ridges that led into the dried-up riverbed. It was dappled with colors of honey, orange, gold, and pink, as if the sun itself had painted the landscape. It reminded Jonathan, oddly enough, of Gaelastad, with the green of their forests replaced by the ribboned sandstone. He looked around. "It's too quiet," he whispered to Kayna. "Between the Dorlíhein and the cry of Alaini-Nah, I have grown accustomed to conversations of wood and stone."

"You've heard naught but sad tales, then," Kayna said. "The forests were not always crying in rage. When I was little they used to talk to me of..."

Jonathan looked over to see the Terakheini's brow furrowed. She shook her head. "I almost had it."

"From here on out, follow me in single file," Nylen ordered. "We'll only stop twice until we get to the lake, and then, Kayna and Kei, you know what to do."

The twins nodded. Kayna had begun to wear the necklace of the Elementarí openly, as Morgan had instructed.

One by one they walked down the ridges of the canyon, following Nylen's steps as best they could. It began to get steep after about twenty feet. They used hands, feet, and knees to maneuver along the smaller ridges that had sharp drops as they went ever downward.

At last they were at the beginning of the canyon proper. Above them towered the jagged tops of the wall, craggy faces peering down. Jonathan felt as if he was being watched, and he constantly looked up until Kei admonished him to concentrate on the task at hand.

"There's no one out here," the Terakheini said.

"Are you sure? How can you tell?" Jonathan said, still keeping an eye on one particularly gruesome face.

"Kayna or I would feel their presence. There's been no movement except for us."

They followed the narrow path around the bends of the ancient riverbed until the tops of the walls closed in. Only a sliver of light dripped down into the tunnel, turning the sandstone into a delicious golden honey. Indentations in the walls formed faces, not like the craggy and grotesque ones in the outer canyon, but smooth contours where the eyes would be, a fluid jutting and drop of the nose, and the plump ridges of lips. It was like walking in between rows of stone people peacefully sleeping.

The rock above became a low ceiling, forcing them to crawl on their hands and knees. Here a quick escape would be impossible. The indentations in the wall continued to divert Jonathan's attention, until at last, on his right, he saw not the indentation of face in stone, but an actual face.

He almost let out a yell of surprise and stopped crawling so that Kei bumped into him. Jonathan pointed to the face protruding from the rock.

"They sleep within the walls," Kei whispered. "Keep moving."

Jonathan crawled, mesmerized by the faces that lined the passageway: ebony, copper, translucent saffron, golden tan, pale white. The rock encased their hair, so that that the honey-ribboned stone blended smoothly onto their foreheads. Some sported soft smiles on their faces, as if dreaming gardens into the world at that very moment. He tried not to think of what would happen should these spirits unexpectedly wake to find intruders.

A little while longer, the chasm walls opened up again, forming a small antechamber. A slit in the cavern roof allowed enough light to see four holes in the limestone wall, less than four feet in diameter, and evenly spaced apart.

"Beyond this is one more narrow passage that we must crawl through," Nylen whispered. "I saw the lake form another tunnel that was its runoff, but that way is impossible, for the wet stone is too slick. If we become separated, you can go through the opening at the east end of the lake and come out on the north end of the gulch. Don't engage any Ophidian if you can help it—we can't automatically assume they are in league with the Three, for Bryn said Phlegon has been trying to rouse others from their sleep to aid us."

And just how will we know the difference? Jonathan wondered.

Nylen climbed into the narrow tunnel on the farthest left, followed by the twins. Once inside, Jonathan had to crawl on his belly rather than on his hands and knees. *Just like a serpent.* The passageway seemed to go on for a hundred feet or more, but it was impossible to tell in that inky darkness. He wasn't prepared for the sheer drop. One moment, he was crawling and the next, he reached out and grasped nothing but air.

"Kei?" he whispered, and poked his head out just enough to get a view of the cavern.

It wasn't a cluster of caves like Jonathan had seen at Kaelest. This was a palace. Low hanging stalactites encircled the right half of the cavern, with mountainous stalagmites twisting up from the bottom to form pillars between them. But the eastern part of the cavern rippled in gold and pink stone, for there lay the lake of healing, its aquamarine waters illuminated with the light of Ashryanna. So brightly did she burn that Jonathan could see the smallest of silver-white bodies as fish darted below. Within these walls, scores of Ophidians rested, all dressed in white that reflected the light of the holy fire. Whatever Jonathan had known of the earth—from tilling its soil, to walking through its forest, both the evil and the good, the ancient and new—crumbled before this vision of loveliness and mystery.

"Jonathan."

He looked down to see Nylen and the twins on some kind of shelf that jutted out from the wall. The tunnel had widened enough to turn around in, and he jumped out, feet first. Walking to the edge of the platform revealed a narrow staircase, worn smooth like bone, that led down into vast darkness. Nylen signaled to move forward towards the stairs.

The light diminished as they descended to the cavern floor. There, sandstone grew in serpentine golden towers, creating a strange maze. Once he touched the floor, Jonathan was plunged into utter darkness, feeling his way around a limestone formation, hoping the others were in front of him. He saw a dim glow ahead and followed it, still trying to orient himself. Soon he was lost, and he realized that the light had not led him to Ashryanna, but to more spires that formed a half circle.

Through the spires, Jonathan saw two lit candelabras on small stone tables, and between them, lying on a limestone bed, was an Ophidian with golden hair. The scent of honey-suckle filled the room, and in the back of his mind, Jonathan knew that something was wrong, but the intoxic-ating aroma clouded his thoughts. Where had the others gone? He crept closer to the circle of towers when a strong hand grabbed him. He turned, expecting to see Nylen. Instead he met emerald eyes, set in a face that he recognized at once as the Ophidian from his dreams.

Adamara!

She towered over him, dressed in white, with golden ringlets cascading down around her face and slim neck. She paused when he turned around, and Jonathan saw the look of surprise on her face.

"Can it be?" A slow smile spread over her face as she leaned in. "Ah, yes—" she said, in a voice as rich as honey.

Her eyes dug into his, feeling, feeding...

"Leave him alone!" Kayna shouted behind him. He dared

not turn away from those eyes, for he feared what the Ophidian would do.

Adamara immediately released her grip, and pushed Jonathan aside, turning her attention to Kayna. "And who do I see before my eyes but Annea's little girl, all grown? My lovely, we had thought all of you to be lost."

In the blink of an eye, Adamara had slipped behind Kayna, her arm tight around the Terakheini's neck. "I tried to save a few of you, but the Nemarons were so eager to kill, so greedy, like humans, and we were ravenous that day." Her voice was sensuously low. "But, oh my darling, how glad I am to have you here now, for my brother is in need of your aid. You remember him, don't you?" She smiled and whispered something in Kayna's ear, causing her to swoon.

Then Jonathan understood. The body lying within the circle was Chalom.

"Kei! Kei!" He yelled, terrified it was already too late. "Get Ashryanna now!" He didn't care if he woke up all of Ophidia. The fire was everything. Running, footsteps, shouts.

"Jonathan, where are you?" Kei's voice echoed throughout the chambers.

Jonathan bolted past Adamara and Kayna, running through darkness towards the sound of Kei's voice. Limestone edges cut him as he felt his way until the thick formations grew smaller and he could finally see by Ashryanna's light. Kei stood a few feet away from the lake. The Ophidians within the walls were opening their eyes, for their shouting had indeed woken them. Where was Nylen?

"Jonathan, what—"

"Adamara has Kayna," he panted. "Quick—get Ashryanna!"

Kei turned toward the fire and put his hand out, uttering the words Morgan taught him. *"Avoci exuro fla nechlac!"*

Nothing happened. All around, the Ophidians were

slowly emerging from the cavern walls. Kei threw out his hands and repeated the words. Again nothing. Over and over again he chanted them.

"Heretheras, desia nom." Seductive voices, almost hissing. Jonathan turned around. Five Ophidians were behind him. He backed away. Suddenly, a crash from above, and Nylen jumped down, brandishing two torches. The Ophidians, momentarily distracted and disoriented, threw their hands up in defense.

"Avoci exuro fla nechlac!" Kei paused, trying to remember. *"I, Terakheini, athelan."*

The flame shuddered, then, in one violent motion, it whirled out of the lake, creating huge waves that spilled out onto the banks. Ashryanna hung there, suspended in the air, and Jonathan squinted his eyes against the blinding light. It was as if the sun itself had descended into the cave and would consume everything.

"Avexi Kayna!" Kei commanded as he threw his hand in the direction that Jonathan had come from.

Ashryanna shot out and knocked Kei to the ground as she flew past them, through the towers of stone and sand, illuminating the cavern as she traveled and created new shadows where darkness seeped in. Someone screamed. Jonathan ran back towards the circle, wondering if Ashryanna had found its way into Kayna's necklace, or if something worse...

He didn't know how many Ophidians were after him or where Kei was, but within seconds he was in front of the stone towers. Kayna lay still on the ground, Adamara kneeling over her.

"Get away!" Jonathan yelled. How could he fight off one of the Three?

"Back again, love? How convenient, for I need my strength to retrieve Ashryanna from our little one here."

She moved forward, and as much as Jonathan wanted to look away, he couldn't. Adamara smiled, two fangs sliding out of her mouth as she began to take on her serpent form.

"*Nemari!*"

Adamara was thrown back against the golden rock behind her as Kei ran past Jonathan to kneel down beside Kayna. Jonathan saw now that the fire had entered her necklace, its flames wildly dancing within the small moonstone.

"I didn't know you were here too, Kei," Adamara said, breathless from the impact. "Both twins with us again? How delightful."

She threw her hand out, and a large rock whistled through the air and crashed against Kei's right shoulder. He fell to the ground, crumpled in pain, as Adamara advanced. "My sweet, don't make me hurt you again."

"The Ogoni burn your lying tongue." A small flame appeared in his hand.

Adamara laughed as she disappeared, her serpent form whipping around the large spire. Kei got up and ran after her. "Get Kayna to safety!" he shouted before he disappeared behind the same sandstone tower.

Jonathan shook Kayna's shoulder but failed to wake her from whatever deep sleep Adamara had cast over her. He picked her up, uncertain of where he should go. Then he heard Nylen's shouts.

Slowly he made his way towards the sound of the warrior's voice; the weight of Kayna was far heavier now that she wore the holy fire, a burden of unimaginable power. When Nylen came into view, Jonathan stopped in horror. Nylen had his back to the lake, surrounded by more than twenty Ophidians who he kept at bay with his Kei-blessed torches. It wouldn't hold them long. He looked down at Kayna, who had suddenly opened her eyes.

"What happened? I was falling..."

"We're in trouble," he whispered. The Ophidians had not seen them. Not yet. He set her down, and for a moment she wavered and held on to him.

"What do we do?" she asked.

To their right, from behind the towers, there came a flash of blue light, and yells from both Adamara and Kei filled the cavern. Jonathan suddenly remembered the body in the circle of towers.

"Where's Kei? Adamara?"

"Fighting. You can't...help him that way," he panted. "Stay here and out of sight."

He sprinted to the circle and through the towers to the body on the bier. Chalom lay there, eyes closed and breathing very slowly.

"Be my guard," Jonathan whispered. "Do you have enough power to give me at least a little time?"

"What are you going to—"

Now you'll know how it feels to lose a brother, he thought as he picked up Chalom, and heaved it over his shoulder.

He bent his head down and charged. He ran through the towers, past the spires and the stalagmite staircase, around to where he saw the Ophidians closing in on his friends, not stopping once to consider what would happen other than what he understood of dreams, of earth and sea, fire and air.

He ran to the lake's edge and heaved Chalom's body into the water.

A scream pierced the entire cavern and shook the very rocks. Within a breath, Adamara was charging the water.

"Now!" Jonathan yelled.

Nylen rushed towards him. "Where's Kei?"

"Here," Kei said weakly, his face full of snake welts like those inflicted upon him in the cave of the Wild Lands. Putting his arm around her shoulder, Kayna dragged him to the steps.

"Nylen, throw your torches down," Kei said when they had gone up a step or two. The fires of both flickered as Nylen hurled them through the air.

"Exuro bitanel, bitanel!" Kei cried, causing the torches to burst into a wall of flame.

They scrambled up the stairs, with Nylen leading and Jonathan taking up the rearguard. He looked back through the flames to see Adamara coming out of the lake bearing Chalom in her arms, the other Ophidians crowding around. The group kept climbing, scraping their hands and knees against the stone. Jonathan helped the twins and Nylen up into the tunnel, and then the warrior pulled him in. They quietly crawled down the narrow corridor. Jonathan held his breath as he passed the sleeping Ophidians, wondering if at any moment the spirits would wake as the others had. Then he saw an earth spirit to his right open her emerald eyes. Jonathan froze.

"Keep moving!" Kei ordered.

"She's waking," Jonathan said and pointed to the Ophidian in the wall, who was looking at Jonathan—neither with malice or fear. Just staring.

"What's going on?" Nylen shouted.

"Shhh." Kei put his hand on the wall. *"Slipatha, Ophidia. Nea wethama."*

The earth spirit's eyes closed as a soft smile played out on her lips.

"Now come!" Kei said. Jonathan scrambled to catch up. They finally reached the antechamber where they could all stand.

Nylen studied Kei. His blue-gray eyes looked too bright. The serpent welts on his face were still there, but not as red. "Are any of them moving yet? Can you hold on until we get to the canyon?"

"I can walk. The snakes aren't, which is good, but the fever is beginning."

"Then we go. I'll lead. Jonathan, help Kei."

They hurried, always listening for pursuit. At times, Kei stumbled and Jonathan quickly helped him to his feet again. The walls slowly grew wider and the afternoon sun bore down on them with unrelenting heat. Soon they were out of the canyon, but they knew the worst was ahead of them, for they had to make the climb over the ridges that led to the canyon of the Alaini-Nah. Kei's eyes were now glassy, his face flushed.

"I need to heal him before the fever gets worse." Kayna felt Kei's forehead. "He can't make that climb like this."

A melodious wail shook the lower canyon. Everyone looked at each other, holding their breath. Answering cries echoed throughout.

"Quickly, do what you can!" Nylen barked.

Kayna sang softly as she ran her hands over Kei's face. Nylen readied an arrow. In a moment they were on the move again.

"How are you doing with Ashryanna?" Jonathan asked Kayna as they began to climb.

"It's...a heavy weight," she said, breathing hard.

They climbed as fast as they could, but all were exhausted now, especially the twins, as the sun beat mercilessly down upon them. Nylen turned to look back down. Against the pinkish brown rock, large, silver white serpents were side-winding up the ridges.

"They're coming!" the warrior yelled as he strung his bow. "Kei, can you make a flame?"

Kei held his hands together, concentrating. His face was very white and feverish, but he was able to call up a small fire. "Send them a message that we are not such easy prey this time," Kei said as he lit the arrow's tip.

Nylen let the shaft fly. It hit one of the serpents, which thrashed about, hissing until at last its body morphed back into the shape of an Ophidian, with the arrow now sticking out his side. A few of the other serpents turned back into their Ophidians forms and gathered around him. One sent out another terrible cry.

"Who are they calling?" Kayna asked, transfixed by the scene below.

"I don't know," Nylen said, "but we must make the canyon before dark, else they will have the advantage with their sight. Look—the sun is sinking low."

Despite their quick ascent up the ridge, the Ophidian serpents were beginning to close the gap between them. Nylen stopped once more to have Kei set fire to another arrow, when a large shadow flew over them. Above their heads, a flock of birds circled.

Not birds.

Cralen.

Nylen pointed to a few of the larger boulders up ahead on the right. An arrow whizzed by Jonathan, followed by another. Two Cralen hit the ground as they ran forward. Jonathan felt a blind terror rising inside him. "Damn it, keep low!" Nylen roared.

Three more Cralen swooped in as they dashed to the rocks. One flew straight at Kayna as she was stringing an arrow. She lifted her arms to protect her face from its talons, but Jonathan had his dagger ready, and with one clean throw, speared the Cralen. Kei conjured an umbrella of fire, but he was still weak, and the two remaining Cralen passed unscathed through the small wall of flames. Nylen's arrow pierced one's neck, and with a terrible shriek it fell while Kayna recovered her arrow to shoot the third as it swerved around. Yet the flock still circled overhead.

"This will do us little good," Nylen shouted. "We can't hope to defend ourselves here. Kei, can you make your fire stronger?"

"I don't know if it would help," he panted. "Ventosus has made them invincible to heat, or maybe the cold venom they release combats the fire."

Jonathan's dagger was still in the Cralen, and he had no other weapon. The snakes slid up the rock, hissing furiously, while, overhead, the Cralen continued to circle, their screeching almost unbearable. And now, a third sound—the howling of wind. Jonathan recognized it even before Nylen yelled out.

"Heads down!"

The dust storm ambushed them from the direction of the upper canyon, which acted like a funnel, turning the fly-ing dirt into miniature tornadoes of dust and rocks. They tried to cover their faces with their cloaks and arms, but the sand flew into Jonathan's mouth and nose. His eyes were tightly shut, yet he saw the talons and the giant wings of Ventosus's ice world. He heard laughter, so loud it drowned out the voices of the Cralen and Ophidians.

Then another voice: deep and lilting, almost musical. It was the woman whose voice he had heard, yet whose face he had never seen. *Fire for darkness, warmth for winter. Call her.*

Call whom? The dust storm continued to thrash them from all directions, causing welts on their hands from the flying stones and dirt. Nylen was shouting something. The laughter grew louder with the howling wind. Jonathan thought of the howling of wolves. Wolves guarding a little girl.

Samara. Jonathan bent every single thought towards finding her. *We can't find you unless you fight the wind for us.*

Sienna's voice cut in now, joining other women's in a chant. *Fire for darkness, warmth for winter.*

"Kei!" Jonathan yelled, reaching out and trying to find him, for the wind was blinding.

"I'm here!" A finger locked into his arm.

Jonathan pulled Kei to him and said, "Use your fire—not at the Cralen. Send out your fire into the wind. Let Samara use it."

Jonathan bent all his thought to the Terakheini. *Help Kei! We'll come find you!*

Kei gathered all his strength and released a cry that resounded over the wails of wind, the howling laughter, and the Cralen's screeching: *"Adustum Nefas! Samara!"*

The words echoed throughout the two canyons as Kei threw a deep blue fire into the maelstrom. Then they heard an answering cry.

Terah chi thero, Ventosus!

Samara's voice rushed throughout both canyons and seemed to shatter the very air. The wind suddenly died.

Cralen alin clath Nemari!

The Cralen screeched and reeled, as if suddenly in pain. Four dropped from the sky, bounced against the ridge walls, and didn't move again. The rest sped away. Jonathan wiped the dust from his stinging eyes. *Thank you*, he told her. Samara suddenly appeared in his mind, surrounded by wolves, just like she had been when he was with Phlegon. She didn't say anything, only looked at him with a sad smile.

A hand was shaking him. Jonathan opened his eyes to see Kei standing over him, holding out a trembling hand to help him up. "You reached her."

"Who?" a raspy voice said. Nylen was pinned under several large rocks. *Neáhvalar, don't let him die.* Jonathan prayed as they lifted the stones the size of a man's head off Nylen's chest and shoulders.

"I'm fine," Nylen said as they slowly helped him to sit up. "Except for a few bruised ribs." He was breathing shallowly. "Are the Ophidians still following us?"

Jonathan peered out from the boulders. "There are only three serpents now, and slow moving, but they'll catch up soon enough."

"One of your ribs might be broken, but I'm not sure," Kayna said, feeling the man's chest. "You'll have to wait for me to bandage it—they'll soon awake. While three Ophidians are better than twenty, three are enough."

"Can you walk?" Kei asked, glancing over Nylen's shoulder. "They're starting to move again."

"I should still be able to climb."

Kayna helped him to his feet. "Jonathan, get your dagger."

Jonathan ran to where the giant bird had fallen and drew the blade out of the creature's entrails. Just touching the bird sent a chill down his arm, and the cold crept into his back. *No time for that now.* The group had already begun the final ascent, and he scurried up the ridge after them.

—◦◦◦◦◦—

They climbed wordlessly, but Jonathan noticed how Kei and Kayna stumbled more on the way up.

"The twins," Jonathan said quietly to Nylen.

"I know. Something happened back there. I don't know what's wrong, but we've got to get them to the canyon."

The remaining Ophidians were close now, so close that Jonathan and Kayna could hear them telling the group to slow down, for they were hungry. Jonathan tried not to listen, although chills crawled down his spine as he remembered drowning in Adamara's eyes. They were almost to the last ridge, and then it would be a race to the voices of the Alaini-Nah. As they reached the plateau, Kayna stumbled, and reaching out, failed to grasp the edge above. Jonathan caught her as she fell back, fainting.

The snakes hissed loudly, and one of them rose up and turned into a beautiful Ophidian with shoulder-length silver hair. It was none other than Trapher.

"Oh dear, now how will you make it?" His voice grew more earnest as his gaze lingered on Kayna. "Our prince is dying. If Kayna comes with us willingly, no harm shall come to her. You may even keep Ashryanna."

"Come anywhere near my sister, and you'll burn until nothing remains, Trapher," Kei threatened, but Jonathan could see that the fever raging throughout his body had taken its toll.

"Tssk, tssk. Always the hotheaded one. I don't remember that helping you before," Trapher said.

Nylen strung his bow. Jonathan was about to sling Kayna over his shoulder when she slightly opened her eyes. "Don't you dare," she said wearily.

"Then stand up. Here," he said as he put one of her arms over his shoulder. "We're almost there."

That hope seemed to wake her, and she was able to run with Jonathan's help. Trapher transformed back into his serpent self as the other two Ophidians began side-winding up the last few ridges. Nylen fired a couple of arrows that merely glanced off their serpent skins as the others climbed up to the plateau.

He quickly caught up to them. "Don't look back!" he yelled as he drew his sword.

"Jonathan..." Kayna whispered as her eyes closed and she slumped forward. The serpents were almost to the plateau.

Jonathan slung her over his shoulder and broke into a sprint. He didn't look to his left or right, didn't listen to the shouts of Nylen or Kei; all he cared about was getting Kayna to safety. Soon he was breathing fire, legs heavy, but he kept running towards the mouth of the canyon.

A voice hissed. "Not yyyet, ssstaaay."

Jonathan's pace was slowing under Kayna's weight.

"It wonnn't...hurrrt."

Jonathan turned his head and saw the serpent to his right. A burst of energy surged through his entire body as he heard the wailing of the lost people begin. With all his might, he threw himself and Kayna over the invisible border created by the canyon walls.

He turned to see the serpent that had been almost parallel to him now crumpled up in his Ophidian form, hands covering his ears. The other serpent, a female, had likewise fallen down. Nylen ran past, Kei leaning against him. Trapher was nowhere to be seen.

"Farther in," the warrior commanded. Kayna still hadn't opened her eyes, and Jonathan wondered if she'd been hurt in the fall. He picked her up gently and carried her to camp where they laid the twins down. Around him, the entire canyon echoed with wailing voices, a roar of angry shouts and battle cries.

"They sense the Ophidians," Jonathan said through the roar. "I can hear them like we were in the middle of the canyon. You should put wax in Kayna's ears, you don't want her waking up to this chaos."

"Did you see where Trapher went?" Nylen asked.

Jonathan shouted no as he clapped his hands over his ears. "If he's hearing what I am, I don't see how he could bear it. Isn't it loud for you?"

"I can only hear distant rumblings, like thunder from far away," Nylen replied. Jonathan could see he was breathing shallowly as he knelt by the twins—neither of whom stirred. Jonathan started a fire and soon he had melted the wax just enough to mold it for himself and Kayna.

"They've fallen into a fever deep enough to kill, I warrant," Nylen said as Jonathan molded the wax into the Terakheini's ears. "Morgan thought the challenge might prove too much for them. I can call them to the surface of their fever, I think." His gaze suddenly darted across the top ridges of the canyons. "Scout the area, but don't go beyond the canyon walls. Let's make sure the earth spirits have found no secret way to slither inside our haven. I will have more answers by the time you come back."

Jonathan walked down one side of the gulch wall, looking up to see if he could spot any movement. He came within fifty feet of the entrance and removed the wax from his ears. The voices of the Alaini-Nah were still excruciatingly loud. He dashed back to camp.

"They're here!" he shouted.

Nylen suddenly stood up. "How do you know? Did you see something?"

"No. The Alaini-Nah are keeping out Trapher and the other two with their cries. The Ophidians are close by, even if we can't see them." He gazed at the twins lying motionless; the spiral imprint on Kei's shoulder was a vivid scarlet once again and had begun to writhe below his skin. *Morgan is not here to save him now,* he thought in despair. "How is he?"

"I need you to heal them," Nylen said.

Jonathan could barely understand him over the heartbreaking cries of the children ringing in his ears. "What?"

"You need to heal them—use Ashryanna."

Jonathan was still unsure he had heard the warrior right. "Morgan said no one could touch the flame."

Nylen leaned close and shouted into Jonathan's ear. "You're not just anyone. Remember, the necklace that holds Ashryanna was given to you first, and you have at least one gift akin to that of a Terakhein. Perhaps, because of your skill, the flame will allow you to handle her. I've done all I can to help them, but Adamara cursed them with some deep fever, and at most, I have kept them from death."

The voices surrounded Jonathan and he closed his eyes, not knowing what else to do. Then he saw them, scores of children running around, tan from the sun and dressed in bright colors. He stepped towards them. They were no longer crying or screaming for their parents in fear and agony; some were laughing and playing tag, others were eating the luscious cacti fruit that once grew there, red juice dribbling down their chins. Jonathan realized that he was seeing the Alaini-Nah as they once were.

"Children!" he cried.

A few of them stopped playing and looked at him. "Your voices are crying out to me, and it is all I can hear. The Terakhein people shared your fate, as did my own village. Yet these two Terakhein are left, and they will die if I cannot bring them out of their fever. Please, help me." Jonathan didn't know what else to ask, even as tears streamed down his own cheeks. The children ran to him. A few of the adults peered down from their high houses. "Help me," he pleaded. "We can't let them die."

A hand on his arm. He opened his eyes to see Nylen staring at him.

"Who are you talking to?"

Jonathan wiped his eyes and knelt down next to Kayna. "Never mind. What do I need to do?"

Nylen retrieved two black river rocks from his sack, the same ones that had been used on Kei in the Terakhein forest, the same kind that Jonathan had seen in Rose and Theo's house. "Pull Ashryanna out," he instructed, "and have her heat the rocks. Her fire must chase away Adamara's fever."

Jonathan gently unclasped Kayna's necklace. He closed his eyes again. The children were still all there, watching him, and now some of the adults had joined them as well. They were a small people, most of whom only reached Jonathan's shoulders. From the crowd, a man and a woman came forward. Their robes were of dark blue rather than the brighter colors that the others wore, and between them they carried a small, ornately-decorated box. The man opened it and withdrew a black river rock while the woman brought out a glass bottle with a small flame inside.

Ashryanna wetha helasme, the woman said as she drew the flame into her hand. Then she nodded once to him.

"*Ashryanna wetha helasme,*" Jonathan repeated, and put his hand over the necklace. A shock reverberated his body as Ashryanna slid from the necklace into his hand.

The woman took the flame and placed it onto the rock the man held. The rock sprung into fire. *Eithuan infervo, haleth Ogoni, siblith di Ashryanna.* Both the man and woman looked at him.

Jonathan suddenly understood. Ashryanna had a sister— and the Ogoni had given her to the Alaini-Nah long ago. He opened his eyes. "Nylen, put the river rock on Kei, right on the spiral." Jonathan held Ashryanna in his palm over the river stone, then he turned his hand over.

"*Eithuan infervo, haleth Ogoni, Ashryanna.*" The flame slid from his palm onto the black stone. Jonathan closed his eyes. The man and woman were gone, as were the children, and he tried not to think that perhaps he had dreamed them all.

"Look!" Nylen said. The spiral on Kei's shoulder had stopped squirming, and the red started to fade as a little serpent once again bore its way out. Nylen crushed it under his heel, cursing. The spiral imprint had turned back to pink.

"That should do it," Jonathan said.

"The spiral's still there," Nylen pointed out.

"Morgan said it wouldn't ever go away, remember? It's Kayna's turn." Jonathan placed the stone on her chest, directly over her heart. *So broken*, he thought, lightly touching her brow. "*Eithuan infervo, haleth Ogoni, Ashryanna.*"

Kayna caruhal, another voice said.

"Who said that?" Nylen stood up, gazing around, then stared at Jonathan in wonder.

"What happened?" Kei opened his eyes and turned his head to see his sister with Ashryanna sitting on top of her. He reached out and took her hand.

"Kei?" she said, barely moving her lips, her eyes still closed.

"I'm here, dear heart," he said as Jonathan lifted the river rock.

"*Avoci exuro fla nechlac.*" The flame gently fell into the necklace in Jonathan's other hand.

"Rest for now," Jonathan said as he clasped the necklace once more around Kayna's neck. He closed his eyes to see the Alaini-Nah gathered around him again. *Denatha*, he said, somehow knowing it was their word for *thank you*. They bowed low. The man in blue pointed at himself. *Amitola*. Then he pointed at the woman. *Galilahi*. They smiled and faded back into the canyon walls.

"And thanks to you, too," Kayna added. Jonathan looked down to see her smiling. "I can't hear them anymore."

"What does that mean for Trapher and the others then?" Nylen asked as he retrieved his bow, flinching in pain as he did so.

Jonathan looked all around him as the canyon grew red in the dusk. "No need for that. The lost ones are still here—you heard one of them just a moment ago."

Nylen sank back against the rock wall. "Then they will watch over us tonight."

Yes, they would be safe tonight, true enough. But how they would make it out tomorrow was another matter.

CHAPTER 18
THE FINAL SPRINT

Jonathan skimmed over the surface of sleep, walked into a room full of mist. Or was it smoke?

"There's still time. You must go with me." The nameless man again. The vision was clearing at least: he could see that the man sat on a horse, his back to Jonathan. In front of him stood the woman, ebony curls that fell past her shoulders—it seemed like she was wearing a dark colored gown, but the picture was still too cloudy. The woman handed something to the man.

"There's nothing left—we've been betrayed," she said. "I hear them coming—"

A great boom silenced her command.

Then, a peal of thunder. Jonathan awoke to a flash as lightning split the sky, and for a moment, he expected a line of fire to rise up and meet it. But no, that was another time. No Elementarí would come and save them here in Ophidia. Jonathan threw off the blanket and went to where Nylen sat, his gaze fixed on the canyon's gaping mouth a hundred feet away.

"They'll not enter," Jonathan reminded him.

The warrior turned slightly, revealing his strong aquiline nose and jutting, stubborn chin. "Didn't stop them the first time."

"The Three were in full power then, whereas Chalom's just had a good dunking." Another rumble of thunder caused them both to gaze at the sky. "Adamara might be preparing something similar for us. Did you see her in the cavern?"

"Had I gotten a glimpse of her face, nothing would have stopped me from wringing her beautiful neck till I sent her back to Neáhvalar himself. It's just as well; she wouldn't have been happy to see me, either." He rubbed his scarred cheek. "I got a good prick of her arm after she killed Cierdwyn, and she repaid me in turn. Could have been worse."

"No man can harm an Elementarí."

"Very true, but Cierdwyn might have taught me a trick or two. That was her way, you know. She always broke the rules." As he spoke of the king's sister, a light spread across his face and softened the lines around his eyes and mouth.

The truth of it suddenly dawned on Jonathan. "Did Cadreyth know about you two?"

Nylen's eyebrows rose in amusement. "You mean that we were lovers? Whatever he thought about me, he kept to himself. I met the king only twice and wisely kept my tongue during both encounters. I thought him a tried and venerable leader, at least until he challenged Truculen. Then I cursed him as a fool." His mouth became grim again. "Don't ever mention my encounter with Adamara in the war to Kei or Kayna. Have you not seen the way Kei's face goes white at the mere mention of her name? She was there the day the Nemarons and Ophidians took over their forest —I'm sure of it."

Jonathan remembered Adamara's delight at having *both twins back again*. A light shiver ran through his body. "When she first saw me, it was as if she *recognized* me."

"Perhaps she did." Nylen scrambled to his feet and started to gather his gear. "Hecthrax was aware of you when you tried to find Samara, so wouldn't it make sense that Adamara has been somehow able to see you?"

I can kill in the shadows of your mind. No dream can stop me, the wolf had said. "That means Hecthrax will know me as well." *And does that mean Sienna can see me, too?* The thought gave him little peace since the widow had turned into Adamara in more than one vision. And if his nightmares held the seeds of truth—

"Where did Sienna get those?" He pointed to the black river rocks that had fallen out of the warrior's sack.

"Never said." Nylen placed the stones back inside the sack and finished shoving everything else in. Then he sat back against a rock and gazed up at the northern star. "I assume they're used among country physicks." The warrior cast a quick glance at him. "Why?"

"No reason." That wasn't quite true. The Alaini-Nah had used those rocks for their healing arts, but Jonathan knew of no such practice in all of Gaelastad, nor had he ever seen such stones as these in any river bed. There had to be some kind of connection between Theo, Rose, Sienna and these canyon people, and he wondered if the answer lay in a sword shooting out of a lake of fire.

―――⊙⸜ⓖ⸝――

They woke up the twins just after dawn. "It is a week to the Cadarian border, then another week to the Camhanaich on foot. If we find a village with horses for sale we can get there in two days with hard riding." Nylen said as they packed up their camp. As they walked the short length of the canyon, Jonathan sensed spirits climbing down from their broken houses, and starting to follow. He momentarily closed his eyes and saw them—dirty children skipping alongside their mothers. The fathers, beautiful warriors with red squares painted over their chests, spoke blessings as they walked.

When they reached the end of the gulch, Kei stopped them, his face pale. "What if Adamara is out there waiting for us? I cannot summon that kind of power so soon after our last encounter, not unless Samara helps us again."

"She's hidden from my thoughts," Jonathan sighed. "She risked being discovered by Ventosus with that display of power yesterday. My guess is that we're on our own, Kei."

The Terakheini blanched at this news, but that didn't stop him or Kayna from walking right up to where the canyon ended. Nylen was about fifty feet ahead of them, peering out into the horizon. Listening.

Jonathan glanced back into the canyon and saw Amitola and Galilahi standing in front of the Alaini-Nah. Amitola whistled loudly and looked up. In the sky, a bird circled. Jonathan had an urge to run back into the canyon and hide, but as the bird descended, he could see its bronze feathers edged with dark blue. It wasn't a Cralen but a desert hawk that landed on Amitola's arm and chattered at the healer. *Ophidian no wearathu. No cimefurath,* he assured Jonathan.

"The Ophidians aren't out there," he shouted to Nylen.

"How do you know that?"

"I just do!" Jonathan could see them, eyes open, and he was in no vision. A little girl, about seven years old, ran up and pressed something into his hand. It was a pale-yellow flower with an outer ring of red petals, in honor of the desert as it once was, before the Three awoke. Jonathan smiled. *Denatha.* He blinked, and the Alaini-Nah were gone.

"Where did you get that?" Kayna was at his side, eyes wide in wonder.

"They gave it to me," he smiled and handed her the bloom.

Kayna turned the flower over in her palm, stroking the furry golden center. She was already tired, Jonathan realized, with Ashryanna sitting around her neck like the sun. Still, she reached up and planted a small kiss on his cheek. "Thank you."

A world of flowers, Jonathan thought, as they filed out of the canyon of the Alaini-Nah, the forgotten ones.

⁓⚬⊙⚬⁓

They kept an even pace as the canyon fell away and the land became dotted once again with silver-thistle brush and Truculen's blue-green flowers. Only stopping twice during the day, the group finally found a place to camp where the land dipped amid a chaotic scattering of large rocks and sage. As twilight fell, the five stone giants stood in the distance, menacing and unmoving.

"I wish we were far away enough for a fire," Jonathan said, reaching for his thick Íarchin cloak. The desert had not been this cool at the start of their journey; what would happen if Ventosus' winter came here, where there was so little shelter?

"I want no more heat!" Kayna said, with beads of sweat on her forehead, as she sank down on her blanket.

"Is it bad?" Kei crouched down beside his sister and reached out to slip the necklace over her head. "Let me take it."

Nylen glanced over from where he was unloading his sack. "Withdraw your hand, Kei."

Kei froze, but kept his hand on the base of Kayna's neck. "I am of the Ogoni, Nylen," he said. "Why should I not be able to handle this holy flame?"

"Morgan's rules, not mine," Nylen replied. He stood up, tall and unmoving. "You're not to touch it, perhaps *because* of your power."

Kei visibly bristled as he, too, stood up and walked up the small ledge of sand and dirt. "Doesn't matter," he muttered. "It's my watch."

—⋆⋅◉⋅◎⋅⋆—

In the early morning, when all was still dark, they were on the move again. The day grew only slightly warmer as the sun slowly climbed into the middle of the sky, and the wind rolled in with strange clouds—neither dark with rain nor gray with snow, but an odd greenish hue that warned of hail. *Not yet, not that.* They were still four days away from the border. In this part of the desert, the small sandstone formations had grown less abundant, and even the gentle dips and rises in the ground offered no easy place to camp. The warrior allowed fewer breaks, always looking up at the sky, that hung down too low.

The rain started as a cool drizzle; by afternoon, it was a downpour, a steady deluge that continued through the evening. For three days and nights the rain washed over the desert soil, turning it into miles of endless sludge. Sleep was stolen in light snatches when they could find a place protected enough that they weren't lying in puddles. The wind blew cold now under gray skies as they trudged on.

"We might make the border by tomorrow," Nylen said.

The worst is still to come, Jonathan thought, peering through the rain and mist and seeing only empty horizon. His boots kept sticking in the mud, slowing his walk.

"This isn't the earth opening up and swallowing us," Kei said, "but it's not much bet—"

Kei disappeared. One moment, he was walking beside Jonathan. The next, the earth had swallowed him, leaving only one arm visible.

Jonathan caught Kei's hand. He pulled, finally wrenching the Terakhein's head and shoulder clear of the mud, but the sludge had locked Kei's legs in the ground. Crouching behind him, Nylen wrapped one arm around his chest, grappling with the mud to slide his other arm underneath the Terakhein's armpit.

"Kayna, make the earth obey you," Kei pleaded, keeping very still, knowing that if he struggled, the mud would only drag him down further.

Kayna wrapped one hand around her necklace and thrust the other into the mud. *"Ophidia ichthrata. Terra kein isi, Nemari!"* she shouted.

The ground trembled so violently that Jonathan and Nylen fell back as Kei's waist and legs came suddenly free. They dragged him free as white lighting cracked across the sky, illuminating the clouds.

Muhalath cometheras. Dormín faleneth. Dormín risent.

The voice reverberated throughout the land along with the thunder. Adamara's voice, calling out in vengeance for the law of Dormín being broken. *The land will rest no longer,* Jonathan thought she had said. Her voice was immediately joined by a chorus of Ophidians repeating the words over and over in different pitch and tone so that it sounded like a holy chant.

"Do not stop," Nylen said, drawing his sword; Jonathan's dagger was now in hand. The voices followed them as they ran, eyes on the ground, leery of holes that would open again and take them. The song grew in volume until they thought they would go deaf, or mad from the noise.

Suddenly, it stopped.

The mud began to churn.

It swirled all around them, kneading itself over and over until it had formed hands that sprang out of the sludge, grasping at their feet. Thickening ooze slowed their running and swirled at their heels. Arms and hands then erupted from the sludge, so their reach was long. Jonathan almost fell as a pair reached out and encircled his knees.

"Put them to sleep!" Jonathan cried. "Before they become fully formed soldiers."

"It's the land itself that is moving!" Kayna replied. "We have no power over it, anymore than we could control the rivers."

The mud was too thick for them to keep running, and as the rain lessened, the kneading bodies grew. Even now they climbed to four feet high with torsos and legs, before melting in the rain, only to simultaneously reform. One of them lunged at Kayna.

Jonathan caught hold of her hand and dragged her to his side.

Another jumped for Kei, and Nylen swung around, bringing up his sword. But such slow strokes were futile against an army of sludge. They were surrounded by mud men continually trying to drag them into the abyss of ooze. Mud flew into their eyes and mouths. They would drown in the desert.

Nylen spotted a creek to their right. "Quick, to the water!"

Clothes caked with mud slowed their swimming, but the rivers still belonged to the Delphini. The monstrous creatures could not follow them into the water, and instead formed towering walls of mud on either side. There was no safe place to climb out and dry off. For the rest of the afternoon, the current dragged them along, numbing their hands and feet to the point where it felt like Jonathan's limbs were on fire. The words still echoed in his mind: *Muhalath cometheras! Dormín faleneth. Dormín risent!* It was either death by fire and ice in the river, or being buried alive up on the banks. No real choice.

By dusk the river had changed course; the mud mountains slowly diminished as they flowed into the Firalis, an offshoot of the Tigechal. Meadows lined both sides of its banks and small trees sprang up all around them. Finally they were able to climb out, and saw up ahead an old wooden outpost about two stories high, long deserted. On its doors, the image of tall flames carved along the sides. They had finally crossed into Cadarn.

"Why is it deserted?" Jonathan asked as they threw their packs down inside the tower and immediately started to build a small fire. "Surely Adolan has not gotten so reckless that he doesn't keep his borders to the south watched, knowing that is where their peril came from last time?"

"It has been some months since anyone has been here, from the look of the tracks inside," Kei added.

"I warrant the king has called all his men up north," Nylen said. "It has been near twenty years since the Ophidians went to war with Cadarn, and they came from the Nemaron border, not the south. No, Adolan would not have kept up these sentry posts, which works to our favor. We should begin to see houses within the next day or two, or perhaps even a village."

They huddled together that night, drying clothes and trying to stay warm. Jonathan didn't mind snuggling up to Kayna and the heat emanating from her necklace. Nylen woke them up all too soon.

During the next thirty miles the rain turned to snow. The night was numbingly cold, and dawn was scarcely better as gray clouds blanketed the sun. Nylen had promised there would be a village within the next day or two, but days seemed like weeks in this blank terrain, with neither rocky caves nor forest to break up the landscape. The snow kept falling. In some places drifts reached just below the knee, forcing them to stay close to the river where the trees gave them some shelter, and the banks were more mud than snow.

"How goes it for you?" Nylen asked Kayna. It was around midday, and already the Terakheini had fallen behind Jonathan, her shoulders uncharacteristically slumping forward as she stumbled behind him.

"It's like a deadweight on my heart," she said. "Can we rest?"

"Soon, but not yet," Nylen said. "If we reach a village tonight, you'll be able to rest and we can get horses—"

A sudden churning in the river splashed more water and mud onto the banks.

Jonathan drew his dagger while Nylen strung his bow. Kei ran to Kayna. But the mud did not rise; instead, a form rose out of the river. A Delphini stood before them, his cloak spread out like a wave. He was shorter than Morgan and her brothers, but clearly their kin. "Put down your arms," he commanded. His violet eyes came to rest on the twins. "I am Elanias—we had word that you would pass this way should you find Ashryanna again, but I've come to warn you that the Nemarons have gathered at Tigechal.

"You have a week before they attack, maybe less. I and others have raised the river and made its current run wild in order to impede their crossing—more than that we cannot do. The winter moves in from the north, and soon even we will not be able to keep the river from freezing over. I believe some of the Ogoni have crawled up from their homes to be closer to the surface and warm the ground. Morwenna, for her part, has commanded the Feállí to stir up the tides in the deepest part of the ocean so that Ventosus cannot use all the winds as he wants. Even so, the Feállí are wild and mischievous, and to let them play in the tides will help you now, yet the price will be great. You do not have much time left."

"What about Peran and Madron?" Nylen asked. "Are they bringing the Íarchins and Lailethans?"

"Have you heard from Morgan?" Jonathan added.

Elanias looked worried. "I've heard from neither the brothers nor the sister. War is coming from both sides to Cadarn, and the Wild is crazed with dread creatures. If they decide to cross the Wild instead of using the mountains, you can be sure they will arrive with fewer men than when they started." He stopped and bent his ear to the water. "I must go now. Fly north and get Ashryanna back to her altar!" he commanded as he fell backwards, arms spread, into the river.

"Neáhvalar could send us more help," Nylen sighed, his brown eyes focused on the tired Terakheini girl before him. Perhaps he was seeing another woman, almost twenty years earlier, tired and beaten in an impossible war…"Kayna—"

"I will keep up," she snapped, with an expression on her face not unlike Sienna's. She threw her small chin out. "I am Terakhein. Let me rest just once, and then I'll not stop until we secure horses and food."

She kept up, much to Jonathan's surprise. It was past midnight when they finally spotted a few wattle and daub houses spread more than a mile apart. Although they had been hoping for a town, that concern ceased to worry them once they came to an old stone house with a stable off to the side.

"Let us go inquire if she's willing to sell them," Nylen said.

"All of us? At this hour?" Jonathan countered. "We'll be more likely met with a dagger than a kind greeting."

"We have no time for traditional courtesies." The warrior strode up to the door and knocked several times. A large woman answered, about Nylen's age or slightly older, her dark hair piled up into her nightcap except for one wayward strand that dangled behind her ear. She stuck her lantern in his face. "Who's there?"

"We have an urgent need to get to Camhanaich, for the Nemarons are gathering at Tigechal. Will you help us?"

The woman looked closely at Nylen, who had exposed his face so he could speak clearly. Her gaze traveled to the twins and then Jonathan.

"Let me see your face," she told him.

Mine is not a look to trust, Jonathan thought as he unwrapped his scarf. Black eyed and black haired, he was the wildest looking of the bunch. She thrust the lantern closer to him.

She looked at him long, frowning, and rasped, "What do you want?"

"Three or four horses, if you have them. We'll pay handsomely for your inconvenience." Nylen produced a bag.

The women took the bag with narrowed eyes. "I've got three horses in the barn you can have. The tackle is there too. Go get them, except for you," she said to Kayna. "Come inside while they get the horses. You look like you're about half dead."

Kayna shook her head. "I must—"

"Go with her," Nylen said. "We'll be back soon."

Kayna went into the dark house and the woman shut the door in their faces. Kei was about to follow them when the warrior threw out his arm, barring the way. "No, let her fix your sister something to drink. We've got to get the horses."

"What just happened?" Jonathan asked.

"Who is this woman, to keep my sister so?" Kei asked, still not moving.

"She's the provider of our horses, and I read neither guile nor treason in her look, merely distrust." Nylen trudged off to the barn, his boots kicking up snow.

Jonathan followed, still having half a mind to grab Kayna out of the house. Regardless of what Nylen said, the look that woman had given him was not friendly. "If we find such courtesy at all our villages, how do we hope to keep up the pace?"

The warrior didn't reply as he opened the stable door. Five good rounceys of fair height stood in their stalls.

"Get the gray and silver," Nylen said, choosing a sable fifteen hands high. "These should bear us well in the snow."

Once saddled up, they returned to the house. Nylen signaled for Kei and Jonathan to remain seated as he went to knock on the door. There was no answer. Nylen pounded on the door. "Ma'am, we come for the lady."

Jonathan saw Kei going for his bow just when the door finally opened.

The heavy-set woman peered out. "She's comin'."

There was a long moment of silence before Kayna appeared. Whatever the woman had given her must have helped, for the Terakheini's eyes were clearer and she seemed more awake. She turned to the woman and embraced her before leaving. "Thank you for all your care."

"'Twas scant fare," the woman rasped, "but you can't expect more in the dead of night and winter. Now, go on."

Kei held out a hand to help his sister into the saddle. They waved their thanks once more to the woman before she shut the door.

"What did she say to you?" Nylen asked Kayna as they rode beside the others.

"Nothing much. She asked a bit about you, Jonathan. Wanted to know where you were from and who your people were. She brought me water and then gave me bread and cheese. After I was done, she asked me if I needed any help, because she could wake her husband and I could stay with them if I didn't want to go." The rest of them looked at her incredulously. "Imagine how it looked to her. One six-teen-year-old girl with three men banging on her door in the late night hours asking for horses. What was she sup-posed to think?"

Kei grunted a protest as Nylen laughed. "I hadn't thought of that."

Jonathan looked back, wondering why the woman had only asked about him. The woman's house had gone dark again.

Together, they galloped through the snowy fields that brightened the midnight landscape. Other small villages now appeared, and the Firalis grew wider. When daylight broke, they saw that it now flowed into the Tigechal River, which meant that Camhanaich was only a day's ride away.

"The river is a mile wide and ten feet deep at the Field of Camholch," Nylen said as they stopped to let their horses drink, "which makes for a good border and easy to defend. Yet we will begin to veer away from it, lest Nemarons camp-ing on the other side spot us. There will be lookouts up ahead."

As they turned northwest, the villages they passed looked empty. They saw few people until they happened upon a band of about fifty men around midday, some on horseback, others walking in the same direction as them. "Keep yourselves bundled up, and stay on your horses," Nylen said as the men slowed down beside them.

"Hail!" Nylen called out. "I gather that you are going to Camhanaich? Can you tell me what news you've had con-cerning the king?"

A tall, large man with a black beard flecked with gray and a bushy head of hair to match looked at him gravely. "Haven't you heard? Nemaron is gathered—the beacon has been going throughout the land for the last week and a half." Jonathan was reminded—in the man's looks as well as tone—of Breoc. The beacon had been launched, which meant that he and the widow had at least been successful in that part of their quest. "We've crossed thirty leagues so far, but it's been a damnable journey. Not even October, and here we trudge through winter."

There were so few. "Are there more coming?" Nylen asked.

"We did not leave our homes unprotected this time; many of us remember the desolation of our villages from before. I've heard that some go east to fight the creatures pouring out of the Wild, and others have gone northwest, for the Nemarons are there too. We are a large country and spread out—obviously you are strangers here, or you would have known all this," the man said, his eyes now surveying the entire group. "Where are you from and what business do you have in Camhanaich?"

"We have urgent news for the king and have traveled far to bring it—from Íarchol—and now we must be on our way. Try to gather more men as you go, for we've heard that the numbers of Nemarons heavily outweigh us still."

"Odd that you strangers have heard more news than me," the man said again, with a wary look in his eye.

"We have heard this from the Ogoni," Nylen said. The man looked surprised. "Yes, the fire spirits are awake once more. The Ophidians are abroad as well, including their prince. The Elementarí come to this war, too. Now, we cannot tarry any longer. Perhaps we will see each other soon enough!" With a courteous goodbye, Nylen set off again.

It did not give them hope to see so few headed to the city. The wind picked up. The gales were like an ocean tide pushing against them, swirling up the snow so that they were blinded by white. By dusk, they could barely see two feet in front of them, and the air was so cold that icicles crusted on their eyelashes. None of them could feel their hands or feet.

Then, in wonder, they saw lights in the distance, a vast array of sparkling lanterns on the top of a great city wall, with lanterns in the turrets, too; a ghostly blossom of light in the snow. It was a beacon, a sign, a thing of beauty that gave hope to any ally or person seeking refuge, that they had come at last to Camhanaich, the city of twilight.

CHAPTER 19
CADARN GOES TO WAR

An endless stream of people were entering the city, mostly women and children from neighboring villages whose men had been called to the king's camp at the Field of Camholch. Nylen looked at them in wonder. "Cadarn wasn't so prepared last time," he said as he gazed up at the tall wall that now encompassed the entire city. He dismounted, as did the others, and they silently joined the throng that swarmed at the city gate.

They waited a long time while the guards checked everyone for weapons and asked what city or town they were from, long enough for the snow to have stopped. The women around them tried to quiet their children and spoke in whispers. Jonathan and the twins anxiously looked at Nylen for signs of what they should do when they reached the guards. As they drew closer to the entrance, the warrior pushed his way through the crowd to the left side of the gate, where five or so guards were letting people through.

Nylen walked up to a broad-shouldered guard whose face was flecked with gray stubble. "We've come to find refuge behind these walls till the war is over. I bring with me my son and his bride, as well as her brother." A small bag of coins was pressed into the guard's hand, which he quickly pocketed and let them pass.

"To our left," Nylen ordered. As the dusk rapidly sank into twilight, Jonathan saw a long cobble-stoned street filled with slushy snow and lined with small trees that had already lost their leaves. They would have looked forlorn except for the lanterns that adorned them with a soft white light. "That street goes to the main square, which we should avoid at all costs for now. You!" he called to two boys around twelve years old. "Where are the stables?"

"On the east side, past the tanner shops. Do you want us to find a place for your horses?"

"Take these three and house them well." He gave the boys a few coins. "I'll come for them tomorrow."

The boys took the reins of all three horses and led them off.

"Now to find lodging," Nylen said. They turned onto a smaller street on the right, away from the temporary housing the king had ordered for the refugees.

Archways over the narrow streets allowed for easy crossing through the traffic that streamed below, and Adolan had constructed dirt paths around the inner perimeter of the walled city for horses and carts to travel, so they would not soil the city streets.

Every shop was illuminated with soft white light, just enough to give an ethereal presence to the very few flowers that were left, frozen in bloom. Camhanaich boasted many gardens and trees, and almost all of the buildings had living roofs, carpets of bugle plants, grass, or other flowers that spilled over the stonework. It seemed as if the landscape had invaded the city rather than the other way around.

"This way." Nylen led them to another narrow street that gently sloped up a small hill, and then curved left again. They went past pink stone houses with richly painted doors in red, green, and blue, until finally, the warrior knocked on a red door.

An old woman answered, older even than Sienna. "Who are you?"

Nylen pulled back his hood and unwrapped the scarf that had hid most of his face. "I am a friend of Cadman's and bring with me his godson and companions."

The woman's eyes grew wide. "In, in," she waved them all through the doorway, not taking her eyes off of Jonathan. "I'm Taralin. Take off your cloaks and scarves—" she peered out onto the street once more, then shut the door. "Throw them over there on the bench. You'll want…"

"Just two rooms, if you have them," Nylen said. "We've traveled for almost three weeks straight with little sleep."

She brushed a thin lock of gray hair off of her forehead. "Is Cadman in the city, then?" she asked hesitantly.

Nylen shook his head. Jonathan wanted to ask a million questions. How had she known the smith? Could it be that during the last war they'd met and fallen in love? It might explain the complete absence of women in Cadman's life— during the entire time Jonathan had known him, whatever lass he'd flirted had never amounted to anything beyond a night's comfort.

A younger woman walked in, although still older than Nylen, for her long hair was all turned to silver. She gave a slight curtsy.

"My daughter, Laurelina. Please get some food for our guests and bring it up to their rooms," Taralin asked her. Laurelina disappeared as her mother motioned for them to follow her up the stairs to two medium-sized rooms. They were lavishly furnished with a large canopied bed, two plush chairs covered in black velvet, an oaken chest, and a marble basin. "You are more than kind for such lodging on the eve of war," Nylen said. He turned to Jonathan and the twins. "Pardon me while I have a word with our hostess."

The twins followed Jonathan into the room he would share with Nylen. Laurelina appeared with biscuits, cheese, and fruit, stealing furtive glances at the twins and Jonathan. She curtseyed again before withdrawing.

Kayna immediately set into piling several pieces of cheese onto her biscuit. "What do you think—"

"Shhh." Jonathan stood at the door, listening to the soft rumble of Nylen's conversation with Taralin downstairs.

The twins ate quietly while Jonathan crept out of the room and stood at the top of the stairs, trying to catch any words.

It wasn't until an hour later that they heard Nylen's heavy boots tread up the stairs. Kei reached over and shook his sister.

"What?" she said sleepily.

"They're done," Kei whispered.

When Nylen walked into the room, it seemed to Jonathan that the warrior looked more worn than when he had left them, his shoulders slumping forward, as if already defeated. "I've told her who you are," he said slowly, looking at Kei and Kayna. "She has promised to lend us aid on account of Cadman."

"Did you tell her what happened to him?" Jonathan asked. "She kept staring at me."

"Taralin hasn't seen Cadman in nearly twenty years, we arrive on her doorstep just as Nemaron is about to invade, and you wonder at her gaze? You've not bathed in weeks and with that hair and beard..." Nylen narrowed his eyes. "You need a shave and a haircut."

"What? Tonight?" Jonathan looked to Kei for help.

The Terakheini rubbed his bare chin ruefully. "My father didn't grow a beard till he had seen twenty-five years."

"I will have Laurelina bring you a razor tomorrow before breakfast," Nylen said. "The guards will not let you into Sethelia looking like a crazed beggar just off the streets." He paused. "It may be that the king will have kept a few Ausels around that remember me, for I was renown on the battle-field in my day. Taralin has sent one of her servants to try to find Breoc and Sienna, if they're here. Now to bed, else we stumble tomorrow in weariness when we need the most stealth."

The twins shuffled out the door. Nylen kicked off one boot, then the other. *You're not meeting my eyes,* Jonathan thought. He had caught something in the warrior's pause a few moments before. A hesitation. "What is it?"

Nylen sat down in the plush chair and rested his feet on a small footstool. Jonathan stood there, waiting. "Nylen."

"Not now, Jonathan," Nylen said wearily as he shifted in his chair. "I've spoken enough of the dead tonight."

Cadman. Jonathan took off his own boots, and threw himself onto the bed, not even bothering to change out of his clothes or bother with blankets. *Too many dead to speak of lately,* he thought, as sleep finally took him.

—⁓◦⊚◦⊙◦⊚◦⁓—

Someone had fallen. He knew that, based on the shouts and screams piercing the air, but he could see nothing through the mass of Nemarons who had crowded into a circle, jeering at what was in the middle. He recognized the hill, knew the battlefield by the stench of burnt skin that filled the air.

"Get out of the way." A violent push sent Jonathan sprawling to the ground. "I wanna see me a spichtren."

A shudder of fear wracked Jonathan as he sank his teeth into the man's ankle. The soldier howled and kicked at him, but it afforded Jonathan enough time to steal the man's dirk and thrust it through his groin. Blood gushed all over his shirt as he hoisted himself back up. He had to claw through the crowd, biting and cursing like any Nemaron would. Quite a few parted for him, so wild did he look, covered in blood. Perhaps they thought he had just come from the field, having done more than his share of the slaughter. What did it matter? Jonathan pushed aside one last scrawny bastard so he could peer into the circle.

Cadreyth's body lay there, his golden hair now drenched red with his own blood, while the warriors continued chanting, *spichtren spichtren spichtren.* The word gave him chills, made him want to run and snatch the king away from whatever desecration they were planning. On the other side of the circle soldiers parted to reveal Truculen, with Hecthrax by his side. The black wolf came forward and sniffed Cadreyth. It smelled something else too, beneath the reek of decay. Hecthrax had smelled *him,* for the great wolf raised its head and gazed at Jonathan, through him even, with those vermillion eyes, so oddly reminiscent of Phlegon's.

Come try to kill me, then, Jonathan challenged, *but leave the dead in peace.* Hecthrax blinked, then bent down and put the king's head in his mouth. The wolf bit and twisted the neck with a great crunch. Jonathan turned away, retching. He looked back up, moving as if in slow motion, to see Truculen holding his standard high, and on the end of it was Cadreyth's head.

—◦—◉—◉—◦—

"The king! The king!" Jonathan screamed, thrashing about until Nylen and Kei threw themselves upon him. Kayna rushed in behind them and, a moment later, both of the older women were at the doorway, holding lanterns.

"Nylen, what is it? Is he having a fit?" Taralin asked in a shaking voice.

"It was Hecthrax!" Jonathan shouted as the men let him sit up. "I saw what he did. I saw what he did to Cadreyth after Truculen killed him." He gulped back air. "You witnessed it, didn't you?" he turned to Nylen. "That's why Cierdwyn challenged Truculen, knowing what he was…"

"Aye, and little good it did."

"He's coming." Jonathan jumped out of the bed, the terror of his dreams becoming reality. "Hecthrax is coming to do it again. He wants the king, just like before."

Taralin made a noise between a gasp and a cry as she buried her head in her daughter's shoulder. From Kei's hand sprang a blue flame. Nylen's mouth was open and moving, but his words were drowned out by horns—great horns, deep, terrifying, and strangely melodious—sounding and resounding. It was beautiful, majestic, but it was not the battle cry of Cadarn. No, for in answer, they heard the howling of wolves, and the howls and horns swept the city awake as dawn broke. Nemaron had declared war.

Nylen threw the front door open onto a city in chaos. Dawn barely cast enough light to distinguish the mass of countryside peasants that now packed into the narrow streets, all crying out for sanctuary amid the wails of babies and shouts of angry men. In the distance, Jonathan could see a wall of smoke against the horizon.

"What happened?" Nylen asked a man who bore the emblem of a city official. "I come from Hethran with others to help the king. How many Cadarians are on the Field of Camholch?"

"Less than twenty thousand, with the Nemarons having thrice that gathered at the other side of the river. But the water froze over in the early hours of the morning and so nothing will stop them from crossing this very hour. I must help the city prepare for the assault. Find a troop to ride out with!" he shouted and ran off.

"Get your stuff," Nylen ordered the twins as he came back inside. "We're leaving now."

"I still need a sword," Jonathan said as the twins ran upstairs.

Nylen sighed. "We do not have time to find you one at the smithies."

"No need for that," Taralin said. "Wait here." She disappeared into a back room. The twins returned a moment later; Kayna had hidden Ashryanna within her cloak, but the fevered light was back in her eyes.

"We'll never get past the king's Ausels, Nylen," she said.

"Aye, there's the point," the warrior said as he drew out three pieces of parchment and handed them to Jonathan and the twins. "Cadman and I had these drawn up at Kae-lest."

Jonathan realized he was staring at a map of Adolan's hall, Sethelia.

"If we get separated, find a way in and return the fire to the king's altar. Then wait by the east wall."

"And if no one meets us there?" Jonathan asked.

"Then use your wits to stay alive!" Nylen barked. "Don't stay in Camhanaich, whatever you do. Head west to Hethran or Daliath, and tell them you know me. People there will take care of you. And by Neáhvalar, keep your hoods on at all times. You too, Jonathan."

"I'm no wilder looking than that lot pouring in here from the country," he retorted.

Nylen had no time to answer as Taralin returned with a sheathed sword. She drew it out and presented it to Jonathan. "My husband was about your height, so I think this will work," she said matter-of-factly. Then in a softer tone, and with teary eyes, she added, "He was part of the king's guard in those last days. He'd want you to have this, as you are here for the same purpose."

Jonathan saw a gleam of envy in Kayna's eyes as he received the blade. The broadsword wasn't decorated, but the hilt was lightly etched with an elongated silver *C*. Jonathan had seen that emblem before—on Cadman's ring. *It's my mark on any work I do.* Apparently the smith did work beyond Gaelastad and even Lailethas.

"Thank you, my lady," Jonathan said as he grasped the hilt. "I'll wield it well in honor of your husband, as well as its maker."

A bewildered look came into the woman's eyes. "Who do you mean?"

"Cadman."

"But Cadman did not make this."

"The *C*—"

"Yes, for Cadreyth. 'Tis the mark for those in service of the king."

Jonathan's heartbeat quickened. *You entire life was a lie, godfather.* Damn it, but he had no time to wonder about the secret lives of smiths or widows, of river stones and hearing the trees speak as Nylen led them through the door that Taralin had just used and down the long hallway to the back door. They filed into the alley, hoods drawn tightly around them, and followed Nylen down two more narrow streets flanked by houses until they emerged into the main square. People ran through the streets, calling the names of their loved ones while scores of men marched out of the gate to battle. The smiths had fixed up temporary stations throughout the city for fixing tackle, and sharpening swords and knives. Since the wind had stopped, their smoke hung dense over the city, the clouds trapping the ash and soot that sought to escape. A band of Ausels rode through the square, their scarlet tunics blazing amid the drab of the city, and everyone momentarily parted for them.

Jonathan walked slightly ahead of the others, trying to get a better glimpse of the guards' blazon coming into view. Jonathan knew what it was, had been dreaming about it ever since he had seen the cup in Theo's house—*A sword, held by a silver hand thrusting out from a lake of fire*. One of the Ausels turned, showing the king's emblem: an emerald tree with gold blossoms, flames cascading down the trunk and along the branches.

"It is the king's Golden Auréus," a voice said in his ear.

Jonathan looked to see an old woman, toothless and grinning.

"You are a stranger here, to be staring at them so."

"From the east. I've come to fight," he said, turning away, but he heard her sudden intake of breath as she caught a glimpse of his face.

A hand lightly cuffed his ear. "Stop dawdling." Nylen grabbed Jonathan roughly and dragged him to the twins.

"What did you think you were doing?" Kayna asked, fury in her eyes.

"I had to see the king's coat of arms," he stammered. Why had it not been the flaming sword in the fire? Whose house was Theo loyal to? "The Auréus in flames—"

"Shows Cadarn's allegiance to the Terakhein and the Ogoni, the Elementarí they honor above all others," Nylen said. "Next time, simply ask, and I will tell you the answer. Don't wander away again."

—⚯⚭⚭⚯—

They wound through the maze of the city, through the open markets still trying to sell their wares before the siege laid in, and around the fountains and gardens that broke up the city with bursts of color. The streets were a tangled mass of people, even with the few Ausels trying to keep order. Eventually, Nylen led them down the shadowed alleyways behind the smithies. Dark smoke billowed over the streets like some storm about to burst.

Soldiers and smiths were running about, giving orders, and yelling news. "Where's Jarafir? Where is he?"

"You, boy! Tell your master his bridle is ready."

"We are to defend the river to the south. Archin led his men there, but still they have too few..."

"Solach, tell the Lady Halim that her son fell in battle this morning..."

Someone bumped hard into Jonathan. A glimpse of a once familiar face, and then it disappeared into the swarm of people.

"Nylen!" Jonathan gripped his arm.

"Do not say my name here," the warrior growled.

"I thought I saw..."

"What?" Nylen put his hand to his sword. "Tell me quick."

Jonathan blinked hard. *Sienna said she had seen him die.* "Never mind, it couldn't have been..."

"Turn here. Half a block up this street," Nylen directed. "Kayna, walk beside me and Jonathan, draw your hood up more. One more block and then we turn right and go up the road that follows the curve of the river. It will bring us to the right wing of the hall."

"Won't that entrance be guarded as well?" Kayna whispered.

Nylen didn't answer.

Jonathan recognized too late the knife positioned against the warrior's back. It was held by a tall, thin man with a grizzled head and beard, wearing a scarlet tunic with the flowering tree in flames. He was of Adolan's Ausels.

"The king would speak with you," he said. "But make a scene and our orders are to silence you in any way we see fit."

Jonathan saw that the king's guards were all around. Eight, by his count, with four built as thick as Nylen. One stood with his massive shoulders slumped forward, like a throck upright on its hind legs. The other two were lean, like their captain, with hollowed-out cheeks and a hungry look.

They were marched up the street, flanked by the Ausels as they turned right and then rounded another corner to a quieter street.

"This is as good a place as any," the captain said, leering at Kayna.

"You're the king's guard," she whispered.

"Nay, sweetling, we merely borrowed their clothes, although they did get bloodied in the exchange."

The throck-like guard pressed the point of his dagger against Kei's stomach. "Your city's easier to breach than a drunken whore," he rasped. "Easier than the forest I helped plunder eight years ago. I watched Trapher finish off a water wench who helped two little red-headed Terakhein brats escape." With a jerk, the Nemaron yanked back Kei's hood to reveal his mop of red hair. "Looks like you're all grown up now." He ran a hand down Kei's cloak and searched his pockets. "We've come to take back what you have stolen from our friends."

Two guards flung the twins' sack on the ground and rummaged through its contents. Finding nothing, he advanced towards Kayna, who drew the necklace out with shaking hands rather than have him forcibly try to retrieve it. Nylen turned his head to follow the movement of the

Nemaron, and with one barely-there nod, gave the signal. Jonathan whipped out his dagger and flung it at the Nemaron just as he reached for the necklace. The other Nemarons rushed in.

"Curse you, Tera filth!" the guard cried as he grasped the knife that had sunk into his arm. He pulled it out and lunged at Kayna. Jonathan threw his full weight against him, yelling out, "Run, Kayna!" while both he and the Nemaron fell to the ground. Out of the corner of his eye, he saw three of the men run after her, but the third wheeled around when the blond Nemaron under him yelled for help. Jonathan grabbed the man's head by the ears and rammed it twice, as hard as he could, into the ground. He rolled off and relieved him of his sword just in time to repel the Nemaron's companion. He tried to scramble back while deflecting blows, but the Nemaron swiped him from the side, causing a bloody line to appear on Jonathan's left arm. He wouldn't last long, sitting and crawling backwards like this.

Nylen was fighting their captain and another man, wielding his blade so fiercely that steel flashed against steel in glinting trails. Jonathan heard a cry to his right. Kei had gouged his Nemaron with a dagger, but another had knocked him to the ground. He was about to drive his sword through the Terakheini's shoulder when he fell, an arrow sticking out of his back.

"Now for some fair odds!" yelled a familiar voice as Breoc barreled down the street and set upon one of the men who had cornered Kei. Nylen leapt towards Jonathan's attacker, swinging left. The soldier's head toppled off in one stroke.

Jonathan turned to see the remaining two guards attacking Breoc and Kei. Breoc had thrust the Terakheini behind him, but was limping from a gash right above his knee. Nylen rushed at the second soldier just as the first was about to cleave Breoc's head in two, but the Ausel ducked and circled back so the Nemaron's stroke went wide. The move let Breoc strike at an angle, slicing clear though the Nemaron's shoulder.

Meanwhile, Nylen had flicked his opponent's sword out of his hand and would have questioned him, but the Nemaron, seeing they had lost, slit his own throat with a dagger. Jonathan noticed how empty the street was now. What few people had been there had fled at the first sign of fighting.

Kei stumbled over to Breoc. "Is my sister safe?"

"Aye," he panted. "Sienna went with her to the hall. We arrived here two days ago and have watched the exchange of Sethelia's guard. I don't recognize any Ausel, and that speaks ill of many things."

"Then take Kei and join them," Nylen said. "Jonathan and I will warn Taralin and Laurelina to find safe shelter."

Jonathan used his dagger to cut off a strip of the Nemaron's tunic. "Bind your leg first."

Breoc nodded as he took the rag and tied it above his knee. "Jonathan, you will be Taralin's guard—the Nemarons know they are our friends now. Nylen, ride on to the Field of Camholch and find Siarl—"

"The Five Captains don't exist anymore," Nylen spat.

"Siarl is still true to the king!" Breoc thundered. "Alert him that there are Nemarons in the city, and that they wear the king's livery. Come, Kei, even with a limp, we must run."

The Terakheini and Ausel were soon out of sight. Jonathan and Nylen found Hammer and Tongs in the stables and rode the outside circle until they came to the end of Taralin's street. Rather than dismount, as was the law, they took to the alley and kept riding until they came to the back door of Taralin's house. It had been kicked open.

"Taralin!" Nylen cried out as he dismounted and drew his sword. Jonathan did the same and they walked cautiously in and down the hall. "Laurelina? Taralin?"

They saw both bodies on the floor of the main room, a thin line of blood across their throats. Taralin's face was frozen in a look of pure anguish, her mouth wide open as if still in the act of screaming.

"Wait here." Nylen ran upstairs.

There was so little blood. Jonathan bent down and gently closed the old woman's eyes. If her mouth were not open in a scream, she could have been simply sleeping. *Just like the girl found in the Seven Woods*.

"No one is here," Nylen said as he jumped off the stair's landing, a linen sheet in his hand, which he laid over them. "The Nemarons must have had men watching us since last night."

"The Nemarons have been hunting us since last *year*," Jonathan said, still not believing the connection he had made between Taralin and the girl. "With Gaelastad's help."

"What is this?" Nylen's face drained of all color.

"A Nemaron moonstone blade did this. Same wound as with the little girl in the woods. Same cut as I saw on Cierdwyn's arm the day Adamara attacked her—with a Nemaron dagger."

Shock quickly turned to subdued rage. "Then today settles the score."

Hoods up, they quietly left the house. Riding the loop once more—except this time to the eastern gate—they deemed it too dangerous to even stop, and barreled through the checkpoint. Jonathan dimly heard guards shouting for others to pursue them as he and Nylen cleared the gate and thundered towards the Field of Camholch.

—◦◉◉◦—

"This way," Sienna said, laying a hand on Kayna's arm. She had run screaming through the streets, begging for help, but, for all anyone knew, she was running from the Ausels. Hands had reached out to catch her for the king's guard and possibly gain a reward. She had stopped yelling then, and only ran blindly down the alleyways until they cornered her at the stables. The shorter Nemaron was swinging a rope in his left hand and a dagger in the other. "Behave now for us. They want you relatively unharmed."

Who are "they"? she had wondered as he advanced, but then Breoc suddenly appeared, yelling in a foreign tongue and swinging his sword with such fury that for a moment Kayna could not believe it was actually him. Not until the two Nemarons were lying in puddles of their own blood did an old peasant woman, her head wrapped in a common woolen scarf, come out from behind a corner.

"Where are the others?" she rasped.

"Behind the stables. Six Nemarons—"

Breoc waited to hear no more. "Get to Sethelia," he said and ran off to succor the others, if they were still alive.

"Come, child." The woman took off her scarf to reveal a crop of white hair. "We have much to do."

—◦◦◦◦—

Kayna couldn't stop shaking, even now, as she followed the widow down a narrow alley, the guard's moonstone dagger in her hand. They turned onto a wider street paved with smooth white stones. Sienna slowed her steps as slim trees with reddish bark and white blossoms began to line the street. Within half a block, they came to a massive silver gate that enclosed a courtyard with a large pool in its center. Around the north and south sides of the courtyard were trees that resembled the Terakhein Auréa, deep green leaves tinged with yellow. On the east side rose a thick wall of vines, supported by an invisible lattice. They heard muffled voices. Sienna pulled her behind one of the trees as five king's guards stepped through a hidden door within the flowered wall.

"We're at the back of the hall," Sienna whispered. "Breoc and I were hoping we'd be able to sneak in between the changing of the guard, but we'd have to scale the gate—it wasn't there before. Adolan added it."

They heard a whistle. Sienna looked over to see Breoc and Kei appear from behind the row of trees directly across from them. Kayna ran to her twin and hugged him fiercely. "Next time you come with me," she choked out.

"Next time, you'll have a sword, and we'll fight together," he said, the thrill of battle still in his eye.

"But where are Jonathan and Nylen?" Sienna asked, her face pinched in fear and pale as the moon.

"Fear not for either," Breoc said, and kissed her cheek. "They're getting Taralin and Laurelina to safe shelter. Now, follow me."

Kayna breathed a sigh of relief. At the mention of Jonathan, she had felt a sense of foreboding. *Something bad is going to happen to him,* she thought, and felt sick inside. She and Kei would find him after they returned the fire. *We'll protect him from...From what?* she wondered. What was she was so afraid of?

"This way." Breoc led them back through the alleyways to the stables, where they entered the last on the right. He went to the northwest corner and, reaching up with his sword, pushed on the stall's back panel. A trapdoor sprang open beneath them, flinging straw everywhere.

"When you get to the bottom, stay close to the wall," Breoc whispered as he motioned for Kei to go first. The widow followed and then it was Kayna's turn. They must have descended about thirty feet, for soon all was pitch black and in the distance Kayna heard only the sound of rushing water.

"Don't move!" Breoc shouted once they had touched the ground.

Kayna blindly reached out for her brother's hand, but felt nothing. "Kei?" She was about to take a step forward when light suddenly illuminated the cavern. Breoc had lit a mounted torch over by the far wall, and now she understood his warning. They were on a narrow path that ran parallel to an underground river, large chunks of ice floating along its waters. "This river feeds the pool of Lestár that sits in the courtyard," he explained. "We'll be at the hall soon."

"How did you know about this?" Sienna asked, looking in wonder at the tunnel around her. It was small, the curved earthen ceiling only a few feet higher than the top of Breoc's head, and just wide enough for two people to walk side by side on the path next to the river.

"Evanna had it built a year before the war due to horrible visions of the hall engulfed in flames. She told no one but Cadreyth and his herald. Eventually I learned of it, though."

"And Adolan?" Sienna drew up beside Breoc. "Did he ever know about this place?"

"Not then," he said, as if in sudden doubt. "But who knows if in so long…"

"I've never been to the dungeons, Breoc, and, at my age, it wouldn't be a great time to be introduced to them," she warned.

Kayna glanced questioningly at her twin, but Kei merely raised his eyebrows. *Later,* he mouthed. This was not the time for questions.

Eventually the path widened, and they came to another half room with a ladder. "I'll go first," Breoc said. "But if I yell for you to retreat, then flee to the wall of the city until either I or Nylen come find you."

"And do not stop to help me," Sienna added. "Let me assure you I can take of myself."

One by one they climbed thirty feet up to another trap-door. *She moves like a woman half her age,* Kayna thought as she followed the widow up the ladder. At last Breoc pulled her up into a small storage room crowded with extra chairs, musty pillows, and silk drapes. He then led them down a great white hall with an arched, fresco-painted ceiling. At the end of the hall large, stone columns carved with the images of golden flames flanked the double doors. They heard the sound of footsteps as Breoc rushed them into the room. He kept the door cracked a moment as he peered out, then shut it softly.

"The guards are searching, it seems, for someone or something. I'm not sure they keep a post at this room like they used to. Still, we'll position ourselves at the entrances," he pointed to the two doors at either end of the left and right walls, "while you return Ashryanna to her rightful place."

"There's the altar," Sienna said, indicating the back wall where there stood a dais, richly decorated in blue, green, and gold. In its center sat a long rectangular block, carved out of dark blue crystal that sparkled like the ocean on a sunny day. Emerging from the crystal was a golden sword, its hilt hidden inside and the blade exposed. Kei and Kayna walked over to it and positioned themselves on either side of the block.

Kayna removed the necklace and held it over the altar, relieved by the weight she felt lifted from her. Kei grabbed her hand.

"Ashryanna Avexi tego illis. Icthu flumaste, helath Celarise!"

They repeated it four times before Kei put his palm over the necklace and began to draw the golden flames out. "Slowly, brother," Kayna breathed as Kei dangled Ashryanna from his hand and gently lowered her onto the sword.

The fire dripped down the blade as Kayna began her song and Kei resumed his chant. The yellow flames rapidly grew brighter, blazing high, threatening to catch the dais tapestries on fire. The entire room heated up as if it were the desert of Ophidia under the noon sun, and the fire took up Kayna's song. It grew louder as the fire intensified, until the room and the ground began to shake, as if the world itself would split apart from the song.

Then the tremors stopped and the air cooled. A blue flame erupted to fill the room, the hall, the palace. Onward and outward it spread, into the city and the Field of Camholch, then into Cadarn and throughout the land. The great thaw had begun.

As if in response to Ashryanna's song, trumpets sounded throughout the city and outside its walls.

"The horns of Kaelest and Cúrmhangon, and listen—"

Kei said in wonder, "those are the drums of Lailethas. They've come!"

"Then let's find a safe place to hide you two," Breoc suggested, "before—"

The arrow caught him in the shoulder before he could finish. Breoc's eyes widened with surprise. "Too late," he said with shallow breaths as he fell against Kei, and the door swung open to reveal a garrison of soldiers.

—◦◦◎◦◎◦◦—

Jonathan dug his heels into Tongs while straining his ear for any sign of pursuit behind them. The thunderous clamor all around put an end to their fear that they'd be found amidst the other horsemen and Cadarians racing on foot to the Field of Camholch.

Black smoke filled the sky as they rode to where two small hills stood against the field of battle where Cadarn had set up its defense. A narrow gully opened in-between, with a smattering of shrubs and scraggly trees. Down below and less than half a mile away, scores of Nemarons were crossing the frozen river, bringing with them so many catapults and siege machines that the snow was muddied and brown. The river shimmered like a silver sea with the mass of their moving bright mail. Leading them was a large man with an orange braided beard. He was dressed all in black, and his herald bore his silver-on-red standard, with one bright gem in the middle of a mountain and a war hammer on top of its peak.

"Is that their king?" Jonathan asked as Nylen slowed Hammer down around the bend of the northern hill, where a few trees provided scant cover.

"No, that's Lacrimas, their captain," Nylen spat, surveying the field. "Stay here. I see Siarl over in the rearguard. I'll be back in a moment—don't move!"

Jonathan studied the field. The Cadarians were hopelessly outnumbered five to one, yet Adolan's orders were to hold the Nemarons at the river at all costs. That was their only hope of keeping Camhanaich safe until the allies arrived, for the city was still taking in refugees from other villages and was not ready for a siege.

The Nemaron pikemen, with their twelve-foot spears, marched relentlessly towards the hills while the rear and the flank were guarded by archers and foot soldiers wielding morning-stars. Cadarn's archers were taking out many Nemarons, but not enough, as more pikemen kept advancing over the bodies of their slain. The siege engines were now over the river, ready to be brought to Camhanaich as soon as the Nemarons breached the vanguard. But two of Cadarn's captains were still holding the line, refusing to retreat lest it become a rout in the ensuing panic.

Jonathan swept over the battle and came to rest on Nylen. He was in a kind of natural trench at the base of the left hill, talking to a tall broad-shouldered man with thin gray stubble. The older man shouted orders, and thirty Cadarian horsemen spurred eastward towards Camhanaich. Spotting Jonathan, Nylen signaled that he would be a few moments. He was talking excitedly to the captain, who flashed a look at Jonathan—*ah, he must be telling Siarl about the Terakhein.*

Something hard and cold was roughly thrust into his hand. Jonathan looked down to see a shield and the burly Cadarian who put it there.

"Why are you just sitting there!" the soldier yelled hoarsely over the din. "Whose command are you under?"

He knew no other name here. "Siarl's company."

"Then go report to him, damn it, and find yourself a helmet before your head is bashed in!"

Jonathan spurred Tongs around the back of one hill. Nylen disappeared from sight as he wound around foot soldiers and horses to come out through the small gulch in between and cross over behind the rearguard. He saw Siarl point to him, and Nylen's glowering face.

"Why didn't you stay where I told you to?" he demanded

as Jonathan dismounted.

"When commanded to fight, with a shield thrust in my hand during war, what else was I supposed to do? Is this captain equipped with as many men as he needs that I can stay safely tucked away?" Jonathan shouted back. He was scared, although he didn't want to show it in front of the captain.

Siarl didn't say anything during this exchange, but he had fixed his stern eyes on Jonathan. "I need to order my men upon the field. You will do as Nylen bids, for you have no armor and are not fit for battle."

"Neither do half the farmers out there fighting for the king," Jonathan retorted. "Why should I be any different?"

"Because you—"

A roar surged up from the front, a mix of great explosions and battle cries, and the Nemaron wolves howled in earnest. Siarl quickly mounted his horse. "Flee to the city or else take refuge behind the hill. I will not have your deaths on my conscience, when I will have so many others today!"

The ground shook, and they heard not the yells of battle but the screams of men in terror. They rode up the side of the trench to see that the wolves had infiltrated the vanguard. Not the normal gray wolves of winter, starving and looking for wounded prey. These beasts were twice the size of any ordinary wolf and pure white: Tréasa's brood. And following them, more dreadful than wolves or Nemarons alike, were silver white serpents that slithered across the frozen river floor. As soon as they reached the banks, they changed into their Ophidian bodies. Jonathan counted at least fifteen earth spirits, towering over all other men and robed in white. Just one could take out a quarter of the king's army. The trees around the hill fell down at their command and crashed into bands of men; horses ran witless, overthrowing their masters.

Nylen's face contorted in fury as he shouted at Jonathan "Fool—you must fly! Head south to Hethran, to Galena's house. We will not survive this. Not with fifteen of them."

The ground jerked again, creating an avalanche that thundered down the hill, folding soldiers into its massive sheet of ice and snow. Then something else sprang out of the ground, white hot, with flames streaming down its legs like a fountain of fire.

Bryn.

The Ogoni cried aloud, his many voices sounding like the rush of a fire that devours everything in its path. Immediately he threw himself at the Ophidians—six of them morphed back into their serpent forms. It was fang against fang as the snakes encircled the giant spider. Wolf howls mingled with the screams of men and the war cries of Nemarons as the Ogoni became lost in a tangle of silver white, and great tears formed in the earth all around them.

"Go find Samara!" Nylen commanded Jonathan once again. "This is not your war!"

With the host of Ophidia here along with Hecthrax's children? "It is now," Jonathan said, and spurred Tongs towards the gulch, with Nylen in pursuit.

A tide of Cadarians joined to strengthen the vanguard. Horsemen pounded down the north side of the hill while the archers renewed their attack from up top. The only direction to run was to the south towards the king, but the wolves were sprinting the same way, and Cadarn's arrows did nothing to stop them. Jonathan was riding out of the trench when a small party of Nemarons and their wolves who had breached the vanguard charged. One white wolf, larger than the others, swerved aside and took a running leap at Nylen, knocking him off Hammer.

Jonathan jumped off Tongs and drew his sword. Instinct told him to duck just as a morning-star swung past him. He turned to see a swarthy Nemaron grinning. "I can't wait to see your fucking brains all over the ground."

"Go to hell," Jonathan shouted, feigning to strike low until the Nemaron brought down his mace to block. Jonathan swung his sword up to slash the man's side wide open. *Your guts for my brains.* He dashed to where Nylen had fallen, but warrior and wolf were nowhere in sight. He stumbled down a small incline to find the snarling wolf on top of Nylen, its massive jaws kept at bay by the warrior's sword, held up against the wolf's shoulders. The wolf bared its teeth, letting Nylen's blade sink into its skin as it lowered its head to close its jaws over Nylen's face.

"Sona Tréasa, Nemari!" Jonathan drove his sword into the White's back. The beast howled and reared back, just enough for Jonathan to push his blade the rest of the way through. The great body shuddered once and went still.

Nylen struggled to his feet as a group of Íarchins and Nemarons broke out into a melee. "I'm all right," he said as Jonathan's eyes widened at the bleeding gash on his head. The warrior drew his sword, and put himself at Jonathan's back. "So, you would leave the last Terakheini to her fate?" he spat.

"I will not run from battle," Jonathan said.

"Then at least stay alive!" Nylen shouted as three Nemarons attacked.

Swords flashed and Jonathan found himself fighting two Nemarons at once, but this wasn't the Jonathan who had been a simple smith's apprentice from the country. This Jonathan had been wounded by talon and ice, had braved serpents and fire. Soon one Nemaron was dead, but the other was quicker and forced Jonathan backwards towards the trench. He was dimly aware of horns blowing, deep and long. They were not the horns of Íarchol or Gaelastad. In desperation and fear, Jonathan heaved his shield up into the Nemaron's face, breaking nose and teeth before gutting him with Taralin's sword.

Jonathan lifted his gaze, but Nylen had disappeared into the melee of soldiers swinging maces and swords, and the horns were growing louder as a new surge of forces swarmed onto the fields.

But it was not evil those horns pronounced, nor death.

Instead they heralded the arrival of the ocean in its wrath and glory as Madron and Peran rode to battle. All parted before them or were slain, for the children of Morwenna were terrible in their anger, giants towering over Ophidian and Nemaron alike, violet eyes black with rage and their cloaks spread out behind them like a flood.

"Withdraw from the river!" Peran boomed in his thunderous voice to the Cadarians. "The Feállí will have no mercy on any who tread their waters."

The Cadarians beat a hasty retreat as the Lords Morvoren rode to the very middle of the frozen river, dismounted, and smote the surface three times with their swords. With a flash the ice broke and burst asunder. Water gushed up as the wild Feállí underneath, furious that their river had been trammeled by steel and ice, were freed. With foamy webbed hands the Feállí caught anything between the banks—the siege machines with their smoke, metal, and death, the Nemaron soldiers who, lost in battle lust, tried to fight them, and the few Cadarians unlucky to have remained on the ice—dragging all down into the river's boreal waters. The Brothers and their horses, however, the Feállí bore to the bank on the back of a great wave at least two stories high.

Thirty thousand Nemaron soldiers or more were stranded on Cadarn's side of the water, most on horse. Enraged at the sight of their comrades screaming and sinking to the bottom of the river, the enemy renewed their assault, calling for the wolves. Only ten Ophidians remained as the brothers had already slain two upon their arrival at the battlefield, and the Feállí had born off three more into the depths. But ten were enough to still swing the war in favor of the Nemarons. The Lords Morvoren strode to meet the Lords of Ophidia, and the ground cracked apart wherever they fought, leaving deep fissures behind.

So it was that in the tumult of battle, no one felt the tremor of joy running throughout Cadarn as the twins placed Ashryanna back onto her altar. Those who noticed the blue flame that flashed quickly through the land thought it the magic of the Ophidians, and merely fought on.

The great thaw was only just beginning, so the battle continued in snow two feet thick, muddied from horses and boots, stained bright red with blood. Jonathan was still searching for Nylen when he spotted the giant black wolf, as tall as Hammer and thickly muscled, with eyes that smoldered like burnt rubies. Behind the wolf strode a tall man, wearing all white, with a circlet of silver set on his raven hair, and wielding a great jeweled sword in his hand. Truculen and Hecthrax were rushing towards the king's party, leaving a trail of wounded in their wake: live meat offerings to their brethren.

Jonathan ran, jumping over bodies and thrusting his sword into whichever Nemaron chanced to be in his path. He had to head Hecthrax off, for he knew what the wolf intended to do to the king, just as he knew that it would never stop hunting Samara as long as it lived. Never. Worse, they were still losing the battle, even with the Brothers' help, for the Nemarons still outnumbered their army three to one. Cadarian bodies now littered the field, and Jonathan vaguely wondered who was going to keep the enemy from sacking the city when all was done.

But at that moment, he heard more trumpets and drums, joyful and ferocious in their glory. The hosts of Lailethas and Íarchol had broken through the gulch from the northern hill, and the field was suddenly thick with the clash of steel and the thunder of hooves. Íarchol raised its standard, embroidered with the Meristán gem of the blue-gray caves of Kaelest, and Lailethas displayed the towering, ice-capped Akrates Mountains. The king's banner was on his right, a wash of scarlet, green, and gold; on the left, Adolan's guard mustered against the advancing host of Nemarons and more Ophidians. But there was no time to wonder. Hecthrax had now caught sight of him. He was just as majestic in real life as he had dreamed—as large as any horse, thickly muscled, with eyes like rubies.

Jonathan held his sword up to the wolf in challenge and let out a battle cry: "For Cadreyth and the King!" He caught a glimpse of Truculen's green eyes, and then they were lost in the fray. All around him the men heard his cry, and the many who remembered the first war now took up the chant as the great Black charged.

Ictuneri heracth norifram, Hecthrax growled.

Jonathan threw his shield aside.

You are the son of no one.

He locked his sword with both hands straight in front of him.

And no one you shall become. It wasn't until the wolf was two feet away and leapt upon Jonathan that he intentionally fell back, shifting the sword's position just to the left. Hecthrax's shadow blocked out all light as it landed on him, the great jaws clenching down on Jonathan's head as his blade traveled deep into its entrails, finally piercing its massive heart.

—◦◦◉◦◦—

As Jonathan impaled the wolf, Kei caught hold of Breoc as he fell.

Don't die, Kayna prayed, as five Nemarons swept through the entrance, weapons at the ready. Ten more charged through each door on the sides of the room. Sienna threw herself in front of Ashryanna while Kayna quickly hid the necklace within the folds of her cloak. The widow motioned for Kei and Kayna to be very still, and even she did not draw her dagger.

Their captain strode up to Kayna and snatched up the folds of her cloak in his massive hands. "Where is it?" His breath was hot and sour. "How did you carry the fire?"

"It…it was in a necklace. We used it to hold Ashryanna, but the moment we put her back on the altar, the necklace burned me, and I dropped it into the fire."

The Nemaron threw her so hard against the wall, she was sure her head had cracked open. Kei yelled something. *Don't,* she thought as her eyes closed, and she temporarily lost all feeling.

When she opened her eyes again, Breoc had his hand clutched around her brother's arm. The captain was standing next to the altar, staring intently into Ashryanna's golden light. He scowled and turned back to Kayna. "I don't believe you."

She scrambled backwards from those beastly hands as he lunged for her.

Kei thrust his hand into Ashryanna. "You want fire? Take it, fools!" He threw out a blue blaze that spread like ripples in a pond.

The Nemarons ducked, distracted just long enough for Kei and Sienna to pull Breoc behind the altar and draw out their daggers. Still dazed, Kayna had nevertheless managed to get Breoc's bow and arrows. Swiftly she strung it and let an arrow fly at the Nemaron in front. The captain fell to the floor, blood bubbling out the hole in his neck as he struggled for air.

Kayna nocked another arrow and held the string at the ready.

Kei put his hand to Ashryanna again. "Retreat, or you'll be nothing but ash."

A lean soldier with fierce blue eyes advanced with his guard. "Terakhein fire hurts no man, from what I remember. Don't assume you understand this war little ones. Your people were responsible for the destruction of my country. I'm sure your historians never gave you that part of the story."

"Lies!" Sienna said, and, with a grip stronger than any man, threw Kayna behind her.

"You think your precious fire is only for Cadarn," he spat. "When did you last visit the dying cities of Nemaron?

I'm sure you never asked why or who woke up Ventosus or the Three. Oh no, some questions are better left unanswered."

"I'd much rather know who let you into the king's hall," Sienna retorted. "What bedmates did you make among the Ausels that procured such a favor?"

One soldier on the far right lunged at the widow, but Kei cut him off with a fierce slap across the face.

Blood poured down the soldier's cheek. "Tera-scum!"

"Wrong family." Kei opened his hand to show a thin blade an inch long wedged between his fingers. "That skill came from the Íarchin army."

One half of soldier's mouth twisted into an appreciative grin. "Just remember that every family has a traitor, boy." Then he gave the signal to attack.

But the Nemarons posted at each of the doors suddenly slumped to the ground, their throats cut. The remaining soldiers turned around and swung their maces as the king's Ausels poured in.

The battle for the holy fire had begun.

-–·◎,◎·–-

I'm going to die, Jonathan thought as the weight of the wolf crashed upon him, its teeth sinking into his head. As the sword went in, Hecthrax had unexpectedly relaxed his jaw and looked down at him with those awful ruby eyes, full of such malice that Jonathan had turned his face away, unable to look, even as the light of them burnt out forever. Then the weight of the wolf began to crush him. Because of the angle of his strike, Jonathan couldn't use his arms to roll out from underneath the monstrous body. He tried shifting and kicking—anything to get out, but to no avail. He was certain he would die here.

Then the brute's body started to roll, back and forth, back and forth, until it was rolled right off him. Jonathan's sword came free. Nylen grinned down at him, despite a black eye and blood running down his arm, and reached out a hand to help him up.

"About time," Jonathan said as he grasped the other man's arm.

But Nylen's smile became fixed, and his eyes widened in wonder as a blade came out through his chest.

The warrior instinctively let go of Jonathan's hand, mouthed the word "run," before he fell forward as the sword slid back out. Jonathan rolled out of the way as Nylen's body crashed to the ground.

"You took my wolf, young prince," a voice said, more sonorous than Trapher's and more sensuous than Adamara's. Truculen now towered over him like a god, white robed and beautiful even in his fury. In his hand was Cadreyth's sword. "I demand repayment."

Jonathan scrambled to his feet as the Ophidian charged towards him. The sheer force with which Truculen hit Jonathan made him reel and stumble. He parried only twice before their blades locked, and with a flick of the wrist, Truculen wrenched away Jonathan's sword. With one hand the Ophidian grasped Jonathan's head from behind and brought it close while he positioned his sword against Jonathan's stomach.

"You look nothing like your father, you know," Truculen whispered as the blade began to sink into his stomach, "but you're the spitting image of your mother."

At that same moment, Jonathan felt another set of hands on his shoulders.

Avexi tegosaleth. Kairo flumaste, Neáhvalar illis, Avexi Celarise!

He was pulled back by a violent ocean tide as the waters of time and space enveloped him. Jonathan felt the blade retreat as Morgan's face swam in front of him, her eyes already turning black. *I believe in you.*

He reached out to stop her but the waters closed over him.

"That was impressive, Morgan," Truculen gasped as

Jonathan disappeared in an instant. "I wasn't expecting you; did Morwenna feel like losing all her children in one day?" He swung his sword to the left.

Morgan's blade flashed with the blue-green sea stones of the Delphini as she brought it up to block Truculen's strike. "You've drawn yourself in, brother. I return to Neáhvalar should the day go ill, but I am not afraid of such a home-coming." She counterattacked and pricked his right arm as he leapt back.

Truculen looked down to see a bright spot of blood. "So pretty, don't you think, the way these bodies bleed?" He raised his sword again.

—⚬⊙⊙⚬—

Jonathan landed on his back across the field. He jumped to his feet and raced towards Truculen and Morgan in the distance. His shirt was wet, and he felt the cut where the blade had pierced him. The wound wasn't deep; he would tend to it later. He darted in and out of the skirmish, swooping down to pick up a fallen sword. He was still sev-eral hundred yards away from Morgan when a Nemaron suddenly planted himself in Jonathan's path. With a quick stroke across the neck, the soldier fell dead. He looked back up. Morgan had just wounded Truculen and now he lunged at her with such fury that the flash of swords was all Jonathan could see.

The land around the dueling Elementarí had already become scorched, and large rents—deep and wide enough to bury five men—continued to form along the ground. Nemarons and Cadarians were caught in small landslides, while their allies tried to extricate them, and towards this chaos, Jonathan ran, weaving through the mass of soldiers.

He shoved a Cadarian out of his way in time to see Mor-gan wound Truculen in the side. The Ophidian staunched the wound with one hand while he parried Morgan's second attack with the other. Jonathan was only a few hundred yards away now, numb to the pain and his own bleeding.

Morgan spun around, striking to the left. Truculen ducked under her swing, and in the next instant, drove his blade up, straight into her heart.

I believe in you... The words, sprung from Morgan's mind, quickly faded into darkness.

Truculen smiled victoriously as he slid his bloodied sword out of her crumpled body. The smile vanished as the earth quaked violently, and both Truculen and Morgan fell into a great pit. Then a roar of fire as Bryn appeared—he too was hurt: one leg gone, another badly damaged, yet that didn't affect the speed with which he leapt into the basin.

She's still alive. Jonathan said to himself, dodging swords and soldiers to reach them. She was Elementarí and now Bryn was there. *She's still alive.* He could pull her out and take her to Kayna for healing—

A sharp pain ripped through the back of his right calf. Jonathan tried to keep running but the leg couldn't hold his weight and he fell face down. He raised himself up and rolled halfway over, the knife driving even deeper into his flesh. He dimly registered the bulk of a shield as it crashed down on his head. A few moments of trying to breathe, and then only darkness.

—◦—◉—◉—◦—

Noises coming through, muffled and slow. He was being dragged over the ground. His back hit a rock or two before he was lifted up.

"Morgan?" No answer. Pain shot through his leg, stomach, and head, pushing him back into unconsciousness.

Someone's hands were on his calf, moving up his knee. Then hands on his stomach, where the blade had entered. He heard a special language being sung. Morgan? The person kept singing, and Jonathan partially opened his eyes to see Kayna bending over him, her hands gently pressing herbs into the cut. He willed himself back into the dark.

"Put him on Tongs," someone said. "That knife had the royal seal. He knows. We must leave the city immediately."

Rough hands grabbing him again, and then he was facing the ground over Tongs' back. The world tilted, throwing him headlong into deep water.

Morgan's face floated in front of him, eyes like onyx, face ghostly white. *Two daughters lost now,* she whispered. *A mother's wrath, and a mother's hope. Find the fourth Terakhein of the sea, son of the fire, before the power of the Three is restored, before Morwenna fully wakes. Against water's wrath, none can stand.* With one forceful push, she sent Jonathan up through the abyss to the surface. He awoke alone, surrounded by trees with golden bark and snow white leaves shaped like coins.

He was in the center of the Seven Woods.

ACKNOWLEDGMENTS

Thanks to Tara Miller, Carissa Ward Sheenan, Jennifer Wagner, and all the peeps over at Absolute Write who looked at early drafts and provided helpful feedback.

Eleanor Boyall, D. Adrian Hall, and Molly Tanzer helped me get this draft polished enough so it actually looked like a book.

Also all my thanks to Siolo Thompson who envisioned Morgan for the artwork, Duncan Eagleson for such great design, and my awesome editor Rose Mambert.

ABOUT THE AUTHOR

Nancy Hightower's short fiction and poetry has been published in *Strange Horizons, Word Riot, story/South, Gargoyle, Electric Velocipede, Danse Macabre, Prick of the Spindle, Bourbon Penn, Prime Number Magazine,* and *Neon,* among others. She did the majority of her graduate work on Henry James, but asks that you don't hold that against her. She has taught classes at the university level on memoir writing, the grotesque in art and literature, writing in the visual arts, and the ghost story. Currently, she resides in New York City.

You can see more of her work at Nancyhightower.com

OTHER TITLES FROM PINK NARCISSUS PRESS

AT TIMES I ALMOST DREAM
Modern feminist fairy tales by Amy E. Yergen
ISBN: 978-0-9829913-5-0

COURT OF DREAMS
A comic fantasy novel by Stuart Sharp
Join unlikely hero Thomas Greene on his journey through
the hidden world of the Court of Dreams.
ISBN: 978-0-9829913-2-9

DARKWALKER
A post-apocalyptic crime novel by Duncan Eagleson
The Railwalkers – an Order of warrior shamans – must stop
the supernatural killer known as "The Beast."
ISBN: 978-1-939056-04-7

FEASTING WITH PANTHERS
A literary fantasy by Lyle Blake Smythers
Warrior-poet Catalan and his band find themselves at the
center of a War Game between two mysterious sorcerers.
ISBN: 978-0-9829913-7-4

PEOPLE WITH HOLES
Stories by Heather Fowler
These magic realism stories are bound together by sex,
metamorphoses, and love's inevitable consequences.
ISBN: 978-0-9829913-9-8

RAPUNZEL'S DAUGHTERS and Other Tales
What happens after the "Happily Ever After"...?
ISBN: 978-0-9829913-1-2

CPSIA information can be obtained at www.ICGtesting.com
Printed in the USA
BVOW02s2258130114

341378BV00006B/11/P